"You're not on Facebook, are you?"

My daughter only cried harder.

Fear was making me into a bully. "You are. Please tell me you haven't put where we live on it. Daisy! Show me. Show me now." I ran over to the computer.

I nearly caved in when Daisy's fingers fumbled on the keyboard. My poor girl who could never be a normal teenager. Because of me.

Eventually she brought up her account, which had a daisy as the profile picture. My heart slowed again as I read "Lives in Peterborough." Thank God she hadn't updated her location to our new home.

There must be thousands of Daisy Joneses in the world. Which was exactly what I wanted.

Praise for Kerry Fisher

The Woman I Was Before

"It's been a long time since I read a whole book in 24 hours but there was no way I was putting down *The Woman I Was Before*. No one writes complex, painful family love like Kerry Fisher. Real and raw but funny too. Loved it!"
— Iona Gray, award-winning author of *Letters to the Lost*

The Silent Wife

"A compulsively readable novel about family skeletons."
— *Publishers Weekly*

"A wonderful, poignant, heart-breaking, heart-warming story of families and secrets, of hidden strength and unexpected friendship. Brilliant! Very highly recommended. Cannot wait for Kerry's next!"
— Renita D'Silva, Pushcart Prize–nominated author

ALSO BY KERRY FISHER

The Silent Wife

The
Woman
I Was
Before

The
Woman
I Was
Before

KERRY FISHER

FOREVER
New York Boston

Copyright © 2019 by Kerry Fisher
Reading group guide copyright © 2020 by Kerry Fisher and Hachette Book Group, Inc.

Cover design by whittakerbookdesign.com. Silhouette of woman by Arcangel Images. All other images by Shutterstock. Cover copyright © 2021 by Hachette Book Group, Inc.

Forever
Hachette Book Group
1290 Avenue of the Americas, New York, NY 10104
read-forever.com
twitter.com/readforeverpub

First published in 2019 by Bookouture, an imprint of StoryFire Ltd.
First Grand Central Publishing edition: October 2020

First U.S. mass market edition: December 2021

Forever is an imprint of Grand Central Publishing. The Forever name and logo are trademarks of Hachette Book Group, Inc.

The publisher is not responsible for websites (or their content) that are not owned by the publisher.

ISBN: 978-1-5387-0878-1

Printed in the United States of America

CW

10 9 8 7 6 5 4 3 2 1

*To Michaela—for your resilience,
your kindness and your sense of justice.*

CHAPTER 1

Kate

Friday 30 June

Of all the emotions I felt as I walked into my new house, hope was the most unexpected. But there it was, against the backdrop of fresh paint, a fragment of belief that this time, in the first home I'd owned since it all went wrong, Daisy and I would know good times.

Of course, right behind hope was the familiar rush of caution—"Keep yourself to yourself"—tagging along like a truculent toddler I'd been unable to shake off for the last sixteen years.

I glanced at Daisy, trying to read her face. I had no right to need anything from her. No right to expect excitement or gratitude. I was still willing her to show some enthusiasm, if only to dissolve the big knot of guilt sitting in my stomach like a doughnut I should never have eaten. She didn't disappoint. Despite growing up with just me, my daughter had sidestepped my tendency to look backwards, to dwell, to live in the past. Instead she gathered herself in and headed towards the next thing with a quiet determination I hadn't mastered at forty-three, let alone at seventeen.

As she stepped into the living room and whirled round and round, her olive skin standing out against the light walls, her dark hair swirling behind her, I managed not to suggest she took off her Dr. Martens. I itched to hurry out to the van to fetch the Hoover, to smooth out the pile in the carpet again, to keep our lives blank and uneventful.

Daisy picked up my phone from the windowsill and started taking photos. I longed to snatch it back, but I didn't want to dampen her enthusiasm. She scowled as I said, "Don't put anything on social media."

"I'm just sending a photo to Maddie. She wanted to see where I'd moved to."

I made myself smile. "She'll have to come and visit."

Daisy shrugged as though she knew that the forward motion of the teenage world would wash the traces of her away within a matter of months. One hundred and twenty miles might as well be the other side of the world "in real life."

I moved out of the shot and let her carry on. There wasn't much in the empty room that would announce to all and sundry that we'd moved onto a brand-new estate built around an old hospital in Windlow. I hoped this move to Surrey would be the last time I'd have to pack up—and erase—our lives.

"I could have an amazing party in here."

I ignored the comment. Even if I could bear the thought of a gang of teenagers rampaging through the house, I hated the idea of a whole group of new people knowing where we lived.

Daisy rushed through to the kitchen to look out at the garden. "There's room out there for one of those blow-up swimming pools. We might be able to get one cheap on eBay." Then she frowned and laughed at herself. "Not that I know anyone to invite round, obviously." She nearly kept the resentment out of her voice.

I was tempted to agree to anything she wanted, just so I could stop feeling so bad about dragging her to another town, away from her friends for the third time in her short life. Instead I promised myself that this time no one was going to hound me out.

I put on my cheeriest voice. "You'll soon meet new people. I bet there'll be loads of teenagers on this estate." I pointed through the double doors. "That girl in the house opposite looks about your age."

Daisy raced through into the living room and hovered behind the curtain, peering at the driveway over the road. I stood back, not wanting to get a reputation as the community curtain twitcher. Naturally, the biggest house on the estate would have to have a conventional family setup, like the Topsy and Tim books my mum used to read to Daisy when she was little. There they all were, Mum, Dad, son and daughter twisting into a back-breaking pose, all four of them laughing with their hands on the door handle while the daughter tried to capture them all in a selfie. The big sign that said "21 Parkview" would probably be in the corner of that picture, for any casual Facebook observer to see. I couldn't imagine living a life where it didn't matter.

Daisy stopped me disappearing down those familiar, well-trodden routes that never led to a solution, by saying, "Shall we go over and say hello?"

I hoped she didn't see me shudder. It was years since strangers had recognised me, horrified fascination passing over their faces before the most brazen dared to ask, "Aren't you that woman who was in the newspaper?" I still dreaded that flicker of puzzlement, followed by wary curiosity. "They won't want us going over now. They'll be getting on with their unpacking. We'd better make a start with ours if we're not going to end up sleeping on a mattress on the floor. There'll be time to introduce ourselves later."

And with that, we went outside, where Jim and Darren, the blokes I'd found to bring us from Peterborough to our new home in a little market town in Surrey, were tag-teaming alternate scratches of man boobs and balls. Jim was muttering about his back already aching. "Hope you're going to give us a hand up them stairs with that wardrobe. Mind you, looks a bit narrow at the top there. Going to be tight to turn."

Darren nodded. "These new houses aren't meant for big pieces of furniture like that," he said, his face arranging into some kind of satisfaction that I might end up with a pine wardrobe wedged between the banisters and the landing.

Over the road, my new neighbour let out a shriek of delight. "The kettle! Who wants a cuppa?"

I resisted shouting, "Me!" as a team of professional movers made manoeuvring a solid oak table through her front door look like they were flipping a piece of balsa wood on its side.

I dragged my eyes back to the battered van and smiled. "Come on then. Let's put our backs into it. You too, Daisy." I fought the temptation to snap, "Put my phone down and grab the toaster!"

There was a waft of BO as Jim reached for the bin bag full of coats I'd grabbed off the pegs as we left our old house. A wave of loneliness washed over me at doing all of this on my own again. But nowhere near as acute as the day when my husband, Oskar, told me he was leaving to go and work with his cousin in Argentina "where I can start again and forget about all of this."

Even if I moved to the furthest corner of Australia, I would never forget.

CHAPTER 2

Gisela

Friday 30 June

Every time I turned round to ask Jack where he thought we should put something, he was waving his hand in that "don't bother me right now, big businessman on a very important call" way of his. God forbid he should actually have a day off and help with something as mundane as sorting out the home we were going to live in. He'd done the grand gesture of organising a bouquet of roses to arrive mid-morning and clearly thought that was his contribution to proceedings.

"Ollie, while Dad deals with his 'urgent business,' could you just make sure all the boxes that say 'spare room' go up to the top floor?"

"Sure. My stuff's going in the room at the front now, right?"

I frowned. "You're having the bedroom overlooking the garden."

"Hannah says she wants it."

I shook my head. "We sorted all of this out ages ago, when we first saw the house."

Ollie shrugged. "She says because I'm away at university, she should have the biggest room."

"I thought we decided you'd probably look for a job in London next year and commute for a while?"

Was it so wrong to have a little jolt of joy at the thought of Ollie moving back home again, even though he'd be twenty-two by then and should be making his own way in life? The one person who sometimes managed to ask me, "And how was your day?" Unlike Jack, who often came into the house still on the phone without making eye contact. Or Hannah, who frequently didn't even bother with a greeting, just defaulted straight to "What's for dinner?" more often than not followed by a big sag, like she'd been punched in the stomach and a strangled "Again?" as though I'd offered her dried yak in prune sauce.

Ollie became intent on peeling off a piece of brown tape from one of the boxes. "I might stay down Bath way if I can."

I frowned at real life intruding on my fantasy. "I'm not messing about changing everything around now. Her room is only an alcove smaller anyway. Let's stick with what we agreed and we can have another think next year when we see how the land lies. Where *is* Hannah?" I asked.

"She went out to explore."

Scouting for boys in the neighbourhood more like. Little monkey. I crossed my fingers that the handsome bad boy didn't live two doors down and hauled the ironing board into the utility room. Titch, our Great Dane, saw his moment to escape and barrelled past me. He barged into the removal man and nearly got squashed by an incoming sofa, causing a flurry of swear words. That would be the last cup of tea I'd be making for him. I was the only one allowed to drop an F-bomb in my house.

"You'd better shut the dog up before he causes an accident."

I raised my eyebrows. The removal man clearly didn't understand that Titch was not a dog to be "shut up." Titch thought he had superior rights to any of the humans in the family. I called Titch to me and he swaggered over, wagging his tail and managing to sweep one of the vases I'd unpacked onto the floor. Not that it was a great loss—definitely in the category of things I felt guilty about chucking out because it was a wedding present. Jack would never notice. Apart from the bowl from

my Great-Aunt Sybil that had *Jack and Gisela 7 October 1995*
engraved on it, he'd struggle to point out another thing in the
whole house we'd been given when we got married.

I shouted to Ollie. "Get Dad off the phone. And go and ask
the removal men if they can see the box marked 'kitchen cleaning' so I can get the dustpan and brush. If you see Hannah out
there, ask her to come in. She can start putting the glasses away
before Titch smashes anything else."

Ollie wandered off outside, showing as much urgency as
Titch on the way to the vet's. Trust us to pick the hottest day
of the year to move house. I was sweating already and I'd only
opened a couple of boxes. I was conscious of the big wave of
irritation filling the space where excitement had been, my illu-
sion of the happy family working together to take responsibility
for creating a home disappearing into mist. I glanced over the
road at the woman at number seventeen. Her daughter was
racing in and out, heaving boxes and grabbing hold of bits of
furniture with a smile on her face. I'd obviously gone wrong
somewhere. Hannah would be all sweetness and light when it
came to choosing a sound system or wheedling a new TV out of
Jack but doing the boring shit of unwrapping the crockery and
running it all through the dishwasher, not a chance.

I started poking the bits of broken vase with my toe, peering
through the front door to see if anyone, any of the three other
people in my family, was actually going to put away so much
as a fork.

When no one appeared, I stomped outside, doing that sweet
"Are you winning?" to the removal men who were having a
fag break. I wondered how many houses they drove away from
going, "I give that marriage six months." Ollie was on the other
side of the road—standing in an unnatural "biceps flexed"
pose—chatting to the girl at number seventeen. I hadn't seen
any evidence of a dad about, unless he was that bloke with the
Black Sabbath T-shirt lifting the sofa.

Hannah was idling up the street, so I beckoned at her to

hurry, which led to her throwing her hands up. "What?" At the same time, Jack was waving the "five minutes" fingers at me through the windscreen of his car.

Bugger the roses. Just get off the sodding phone.

Photos: All four smiling widely into the camera at the front door, Gisela's face pressed against Jack's.

Boxes stacked neatly in a white kitchen with gleaming grey granite and a huge bouquet of roses in the middle of the island next to a bottle of champagne.

Caption: So the day has finally arrived—we're in our new home! Just a "few" boxes to unpack, but at least the hubby remembered the essentials . . . roses and bubbly!!

#GottaLoveTheHusband #Newhome #Moving #Excited #FamilyAdventures

CHAPTER 3

Sally

Saturday 1 July

"Breakfast in bed for the love of my life," Chris said as he walked in with a tray. "You need to go and check out that shower. Got much more power than the old one. Good choice to have two shower rooms instead of bathrooms." He passed me a glass and clinked it with his own. "Cheers. Here's to us and our happy home."

I refrained from asking which champagne he'd polluted with orange juice (*please* don't let it be the vintage Henri Chauvet I'd stocked up with during my last trip) and ruffled his wet hair. Apart from a few tiny wrinkles around his eyes, he barely looked older at thirty-six than he did when we'd met at work a couple of years after I'd left university.

He took my glass from me and started kissing my neck. "Time to christen our new bedroom, I think."

My eyes darted towards the landing. I couldn't help it. Ever since we'd first seen the house on the plans, that little room across the corridor kept calling to me. The room that every time I walked past, I imagined with a frieze of sailing ships against pale green walls and one of those mobiles made from bamboo hanging from the ceiling. No bright primary-coloured plastic anywhere or stupid wind-up lamps blaring out a tinny

"Twinkle, Twinkle, Little Star." Chris would never tolerate that. But maybe, eventually, he'd come to see that a four-bedroom house required more than just bookshelves of military history and a scattering of the latest chrome gadgets.

His hands pulled up my nightdress and he pushed himself against me.

I hesitated, allowing myself a second to luxuriate in the romanticism of explaining to a sandy-haired teenager, eighteen years from now: "You were our surprise house-warming present."

Maybe this would be the opportunity I needed. I didn't have to say anything. I could claim heat of the moment, my brain overwhelmed by the move. He obviously hadn't remembered. I'd always despised women who shrugged off things, saying, "What he doesn't know won't hurt him." I didn't want to be that wife. I didn't want it to happen like this, by trickery.

I wriggled free. "Don't forget I had the coil removed last week."

Annoyance flashed across his face and he immediately swung his legs over the side of the bed. I pulled down my nightdress, feeling exposed and vulnerable. "Oh Christ, good job you're on the ball. The Buck's Fizz must have knocked the sense out of me. Any idea where the condoms are?"

I almost laughed at the frustration on Chris's face. When I'd been dropping with exhaustion the night before, my hands sore and dry, irritated by all the paper and cardboard, he'd refused to go to bed. "I can't get up tomorrow and come down to all this mess. I won't be able to sleep." And now, although we knew where the tea strainer, garlic press and lemon squeezer were, neither of us recalled seeing the condoms.

In the end, we didn't need them. Just as I was offering to nip down to the garage and see if there were any bathroom boxes left in there, tidied away last thing so they wouldn't affront Chris's eyes in the morning, a great racket broke out next door.

We looked at each other, trying to place the noise. I peeped through the bedroom curtains into the neighbour's garden, where a man was filming his brood of children leaping onto the newly erected trampoline pushed right up against our fence. "It's the kids next door."

Chris rolled his eyes. "At 8:30 on a Saturday morning? They'd better not do that every weekend or we're going to have words."

I cuddled him from behind. "They're just excited because it's all new. The same as it is for us. They'll settle down."

"We should have double-checked who was moving in next to us. If I'd have known there were four kids, I might have had second thoughts."

I forced a smile into my voice. "These houses are built for families really, though, aren't they?"

He tensed as though he caught a hint of suggestion rather than mere statement. "No. They're big houses with lots of space, but not everyone is going to use that for kids. It's perfect for us—we've both got an office each and still have a guest room for our friends."

Who no longer came to stay because they all had children. Even the best-behaved child couldn't meet Chris's standards for low decibels, scarcity of spillage and absence of interrupting. Coupled with his crinkled expression of bemusement that the parents thought he might be remotely interested in anything their child had to say, our Christmas card list was thinning out nicely. The only people likely to occupy our guest room were my mum and dad, and even their visits were few and far between. Though I couldn't entirely blame Chris for getting fed up with my mother and her subtle hints: "Can't believe you and Chris have been married ten years. And together for thirteen!" "Thirty-seven next birthday, Sally!" She might as well stand there making a pendulum movement with her arms.

Now wasn't the moment for that battle. I gave Chris a hug. "We're very lucky to be able to afford so much space."

I'd have to be smart about this.

Photo: Two glasses of Buck's Fizz, poached eggs and salmon on a tray, perched on a white linen duvet.
  Caption: First morning in our new love nest!
  #ForeverHome

CHAPTER 4

Gisela

Saturday 8 July

Photo: Long dining table stacked with plates and glasses, with an enormous vase of lilies. Huge buckets filled with ice and beer. Wine fridge with all the gold tops of champagne lined up.

Caption: Gearing up for house-warming with all the new neighbours. Hope they don't think we're alcoholics!!! #MeetTheNeighbours #LoveMyCommunity #Excited

With an hour and a half to go until everyone arrived, Jack emerged from his study with one eye still on his phone.

I stood with my arms folded. "Is there any day of the week where you could actually give your full attention to your family? I'm sure the caravan-rental business can survive without you for one weekend out of fifty-two."

"As you well know, it's our busy time of year, so I'm always going to have to do a bit of troubleshooting at weekends. On the upside, Painted Wagon Holidays affords you a very nice standard of living, Gisela."

Only the desire not to have a massive row just before our guests arrived stopped me responding to the family folklore that Jack worked his arse off while I booked pedicures and lunches out.

Jack's face told me he knew he was lucky to get away with that. He put his phone in his pocket and said, "What do you want me to do?"

I was tempted to fling out my arm and point to the whole house, saying, "Pick a bloody job—any one." Instead I settled for, "Just go and check that you cleaned the barbecue last time we used it." For a man who didn't know the difference between a J-cloth and a duster, he was surprisingly precise—and possessive—about his barbecue, the twenty-first–century equivalent of standing growling in front of a cave.

I'd just finished bleaching the loo when he came rushing back in. "I put the gas on to freshen up the grill and it's run out. I'll just nip down to the garage and see if they've got any canisters."

My stress levels soared. Not only did we have forty people coming who would need more food than a few rocket leaves and a couple of slices of baguette, but I'd also been counting on Jack to give all the garden chairs and tables a good wipe down. Based on the women I'd met on the estate so far, I was pretty sure white jeans would be a popular choice. I contented myself with, "Be as quick as you can, I'm getting a bit nervous."

He smiled and waved his hand at the dining room. "Looks lovely. You've done a great job. Anyway, if they don't like us, we won't invite them again."

If they all had to charge down to the kebab shop later because the "barbecue" failed to materialise, they probably wouldn't rush to come again.

I shouted upstairs to Hannah and Ollie. "I need some help down here."

Ollie appeared, in an ironed shirt and clean-shaven instead of the non-designer stubble he usually sported during the holidays.

"You look smart."

"My girlfriend's coming over. Thought I'd better make an effort." He looked down.

A herculean effort managed to push back the hurt he'd never

mentioned a new girlfriend to me. Instead I raised my eyebrows, comedy fashion. "Well, aren't we honoured? She must be something special if you've actually had a shave."

He didn't answer. "What was it you wanted help with?"

I handed him a bucket of hot soapy water and a cloth, all the time dancing between wanting to know more about the girlfriend he'd never mentioned before and wondering if she was "the one" given Ollie's bashful reaction. He'd rarely bothered to change out of his tracksuit bottoms before. I'd always been able to tease information out of him; I couldn't let her arrive without knowing the basics. "So, go on then, what's her name?"

Ollie smiled, the sort of smile that meant he was remembering things I really didn't want to know about. A smile that excluded me from his life. "Natalie. Nat."

The name conjured up someone small, slim and dark. A contrast to Ollie, who'd stayed incredibly blonde, like some Norwegian god. I told myself off for even imagining what a mixture of those colourings would look like in a child. "Have you got a photo?"

He did that shruggy "I don't spend my time taking photos of her" thing. "She'll be here in an hour, then you can see her for yourself."

I started decanting the mayonnaise into a pretty bowl. "I think it's a bit rude if she gets here and we don't know anything about her. Where did you meet her? Is she from your university?"

Ollie glanced down at his phone. His face softened, then he frowned up at me again. "Yeah, sort of." I waited, feeling curiosity puffing up inside me. He wrinkled his nose. "I met her this year in Bristol when I was doing my placement."

"How long have you been seeing the lovely Natalie, then? You kept that quiet."

"I knew you'd have hundreds of questions, so I thought I'd save myself the aggro. I've been seeing her for a few months, maybe four or five."

I pretended not to hear the impatience in his voice and plugged on with my next question. "Do you think you'll stay in touch when you go back to Bath for your final year?" Before he could answer, I had another thought. "Have you sorted out a house yet? We haven't paid a deposit or anything."

"I'm on it. Just working things out now."

And with that, he sloshed off outside, dripping water through the kitchen.

As I followed in his wake with a cloth, I puzzled away over his reluctance, his hesitation to talk about her when he was clearly smitten. I felt the sting of sadness that he'd grown away from me. There'd been someone in his life for several months and he hadn't even mentioned her. Someone else who'd be the keeper of his secrets, the worries he could never tell his friends for fear of appearing uncool, the person who noticed minor ailments and insisted he go to the doctor. She'd better be kind. If he met her on his placement, at least she was at university or work. I'd hate him to end up with someone directionless, bumbling through life with no real plan. Like me, at his age.

The excitement I'd felt about the party was in danger of seeping away. I grabbed my iPhone and flicked through to my "Happy times" playlist with all the *Dirty Dancing* songs. I ran up to get Hannah, who was standing admiring herself in the mirror, dressed in a crop top and knickers. I used to have a stomach that flat. I did. Hipbones even. No amount of sticking my arse in the air at Body Balance would ever give me that taut smooth stomach again. I looked down at my boobs, which were ridiculously big for my small frame. A selling point about twenty years ago, now requiring a shopping trolley of their own.

"Hannah, can you come down and give me a hand?"

"I'm still getting dressed."

"You've had all morning to do that. Just come and put out some olives and cut the bread for me."

Hannah looked at me as though I was the most tiresome

creature on the planet. "I'll be down in a sec." She paused. "Are you getting changed?"

"No, I thought I'd wear this. Why?"

"Isn't it a bit frumpy?"

I looked down at my jeans and tunic top. "What about if I put some heels on?"

But Hannah was busy filling in her eyebrows, obsessing over the two hairs that grew in the opposite direction from the others. "You just look a bit old-fashioned, more like Grandma."

I marched out of her room to my wardrobe and started pulling out different tops. The jeans were new, those butt-lifting jeans for middle-aged women, which appeared in all the papers. They couldn't be frumpy. I sieved through the options—the sheer top that was a bit transparent—not sure a glimpse of the thick-strapped scaffolding required to prevent a G-cup from free fall was going to improve anyone's burger experience. The silky vest top. Ugh. My bingo wings were so bad everyone would be shouting out "full house" if I appeared in that. I wondered about getting Hannah to help me, then decided it was entirely possible that her advice would act like a pestle on the mortar of my self-esteem.

I went for a long-sleeved top with a fat-disguising frill down the front that finished below my bum. If only I'd known at Hannah's age that I would never look better than I did then, that thirty years down the line I'd rate clothing not for its cutting-edge fashion but for its ability to skim the stomach.

I ran downstairs, whirling around, putting crisps into bowls, wishing Jack had bought something other than Pringles. How I missed my twenty-year-old self who swigged cranberry juice out of a carton then gargled in a slug of vodka, sunbathed half-naked, laughed long and loud and felt sorry for anyone who had a problem with my behaviour. Now I was worrying about what people would think of my crisps.

Thankfully, Jack came bowling in through the door, brandishing a couple of Calor gas canisters like hunting trophies.

"We're in luck!" Relief Jack was going to take charge of the huge mound of meat rather than it becoming another job for me in an oven I hadn't yet mastered outweighed my pissed-offness at the fact he was breezing in at the last minute. I didn't have time to get any further because the doorbell went, ten minutes early.

"I hate people who arrive early."

Jack laughed. "Good job you're so organised. Looking on the bright side, at least someone's turned up."

I arranged my face into one of welcome as I opened the door to a woman in her early thirties, who was so tall I found myself looking up at her. I stuck out my hand. There were a few families I hadn't managed to speak to, so I'd popped a note through the door. "I'm Gisela. Are you the lady from number seven? Or number thirteen?"

She laughed, the big, confident laugh of someone who'd decided long ago that being several inches taller than the average woman was an advantage. "No, I'm not from number seven *or* number thirteen."

I waited for her to say, "I live diagonally opposite—I've got the two little girls" or "Number fifteen with the boy who's always riding up and down on his bike." She paused as though she was expecting something from me. I had the sensation that she was looking me up and down, though her eyes never moved from my face.

"You must be Ollie's mum. I'm Natalie."

I knew. Of course I knew it was his girlfriend. "Natalie. Nat." But I was still waiting for her to say that she was his mentor, or boss, or I don't know, climbing wall partner, personal trainer, physiotherapist.

Because a six-foot woman, at least a decade older than Ollie, in an expensive shift dress and wedge sandals revealing pillarbox red toenails that I recognised as professionally pedicured did not fit my parameters of what Ollie's girlfriends looked like. I felt compelled to look behind her for a thin little thing with swishy blonde hair and ripped jeans.

She put her head on one side, with a confidence that spoke of life experience way beyond a muddy weekend at Reading Festival and a season as a chalet girl. "I'm Ollie's girlfriend."

I suppressed the instinct to say, "What the hell are you doing with my son? He's just a boy. He can't find his sports kit without my help. I still make his dental appointments. And he never cuts his toenails until they're making holes in his socks." Instead I shook her hand so enthusiastically a flash of discomfort crossed her face. "Of course! He said you were coming. Lovely to meet you."

God only knows whether I managed to bring my eyebrows back to earth before I ushered her in to meet Jack, doing a "Don't say a word" warning face.

My voice bounced around the hallway, gathering speed and urgency. "Ollie's out in the garden. I'll take you through."

There was no mistaking the delight on his face when she stepped onto the decking. It took him a few moments to tear his eyes away from her to focus on me and gauge my reaction. He wasn't going to catch me out that easily. I offered her a drink and rushed inside to fetch it.

Please, God, let Natalie be just a phase.

CHAPTER 5

Sally

Saturday 8 July

Chris's Facebook page:
   Photo: Selfie of Chris with a bottle of bubbly and Sally in a white denim dress.
   Caption: Off to a barbecue with our new neighbours. Only right to take champagne.
   #Anyexcuse #TheGorgeousMrsGastrell

Chris whistled when I came downstairs. "Like the new dress. Looks really good on you." He whipped out his phone. "Going to make my work colleagues so jealous. Here, grab this bottle of champers."

He cuddled in close. He turned the bottle to make sure that the Taittinger label was visible. I didn't even know why it irritated me, when one of the things that I loved about him was his refusal to buy cheap. In the beginning, I'd loved the fact that he always wore a shirt with a discreet logo sitting somewhere, long before we considered ourselves affluent. And today was no different. The white Ralph Lauren polo shirt, the tailored shorts, the deck shoes. Not for Chris, sandals or Hawaiian shirts.

"Let's see," I said, reaching for his phone.

"Good enough for Facebook?"

"It'll do. We'd better go, otherwise we're going to be late."

"Yep, terrible shame if we miss a few burnt burgers."

"Don't be like that. We might make some local friends. It would be great to be able to pop down the road for a few drinks without having to get a cab anywhere." I fiddled with my hair in the mirror, noting even without Chris pointing it out that my roots needed doing.

"Rather have you all to myself. You're disappearing again on Monday, aren't you?" Chris said, as though I was jetting off on a jolly with the girls rather than a business trip to Ribera del Duero as an international wine buyer. International had been part of my job title for at least five years, but Chris still seemed to find the reality of it a personal insult, even though his job at a global logistics company took him away as often.

In a rather smart pincer move, I said, "Perhaps I should just become one of those stay-at-home mums instead, then I'd never have to travel?"

Chris barely even flickered his attention in my direction. "You'd be bored in no time. Can't imagine you with a posse of kids clamouring round your knees, you'd go mad with all that colouring and making fairy cakes shite."

He said it as though I was so abnormal, so lacking in maternal instinct that I'd be beating them back with a stick. I tried to remember how our agreement not to have kids had come about. I couldn't recall ever sitting down and saying the words out loud. At some point, without great ado, it had passed into unwritten law, a bit like whose responsibility it was to renew the house insurance. Initially children hadn't even been on our radar. We'd been young and ambitious, fast-tracking up the career ladder, which had somehow morphed into accepting that we'd always be like that. As time went on, I didn't know how to say, "I really want a family" when Chris only had to see a toddler covered in chocolate in a café window to scoot on by.

He handed me the pot of lavender I'd bought for Gisela.

"Right, off we go then. If it's really dull, let's just tell them you need to get ready for your trip."

I walked down the drive, feeling the July heat through my sandals. Chris was muttering something about "There better not be a bloody bouncy castle on their lawn, or I'm coming straight home." But the baking sunshine and the shouts of the kids in the various gardens, the splashing of paddling pools carrying on the hot air reminded me of my childhood. My mum coming out with lollies she'd made out of orange juice. My dad digging a few squares of turf out of our lawn so my friends and I could cook sausages on a campfire. Lying in a deckchair slathered in Hawaiian Tropic, refusing to go into the shade until I was at least a bit burnt. I wanted my kids—our kids—to have these experiences. Without the burning, which Chris as Mein Führer Factor 50 would never allow anyway.

We rang the bell. I mentally rehearsed my devil-may-care laughing off the question "Have you got children?" In my mind, I reserved a special spear-studded place of hatred for people who asked, despite my offering up absolutely no evidence of procreation. What if I'd had a stillbirth? A miscarriage? Had a child die?

I put my game face on as Gisela opened the door, sweeping us through to the garden, all warm and welcoming and nowhere near as stressed as I'd have been if I had a whole houseful of strangers to meet and greet. She beckoned over a young man with a tray of champagne. He had bright blue eyes so like Gisela's, he could only be her son. "This is Ollie. He's just home for the holidays from uni," she said, passing us drinks then dashing off as the doorbell rang again. Ollie apologised for not being able to shake hands and made a joke about having a wonderful future as a waiter.

Chris immediately set a little trap. "What are you studying?"

I sent up a little prayer that he wasn't studying medieval poetry, because under the guise of being interested, Chris would ask him what he was intending to do with that until he was backed into a corner. Chris wasn't a man who believed in following your dreams if there was no guaranteed crock of gold at the end of them.

"I've just finished my third year of engineering at Bath. Just had my placement year. I'm hoping to get a job on the oil rigs." One-nil to Ollie. He'd escaped Chris's eye-roll by coming up with a "proper degree."

Ollie stood chatting for a couple of minutes before glancing round and excusing himself to deliver more drinks.

Chris nodded after him. "He's rather charming, isn't he? Not your average grunty student."

I wanted to grab his upper arms and shake him. He acted as though children were just one big snot machine designed to drain the bank balance. His surprise when any child said something that interested him was akin to discovering a species he'd thought was extinct.

Gisela whirled past, dragging with her my next-door neighbour, whom I'd waved at but not yet spoken to. "This is Kate, and her daughter, Daisy. Oh sugar, that's the doorbell again. Hang on, I'll be right back."

Kate was the complete opposite of Gisela, the sort of woman who would sit through a whole conversation on a niche topic, then reveal herself to have a PhD in the subject just as everyone had made a fool of themselves stretching out their two fragments of facts to make an argument. I knew Chris would be working out how to shake them off, intent on finding the big businessman at the party, "the chap who might be a useful contact," "the bloke who'd be interesting to get on board."

I targeted Daisy in some perverse attempt to show off my bonding skills with teenagers.

"Are you still at school, Daisy?"

"I'm starting at the college in September to finish my last year of A levels."

"You're halfway through already? That's a tricky time to change schools."

She glanced at Kate. "I don't mind. It's the same syllabus for languages as my old school."

I waited for one of them to explain why they'd moved now but nothing was forthcoming. I rattled on. "Which languages do you speak?"

Kate rushed in with, "You're best at Spanish, aren't you?"

Daisy frowned and then nodded. "I'm doing French A level as well. And psychology."

There was a little beat of silence. "That's an interesting combination. You could *be* Spanish with your lovely hair and olive skin? Or maybe Eastern European with those beautiful cheekbones."

Kate answered for Daisy. "Perhaps we had some exotic ancestors." She was glancing round, nearly as obvious as Chris in her desire to escape. "Daisy, why don't you go and see if Gisela's daughter wants any help pouring the drinks?"

Daisy pulled a face. Even I could see that Daisy wasn't confident enough to introduce herself to Hannah. But Kate was shuffling her along as though she was a tiresome toddler who needed to go and make some friends in the sandpit.

I gulped down the rest of my champagne and wiggled my empty glass at her. "I'll come with you and get another drink— that one hardly touched the sides."

I ignored Chris's "Don't leave me with a dud" semaphoring. As I walked away with Daisy, I heard him ask, "Do you work?" If she didn't, he wouldn't still be standing with her when I got back and I'd definitely be in for the "What do women who don't work *do* all day?" speech on the way home.

I'd never managed to convince him that staying at home with children was not the easy option. Fortunately I caught Kate saying, "I'm a paramedic."

Chris would be in his element. He considered himself an expert on how the NHS could save billions if they made everyone produce their passport when they went to hospital but stopped paying for "stupid things like IVF." I also knew he'd take the opportunity to get some free advice on his latest ailment of indigestion rather than go to the doctor.

As we headed towards Hannah, Daisy surprised me by engaging in a discussion all about my job. "Sounds awesome, going to different countries every few weeks. Do you get to travel round while you're there?"

"Not as much as I'd like to. We're usually at trade fairs, then, beyond that, we arrange visits to the vineyards that interest us. But I did go to a new wine area in Argentina, the Chapadmalal, and I managed to tag on a few days in Buenos Aires as it's so close."

"My dad lives in Argentina, near Buenos Aires, in fact." She trailed off at the end of the sentence as though the words had run away from her.

"Wow. How often do you see him? Have you been out there?"

She coloured up. "No, I haven't."

I noticed she didn't answer my first question. Mother and daughter shared that trait of not feeling obliged to satisfy anyone else's curiosity. I didn't get a chance to investigate further because Gisela's daughter burst straight into our conversation without waiting for a natural pause, brimming with the sort of confidence that comes from growing up thinking you're the most important person in the room.

"Hi! I'm Hannah." She turned to Daisy. "Were you the girl talking to Ollie the day we moved in? Thank God there are some young people on the estate. When Mum and Dad said we were moving to a gated community, I thought I'd be trapped with a load of old crinklies."

Daisy smiled, not exactly shy but there was something cautious about her, a reticence that was a charming contrast to Hannah's boisterous enthusiasm. Hannah was full of how she'd just left school and was going to party every day until she went to Exeter University in September. She didn't bother trying to include me in the conversation, launching into a discussion about the best nightclubs in the area. "You eighteen yet? Not till June next year? That's bad luck being the youngest in the year. We'll have to try and get you some fake ID then—you won't get into Shalimar without it. I know a guy who sells other people's driving licences for twenty quid. Thursday night's a good night to go; drinks are half-price."

I marvelled at the fact that Hannah was totally unabashed about having this conversation in front of me.

Daisy was fiddling with the hem of her top. "Mum normally works the late evening shift on Thursdays. She's not keen on me being out when she's at work."

"What time does she finish?" I asked.

Daisy shrugged. "Depends. She's supposed to finish about midnight, but if there's a delay in handover at the hospital it might be one. Sometimes two."

Hannah did a little wink as though parents were just a peripheral inconvenience.

I surprised myself by blurting out, "Don't you mind being in the house that late on your own?"

Daisy wrinkled her nose. "Not really. I'm used to it."

I wondered how young she'd been when Kate had first started leaving her that late.

"I still get a bit jittery in the house at night when Chris is away. You can always pop over to me if you get nervous or lonely. We've got a spare bedroom."

She thanked me with the air of someone who would never dream of asking for help.

Hannah topped up my glass. "There you go," and I realised, as she moved the conversation onto what sort of music they liked, that she was dismissing me. Daisy kept glancing at me, as if she wanted to involve me, but Hannah had that sort of hardness about her that reminded me of the cool group of girls at school, not outright unfriendly but not allowing you to think for one minute you'd ever break into their ranks. If I ever had a daughter, I'd make sure she included everyone.

I hesitated for a second, trying to understand how someone half my age had taken control of who I spoke to, then I headed back over to Chris. He put his arm round my waist. "Kate has kindly said she'll keep an eye on the house if we're both away at the same time."

Kate leaned towards me, a bit intense as though she was ready to concentrate on every word I said rather than a quick discussion about watering my spider plant. "Your job sounds very glamorous, jetting about all over the place. I bet you see some gorgeous scenery."

I told her about a little village called Laguardia that I'd visited recently, right in the middle of the Rioja, full of old-fashioned tapas bars and surrounded by vineyards. "If you friend me on Facebook, you'll be able to see the photos."

She shook her head as though I'd suggested we started sexting each other. "I don't do social media."

Chris rolled his eyes. "I don't understand people who 'don't do social media' in this day and age. It's such a good way to keep in touch with people." So much so he had more conversations with people he hadn't seen for ten years than with me.

Kate crossed her arms. "Maybe. But I can't see the point for me. God knows what I could post that could possibly be of interest to anyone else. No one needs to see pictures of me running around Morrisons at the end of a shift. It's a bit different for Sally with all her exotic globetrotting."

Chris spotted an opportunity. "I'm always telling Sally she needs to take things easy and travel a bit less."

I hated it when Chris enlisted other people's help to get his own way. I tried to keep my voice neutral, without alerting Kate to the fact that this tricky little subject was the gift that kept on giving. "I don't travel as much as you do."

"You're away for longer stretches. I only ever go for a couple of nights at a time."

Kate must have sensed the tension between us because she said, "Whatever you do, it's hard to get the right balance, isn't it? So I can be at home three days a week for Daisy, I work two really long shifts. I hate not being there for her when she gets back from college."

"She's very welcome to pop over to ours for the evening if she gets lonely."

Out of the corner of my eye I could see Chris furrowing his eyebrows. Fortunately for him, Kate said, "Thank you but we've got our own routine now. She's very capable and doesn't mind being on her own."

More to stop Chris thinking that he had the ultimate control over who stepped through our front door, I persisted, "Keep us in mind. It's not as though you can walk away from a car accident because you've got to get the dinner on."

"We don't get called to as many crashes as you think. Our most common call-out is abdominal pain—which is usually a bug of some sort," Kate said, with the same air of stubborn self-sufficiency about her as Daisy.

Chris did one of his false laughs. "Can't imagine how things would work in our household if we had kids. No way Sally could do what she does with a family."

Sometimes I felt as though I'd married a policeman from one of those 1960s cop shows. I was sure Kate would think that too and wonder what I saw in him. I didn't want her pity, didn't want her looking at me, judging my life and finding it lacking, especially because I didn't have children. "That's the choice we've made, though." I breathed out, glad to have got the "choice" out there. I hated people speculating on why I hadn't had a baby, whether the "fault" lay with me or him.

Kate's expression remained blank. I couldn't decide whether she was disinterested or disapproving, which immediately led to me wittering on.

"But nowadays, having a family doesn't mean that women have to give up their jobs. It's so much easier to work flexibly now. There's a woman in my office who does three days a week while her husband looks after the kids."

"On your bike with that one," Chris said. "Career death, that is."

I wondered when Chris's opinions had started to embarrass me. I used to love the way he added spice to dinner parties with his outrageous comments, getting everyone fired up before raising a glass and saying, "We'll have to agree to disagree" when he got bored with hearing other people's bigoted views. Over time, his statements seemed less of a strongly held belief and more like something he'd seen on a fridge magnet.

Kate sipped her drink, her face neutral, her dark eyes watchful as though she was running through a few columns from the *Guardian* about stay-at-home husbands in her head.

Thankfully, a woman in her late twenties whose looks had probably acted like an automatic door-opening mechanism throughout her life appeared with some mini bruschetta. She had such a posh voice that the bee tattoo on her wrist surprised me. I was obviously turning into my mother: "I don't understand these young ladies disfiguring themselves like that." I wondered if people like her, with that blonde hair falling into luxurious corkscrews, all fresh-faced and slim-hipped, did have easier lives than people like me who were a bit lumpy-bumpy ordinary. But regardless of how privileged her life, I welcomed her with such enthusiasm I bet she was asking herself where we'd met before.

"What number do you live at?" I asked.

She laughed. "I love how we've all become numbers here. I'm number five—Sophie—but it's actually my friend's house; I'm house-sitting for a couple of months until she moves back from Australia. I'm waiting to move into a new-build on the other side of town, by the old bread factory." She paused, tucking a blonde curl behind her ear. "Love living here though. It feels really safe with all the families around, even though I'm on my own. I never feel as though I'll come back to French windows that have been jimmied open, not like when I lived in London."

"Does procreation make you more law-abiding, do you think?" Chris asked, with an edge to his voice.

Quick as a flash, Sophie laughed and said, "I don't know yet. Have you found out?"

I tried to catch his eye, to stop the big sore at the heart of our marriage becoming a free-for-all bun fight. He didn't even glance in my direction. "Haven't got any kids. But I'm not going round stealing cars or breaking into the neighbours' sheds despite not adding to the world's population."

Sophie didn't scuttle into her shell in the way that I would have done if someone I didn't know had taken a flippant comment as an insult. She simply lifted her chin and said, "I didn't suggest you were."

Chris shrugged as though what she thought about him was no concern.

Sophie raised her eyebrows at him in a "Get you, Grumpster" way. I felt that familiar knot of tension in my stomach, that need to step in and smooth over any niggling even when I wasn't the source. "Do you work locally?"

"Yes, I've just opened my own veterinary practice near Albert Park."

Chris's head shot up. "Crikey. That's good going for a woman, especially your age." Chris was clearly running down a checklist of contentious topics to piss off women at parties.

I turned to Kate, hoping to speak loudly enough to drown out Chris and his stupid comments, blurting out the first thing that came into my head. "Is Daisy's dad in Argentina permanently?"

Her response: "I hope so"—delivered with a finality so raw and vehement that I was obliged to readjust my view of her as someone who would never let an unfiltered comment out into the world.

CHAPTER 6

Gisela

Saturday 8 July

Photo: Jack standing next to a mound of uncooked sausages surrounded by lots of men raising their beer bottles to the camera.
 Caption: Let the cooking begin!
 #ChefJack #KingOfTheBarbecue

Every time I went up to Jack to suggest he get started on the barbecue before everyone in Parkview fell into the flower bed with booze leaking out of every pore, he nodded and said, "Just going." Except he wasn't just bloody going, he was pouring another beer and yakking to some other bloke about the merits of bitcoin, or in one thrilling conversation I caught a snippet of, the hi-tech composting loos they were installing at Painted Wagon caravan parks.

By two-thirty, I'd got to that gritted-teeth, fixed-smile stage, which after twenty-two years of marriage, Jack knew enough to act upon.

He beckoned Chris over. "You look like a man who knows one end of the barbecue from the other."

"As it happens, Sally bought me a course one year for my birthday, so I do know the basics. Might be able to stop the burgers burning at least."

As he passed me, Jack whispered, "Christ, didn't know we'd invited Jamie bloody Oliver. Old MasterChef here has had barbecue lessons."

"Sssh!"

From the way Jack was gesticulating with his hands and slapping people he'd only just met on the back, Chris was my lifeline to putting something on the table that wouldn't be burnt on the outside and raw on the inside. They bonded immediately over cars, with Jack saying, "Love the purple Lotus, mate. Really distinctive. Don't see many of those around." The conversation moved on to comparative engine size between Chris's Lotus and Jack's Jag and I left them to it, heading over to Sally and Kate.

"Very impressed your husband did a barbecue course."

"He really likes cooking. Does most of it."

As always I was in awe of any woman who managed to find a man with domestic skills.

"Nail him to the floor. Jack can just about pour a bowl of cornflakes without needing supervision."

Sally looked a bit taken aback at my lack of loyalty. I didn't really get these women who thought their husbands were perfect. Surely the point of having a husband was to have someone to blame when things went wrong? It was only a matter of time before I blamed Jack for Ollie making a fool out of me by bringing home a woman who—according to Hannah's sleuthing skills—was thirty-four. Closer to my age than Ollie's.

Sally's disapproval on top of the alcohol I'd consumed brought out a tiny desire to shock. "When the kids were small, I never seemed to organise myself to cook or shop. I used to be able to recite the local takeaway menus in my sleep. I think Hannah's first words were 'Peshwari naan.' "

Sally did a tight little smile as though admitting to anything other than puréeing sweet potato with a smattering of chia seeds was a complete motherhood fail. Christ, she only had to look over at Ollie and the perverted picture of his hand round

Natalie's waist to know that my parenting hadn't yet shown itself to be a roaring success. God only knows what on earth a grown woman found to fancy in a boy who wouldn't clean his ears unless I ran after him with a flannel.

Kate stopped me from digging myself any deeper by saying, "If you'd been born in Europe, your kids would eat out all the time. Sally was just telling me about her time in Rioja, with all the lovely tapas bars."

I was grateful to her for rescuing me and diverting me onto a less contentious subject that wouldn't end up with me bursting into drunken tears. I was definitely reaching the stage of needing ballast, burnt burger or otherwise.

As I listened to Sally talking about her travels, all I could think was how much I'd love to be getting on a plane in the morning, just like I used to, with a tiny rucksack and a belief that booking ahead was for old farts when everyone knew that a slice of watermelon, a packet of Benson and Hedges and a sleeping bag was all anyone really needed.

As Sally moaned about the loneliness of visiting places on her own "because in the end, you're miles from home with no one to share any of the lovely views or restaurants with—that's why I put so many photos on Facebook," I thought it sounded like paradise. I'd give anything to explore, with no timetable, no constraints, just the freedom to take whichever road I fancied without someone arguing that it would be quicker another way. To wander round a market, a gallery, or watch the world go by in a square without someone needing feeding. Or needing anything. The only trouble was, after all these years of travelling about as a homogenous pack, with Jack in charge of the passports and tickets, Jack making sure that we had the right travel insurance, with me trailing behind double-checking that we hadn't lost a bag, a coat, a child, I wasn't sure I could find my way to a Pret without someone pointing me in the right direction.

That was quite a lot of deep shit to park on someone I'd probably have never met if she hadn't moved into the same street. Instead, to cover up the fact that I was a middle-aged mother seemingly held together with a paper clip, I blathered on about Facebook. "Oh yes, it's brilliant for keeping in touch and seeing what people are up to."

With that, Sally whipped out her phone and started searching for me. She thrust the screen under my nose. "That's you with Ollie, isn't it? I'll friend you."

I nodded. "That was us last year, when we took him to Bristol for his work placement." I didn't add Hannah had moaned her arse off for the whole journey about getting up at the crack of sparrows. We'd ended up having the sort of row that starts with the current infuriating behaviour and spirals into a catalogue of irritations about stealing phone chargers and piling bowls on top of the dishwasher instead of risking opening it and finding that it needed emptying. By the time we finally rolled out of the car down by the waterfront, I was on the verge of stomping off and shouting that I'd get a train home. Ollie was monosyllabic, his first-day nerves shredded by the vicious trading of insults between Hannah and me. Just before we waved off Ollie, I'd asked Jack to take a photo, craving evidence that I'd done a good job with one child at least. Ollie had obligingly put his arm round me, despite being in a hurry to get away from us. I smiled up at him, all six foot two of him. You couldn't see that my eyes were glistening with tears.

At that moment, Ollie came past with a tray of the first sausages off the barbecue, with Natalie strutting along beside him.

Sally said, "We were just talking about you working in Bristol. I started my career in a wine warehouse there. Will you miss it when you move back to Bath in September?"

Ollie's eyes darted to me and then to Natalie. Her eyebrows were raised in expectation. Ollie flushed. "I'm not going back to live in Bath. Nat's got a house in Bristol so I'm going to stay at hers."

Suddenly his unwillingness to tell me his plans for accommodation for next year made sense. I heard the plea in his voice, the "please don't make a scene and show me up in front of this middle-aged woman who happens to be my girlfriend."

I kept my voice light. "Won't you get fed up with commuting? Especially when we move into winter? You won't feel like you're missing out on the last year with the lads?"

Ollie shrugged. "Not really. I'll still see them at uni. I'll probably get more work done as well. Anyway, it's really hard to find a decent house for five people." He reached for Natalie's hand, the tray of sausages wobbling precariously. "It's what we both want."

I felt the "we" land like a blow to the stomach. This was it. My son had ripped away the last piece of Velcro binding him to me and stuck himself to another woman, years before I thought it would happen. Without me even preparing myself for it.

Apparently that twenty-year-old boy in my profile photo, nervous about who to ask for at reception on his first day at work, was now a twenty-one-year-old man moving in with a woman who was probably already paying into a pension.

I smiled brightly. "Well, thank goodness you've got your accommodation sorted for next year. That definitely calls for more champagne."

I ran into the house and locked myself in the bathroom. Then I cried big tears for the man-child who wouldn't let me throw out the blue bunny he had when he was a baby but was going to miss out on his last carefree year at university for a woman who should have known better. Hopefully, the towels on the bathroom floor, empty loo rolls and crumbs on the work surfaces would turn out to be passion-smotherers to a girlfriend old enough to possess a mop, pan scourer and a loo brush and to get properly pissed off when they didn't get used.

Fingers crossed.

CHAPTER 7

Kate

Friday 28 July

That Friday, work was quiet: a ninety-year-old woman who'd fallen and a bloke who thought he was having a heart attack in a curry house but it turned out that he'd eaten four raw chillies as a bet and had raging indigestion. So when my boss offered to let me go early because of how long I'd been held up at the hospital the day before, the temptation to be home by midnight was too much to resist.

I drove up Parkview. Out of habit, I scoured the road for stationary cars that had anyone sitting in them. I passed Gisela's house, with candles burning in the front window. She must single-handedly contribute to global warming. I could see her next to Jack on the sofa, a wine bottle on the table in front of them. I couldn't quite pin down the emotion I felt. Something like jealousy but without a desire for Gisela to be miserable instead of me.

I was just thinking about how long it was since I'd done something so simple as have a glass of wine in front of the TV with anyone other than Mum—and now I didn't even have her—when I realised all the lights were on downstairs in my own home. I turned into the drive, irritation fizzing through me. Daisy always promised me that she'd be in bed by eleven when I wasn't around.

Waking her for her 5:30 a.m. Saturday job at Tesco was already a strain on my patience, exacerbated by guilt. I couldn't afford any of the things she saw Hannah doing—"Just off to the Shard for lunch with Mum," "Just going to the cinema then to Nando's," "Off shopping in Guildford."

I pushed open the front door and heard a muffled noise in the living room. I marched in, ready to tell Daisy to go to bed, to find Hannah scrabbling into a sitting position hauling up her bra straps, with a boy I didn't recognise pulling his T-shirt back over his head. Daisy was disappearing into the kitchen, followed by a tall, skinny lad who had not improved his looks by the huge plug in his ear.

"Daisy!"

She appeared in the doorway, her cheeks flushed.

Hannah was first to speak, plummy little words falling from her lips with all the self-assurance of someone used to being forgiven. "Hello, Kate. Hope you don't mind us being here. Daisy texted me because she could hear a noise, so we thought we'd keep her company until she felt safe enough to go to bed."

It was a measure of how much I liked Gisela that I didn't tell her to shut up. Cocky little madam.

Daisy slouched against the door jamb, looking as though she might cry.

I took a deep breath. "Who are your friends?"

I was waiting for her to tell me that they were from Hannah's old school, but she bit her lip and nodded towards the lad next to Hannah, the one with a smirk I would dearly have loved to scrub off his face. "That's Ryan, and this is Joe."

Joe managed an "All right?"

I swallowed. "Right, well, it's quite late, so it's probably time for you two to get off home as Daisy has work tomorrow."

Hannah hopped up to leave, but not before I'd seen the love bite on her neck.

I put up my hand to her. "Let me just see the boys out."

I picked up the packet of Rizlas from the table and thrust

them at Joe, who shot out of the door with his feet hanging out of his trainers.

Ryan took his time, leaning round me to wink. "See you soon, Helen. Great evening. Cheers, Daisy," he said, like he was starring in his own soap opera.

I slammed the door behind them.

I looked past Hannah, who was tucking strands of hair behind her ear and trying to make eye contact with me. "Who are those boys, Daisy? I didn't know you knew anyone around here yet."

She hesitated and looked to Hannah for support. Hannah opened her mouth to speak, but I glared and she decided against it.

"Daisy?"

"We just know them from around."

"Around? How around?"

Hannah was like the girl in class who knows the answer and couldn't stretch her fingertips any higher. "I know them from school."

"I thought you went to an all-girls' school?"

She paused for a second. "I did, but we shared the playing fields and the pool with the boys' school up the road, St. Ethelburga's."

I drove past St. Ethelburga's on the way to work. It was the local answer to Eton, with an Olympic-size swimming pool and rugby fields as far as the eye could see.

"They're friends of yours? Does your mother know you're over here with them?"

Hannah smiled. "We didn't realise they were coming over. It was all a bit last minute. She knows I'm keeping Daisy company. She'd be fine with it."

That little tone of resentment, as though I was making a fuss about nothing, finished me off. "I'm not sure she'd be fine about you canoodling with a boy and going home with a great big love bite."

One-nil to me as Hannah did look down briefly. A sulky

shadow passed over her face. Daisy's face was a mixture of rebellion and trepidation.

"So, let's be really clear that when I am at work, I am very happy for you to come over, Hannah, but no one else. Ever. Is that clear?"

"Perfectly." The sass of the girl. An eighteen-year-old thinking she could outsmart me.

"Just one thing, though. If they were friends of yours, why did Ryan call you Helen?"

"He didn't."

"I think you'll find he did."

Daisy's eyes were beginning to fill. I'd dug myself into a hard place. Given how I'd dragged Daisy away from all her friends, I should be grateful that she'd found someone to hang out with so quickly. But why did it have to be Hannah? I couldn't wait till she trotted off to university in September.

At the sight of Daisy's pleading face, I gave way. "Think it's time for bed for all of us now anyway. Early morning tomorrow."

Hannah turned to Daisy. "Bye. I'll text you tomorrow."

I saw Hannah out.

Daisy was crying by the time I got back into the living room, but I couldn't relent until I knew the truth.

"How did you meet those boys?"

Daisy pulled a cushion onto her knee.

"Like Hannah said. She knew them from school."

"Daisy, there is no way that a skinhead with a great gaping hole in his earlobe would have been allowed to go to St. Ethelburga's looking like that."

Daisy stood up and bustled about, picking up glasses and pizza boxes.

"If you don't tell me, I'm going to talk to Gisela."

She turned round, her face a picture of panic. "You can't do that."

"So how do you know them?" Fear was making me into a bully.

Her voice was only just audible. "We met them in a Facebook

group. It's one that Hannah belongs to for people who like the Shalimar nightclub in town. I didn't really want them to come round, but she thought it would be a laugh."

"You're not on Facebook, are you?"

Daisy cried harder.

"You are. Please tell me you haven't put where we live on it. Daisy! For Christ's sake! Show me. Show me now." I ran over to the computer. "NOW!"

I nearly caved in when her fingers fumbled on the keyboard. My poor girl who could never be a normal teenager. Because of me.

Eventually she brought up her account, which had a daisy as the profile picture. My heart slowed again as I read "Lives in Peterborough." Thank God she hadn't updated that. There must be thousands of Daisy Joneses in the world. Which was exactly what I wanted.

I put my hand on her shoulder. "I thought we'd agreed that you wouldn't go on social media. When did you set this up?"

"Four years ago."

"When you were thirteen?"

She nodded. We'd been in Peterborough for about a year then. She'd started a new school in the second year, by which time all the cliquey girls had pulled up the drawbridge. Her wan face was almost my undoing as she walked into school every day, unsure whether she'd spend her time trying to join in. Or resign herself to being left out.

"I just wanted to fit in, Mum. Everyone else was on Facebook and I was missing out on everything. I'm sorry."

"Will you close your account down?"

She sagged over the computer. "I can't."

"You're not keeping open some stupid Facebook account just so you can talk to boys like Ryan and Joe." I tried to keep my voice on the right side of shouting but it didn't feel like a battle I was winning.

She lifted her head up, her voice a mixture of begging and refusal. "Mum! I can't close it down."

"Do you want it all to start again? Being afraid to step outside our own front door?"

I felt sick. That voice so raw with rage and grief. That face, once the safe haven, the welcome I'd search out in a crowded room, now contorted and vengeful.

Daisy wiped her nose on her sleeve. She stuck her chin up in a gesture of defiance that I so rarely saw. "I'm not closing it down because it's how Dad and I talk to each other."

I sank onto the sofa. "I didn't know you were in contact with Oskar. I wondered why he'd stopped sending cards and letters."

Sixteen years and my heart still felt as though it was swaddled in bubble wrap and tucked deep into a freezer. I only knew I was capable of emotion when I thought about something happening to Daisy.

"He's rubbish with his phone. Never answers my texts. But he always replies if I message him on Facebook. And I can see all his photos too."

I forced myself not to ask what she'd seen, what his life was like now. "I need to understand what you're doing on there, who you're connecting with. There are some horrible people out there."

"I'm not giving you my password. I won't be able to write what I want to Dad if I know you're reading it."

I dreaded to think what she was telling him. I bet he had hundreds of bloody opinions on how I was bringing her up. Lucky him that he was thousands of miles away and his parenting wasn't under scrutiny, though I bet he didn't see it like that.

Daisy looked at me hopefully. "I could set up an account for you? Then you could friend me and see what I'm doing. You still won't be able to see my private messages to Dad."

The words I meant to say were, "Don't be so stupid."

The words that left my mouth, desperate to make amends for everything she'd had to put up with, were, "All right then, but don't put a photo of me on there or anything that shows where we live."

CHAPTER 8

Gisela

Thursday 17 August

Photo: Hannah doing a dramatic and terrified look into the camera.

Caption: Awake since 6 a.m. waiting for UCAS to update!

#FingersCrossed #ALevelResults

The UCAS page that would tell us whether Hannah had got into Exeter University or her second choice of Sussex still hadn't updated by the time we left home at 7:30 a.m. to pick up her results.

Hannah refreshed the page all the way to school, swearing away. "Why they can't bloody put the results up earlier, I don't know. The universities must have known what our grades were last week to have time to decide who they're going to give places to."

"It was the same when Ollie got his results. We'd already arrived at school when he found out he'd got his place at Bath."

There was a long queue of traffic into the car park. She opened the door. "You find somewhere to park and I'll get the results."

"Don't you want me to come in with you?"

"No. I'll be fine."

I pushed away the disappointment I wouldn't be there to see her face break into relief. I knew she wouldn't wait for me to arrive.

I eventually parked miles down the road and hurried back towards school, doing that whole "good luck" thing with all the mothers walking past and feeling irritated that the ones who had the straight A* students, grade eight piano and all-around wunderkind were the ones bigging up the disaster potential— "Oh well, we'll see, there's always clearing"—which was code for "Definitely on for four A*s."

The first students poured back out towards the car park, some rushing and waving papers, some doing the uber-cool saunter, others keeping their parents in suspense for longer by messing about taking selfies on the wall, leaning in, their youthful faces vibrant and joyful. I scanned the melee for Hannah, preparing the camera on my phone, ready to capture that moment when she hit the springboard to the rest of her life.

The crowd was thinning. A little dot of unease spread in me. I walked to the corner of the car park, where I had a view of the steps that led up to the great hall. Still they came bounding down, towards their new lives, to the freedom of leaving home without yet having to shoulder the burden of adult responsibility. All those happy faces, expecting good things from the future, carrying within them the certainty of their own invincibility, of their own importance in the world. There was a roundness to them, the sheen of youth, as though their faces hadn't yet worn the tribulations of adulthood. Shouts of "Got into Bristol!" "Politics at Manchester!" "A* in Maths!" filled the air.

Still no Hannah. My phone vibrated. I glanced down, expecting a message from Hannah telling me there was a queue, or she was comforting a friend, or they were doing a group photo.

I've done really badly. Pick me up from the staff car park so I don't have to walk past everyone.

My stomach clenched. What did "badly" mean? A "C" instead of an "A"?

I rang her.

She barked a sobbing "What?" down the phone.

"Darling, what's happened? What did you get? It can't be as bad as all that. Did you get your insurance choice?"

"I'm not talking about it now."

"But don't we need to speak to someone about clearing if you didn't get the place you wanted?"

"I'm not FUCKING GOING TO UNIVERSITY. Just bring the bloody car."

I hung up. There was no talking to her when she got like that. I hoped the teachers couldn't hear her.

I decided the quickest way to limit the damage was to go and find her on foot. I ran up the steps, cursing my choice of a school on a hill. I huffed past all the cheers and jubilation, the students punching the air and singing, "We Are the Champions." Hannah was slumped on a bench, her A level result slip in tiny confetti pieces.

I sat next to her. "Shall I just go and have a quick chat with the teachers to see what we should be doing?"

"Muuu-uuum! There isn't anything to be done. I got a C, a D and an E."

Which did make Exeter with its "If you make us first choice, we'll accept AAB" look a little on the ambitious side.

In that moment, I wanted to march into the hall where all those teachers would be congratulating themselves on pushing so many students up to an A* and ask for my bloody money back. God knows how much we'd spent on private school over the years, but I now wished I'd blown it on seeing the orang-utans in Borneo.

I pulled Hannah to her feet. "Come on, let's get you home."

She sobbed all the way down the steps, with various mothers pressing their lips together and looking like I'd suffered a bereavement. Which I had. The death of my dream for my daughter.

I'd spent years going to Jack's company dos sandwiched between a couple of corporate bigwigs, who would turn to me at some point in the evening and say, "And what do you do?" their eyes darting around for someone worthier of their intellect when the answer was "I'm at home with the children." On one occasion, a portly man with nostril hairs that looked as though they could be recycled into a scrubbing brush said, "Isn't that a waste of a university education?" and I'd muttered that I'd gone straight to work from school. He'd glanced over the table at Jack and said, "But your husband is so bright. You're a pretty little thing, though. I'll give you that."

Jack dismissed it. "Stupid old git. If you weren't at home looking after the kids, I couldn't do my job." And every time it happened, he turned up with a diamond bracelet or a fancy handbag—"*I* appreciate you." Which I loved—but I would have loved being a big important lawyer rather than the "pretty little thing" at home much more.

Even before Hannah was born, I promised myself if I ever had a girl she'd get the best education money could buy. In my mother and baby group, the competition between the mums over who sacrificed more reinforced that view. The women who went to the best universities and ended up with a recognisable career—solicitor, teacher, accountant—somehow felt they had the monopoly on finding motherhood the most challenging. "I feel guilty saying this, but I'm looking forward to getting back to the stimulation of work." "I find it so hard after running my own team to be at the beck and call of a tiny person who won't follow orders," followed by a self-deprecating laugh. There was an assumption that the rest of us were too thick to need any intellectual stimulation, as though our brain cells were satisfied by measuring out Calpol in 5ml doses.

And now history was going to repeat itself.

*   *   *

When I got home, Jack looked at Hannah, who by now was a bright red beacon of misery, yet still said, "Did you get what you needed for Exeter?"

She screamed at him and stormed upstairs.

"For fuck's sake! You could see she was upset. Did you not make the correlation between Hannah crying and not getting the grades she needed? On A level results day?"

Jack shrugged. "Sorry. I was just trying to—"

"Trying to what? Trying to make a shitty situation just a little bit more tense and shitty than it already is? Well, you've done that."

After I'd slammed about in the kitchen for a few minutes with Jack hovering behind me, I blurted out the results then burst into tears myself. He moved towards me, but I shook him off.

"How did she manage to do so badly? I thought she worked quite hard," he said.

I wasn't sure how Jack would know when he'd seldom been at home in the last six months. He certainly hadn't been bothering himself with the tedious biology testing. I only had to hear the word "yeast" to want to shout "Unicellular!"

I muttered a bad-tempered "God knows" and buried myself in my laptop. I opened up my Facebook account to delete the picture of Hannah all bright-eyed, waiting for her university place to be confirmed a couple of hours earlier when I'd still been quietly confident that any disaster would be confined to a B in Geography.

My timeline was crammed with pictures of smiling teenagers. Every mother in the world was #SoProud, apart from me who was #SoBloodyPissedOff.

I went back to read the comments under my original picture of Hannah. In amongst the "Good luck!" and "Bet she'll do brilliantly" was Sarah, a mother from primary school, whose daughter, Faith, went into a decline if Hannah ever beat her in a spelling test: "Did she get into Exeter to do Business? Faith off to Bristol to do Classics—her first choice!" followed by a line of champagne bottles and fireworks going off. I bet she knew already that Hannah had screwed up. Her A level catastrophe radar would be overheating. The fact that she'd be gloating away with Faith, shaking her head and saying, "I wonder what went wrong there?" made me want to put a fist through the laptop screen.

Instead I wrote "Hannah still debating whether it's worth running up such a large debt, even though business is much more vocational than many other degrees." The second I pressed "post" I knew I'd made an enemy for life. Sarah wouldn't take that comment lying down but right at that moment, I was up for a fight with anyone who was brave enough.

I went upstairs to find Hannah. She was face down on her bed, the perfect picture of teenage devastation. She lifted one cheek off the pillow. "Go away."

"Darling, just let me talk to you for a moment. I know you're disappointed," I said, while forcing down the desire to shout, "I am too!" "But there'll be a solution to this. We can look into clearing, or retaking, if that's what you want."

She swung her legs round and sat up and I prided myself on being able to reach my daughter even in her worst moments.

A look of disgust flashed over her face. "I'm thick. Like you."

I ignored the big stab of hurt and kept my tone steady, protesting that I hadn't been lucky enough to have the wonderful education she'd had and that when I was her age, I hadn't had any encouragement from my parents to go to university. They'd seemed quite happy with the idea that I'd twit about in an office for a few years, then find someone to marry. Which was roughly what happened. I didn't think it was the right time to point out that I'd actually got better A levels than Hannah.

"Oh, get the violins out, Mum. Just go away. You're not helping."

I went downstairs without replying, half wishing I'd had a good bellow about Hannah's sense of entitlement instead of letting her take out her disappointment on me. Jack had found urgent calls to make, which would no doubt last until the chance of him being called in to deal with any of the drudge, rather than the highlights, of family life had faded.

I logged into the computer to email the school and ask them what the next steps were. The screen was still on my Facebook page. Where bloody Sarah had written, "Faith has a real passion—and flair—for her subject and I'm confident employers will see that anyone who can do a degree in such a difficult subject is head and shoulders over someone with a degree that on the surface appears more vocational."

Stupid cow.

Someone else waded in. "Too many kids going to university these days. Too many Mickey Mouse degrees! Should get a job instead and learn the value of real hard work."

To which Jack's business partner, Mike, replied, "But university is not just about the degree. It's the whole experience, meeting new people from all walks of life."

A bloke we'd met on holiday in Sri Lanka chipped in: "You can go down the pub and do that without spending nine grand a year."

And then, like Prime Minister's Question Time, it spiralled out of control, with people I barely knew chiming in—my old dog walker, some bossy moo from the tennis club, an old schoolfriend I hadn't seen in thirty years.

"We need fewer degrees in Sport Science and more young people who can show up on time knowing their eight times table."

"Snowflake generation! Half of them don't even finish their degrees and they have the benefit of the internet. Don't even have to go to the library and sift through hundreds of textbooks to find out what they need."

"Much better off doing an apprenticeship!"

A personal trainer I'd once had for about two weeks before deciding I liked drinking too much wrote: "Total waste of money. Sorry, but who needs a bollox degree in Ancient Greek?"

Sarah replied: "I suppose you think libraries, museums and art galleries should be closed because 'culture' is irrelevant? Or spelling for that matter! People like you are what led to the UK voting for Brexit!"

I loved that Brexit became part of any Facebook argument. I reckoned there could be a debate on the best way to stop rhino poaching in Africa and Brexit would somehow get in there.

I tried to call a halt to the nastiness I'd set in motion: "Shall we all agree to disagree? Good luck to the students who want to go to university and good luck to those who'd rather get a job. Lots of ways to get from A to B in life."

But Sarah, who had complained to the teacher when the girls were six years old that Hannah had copied from Faith in a maths test and beaten her by two marks, was not going to agree with anyone. "Great philosophy to hide behind if you don't manage to get the grades you need for university."

I slammed the laptop lid down. I'd let my other "friends" deal with her.

CHAPTER 9

Sally

Friday 1 September

Photo: Sally and Chris on their wedding day.
   Caption: Happy tenth anniversary to my darling husband.
   #Allthelove

I'd held it to me, waiting to surprise him on Friday morning, the day of our anniversary. I'd given him a card with a picture of the boutique hotel in Hove that I'd picked, adults-only. The last time, if everything went according to plan. But I had more chance of success if there weren't any actual children there to show Chris what the future might hold.

"I know you're working from home today, so do you think we can head off a little bit earlier?"

He ran his fingers through his hair. "I didn't know you'd got all this planned. I've got a presentation to work out for the board, I've got a con-call at 5:30 and I need to speak to the FD about our Q3 forecast. I chose to work from home so I could get a long day in."

I tried to overlook Chris's pompous super-important abbreviations. It was as though he wanted to bombard me with his business terms, waiting for me to go "FD?" so he could patiently explain he had an audience with the Financial Director and reassure himself I wasn't quite as far up the corporate ladder as he was. "Even though it was our anniversary you weren't worried about finishing early?"

He shrugged. "I thought I'd do all the flowers and stuff tonight, when we're not rushing about for work."

I could see all the joy of my treat turning into another tick on the chore list—Have fun with wife. Have dinner with wife without checking mobile. Have sex with wife.

"Sorry. I was probably trying to fit too much in. You take your time. Even if we get there at nine, we'll probably still be able to get dinner. I'll ring ahead."

Chris nodded and disappeared into his study, looking as though he'd discovered he had shingles. Not life-threatening but a serious irritation.

Happy bloody anniversary.

I spent the day catching up on paperwork, half expecting him to pop into my office and tell me that he'd rearranged the flaming "con-call" and we could head off. The temptation to take out the silk underwear I'd splurged on at Victoria's Secret and pack the nude no-VPL bum huggers instead was overwhelming. Except that would scupper my plan.

I tapped on his office door and then checked myself. Knocking on doors in my own home like a ruddy secretary. I marched in.

He glanced up irritably, snapping "I'll call you back" into the mobile.

"Sorry. I didn't mean to interrupt. I just thought I could pack for you to speed things up tonight."

He smiled. "You are lovely. Sorry to be such a grump. Just one of those weeks."

I went to our bedroom to pick out some shirts and trousers for Chris, forcing myself to fold them properly rather than fling everything in. I put both of our cases into my car, then sat downstairs waiting, trying not to watch the minutes ticking away or think about how I wouldn't have time for a swim before dinner.

I flicked open my Facebook feed, scrolling down the page. Gisela had posted a picture of their curry takeaway—#classyFridaynightcooking #takingiteasy. To my mind, Gisela was always taking it easy. I wasn't quite sure what she did, except shop online for perfumed candles, throws and what my mother would call knick-knacks—funny little dishes that were no good to man nor beast for actually holding anything, glass prisms and silly little signs about wine o'clock. Her timeline was full of #makingitourown #houseintohome #interiordesign. Her house did look beautiful, but I was pretty sure that with endless money and time, most people could pull together something that wasn't half bad.

I kept straining for the noise of Chris finishing up, listening for the telltale sound of the wheels of his chair squeaking backwards, but I could only hear the low murmur of his voice.

Just as I was wondering whether to cancel dinner, Chris appeared at the top of the stairs. "Right. Finally. Sorry. Let's go and enjoy ourselves."

I jumped up. "Everything's ready."

Chris set the alarm and I opened my car.

"Why aren't we taking the Lotus?"

I had an urge to say, "You drive way too fast, have zero lane discipline and the half a finger on the steering wheel of a ridiculously powerful sports car while the rest are stabbing at your phone for those last-minute calls that can't possibly wait till Monday scares the shit out of me."

Instead, I placated him with "I thought you'd be able to unwind on the journey so that you're in party mode when we get there. Come on, my car's all packed."

I held my breath. If my mother had been there, she would have told me off for "emasculating him," as though the mere possession of a penis equalled the right to drive.

He looked as though he was going to argue, but in the end he huffed into the passenger seat. I tried not to squeal out of the drive, but I just wanted to get there, have that first glass of wine and be like any normal couple. I bet Gisela didn't have to scrape Jack into the car like a barnacle off a rock to get him to go to a posh hotel for a guaranteed shag.

I glanced into their home as I turned the car. They all seemed to be up dancing. Gisela was really giving it some, her boobs flinging from side to side and Jack twizzling her round. What family spontaneously gets up after a bellyful of chicken tikka masala and starts twirling about their sitting room? I swore she never shut her curtains—Designers Guild, £100 a metre when I'd looked online—so the rest of us could look into the window of her life and find ourselves lacking. The contrast between the warm fuggy fumes of cinnamon and coriander in her house and the chill of Chris's lemony aftershave and pissed-off manner in our car wasn't lost on me.

By the time we made it to Hove, Chris was at least speaking. "Shall we walk the Seven Sisters tomorrow?"

"Love to. I've packed our walking gear. Let's see what the weather looks like." If I had my way, that's not what we would be doing at all.

Thankfully, as soon as Chris saw the room, he cheered up. "Wow. This is gorgeous. Thank you. Sorry for being such a grumpy bugger."

He gave me a hug, lowering me onto the bed and undoing my blouse.

I didn't want to spoil the moment, but I knew he'd shout about "sodding British hotels shutting so early" if we ended up with a club sandwich from room service. "Kitchen closes at 9:30. Shall we go and have dinner first? We don't have to get up early tomorrow."

Contrarily, I was a bit offended that he called a halt to proceedings so readily in favour of making sure he didn't miss out on his triple-cooked chips.

Once we were settled in the restaurant in an intimate booth perfect for a romantic celebration, we began to relax. I let him order the wine—the Malbec he preferred rather than the Rioja I did. I wanted him to suggest champagne, to think that ten years with me was worth pushing the boat out for. But he just said, "We've got some up in the bedroom. We can have that later. Or tomorrow."

When we first met, when Chris was earning a lot less money than he did now, he'd insist on champagne Fridays. "End of the week is a celebration and I'm doubly lucky because you're here with me."

Then again, I used to spend many lunchtimes browsing La Senza and Victoria's Secret for something new, just to hear him say, "I like that. I like that a lot." Whereas apart from special occasions like today, I often opted for a comfy bra rather than a silky underwired one that dug into my ribcage. Maybe that's how married life evolved, though I couldn't help feeling that frivolous stuff like bras and bubbles stopped married couples descending into the drudgery pit of mortgages and remembering to descale the iron.

My mother always said I looked for reasons to be unhappy, which was rich coming from her given that she'd gone on a cruise in the summer and complained that she didn't like being surrounded by sea. However, since I'd blown a sizable chunk of my pay rise on this weekend, I deliberately looked for a mood-boosting topic of conversation. One that would put Chris in charge.

"So how did the con-call go? Are you making progress with the, er, thingy, the project you were working on?" I asked, realising that if he'd told me what he was doing I couldn't remember.

He frowned and filled me in and either I hadn't listened

or we'd never spoken about it before. Sometimes I just didn't have the energy to listen to his work woes when my own job required me to be super-sharp, especially now they'd promoted me to senior wine buyer with a special responsibility for sourc- ing wine for restaurants. It would mean a bit more travelling, perhaps three times a month, but I figured I wouldn't burden Chris with that just yet.

Anyway, with any luck, I was going to be at home as much as he wanted. "So, do you think you'll still be working in the Staines office in five years' time?" I asked, hoping that he was aiming for one of the top jobs in London.

"That's an interesting question," he said, as though my usual conversation was banal. He topped up our wine glasses and clinked his against mine. "There is a possibility that I'll get promoted to an international analyst manager, which means I'll be away a lot more. One of the areas I'd have to cover is North America, so I could be gone for a week or two at a time. Would you mind? Would you be lonely?"

I felt my adrenaline push itself off the starting blocks. If Chris was doing what he wanted to do, then, in theory, I should be able to follow my dream and have a baby. "It's not so much about me being lonely but about us overlapping at home. I'm not sure it's going to be great for our marriage for both of us to be away a lot."

Chris jutted his chin out. "So it's all right for you to be gal- livanting about?"

Before I could answer, our starters arrived. I made a big show of taking photos—"That asparagus is gorgeous. Don't those calamari look good, Chris?"—and being very jolly with the waiter. I'd told them it was our anniversary when I made the booking and I didn't want him going back into the kitchen and laughing about the couple who'd be lucky to make it through another year.

I waited for him to leave then said, "I wasn't saying you shouldn't take a job covering the States if the opportunity arises." I stretched my hand out to cover his. His fist remained rigid under mine.

"What then?"

"Maybe it's time to rethink the direction I'm going in. Someone needs to be at home, otherwise we're going to be like two ships that pass in the night."

"So you're going to volunteer for a demotion?" Chris was forking in his calamari, which wasn't receiving sufficient homage at about £1.50 per crispy tentacle.

"Not exactly." Now I'd created the moment, I was finding it hard to take the final leap, to let the words out there.

"What then?"

I cut the tip of an asparagus and took my time sweeping up the hollandaise sauce. "I'd like to have a baby," I said, counting the remaining asparagus spears before I looked up.

Chris had a tentacle hanging out of an open mouth. "You want to do what?" Incredulous as though I'd suggested setting up a gorilla sanctuary in the back garden. "But you never wanted kids. *We* never wanted kids."

I tried to keep the break out of my voice. "I'm not sure we ever had that conversation, Chris. I think we just didn't make a conscious decision that we did want them and because I got the impression you didn't, it got harder to say I did. It really is what I want. When I think about being fifty, I can't imagine a future without children. And if I don't do it soon, I'm going to run out of time."

Chris squeezed some more lemon on his calamari. "When I think about being fifty, I imagine us going on some fantastic holidays—Sri Lanka, South Africa, Australia. All the places we talked about going to when we first met and couldn't afford."

"But don't you think that's a bit empty in the end? What's the point if you're not sharing it?"

"I don't think it's empty at all. I'd be sharing it with you."

"And that's enough? Job, holidays, staring at me across the table for the next fifty years?"

Chris looked away. "Yes. That is enough. For me."

The waiter collected our plates as we sat there in total silence. Tears were starting to gather. "Will you at least think about it? You could pursue your career one hundred per cent. I'll stop work completely if that's what you want. I wouldn't be travelling anymore and I could make our house into a proper home, instead of just somewhere we breeze in and out before we're off to the next place."

The waiter returned with our main courses. "Is everything all right?"

I brushed my eyes, managing to say, "Yes, yes, this all looks amazing." To divert attention from the fact that fat tears were plopping onto my linen napkin, I dug into my bag for my phone waiting for his shiny shoes to head back towards the kitchen. Before I could sort myself out he returned with a jug of salsa for my sea bass. I dolloped it onto my plate and pretended to be engrossed in taking photos of my food until he stopped doing the "Any more wine? Any more sauces? Water?"

Then I got up and walked out, leaving Chris celebrating our tenth anniversary with a miso-blackened salmon and sweet potato fries for company.

Photos: Dainty plates of asparagus, calamari and sea bass.

Hotel with beautiful geraniums and benches under pergolas covered in sweet peas.

Caption: Celebrating ten years of marriage to Mr. G!

#PerfectDay #LoveOfMyLife #Adult-onlyBliss #Child-freePeace

CHAPTER 10

Kate

Friday 1 September

I'd been on shift since 6 a.m. and was just looking forward to a long soak in the bath when we were called to the scene of an accident where an eighteen-year-old girl had rolled her car. I was trying to do everything kindly and calmly, but I had more adrenaline pumping than usual.

As I assessed for spinal injuries, I stared down into her face, talking to her. "I know you're frightened, but you're doing fine, we're going to take care of you." I'd be lying if I wasn't saying it as much for my benefit as hers. Lacerations to the face and chest. Open ankle fracture. And blood. Blood everywhere.

She was too shocked to cry. Just kept asking, "Can I phone my mum?"

"You can in a minute. Let me get you comfortable and give you something for the pain." Please, God, never let me have to receive that phone call from Daisy. I never wanted to hear—or say—those words, "You'd better come" again. I could almost feel them reverberating in my brain, even at the distance of nearly seventeen years, heavy and forbidding.

My voice sounded wrong. I could hear the tremor in it as I kept talking, kept reassuring her. Bella, her name was. Despite my training, and the knowledge that I'd signed up for this, I wanted to get out of the ambulance and distance myself from another mother's random bad luck. From that mother who right now was probably standing staring into the fridge for the miraculous ingredients that would constitute dinner without a trip to the supermarket. The thought that this could be Daisy, that somehow there'd be a payback, was swamping me, making me only marginally less terrified than Bella.

Even after I'd done the handover to the emergency staff at the hospital, I kept seeing the blue lights in my mind, lights I'd seen a thousand times, that were a part of my daily job. But now, I could only see *those* lights from that day, lighting up the horror on *her* face. I drove home, my breath coming in bursts, saying, "Think bike" at the busy junctions, reminding myself to use the wing mirrors.

When I got in, Daisy was folded over her books, sitting with her legs tucked under herself in a way I was sure was bad for her posture. I wanted to beg her never to learn to drive or, if she did, never to go on the motorway, never to text while driving, never to hurry, to get there late but alive. I longed to burst out with how much I loved her, how proud she made me, the sort of thing Gisela said to Hannah with such ease. I was almost afraid to say it in case some higher power heard and totted up a tally of whether I deserved to keep her. I was just working up to it when she said, "I'm going over to Hannah's in a bit."

"Why don't you invite Hannah over here?" I asked, ashamed that my disappointment about Hannah not getting into university had nothing to do with her education and everything to do with the fact that she'd be over the road for the foreseeable future, a siren call to Daisy every weekend.

She shrugged. "Maybe next week. We're going to have a Netflix night then get a Domino's."

I'd forced myself to squash the stab of hurt when I discovered that Gisela and Jack often watched films with them: "Jack even cried at *Gnomeo and Juliet*!" I couldn't compete. Gisela was the perfect mother—always at home, with the right banter for the teenagers, much more relaxed about spills on the carpet and water marks on the table, unlike me who was the "shoes off" police and slapped down a coaster the minute I heard the top coming off a bottle of Diet Coke. But the real clincher was that Gisela liked shopping and make-up and clothes. I wanted to share this burning passion of Daisy's, but whenever I got to the shops, I'd be muttering about not needing any of this crap and say things like, "But you've got a pair of black jeans. I saw a red lipstick in your bedroom," seemingly unable to grasp that the minute differences were worth Daisy blowing her hard-earned Tesco money on.

When I peered into the background of the photos Gisela sometimes posted of Daisy and Hannah on Facebook, it didn't surprise me that Daisy preferred being over there. The Mac laptop, the flat-screen TV, the cream sofa. There were always so many wrappers—crisps, biscuits, sweets—lying around. Made a mockery of me racing into Morrisons before work to pick up mango or watermelon for her.

Daisy gathered her belongings to escape over the road. "You should try and get to know Hannah's parents better. They're really nice. And they do stuff they can invite you to. They have loads of parties. According to Hannah, Gisela really likes you."

I laughed at how surprised she sounded. "Maybe I'm not so bad after all."

"Mum, you know what I mean. I just want you to do something normal, like have lunch with friends or go out for a drink." It sounded so easy. But the fear that they'd find out who I was, that the moment would come when I'd sit opposite them, watching the cogs whir and fall into place, paralysed me. And, funnily enough, most people weren't so keen to hang out with me after that, with the invitations and texts gradually dropping off. Then the weeks would stretch into months of silence, the "sorry we haven't caught up lately, it's been manic, you know how it is" if we bumped into each other accidentally.

For the moment, though, Facebook had opened up a

potential new social life with Sally and Gisela. Daisy had only just created my account, with a profile picture of a cat, when a friend request arrived from Gisela.

"How does she even know I'm on here?" I'd asked.

"I told Hannah."

I didn't have the heart to tell her off. Then Sally had joined in on the act and a barrage of messages from them both followed— "Who's free for coffee tomorrow?" "Who fancies the cinema next Thursday?" "I'm looking at a spa day for February. Who's in?" I'd refused so far, making the excuse of work, but there was something surprisingly uplifting about being wanted, about people with good, ordinary lives finding me worthy of their company.

After I'd reined in the queasy feeling about people springing up from nowhere, I began to be curious again, to snoop about people's lives, the friends I might still have if they hadn't had to choose between Becky and me. I'd even found Becky herself. Frustratingly, her privacy settings were so tight, I could only see her profile picture. She carried the burden of life in the lines around her mouth, but her eyes still held that glint of mischief. I wished I could hate her, but despite everything, I hoped her natural optimism was pushing her forwards.

It was so tempting to look for Oskar, but every time my finger hovered over the "O," I pulled back. If the eleven years since he'd left me had taught me anything, it was not to go in search of things to feed my dark thoughts at three o'clock in the morning.

After I'd watched Daisy head over to Hannah's, I gave in to my nosiness about my new neighbours, despite knowing I'd end up feeling dissatisfied with my own life.

I flicked onto Sally's profile. She'd posted a photo that morning of her and Chris on their wedding day. "Happy tenth anniversary to my darling husband. #Allthelove." She'd done better than me. I'd just about made nine years of marriage.

I studied the picture. Chris in his top hat and tails. Sally all lace and veils. That did surprise me. She seemed so independent, travelling about all over the place. I found it hard to imagine her doing the whole church thing. Chris hadn't changed much, but Sally looked so much softer in her wedding photo. Now she was a person of sharp edges, her face permanently on guard, life a collection of faults to find. Still, I was pretty sure if you looked at a picture of me on my wedding day, I'd be positively dewy compared with how I looked now.

Before I went to bed at eleven, I had another little scroll. Her night away was so well documented, we could have been there ourselves. A four-poster bed against a backdrop of bold flowery wallpaper, with a bottle of fizz in a bucket. Then another of the basket of Molton Brown toiletries and the shower with a massive rainhead. #TenthAnniversaryCelebrations #Don'tMindIfIDo #CheekyWeekendAway.

Sorry, but that was just weird. Surely no one needed to see the precursor to a night of passion? I couldn't be the only one in the world who thought the hashtag should be #BigNightOf-BonkingAhead. Urgh. Sally was so busy making sure we all knew how happy they were, it would be a miracle if they had time to make use of that bed.

I read through the comments, which ranged from the straightforward "Have a lovely time, congratulations" to "You're in there. Lucky Mr. G!"

Twenty-nine people liked the post in about five minutes.

Shame there wasn't a "vomit" button.

I looked further down her posts, though I knew before I started that they would make me feel that I had the most boring, pedestrian life, with not much prospect of it changing.

And I was right. Sally had recently started a jar of joy.

"Day one: Breakfast in bed brought to me by my gorgeous hubby. Poached eggs on spinach and soda bread. #SpoiltRotten #CouldGetUsedToThis"

Nothing so common as a bowl of Frosties for Sally. The fact that I even clicked on the picture and noted with satisfaction that the egg yolks weren't runny was a sign of the petty person

I'd turned into. I should delete my account. I only had two friends, but scrolling through their lives was like mainlining a dissatisfaction drug, a sort of online self-harming without the razor blades. If Sally wasn't careful, I'd start countering her jar of joy with my own jar of pissed-offness—the chair where Daisy should have been sitting rather than over at Gisela's. The alarm clock set for 5:30 a.m. A big turd on my lawn from next door's cat who'd decided my grass was shit central. The masking tape holding on the wing mirror that some bastard had reversed into at work and not bothered to leave me a note. Or maybe a jar of things that should have been mine. Starting with a husband. Then the best friend I'd had since primary school. The girl, and later, the woman, who'd always had my back.

"Day two: Chris taking me to the airport despite 5 a.m. start. #Luckywife #Superhero"

Jesus. When my car had finally given up the ghost at work, I'd waited for the breakdown man in the ambulance station car park at midnight. Half the lights had gone out and the rest had exuded a creepy orange glow. The rain had bashed down onto the windscreen. I'd kept the doors locked but it didn't stop me peering into the back seat in case someone had crept in through the keyhole. When the truck finally arrived, the mechanic was so kind to me. "Poor you sitting out here in this. Bit spooky out here, isn't it? Couldn't you have rung your husband to keep you company?"

I'd felt embarrassed saying I didn't have one and irritated that he'd assumed I had. The mechanic was only being nice, though. He probably wasn't looking for the long answer, the one that involved Oskar gradually withdrawing from me over a five-year period, until we weren't "in this together" but I was "deep in it on my own." I already imagined the mechanic running oily fingers over his bald head, saying, "That's some heavy shit. Anyway, think I've got her going now if you'd just like to hop in," before screaming round the corner on two wheels in relief.

"Day three: Beautiful sunrise glinting off the titanium roof at Hotel Marqués de Riscal #Spain #NoFilter #WorkingLife #LoveMyJob"

I clicked off Sally's page.

My life was #onebigfilter and my jar of joy was #particularlyempty today.

CHAPTER 11

Sally

Friday 20 October

Jar of Joy Day thirteen
    Photos: Fortnum & Mason's sign. Cream scone and
tea.
    Caption: Rare day off with my lovely mum.
    #LondonLife #Bestfriends

I'd booked afternoon tea with Mum before the summer, thinking that October was ages away but at least I could stop feeling guilty about neglecting her. It seemed to fly round and even though it had been in the diary for months, it was just another thing to shoehorn in between work trips and getting the builder round to look at the cracks in the wall in the bedroom.

I'd felt guilty at finding it a chore when I'd seen her Facebook page: "Daughter taking a day off from globetrotting to have posh afternoon tea with me in London—can't wait!"

But her face didn't look like it couldn't wait when she came bustling down Piccadilly towards me, in her best gloves and scarf, practically swatting the *Big Issue* seller out of the way. She gave me a big hug, though, and I got a waft of Je Reviens, the scent of so many goodnight cuddles.

"I don't know why we always come to London. Honestly, the trains from York were right up the creek this morning. And King's Cross, you've never seen anything like it. They'd closed one of the escalators to the Piccadilly line, my feet are killing me…"

Thankfully "It's lovely to see you" finally followed the litany of Transport for London complaints. I hadn't seen Mum since May Bank Holiday. I'd put her off coming down because we were moving and Chris's tolerance of her occupied a space of no more than a cubed centimetre even in times of absolute calm. With all the stress of packing up our old house and sorting the move to the new one, I didn't feel able to summon up the necessary diplomacy to stop her rearranging our drawers and cupboards to her warped logic—Tupperware in the cupboard with the bleach, teaspoons in a drawer at the far end of the kitchen, teapot in with the ironing board. Not to mention putting the dishwasher on as soon as there were more than five mugs in it—"It all gets so smelly." Or worse, washing them up in cold water with a cloth she'd used to wipe up something on the floor.

I pushed away the thought of all the emails piling up in my inbox and concentrated on jollying Mum along. "Sorry you've had a horrible journey. It's probably all the families going on half-term early."

Just imagining getting on a train to York in the school holidays with my daughter or son, my dad walking us round the Railway Museum, Mum with a bag of Opal Fruits in her pocket, filled me with a longing that didn't feel as though it would go away any time soon. I swallowed the sadness down.

"Your dad sends his love. Spends all his time on the golf course now he's retired. See him less than I did when he was at work."

Dad had the right idea.

I led Mum through Fortnum & Mason, with her clucking away, "Look at that! Twelve pounds fifty for a tin of tea. People have got more money than sense. Suppose it's all the foreigners that buy it, though."

"Sshhh." Mum thought anyone who didn't come from Yorkshire was foreign.

I shuffled her through to the Diamond Jubilee Tea Salon before she spotted someone in a burka and offered her opinion on that.

Once we were settled, I ordered the afternoon tea with champagne.

"Are we celebrating something?" Mum asked, her eyes dropping to my stomach. "Should you be drinking?"

The hope on her face made me desperate to have that moment, the one where I could build a bridge back to her, have something in common with her again, let her be the one who knew more than me, rather than endlessly struggling to pull her into my world.

But that wasn't going to happen yet. "Just thought it would be a bit of a treat for us. I don't see you very often."

Her face fell. Her eyebrows did the little raise that preceded the "a career's all very well, but when you're my age, you'll wish…" lecture. I pushed my back hard into the velvet chair, braced for the "No one ever lay on their deathbed wishing they'd spent more time in the office."

The frustration and injustice that she didn't even consider that I might want a baby and couldn't have one were so strong today, bubbling into my limbs with such powerful force, that I wasn't sure I could tolerate "the speech" without running amok through the restaurant, flipping the tiered cake stands over and sending all the little smoked salmon sandwiches catapulting through the air. I said the first thing that came into my head to distract her. "How's Edie next door?"

Mum looked aghast. "She died. Last year. Dreadful do it was. I told you, I went to the funeral. Her daughter didn't even bother coming back from New Zealand."

I could be forgiven for forgetting Edie had died. Mum often

rang when she'd compiled a full list of neighbourhood ailments and demises. I needed a spreadsheet to keep on top of them.

"How's Chris?" Mum asked, after the waiter had finished talking us through the sandwiches.

"He's fine, in the running for a new job, big step up. Sends his love."

Which he absolutely hadn't. Despite coming in from a company do at 2 a.m. and not needing to get up because he was working from home, he'd run downstairs as I was leaving, to shout, "Don't invite them for Christmas!"

"Do you two ever get any time together? You both work so hard. Your dad and I worry about you."

I tried hard not to hear that as "worry about you not finding time to make a baby." But right now, every conversation I had—not just with Mum—seemed to loop back to the stalemate that Chris and I were in. It was like the first time you split up with someone you loved and every song on the radio seemed as though it was meant for you and your desolate, devastated heart. If only she knew, if only I could tell her about the uncertain days that followed our tenth wedding anniversary, when we'd veered between angry recriminations—"You're just being selfish"—and sad, sane conversations—"I wish I didn't feel like this"—about wanting different things. We'd gone round and round in circles, even putting a tentative hand out towards splitting up, as though touching something we knew would burn, before snatching it back again and hugging each other tightly, telling ourselves we'd find a way through it. What we really meant, though, was that we hoped the other person would eventually see the light and acquiesce.

Sometimes I'd get a late-night text to say he was staying in London as he had an early meeting at his office headquarters. Clearly, a night sleeping next to me no longer outweighed the 6 a.m. cab. Fierce rows erupted whenever we'd had a drink, followed by several days when there'd be a silent race to be the first one out of the door in the morning without saying goodbye.

Eventually, Chris would want sex—the irony—and we'd get through a few days, sometimes a week, before the whole cycle started again.

Mum poured some tea, then peered into her cup, frowning. "They might have told us they didn't use teabags."

I craned round to call over the waiter to bring a fresh cup, using the distraction to send the conversation in a different direction. "You must come and see our new house. We're really pleased with it."

"Your dad feels very put out you haven't asked him over to hang all your pictures and sort your shelves."

"I don't like to ask him down to visit and then make him sing for his supper," I said, thinking back to the time I'd asked him to put a mirror up in the downstairs loo and he'd hung it over the toilet cistern rather than the basin.

I'd laughed about it, but Chris had been apoplectic. "What bloke needs to see their face when they're taking a slash?!"

He wouldn't agree to Dad swinging a hammer anywhere near our perfect Lamp Room Gray walls.

"Do you think he'd be up to planting some daffodil bulbs? The garden could do with a bit of attention."

Mum smiled, the sort of smile I remembered from my childhood when I read *Carbonel* out loud to her, or recited *The Lion and Albert* in a Lancashire accent. I wondered when I'd become a disappointment to them, despite everyone else thinking I'd "done well." I felt the urge to cry.

Mum hoovered up some crumbs of scone with her finger. "Your dad would love that."

I unclenched my stomach muscles, the swell of tears subsiding. "We'll have to sort out some dates then," I said, feeling exhausted at the thought of timetabling in another commitment beyond work, finding the right Russian roulette moment to tell Chris my parents were coming or trying to juggle it to coincide with when I was at home and he was away.

My mum rapped her teaspoon on the cup as though she was

about to make an announcement. "What he'd really love is a grandchild, though. He wouldn't mind if it was a boy or a girl. He's always collecting bits of odd wood 'in case I need to turn my talents to a doll's house.'"

The image that created in my mind, my old dad saving crates, scavenging bits of timber at the dump, filled me with sadness, raw and jagged. I screwed up my eyes to disperse the tingle of tears.

I pushed my chair next to Mum's. "Here, let's get the waiter to take a photo of us enjoying our tea. Perhaps Dad will come with you next time."

Photo: Sally and her mum crooking their little fingers over their teacups and waving a coronation chicken sandwich at the camera.
 Caption: Don't mind if we do!
 #PerfectAfternoon

CHAPTER 12

Gisela

Monday 23 October

Initially I'd been all conciliatory. "So would you like to go through clearing? Retake? Have a gap year, get any old job and think about what you'd like to do?"

Now we were at half-term with no progress, so I had to push Hannah to make a decision while we still had any hope of a civil relationship. She was getting up at midday, coming down in pyjama shorts so tiny that most of her bum cheeks were hanging out, regardless of whether the gardener or cleaners were here. Then she'd go to the fridge, fling open every cupboard until they vibrated on their hinges and complain there wasn't any food—by which she meant Pringles, chocolate chip cookies and that smoked Austrian cheese that came in a sausage—rather than bananas, broccoli or Brussels. Eventually she'd drift off to watch Netflix with a trail of crumbs, smears of butter and empty bagel bags in her wake.

That, coupled with Jack's endless leaving out of the milk and knocking into the dog bowl and slopping water everywhere, led to scenes straight out of a sitcom, where I'd start shouting to no one in particular, "That's right, don't you bother wiping that up, yes, you're all too important and too bloody busy to actually get a cloth out and trouble your hand with a circular motion..."

Hannah would glance up from the sofa. "All right there, Mum?" then go back to watching vampires.

If Jack ever had the misfortune to come into the kitchen during one of my rants, he'd laugh and say, "Been at the vodka?"

After a few weeks, when it became clear that Hannah wasn't going to follow Daisy's lead and start earning her keep down at Tesco, I began looking at courses. "Do you fancy photography? You're good at art."

"Not really my thing."

"What about physiotherapy? They're always in demand."

"I'm not spending my life touching someone else's sweaty back. What if they had groin strain? No thank yoooouuu."

"How about setting up your own business? There's an evening course at the tech college that helps you generate ideas and understand how to do it."

It was a constant surprise how fine the line in motherhood was between protecting your kids from every danger and becoming a threat to their lives yourself.

When she didn't bother even looking up from *The Jeremy Kyle Show* she was watching on catch-up, I just booked her onto a cordon bleu cookery course. Even if she didn't use it in her career, it would be useful in life—and she'd be out of the house on a daily basis.

Her reaction was as I'd predicted: "Why did you do that? I don't want to learn how to make some crappy old lamb casserole."

"You're going."

"I'm not."

It had only taken me forty-three years to learn to bulldoze resistance methodically rather than engage in out-and-out warfare.

Eventually, I had to get the big guns in—Jack—who dipped in and out of parenting but could be shaken into an authoritarian stance in an emergency. Even Hannah would have to have balls of steel to resist him in his current frame of mind. He'd become so snappy. After twenty years of kissing me on the lips when he walked in the door, these days he grumbled out a "Hello" before dashing upstairs to his office, mumbling about "Stuff to do." I'd even wondered if he was having an affair, although he'd always been so disdainful about men who were unfaithful. I'd still been sufficiently worried to glance—with one eye closed in dread—down his credit card bill, but if he was up to no good, Gisela Mark Two was an economy model.

The upside to his tetchiness was that he really did play the bad cop with Hannah. "Sorry, but the party's over. You're not hanging around here sponging off us. So get your arse to the course or that allowance of yours—" He made a snipping motion. "I'm very happy to get you a job cleaning the washrooms at the caravan sites. Your choice."

It seemed to do the trick, because Hannah sulked about, saying, "How many people are on this course?" "Are they all middle-aged *Bake Off* wannabes?" "Am I actually going to cook anything I want to eat?" before agreeing to give it a go.

Though, when the bill for the course came in, Jack stormed into the kitchen, waving it under my nose. "Eight bloody grand to learn how to boil an egg? That's more than a term's school fees and they were nearly crippling me! Who's teaching her? Gordon Bleeding Ramsay?"

I'd flown back at him. "What were you doing to sort her out? It's fine for you, disappearing to the office every day or wining and dining your bloody capital investors in London. You're not having to look at her sitting here with a face like a week of wet Sundays. What bargain-basement solution do you suggest?"

He'd shaken his head as though I thought money grew on trees. It was amazing how over the years, money, even with the most generous of men, became a source of control: "You don't need to work. My money is your money." Of course, the subtext was always "I'll have a say in what you spend it on, but if the mood takes me to go out and splash the cash on a new car, well, so what? I've earned it."

So, there we were, outside the cookery school, with me acting like the poor sod in charge of warming up the audience for the big comedy act to follow. "Love the hat, Hannah! You look like a professional cook! Can't wait to see what you bring home for dinner." I took about fifteen photos before there was one where she cracked a bit of a smile. And that was only because I'd stepped back into a dog poo.

What I needed was a little party for my birthday in a few weeks' time to bring a bit of joy into our lives. And that handbag I'd seen on the bargain designer website. Better pay for a named delivery day when Jack was in London, given what a grouch he was about money. Yep. That would cheer me up.

Photo: Hannah with her chef's hat on.
  Caption: First day at cookery school. Looking forward to sampling the results!
  #NewBeginnings #CordonBleuChef #World'sHerOyster

CHAPTER 13

Kate

Monday 6 November

Facebook was opening up a whole new life for me. I'd actually received an invitation from Gisela: "My birthday party on Saturday 18 November to get us through a cold and crappy month."

I had to admire her. Not only did she not stand paralysed in front of the freezers at Iceland, wondering whether it would be too naff to serve a few Indian platters, cocktail sausages and chicken dippers, she never seemed to worry no one would turn up. If I ever held a party, I'd be like a dog running up and down a chain-wire fence in case no one came and I was left with a mound of quick-defrost profiteroles and crates of Beck's.

When I told Daisy about the invitation, she said, "You are going, right?"

"I feel a bit awkward because I'm never going to hold a party here to ask her back."

"Mum! She doesn't care about that. She's not the sort of person who counts how many times you go over there. Just say yes and chill."

Daisy looked so anxious, so keen for me to join in.

"I don't know whether I want to go anyway," I said.

"You are so weird. Don't you get bored sitting in night after night?"

"Not really." Though that wasn't true. Following the life of my neighbours on Facebook had acted like a maraca shake to wake up the person I used to be. The one who would drag Oskar up to dance, who'd invent new cocktails, who was never happier than when a crowd of people gathered round for my legendary cheese dumplings, *pierogi*. I'd told myself that as long as no one found out the truth, I was happy enough with my box sets of *Game of Thrones*, that work provided more than enough drama in my life. But with Daisy showing every sign of needing me less, I felt as though I was stepping into a void, where the only company I'd have in the evenings would be a whole host of memories scrabbling at a door I was desperate to keep shut. That scream. Those fists straining to get at me. Her complete inability to hear me, to understand what I was saying, what anyone was saying. And Oskar's face, stricken, his arms clutching Daisy.

I spoke, saying the first thing that came into my head, just to have the noise of my voice in my ears, rather than Becky's with those words, those dreadful damning words, burnt into my brain forever. "I'll think about it. Are you going?"

Daisy threw her hands up. "Um, yes. Why wouldn't I? Their parties are brilliant. Get Gisela to introduce you to one of Jack's hot friends. Hannah says he's got some good-looking mates."

I found it alarming that Hannah even noticed what her dad's friends looked like. At her age, my dad's mates had all melded into one in a blur of cardigans and baggy trousers.

"They'll all be married, silly. And anyway, what would you think if I suddenly turned up with a boyfriend?"

"I'd be delighted."

"Really?"

"Yes! You should go on one of those dating websites." She sighed. "Dad's not coming back, is he?"

An image of Oskar fast asleep on the beach and shooting up in shock when Daisy, a four-year-old bundle of mischief in a frilly pink costume, had tripped and spilt a bucket of freezing cold water over him rushed into my mind. That was our last holiday as a family. When we still had hope. When we still thought we'd drag ourselves through. When I thought love would be enough.

I focused again on Daisy. "No, love. It's been eleven years. I don't think he'll come back now."

She frowned. "I mean, you're not that old. And you're a lot thinner than loads of the other mums around here. That one with the twin boys at number nine is a right old heffalump."

"Karolina!"

Daisy's eyes flew open. I never called her that anymore.

I carried on without acknowledging my mistake. "Daisy, don't be so horrible about people. Those boys are still quite young. It takes time to get back to your normal weight. We've no idea what goes on in people's lives. She might be ill and can't get the weight off. We just don't know. She's probably self-conscious enough, without the rest of us joining in."

We knew what it was like to be judged when people didn't know the facts.

Daisy stared at me with her clear dark eyes. I wasn't sure whether she was waiting for me to finish speaking so she could disappear up to her bedroom or whether any of what I was saying was actually going in. She was harder to read these days. Apart from the occasional chat with my colleagues at work, I had so few conversations with other mothers that I had no way of knowing whether or not Daisy's behaviour was normal, run-of-the-mill teenage naivety and selfishness, which she'd later grow out of.

"I still think you should get a boyfriend," she said. "Shall I create a profile for you on a dating site? I could help you sift through them and find someone nice." She sounded excited, as though I was a new project.

"No. Definitely not."

She huffed out a sigh of frustration. "No one will realise it's you. She won't be looking for you on a dating site."

That fear was back. The fear that Daisy didn't quite get it, that she was way too casual about who knew what.

I tried hard not to snap. "I don't even want a boyfriend. We're happy as we are, aren't we?"

Daisy's face closed down. "Guess so."

I knew the real answer. The responsibility of me, on my own, worrying away, weighed on her. If she could shift that burden onto someone else, she could fly free.

But how could any relationship even get past the first hurdle if I never admitted who I was?

I plonked myself down on the sofa with the laptop on my knees. Daisy was shuffling up her homework and phone, ready to disappear. I wanted to keep her there, to talk to her, to stop her rowing ever further out of reach.

I glanced back down at Gisela's message and saw something I'd missed before. "Oh for God's sake!" That got Daisy's attention. "It's a bloody fancy dress party. I'm definitely not going."

But, of course, "sorting me out with an outfit" was right up Daisy's street and if googling fancy dress suggestions was what it took for my daughter to be fully engaged without texting away on her phone, then I was prepared to spend an evening debating the merits of Wonder Woman/Marilyn Monroe/ Queen Victoria.

"It's got to be something we've already got or can make ourselves. I'm not spending a single penny on something I'll never wear again."

Daisy's head shot up. "Would you fit into Babciu's dress, the one with the white blouse and sort of peasanty skirt?"

"I might, but I'm not wearing that." Too Polish. Too much of a giveaway.

"You'd look beautiful in it."

"Thanks, but no."

"Why not? It's just sitting in a suitcase. Babciu would love to know it had some use."

I hadn't been able to part with it when we'd cleared my mother's house. Although the big puffy skirt took up a whole case of its own and definitely fell into the category of "stuff I'd never look at or use," it was one of those items that was impossible to get rid of, holding within the folds of its bright blue and green striped skirt the essence of Mum. It reminded me of the Polish summer camps we went to in Pwllheli, when my whole family—my grandparents and parents—seemed to come alive, relax, as though they were breathing in familiarity, the customs and traditions they held in their hearts, after the effort of forging a life in a country that they loved and respected but didn't *feel*.

Despite moving here at sixteen, my mother remained resolutely foreign, other, different from my friends' mothers, married to a Pole and living in a community that defined itself by the nation they'd left behind. My surprise arrival when she was forty-six, having long given up hope that she'd have a baby, changed the way she lived, determined as she was that I should embrace Britain and the opportunities it offered. And I had. She'd been so proud that I'd trained as a paramedic. "My daughter saves lives." I tried never to dwell on the irony of that statement.

Reluctantly, I allowed Daisy to chivvy me upstairs. I pulled the suitcase down from the top of my wardrobe, thinking back to all the things that embarrassed me about my mother when I was a child, the sheer Polishness of her. The way she slightly rolled her r's despite thirty-odd years in England. The dumplings in my packed lunch, still warm in the tinfoil, instead of ham sandwiches like my friends. How she watched me on the swings, nattering to my dad in Polish and offering complete strangers her homemade doughnuts, which they inevitably refused.

How I wished I could hold her hand one more time and tell her how much I loved her. How proud of her I was. How much her support, her absolute belief in me, meant. I wished I could tell her I was proud to be Polish and even if I had to keep my background a secret now, it sat within me, curled around my heart.

Daisy was on her feet. "Just try it on. I've never seen you in it."

She was excited, not yet old enough to know that messing about with things belonging to dead people was like prising off a lid, which was sometimes best kept tightly sealed.

In the interests of "living my life," as Mum had urged me to do, even in her last few days when any words were a struggle, I allowed Daisy to carry me along with her enthusiasm. At the first click of the suitcase, the first rustle as I smoothed out the rose border along the bottom of the skirt, the emotions I tried so often to suppress swirled around me. Regret for all the time Mum had missed out on with Daisy because we'd moved away, for the fact that her life had been so much worse because of what happened to me. I could hear her now. "If I could give you back who you were before at the expense of being unhappy myself for the rest of my life, I would."

I wanted to bury my face in those petticoats and fabric and cry. My ordinary mum. Not educated. Not wealthy. Not stunningly beautiful. But the person who loved me no matter what.

Daisy shook the skirt out. "That's awesome. Put it on."

I wriggled into the blouse with the embroidered sleeves, then passed the skirt and bib over my head.

Daisy clapped her hands. "You look amazing."

It was so long since I'd seen myself in anything other than my work uniform or my leggings and a long top that I barely recognised myself.

"Can you do any of the dances?"

I put myself in the starting position, recalling Mum's voice telling me what to do, a feather of a memory rolling across my brain. It soon became clear that I'd been far more interested in messing about on my roller skates and hanging out in the park with my best friend, Becky. Just allowing Becky's name to take shape in my mind made me feel as though I needed to run outside and take great gulps of fresh air. I started unzipping the skirt.

"Nope. Can't remember how to do it at all. Good idea, but I don't think I'm going to be wearing this."

"You've got to! Give me your phone so I can take a picture of you."

I handed it to her, clamping my lips together to stop me commenting.

"Go on, do a proper smile, Mum. You look so much like Babciu."

I took pleasure in her pleasure, and although I hated having my photo taken, I did a few lively poses.

"God, this dress is making me hot." I pulled it over my head, loving the weight of the petticoats. In my mind's eye I saw the image of Mum pulling on her little black boots, burrowing through the heavy layers, adjusting the frills of the sleeve.

I hung it on a hanger and put my clothes back on.

Daisy was still looking at my phone.

"Hannah's just messaged and said you look amazing." She was all flushed and smiley.

"How does Hannah know what I look like?" I glanced at the curtains in case there was some flaming telescope trained on my bedroom window.

"I just sent her the picture."

"Please tell me that you haven't told her it's Babciu's? Or that we're Polish?"

"I'm not stupid. I haven't told anyone we're Polish. What, me, be honest about who I am?" She threw down my phone and marched out.

Yet again, I'd managed to turn a tiny moment of connection with Daisy into another chasm between us. Sighing, I went back downstairs and sat at the laptop, ready to contact Gisela and turn down the party invitation. Before I could, a message popped up. "Just seen your fancy dress outfit! You look amazing. Raised the bar for all of us. Any ideas for me? Michelin Man? Bouncy castle? Shrek?"

I shook my head. Bloody phones and photos. I couldn't back out now without looking rude. I'd have to say I picked it up in a second-hand shop and I'd come as an exotic milkmaid. Let's hope it wouldn't be the little Jenga lie that brought all the others crashing down.

CHAPTER 14

Gisela

Saturday 18 November

Photo: Chocolate croissant, cup of tea, pile of cards.
    Caption: Twenty-one again!
    #HappyBirthdayToMe #SpoiltRotten

Jack leapt out of bed, singing "Happy Birthday to You-u-u-u." "Stay there! I'm going to make you breakfast in bed!"

I stopped myself saying, "No, it's fine, I'll come down." I knew that even after two decades of marriage, Jack would present me with a mug of tea that was too weak to crawl out of the cup, instead of the stand-your-spoon-up syrup I liked to drink. He'd been such a grump lately, I was just grateful he was in a good mood. And today I could have some new things without having to feel guilty. Every time I'd bought something lately, he'd made some snide comment: "Haven't we got enough bloody photo frames by now? It's like living in a fricking art gallery." And when I'd told him I'd invited forty people to my party instead of the twenty I'd originally planned, he'd told me that I could forget about ordering champagne for them all.

As always, though, like a demented optimist who'd never

seen *Titanic*, I approached my birthday with a rush of expectation, which no doubt meant I'd be misunderstood and resentful for the next couple of days.

Jack came in with a big box with a bow round it. Yet again, I had that ridiculous surge of hope, that this year he would have found the present that would make me feel twenty-three again, before that wrinkle above my lip took up permanent residence, like a crevasse in a mountainside that my lipstick could disappear down at any moment. The gift that would say, "I know we didn't plan to get married so early and have kids so quickly, but I'm so glad we did."

I rattled the parcel. "This sounds exciting."

I peeled back the paper.

A thin white box containing a toilet brush.

Albeit a designer toilet brush that I'd pointed out to Jack in one of the home catalogues that dropped through the letter box on a regular basis. He'd taken one look and said, "Seventy-five quid to clean up some skid marks? Jog on!"

So now I knew, that when he scratched his chin and thought deeply about what he was sure I'd love for my birthday, a loo brush sprang to mind.

He looked at me, all expectantly as though I was about to break into applause. His smile faltered. "You did say you didn't need any more jewellery."

Jesus. Since when did "not need" equate with "not want"?

I muttered a "That's an unusual gift, thank you," thinking there was every chance that before the day was out, I might have jammed it up his arse, designer handcrafted ceramic handle and all.

"Hannah has got something for you as well, but she's not up yet."

I just managed not to say, "If it's the matching loo roll holder you can take it back to the shop."

The days when the children would stand over me on my birthday, prising my eyelids open at 6 a.m., hiding their handmade cards behind their backs like precious treasure, seemed a million years ago.

From being the boy who came home from uni as a surprise on Friday nights—often with a bunch of his scruffy mates in tow, all looking as though they could do with a good plate of sausage and mash and a reacquaintance with washing powder—Ollie had gone quiet. "I don't suppose you've had any communication from Ollie? I guess it's too much to hope he's going to make a surprise appearance for my birthday?"

"Gisela, you can't expect him to come back every year. I never went home for my mother's birthday after I went to university. I think that's fairly normal for a young man getting on with his own life. Especially when he's got a serious girlfriend," Jack said.

"You're not bothered about the fact that she's thirteen years older and it's actually a bit obscene that she's taken up with Ollie?"

"Don't be so dramatic. Look at Macron, the French President. His wife is tons older than him, but no one bangs on about that."

"That's completely different. The French have a weird attitude to sex."

Jack laughed. "He's an adult. He's got to make his own mistakes. Like we did." He held his hand out to me. "Come here, my ferocious mother bear. You weren't a mistake, though. And although your parents didn't think I was much of a catch, I've turned out all right in the end."

I smiled, momentarily forgetting about the loo brush. "My dad was just disappointed I didn't go to university after all that effort of retaking my A levels. Anyway, it was completely different; I wasn't thirteen years older than you. Could you have a word with Ollie?"

Jack shook his head. "Just let him work it out of his system. He's with Natalie now, but when he finishes university he might decide to spend a year surfing in Australia, he might live in

Ireland and open a pottery, work in the vineyards in the South of France...There are loads of ways of finding your path in life—and Ollie will find his."

Intellectually, I knew Jack was right. It didn't stop me feeling sick every time I imagined Ollie diving straight into a life arguing about who used the last of the milk and who opened another box of Weetabix before the first one was finished.

I'd asked Hannah to invite him and Natalie to my fancy dress birthday party. It felt too needy to ask him myself when he knew exactly when my birthday was. But she either hadn't had a reply or was retaining the knowledge to punish me for forcing her onto the chef course. "I don't give a shit about lamb bloody noisettes and lemon posset. I'm going to become a vegan anyway."

So, by six o'clock on the evening of my birthday party, when I hadn't heard a peep from Ollie and Jack had thrown a fit when he realised I'd paid a hundred and fifty pounds to hire a Cinderella dress complete with a blow-up carriage that was now gracing the corner of the living room, I felt like cancelling the whole bloody thing.

As usual, though, the doorbell signalling the start of the party acted like curtains up on the Andersons' best behaviour. Hannah came swanning down the stairs in her Black Widow Avengers costume and Jack appeared with a tray of Prosecco, which after a few glasses might allow some people to see his passing resemblance to Daniel Craig's 007.

First through the door were Chris and Sally in their *Grease* outfits. Hannah made us all feel ninety-five by not knowing who the T-Birds were, so I felt obliged to make up for her sneering at them by raving about their costumes and immediately posting a photo of them on Facebook. I stamped on the thought that it was always the people who need the most entertaining who arrive first at parties. Especially as there was some sort of atmosphere hanging between them, as though one of them hadn't been keen to come. Maybe I could tell them that I hadn't

wanted to hold the bloody party either and we could all just
bugger off home and watch Netflix with a tub of Ben & Jerry's
and save the small talk for another time.

Within minutes, there was a steady stream of people and
the familiar hubbub of tops being screwed off the Sauvignon,
the pop of the Prosecco, the introductions "We're at number
nine," "Oh, you live to the right of the chap with the Lotus," "Is
it your garden that backs onto the corner of the old recreation
ground?"

No Ollie. It didn't matter who I was talking to, how fascinating the subject—one of my neighbours turned out to be
a make-up artist for a mortuary—I was on red alert for the
doorbell, like someone marooned on a desert island waiting for
a ship to appear on the horizon.

Kate's arrival shook me out of my gloom. Without her paramedic scrubs, her hair clipped back and adorned with a pink
flower, the swirling skirt, she was like a completely different
person, as though a stubby garden sparrow had emerged as
a brightly coloured parakeet. I hovered between paying her
a compliment and insulting her by gawking at the incredible
transformation. I stuck to the facts. "You look gorgeous."

And it wasn't just me who noticed. The entire room did a bit
of a meerkat sensing danger, with a whole lot of heads swivel-
ling in her direction.

"Thanks. Now, what can I do to help?"

I was about to wave her away and tell her to go and mingle,
when I noticed the pleading expression. This was not a woman
who was used to the limelight. "Could you hand round these
bruschettine—they're halloumi and mushroom—and these
little salmon Wellingtons?"

Kate grabbed the plates. "Oh my life, did you make these?"

From anyone else I might have felt criticised by the question
because it was pretty obvious by their uniform shape that I'd
emptied them onto a baking tray from a packet. But there was
something about Kate, as though the question came from genuine

admiration. She was so unassuming and—I suspected—not very used to entertaining. Apart from Hannah, I hadn't seen a single person visit their house. So I laughed. "God, no. I'm keeping the COOK shop in town afloat."

She glanced at the rows of platters housing all manner of little Yorkshire puddings, blinis and pastry puffs. "You're extremely generous and very kind."

For a second, I felt as though I might cry. I covered it up with a wave of the hand. "Thank you. It's just a few bits and pieces to stop us all falling flat on our faces after the first glass," I said, snatching up another platter and diving into the crowd.

I was just dealing with the woman from number seven who seemed to have every allergy under the sun—"Does it contain dairy? Gluten? Any egg?"—which meant I had to scrabble in the bin for the packaging, when Ollie burst through the door dressed as a caveman.

My heart lifted as he swept in and swung me off the floor, my five-foot-three frame dangling helplessly.

"Happy birthday to you-u-u-u," he sang.

I dusted myself down. "You're here! Great costume." I stopped myself from asking if Natalie had come with him, restricting myself to adjusting the shoulder of his furry outfit so I could scan the room without him seeing.

The strength of my disappointment when I spotted Natalie laughing with Jack by the door shocked me. And it pissed me off that Jack was all backslapping welcome.

I pretended not to see her and turned back to ask Ollie how he was finding university. I even managed to run up to the question of how he was getting on living with Natalie but backed away at the last minute, retreating to, "And do you like living in Bristol?"

Before he could answer, Natalie appeared at his elbow, dressed as bloody Bo-Peep, with some kind of wired sticky-out skirt that made me want to cup my hands around my mouth and say, "Big bus coming through!"

She handed me an envelope. "Happy birthday! Here's your present. You can't open it until we've gone though."

Someone I didn't know telling me what I could and couldn't do made me want to rip open the envelope, whip the present out, wave it about and say, "What're you going to do about it then?" I really needed to find my grown-up.

I looked at Ollie.

"It's a very special surprise," he said, before putting his arm around Natalie's waist and hugging her. I still felt as though he was cuddling his teacher. I hoped it wouldn't be a "special surprise" that involved me spending any more time with Natalie.

"That's extremely thoughtful of you. Thank you so much." To be fair, I had to credit her with actually getting a present and card to me on the right day, instead of Ollie's norm of recent years: "Sorry, I missed the post but hope you have a good day."

I forced myself to be that mother about whom girlfriends would say, "I'm so lucky with Ollie's mum. She's lovely."

I glugged down the last of my drink. "So, Natalie, is Ollie behaving himself? I'm not sure I did a brilliant job of housetraining him. I did my best, but I think he's inherited Jack's non-domestic gene."

She looked at me as though I was some kind of unusual exhibit in a museum, an Enigma machine, or perhaps a mangle. "He's far more capable than you think." Which should have been music to my ears, but instead there was such a dollop of "I'm not sure you know your son anywhere near as well as me" that I was tempted to run through every idiosyncratic domestic failure he'd exhibited in the last decade in a display of maternal one-upmanship.

Thankfully, Sally popped up at my side to ask me where I'd bought my salad servers and I took the opportunity to escape, leaving her talking to Natalie.

A great weariness washed over me. I needed more Prosecco and headed over to Jack, who was chief cork popper. He was chatting to Chris, Kate and a woman whom I vaguely recognised but had no clue about the name. She was dressed in a white coat with a stethoscope hanging around her neck and a plastic parrot on her shoulder. I darted the "Help me out here" eyes to Jack who smiled and said, "Have you met Sophie from number five?"

We shook hands. She smiled and said, "We met briefly at your barbecue in July. I feel like a bit of an impostor here—I've been house-sitting down the road, but my own house is finally ready next week, so I won't be here for much longer."

I did that British thing of pretending to remember exactly who she was now she'd reminded me we'd met before. "Of course. I'm sorry, there were so many people there, I didn't get to have a proper conversation with everyone."

Chris leant towards me and said, "Sophie's a vet."

She smiled as though she was used to people being impressed by her job. Lucky her. I had to make do with people being impressed with my lemon and pomegranate salad dressing.

She indicated her outfit—"Hence the Dr. Dolittle costume."

"Do you work locally?" I asked.

"Yes, I've got my own veterinary practice near Albert Park."

I bet she grew up in one of those rambling vicarage-type places with a posse of cats crowding into the kitchen for milk and scruffy dogs lying in front of the hearth, plus a couple of ponies to experiment on and the original free-range chickens scrabbling around the garden.

"She was just telling us about her hydrotherapy pool for dogs," Chris said, tilting his head on one side.

Jack said, "Is there much demand for that round here?"

"You'd be surprised. It's great for dogs with arthritis or ones that are recovering from an injury because it's not weight-bearing. It increases the rate of healing." She had that way about her, that assurance that well-educated people have, that they can stand their own in any intellectual debate, because somehow they absorb all the facts and figures in newspapers rather than—like me—only remembering the pictures of a mother duck waddling into a pond with her babies on a spring day or deer rutting in the park.

Jack looked as though he'd like to pop her on a platter and

eat her with a squeeze of lemon. Maybe he was capable of having an affair. I pushed that thought right away. I didn't need to find out my last bastion of sanity was a quicksand quagmire.

Jack was hanging off her every word. "We need a new vet. Titch's vet has retired and Great Danes aren't known for making old bones."

Sophie whipped out a business card and handed it to Jack. "Any time."

Jack winked. "Do you do mates' rates?"

I could have throttled him. Making us sound all grabby and greedy when we hardly knew her.

She just laughed. "I might be able to offer a discount. Mention that you were a neighbour of mine to my secretary if you come down and she'll make a note of it."

In her twenties with her own secretary. I was forty-three and hadn't yet managed to delegate hanging up a jacket to anyone in the last two decades.

I picked up the card from Ollie and Natalie from the side and stomped upstairs to have a quiet read in my bedroom. Hopefully he'd written some lovely words to soothe me. I opened the envelope to find an ordinary card—no "To a Special Mum" or "To a Brilliant Mum"—and a smaller envelope: Dear Mum, Have a very happy birthday. Hope you like your surprise! Love Ollie and Nat.

So far, so unimpressed. I studied the smaller envelope. A day at a spa? A makeover? A voucher to get my colours done?

I slit open the flap and pulled out a flimsy bit of paper.

An ultrasound picture of a baby.

Photos: Sally and Chris in their Grease costumes. Gisela holding a stuffed rat.
    Caption: Such a fun birthday!
    #ParkviewPinkLady #T-birds #Cinderella #Birthdaybash

CHAPTER 15

Kate

Saturday 18 November

I looked for Daisy, to let her know I was going to head off. I'd handed round the blinis, collected up the stray glasses, sat stroking Titch until my hands smelt and still I hadn't managed to fit into any of the little pods of conversation orbiting around me. It was as though I'd forgotten how to make small talk, how to insert myself into the to and fro of social pleasantries. It was probably a bit ambitious to think I could get to know people while stopping them finding out about me, a bit like swimming while trying not to get wet. Sally had unnerved me by saying, "Wow! That's an amazing dress. You look like one of those little dolls in traditional costume that you bring back from holiday. Where's it from? Russia? Bulgaria? Must be somewhere Eastern European. Poland maybe?"

My heart gave a surge of fright. "I've no idea where it came from. I didn't want to spend a lot of money on an outfit and saw it in a charity shop and liked the colours. I hate fancy dress parties anyway."

She blinked at how ungrateful I sounded, but to be fair, she did offer me an escape route by saying, "It is hard to know what to wear, isn't it?"

"Anyway, I'm going to make a move. Nice to see you. Catch

up with you soon." And I'd dashed off, leaving Sally standing on her own, probably wondering how a compliment from her turned into a grumpy retort from me.

I spotted Daisy whispering in a corner with Hannah, who, as usual, had that satisfied look on her face, as though she'd set a trap for someone and was just biding her time until they dropped right into it. I'd never managed to work out how some individuals with less than half my life experience could make me feel stupid, fat and clumsy. I tried not to care what anyone else thought anymore but had come to the conclusion that was reserved for the good-looking, the super-intelligent and the wealthy, who were so far ahead of everyone else that they didn't have to care. The rest of us were still working out how to get people on our side. Or at least off our backs.

Daisy did that smile I was seeing a lot these days. The "Hello Mum, could you just leave me alone now?" face.

"I'm going to disappear now."

"But it's only 9:30!" Daisy said as though I was the biggest party pooper in the whole world.

"I've got a bit of a headache."

Her eyes boggled with the effort of not rolling.

"Don't be too late. You've got work in the morning."

"I won't," Daisy said with that little tone of "I'll do what I want" I'd noticed creeping in over the last few months.

I almost leant forward to kiss her, but instead I did an awkward wave and walked towards the front door, wondering if I could slip out without Gisela seeing me.

I glanced around to locate her but couldn't see her anywhere. I hadn't seen her for a while in fact. She was probably digging more booze out of her Aladdin's cave of a garage.

Just as I walked past the downstairs loo, a man came out in a furry black and orange spider costume and banged into me with one of his many legs. "Oops. Sorry! Not used to having eight legs." He looked down. "Love your skirt. Have you just blown in from the Austrian Alps?"

I didn't miss a beat. "Nope. Sorry. From over the road. Nothing like as glamorous."

"But I detect a little northern accent?"

"Lancashire, years ago." I hoped he wouldn't push me to a precise location. Luckily most southerners couldn't tell the difference between a Manchester accent and anywhere else in the north.

He pushed some legs out of the way and stuck out a hand. "I'm Alex."

"I'm Kate. Nice to meet you. Don't take it personally, but I'm just leaving."

He did a dramatic step back. "Noooo! You're the first friendly person I've spoken to."

His honesty made me laugh. I'd had moments this evening when I swore people were rationing their smiles in case they got laughter lines.

"I'm an interloper. I don't live down this road. I'm Jack's best friend from university. You know the sort, the friend who lurches from one disaster to the next and keeps getting pity invites from his sensible married friends hoping that their sane lifestyle will somehow rub off on me."

I wanted to tell him that I was so disastrous I didn't even get pity invites anymore. "It's hard for me to judge how true that is when you're dressed as a tarantula. It kind of muddies the waters a bit."

His eyes flickered with amusement and I blushed because he had that look about him. The one that meant he could be naughty. I knew what he was going to say and he knew I knew.

"I could take it off if you like, so you get a better idea."

"Just no." I tried to sound dismissive and disapproving, but I sounded teasing and giggly. God only knows where that came from. Some crevice in the concrete of my soul.

"Are you single?"

I was way out of practice. Were men this direct now?

"Do I look single?" I immediately felt defensive, as though there was something of the "Don't fancy yours much" about me.

The tarantula man sighed, his face lighting up with a grin. "I'm not sure what single would look like unless you were pushing a trolley-load of Pot Noodles, with a parade of cats following you down the street. But I had to ask because a) you were leaving on your own, and b) Gisela and Jack will *kill* me if I cause trouble for one of their married friends. And then I probably won't get even a pity invite. Which would be the end of my social life. Everyone else has given up on me."

Alex was his own worst publicist.

I moved towards the door. He put his hand towards me but didn't touch me. "Don't leave me to any more conversations about whether the properties on this road have increased in price since everyone bought them. Or whether that fancy school Hannah used to go to is worth the money. Or whether BT are going to put in a fibre-optic broadband along here in the next millennium."

I don't know what got into me. Probably that I had sympathy with him over the repetitive conversation topics, but I ended up agreeing to one more glass of Prosecco. He guided me back into the sitting room.

And, half an hour later, it was so satisfying to see Hannah nudge Daisy in surprise that dead-in-the-water me was doing the Macarena with a tarantula.

CHAPTER 16

Sally

Thursday 30 November

Photo: Little Provence Market, mound of cheese, strings
of garlic.
   Caption: Autumn in Provence.
   #HardAtWork #SomeoneHasToDoIt

Every time I went away for work, I was frightened the elastic
band pinging me back to Chris would stretch a bit further until
one day our relationship would end up like an old bikini, too
baggy around the bottom to snap back into shape. Tonight
I'd arrived home after an exhausting few days trekking round
vineyards in Provence with bad-tempered vintners who clearly
didn't give a hoot whether I bought their Bandol Rouge or Côtes
de Provence Rosé. I was the only woman on an exclusive tour
for a hand-picked selection of wine buyers and most of the
proprietors talked to me as though I'd never heard of the grape
variety Mourvèdre before.

   As I'd driven back from Gatwick in the pouring rain, I
entertained a fantasy of walking into the sitting room, Chris
relieving me of my case while a chicken casserole bubbled on
the hob.

Instead I found a note on the kitchen table:

*Hope you had a good trip. Sorry to have missed you.
Had to go back to work because we need to draft a
document to present to the Board tomorrow. Don't
wait up. I'll see you in the morning. Chris x*

Bit of a contrast to when we were first married and I'd walk
into a room full of flowers. Clearly I was now only worth a bald
little kiss and should probably count myself lucky if there was
some milk in the fridge.

I stomped upstairs, bumping my suitcase up every step, not
caring that the wheels were leaving black marks of airport dirt on
the treads. I picked up my phone and stabbed out a text message.

Thanks for the welcome home. Much appreciated.

No response.

I poured myself a large glass of wine, ran the bath and did
all the things Chris used to do—lit the candles and joss sticks
and put my pyjamas on the radiator. I took a picture of it, then
peeled off my clothes and lay in the bath, adding more hot
water. I tried to read, but my mind kept turning to that terse
little note. Was this how life was going to be? Drifting towards
old age, resentment creaking up a notch year on year, until we
were keeping count of who made the last cup of tea and sitting
in our armchairs dying of thirst rather than letting the other
person "get away with being so idle." But the alternative. God,
the alternative. Just imagining my mother's reaction made me
want to start googling places to live where you can't get a phone
signal. "But married life isn't a bed of roses. Look at your
father. What you need is a baby to unite you. You've got too
much time to think about yourselves."

Eventually, I got out of the bath, ignoring the mat and dripping water as I went, wandering into our bedroom, leaving

damp footprints on the cream carpet. Tonight was the start of my rebellion. Over the last decade, little bits of me had tidied themselves into the orderly pattern that Chris required. I'd gone along with it for a quiet life, or because he just had more opinions, more rights and wrongs than me. I used to be happy to follow where he led. But now I wanted to take another path.

I snuggled into bed, propped myself up with my book and waited, allowing myself to imagine a life when I couldn't count on another body next to me at night.

The radiators clicked off. Car doors slammed. The voices of people walking home from the pub died away. Still no Chris.

I texted him: *"Are you on your way home yet?"*

I tried to read, but my eyes kept flicking to my phone. Still no answer.

After half an hour, I rang him, but the phone clicked onto voicemail. It was hard to see what could be so urgent that he'd be at the office until gone midnight. I vacillated between fury and alarm. By twelve-thirty, alarm was starting to gain the upper hand. My mind—hewn straight out of my mother—headed towards the catastrophe spectrum of events. Locked in the office by accident. Car crash. The victim of a stabbing. I wondered what the law was regarding posthumous gathering of sperm.

At one o'clock, a car door slammed. I peered through the curtains in time to see a taxi taking off at speed, then heard Chris's key in the lock.

I ran downstairs. "Are you okay? I thought something had happened."

"I said I'd see you in the morning. Why are you still up?"

I stared at him. The sigh of annoyance that I hadn't got home from my business trip and trotted off to bed as instructed pushed the detonator button.

"I'm still up because I was bloody worried about whether you were safe! What crisis at work could possibly necessitate you staying there till this time?"

His movements were slow and deliberate, unwinding his scarf, unbuttoning his coat.

"You've been at the pub."

"Just took the team for a quick one. It's been a hell of a day. Please don't start having a go, Sally, I'm absolutely knackered and I've got to be up early."

"This is ridiculous. I've been away, you come home late when you could have been back earlier and don't seem to give a shit that your wife is upset? What does that mean? That today's a bad day and tomorrow you'll realise that you've been pretty out of order? Or are you hoping that I'll be the one to decide our marriage isn't really working?"

My voice was rising into the sort of high-toned hysteria that would have Chris telling me not to get my knickers in a twist.

"I don't know what you're talking about. I'm a bit late home after a hard day." He raised his eyebrows. "Is there any tiny part of you that thinks you might be blowing it out of proportion?"

I flew at him. "Shut up. You know this isn't about you being a bit late home. You're punishing me because you don't like it that I won't accept I can't have a baby. I want to accept it. But I can't. I just cannot imagine growing old without children. Instead of helping me work through that, instead of trying to find a compromise, you've withdrawn. Headed for the hills at the first sign of trouble."

I stopped short of telling him to get out, but I could feel the blood pumping, my hands itching to rush into our bedroom and shove his carefully folded underpants into a holdall.

He took a breath. Not a "giving himself time to respond" breath, but one that I recognised as "in through the nose and out through the mouth" from the one time I'd gone with him to a fitness class based around variations of t'ai chi. Chris could never just react from the heart. Everything was considered and deliberate. And having a baby when you weren't sure was the ultimate leap of faith. Not one he was going to take any time soon.

In a very quiet voice, he said, "I'm going to move out for a bit, give us some space to think. I'll stay in one of the firm's flats in London."

I'd pushed him towards this. And now I felt as though my heart was being sieved through a fine strainer, leaving tiny, enduring fragments of love in its net like hard balls of icing sugar. The rest, the building blocks of marriage—the automatic kindnesses, the unselfconscious touching, the celebrating of each other's successes—had been distilled down into dust and blown away.

"How long will you be away for?" My anger was draining away and I was working hard to banish the neediness from my voice.

"Let's see how it goes."

I couldn't pinpoint which emotion was triumphing. Panic was doing quite nicely.

"So shall I tell everyone you've walked out on me? Shall I tell them why? That you're too selfish to have children?"

Again, that quiet, sorrowful voice as though he was pre-scribing some particularly evil medicine for my own good. "Sal. It doesn't have to be permanent, but we can't keep going round and round in circles. All I'm asking for is a bit of time apart so we can think things through. It will do you some good too. You could tell anyone who asks that I'm away on a long trip to LA. Which won't be a complete lie. I will be there a lot of the time for that change management project. It's starting at the beginning of December."

"You will be back for Christmas, though?" I could see my mum going into a decline at having wasted her money on a bumper pack of socks "with special loose elastic that doesn't pinch your ankles. I thought it would stop him getting one of those blood clots when he's flying about." Chris wouldn't have worn them anyway, declaring himself far too young and fit to need anything that had the word "comfort" in its product description.

"Let's play it by ear. I'll sleep in the spare room tonight."

And just like that, I went from a wife hitting a rough patch in her marriage to a woman no longer sure she could count on having a husband.

I lay, till dawn, desperate to creep in with him, to put my head on his chest and beg him to help me make sense of this thing we thought was love but turned out to be a weapon for wounding instead.

CHAPTER 17

Kate

Friday 1 December

I was leaving for my early shift on Friday when Chris came out of the house with a suitcase and several holdalls. It seemed rude to ignore him, even though it was 6 a.m. and if he was anything like me he just wanted to grump himself awake without any dickheads prattling on.

I raised a hand. "Off on your travels?"

"Yes, long one this time. Off to LA for a few weeks."

"Back for Christmas, though?"

"Hopefully."

I thought my shift pattern was bad. What kind of job didn't let you come home for Christmas? He didn't seem to want to get into a discussion about it and, frankly, it was a bit early to get into employee grievances.

I looked round for Sally. When Oskar used to go anywhere, whatever time, I always felt I had to see him off properly as some kind of safety insurance. Sally was obviously still snoring away. They were so hard to make out. On the one hand, they seemed so self-contained as a couple, not really needing anyone else, unlike Jack and Gisela who seemed to thrive on company, lots of it, and not necessarily very selective. On the other hand, Sally and Chris seemed so independent of each other. He never de-iced her car when he did his or ran out to help her when she was struggling in with the supermarket shopping, all the little kindnesses that outweighed the irritations of married life. I relished those tiny things when I was married to Oskar. Putting a hot-water bottle on his side of the bed. Letting him have the last of the milk in his coffee because he couldn't stand it black. Peeling an orange for him because I knew he'd never eat it otherwise.

In the end, those small gestures hadn't been enough to keep him with us, to stop him deciding that our lives were too difficult and that the "for worse" bit of our marriage vows had a limit to it. Nevertheless, day-to-day, I'd loved that moment of softening in his face, "*Thank* you," that fleeting butterfly of connection. I couldn't imagine how I would ever allow myself to be that vulnerable again.

And yet, at tea break, I clicked onto Facebook to see if Alex had sent me a message. I hadn't seen him since Gisela's party two weeks ago, but there was no doubt that a little note demanding to know when I would go for a drink with him made my day. Even if I always said no.

Sally had posted a photo of Chris. "Hubby away for work #Lonely #Sniff #MissingYouAlready."

Even if I did have a husband to #MissAlready, I wouldn't bloody post it on Facebook when he was away in case the local burglars saw their opportunity. It was just slightly tempting to write "But not #lonelyenough to get up and wave him goodbye."

I was just trying to shake out my petty thoughts when Alex messaged me again. "Dinner tonight? Go on. I'm a social pariah and bored of eating M&S dinners for one. I can microwave a dinner for two, but I've also taken the liberty of booking a table at the Jolly Farmer?"

I finished early tonight. Daisy had begged to stay at Hannah's—"Gisela just bought her a whole new thing of Mac make-up so we're going to experiment"—and this would be the weekend the carol singers were out in force. There was nothing like a few tinny verses of "O Little Town of Bethlehem" going on outside my front door to make me feel everyone else was sitting round for a communal wrapping session and cracking open the advocaat with seasonal joy in their hearts. Sally had no bloody idea what #Lonely was. I typed, "OK. What time?"

I laughed as I got a GIF of a boy doing a celebratory dance with "Hell, YEAH" plastered across it. "Seven-thirty."

Six hours to double-check my barriers and make sure they were all nicely in place.

I didn't let him come to the house to pick me up as he suggested. Of course, he already knew I lived in Parkview and Gisela would point across the road without a second's hesitation, but I didn't want him to think he could pop round any time because he'd been here once. In the time between accepting his invitation and leaving home to meet a man for the first time in eleven years, I hovered between not wanting to look like I'd made an effort and wanting to prove I wasn't yet ready to spend my days sorting through fifty-five bits of blue cloud in my latest jigsaw.

By the time I'd walked to the pub, my face was freezing, but the rest of me was clammy with nerves. I marched in, rehearsing my "I'll have a large glass of red wine" so that I wouldn't lose my nerve at the bar. I paused before I pushed open the door, reminding myself that if anyone turned round, it would be from the passing curiosity of seeing who was coming in. Not because they *knew*. Thankfully, Alex was already there, at a table right by the door. Surprisingly good-looking without his orange and black tarantula balaclava.

"Kate!" He stood up. I hadn't remembered him being so tall. I wanted to shrink back, unsure whether to shake his hand, kiss him on the cheek or stand there like a bloody milk bottle. Alex was all warmth and big bear hugs. "I was so prepared for you to blow me out. Come on, you're so cold. Let's sit over there by the fire. What would you like to drink?"

"I'll get them." The words came out abruptly as though he'd offended me, overstepped some invisible boundary of first-date manners.

He leaned towards me, laughing. "You're very lovely to offer, but tonight is my treat. You can pay next time."

How wonderful to exist in a world where you were so confident there would be a "next time."

As we sat down with our drinks, I took my time arranging my coat and bag, putting off the moment when he'd be sitting opposite me and I'd have nowhere to hide. Alex seemed oblivious to my shrinking, hitting conversational bullseye by asking me all about my day at work. With nothing personal to sieve and filter, I relaxed into a story about one of the guys I worked with whose thuggy appearance was completely at odds with his gentle manner. "The old ladies start off watching him like a hawk when he walks in, in case he makes off with their handbags, and by the end of it, they're telling him to pop in for a cup of tea whenever he's passing."

"That's the danger of judging people on their appearance." Alex took another glug of wine, an easy smile lighting up his face. "So what's the real Kate like then? What's behind the cool and collected façade?"

There it was. That little flip of fear. He couldn't know anything.

I swallowed. "If you're hoping for hidden depths, you're going to be disappointed. What you see is what you get, I'm afraid. Pretty dull, really."

Alex threw back his head and laughed. "Says the woman who danced with such rhythm and passion. You are *not* dull."

I released the breath I'd been holding. "That was the wine making me interesting."

A flicker of impatience passed over Alex's face. "I've been out with so many women—" He corrected himself: "I've often been out with women who think that every detail about them, from where they bought their shoes to how often they get their highlights done, is a source of fascination. You, the most interesting woman I've met in months, think you're really boring." He shrugged. "I'm never going to understand women."

"I don't know what to say to that." Though I couldn't ignore the big burst of happiness that Alex thought I was so fascinating. "Anyway, you haven't told me what you do for a living?" I asked.

"Not nearly as interesting as your job." But before he could elaborate, the waiter arrived with menus.

And with the whole "I didn't have you down as a butternut squash risotto type of woman, thought you'd be a carnivore," we started talking about stereotypes and first impressions. From there, the conversation scooted along, diving down unlikely and amusing alleyways. "My sister's lovely but quite bonkers. Turned up at Christmas at my parents' house with two greyhounds she'd adopted from Greece but not bothered to housetrain. Which led to my father slipping on a turd on the rug and trying to chase them into the garden. They thought it was a fantastic game and ran all round the house, with my mother flapping a tea towel at them and shouting that she wished she'd voted for Brexit."

The longer I sat with Alex, the more feelings so long forgotten that I couldn't readily identify them were stirring. The ghosts of good times past transmitting a faint heartbeat. Then, suddenly, the pub was emptying and the awkwardness of winding up the night and wondering whether he'd want to see me again frilled round the edges of the evening.

Alex leant towards me. "You're fidgeting. Have I bored you?" he said with the confidence of a man who knew he was entertaining. "Do you want to go?"

"Sorry. I don't go out very often. Seem to have an inbuilt Cinderella."

"Is Daisy at home?"

"No, she's staying at Gisela's tonight with Hannah." I felt the heat flood through me as though I'd winked and said, "Empty house available for all-night shagging."

Alex tipped his head on one side. "Let me guess. You're not keen on her staying there?"

"Why do you say that?"

"You looked really sad when you said it. One of the very lovely things about you is that your face shows every last feeling."

And then God knows what got into me. It was as though he'd been sitting on the airbed of my life and pulled the stopper out, allowing everything that had been trapped within to gush out into the atmosphere.

Out splurged my guilt at working and Daisy often being in an empty house. My frustration that Daisy preferred being over the road at Gisela's because there was more life, more technology and, frankly, more money.

"It's all 'just popping over to Hannah's for a takeaway,' 'just doing my presentation on Hannah's Mac.' Makes me feel such a failure."

Alex nodded. "You're not. She's lucky to have you. Sadly, she probably won't appreciate that until much later. I was about thirty before I realised how much my mother loved me and what she'd done for me."

I ached with the desire to tell him how much my mother had done for me.

When we couldn't ignore the yawns of the bar staff anymore, Alex said, "Can't believe it's quarter past eleven. Time flies."

I stood up, suddenly feeling exposed. "Sorry. There you were coming out for a light-hearted evening and you got my life story."

He held out my coat to me. "I *loved* your life story. Maybe one day you'll tell me how you ended up on your own."

I didn't respond and he didn't insist. Alex loved the neatly packaged, acceptable-to-all-people version of my life. Not for the first time, I felt tempted to tell him what he asked and see the shock on his face, ending with a little flourish of "Funnily enough, our marriage didn't survive."

This was who I was now.

He buttoned up his jacket. "Shall I walk you home or shall I call you a cab?"

I knew I should say cab. But it was so long since I'd been in male company, I didn't want the evening to end. "Is it too cold and wet for you to walk me back? I don't want to take advantage of your good nature." I peered out of the window. "The rain seems to have stopped."

Again, that wide warm smile. "If you're sure you're happy to walk, it would be my pleasure."

We set off, with Alex talking about how Jack was so popular with the girls at university but never wanted anyone other than Gisela. "All those possibilities on his doorstep and all he could think about was getting the train home." About halfway home, the rain started in earnest. He looked down. "Hmm. Think we were a bit premature with 'the rain seems to have stopped.' You haven't got any gloves. Do you want mine?"

I shook my head, even though my hands were red raw from the cold.

"I bet you would say you were fine if you'd got knocked over by a car and your own paramedics were trying to revive you. Here, we'll have one each. Take my right-hand glove and give me your left hand."

As he pushed my hand into his pocket, his own wrapped around my fingers and my heart surged. I hadn't touched another man with anything other than professional detachment in so long, I felt all the heat in my body rush to my palm, to my fingertips. I had to instruct my legs to keep moving forwards. All of a sudden, every sense was heightened. The noise of the tyres on the wet road. Our feet splashing in shallow pools on the pavement. My fingers rigid in Alex's pocket, slowly responding to the gentle pressure of his thumb and unfurling, despite the jackhammer chatter in my head of "Don't do this. Don't make yourself vulnerable."

We fell silent in that way people do when they've exposed their feelings and are assessing inwardly how the risk has panned out. A couple of times we smiled at each other, tutting at the rain, acknowledging that we should have called a cab. All the talking was taking place through our hands, as though every nerve ending was nodding, introducing itself and settling down on the sofa to see what happened next. I didn't care that my hair was hanging in wet strings, that my mascara would be careering down my cheeks. I cared that when our eyes met, saying much more than any words I'd ever managed to produce, I could feel a fragment of who I was before, almost like seeing a sliver of myself in a shard of a mirror from the past.

Eventually, Alex stopped. "Sorry. Getting you soaked to the skin wasn't part of my plan."

The noise of me swallowing was loud in my ears. "What was part of your plan?"

He pulled me towards him. "I'm afraid to tell you," he said, "in case you run."

I looked down. "I won't run."

And then we kissed, the rain sheeting down until I could feel it squeezing under my eyelids. Still I didn't want to move. I stood there in the moment, unfiltered, original me.

Finally Alex pulled away, ruffling his hair and sending droplets of water flying. "As much as I don't want to move, I'm not sure a first date should include pneumonia. Let's get you home."

I nodded, though I would probably have stayed there kissing until I drowned.

When we reached the corner of Parkview, I said, "I can find my way home from here."

"Don't be silly. I'll walk you to your door. Promise I won't invite myself in for a coffee." He paused. "Unless you want me to."

I wanted him to come in. I didn't want him to come in. I didn't want to get involved. I did want to feel like this—this excitement, this connection, this sense that someone liked me, the me I was now.

The answer came in the rain transforming itself from a persistent shower to a thunderous downpour. I grabbed his hand and started to run. "Come on, we can get you a cab from mine."

I glanced up at Hannah's window, hoping Daisy wouldn't choose right now to look out.

Alex and I dived in through the front door, leaving pools of water in the hallway.

"Give me your coat. I'll put it over the radiator to dry. Let me fetch a towel. Hold on." I ran upstairs and rummaged through the pile to find one that wasn't scraggy and old, wrapping my hair in one before going downstairs.

"Not really how I'd planned to look tonight."

I handed him the towel.

"You look gorgeous to me."

"Would you like a coffee...to warm up? Not '*coffee.*'" I blushed. I didn't know how to do this anymore.

He laughed as he dried his hair, leaving it standing up in sandy tufts. "Either sounds wonderful to me."

I told him to take a seat, but he came through to the kitchen, standing behind me while I spooned coffee into mugs.

He pulled out a few tendrils of hair from my turban, twisting them in his fingers. "I love your hair. You smell nice too," he said, kissing my neck.

I leaned into him, his cold face pressing into me. And then, somehow, we were kissing again, the worktop pressing into my back, and my heart loving that moment where you think the man you've met is perfect, that tiny slice of time before you discover he leaves teabags in the sink and never puts the milk back in the fridge.

We made our way to the sofa. I drew the curtains, smothering a little smile as I thought about how Gisela would immediately try to arrange dinner for four, give me the low-down on Alex's last three girlfriends and provide me with an estimate of his finances.

He turned my face towards him. "Thank you for tonight."

My heart plummeted. I wasn't ready for him to leave yet, to plunge straight into the "Will he, won't he call?" the second he walked out of the door, to sit in the cold space on my sofa where he'd recently made me feel like a woman who might have a future.

I said, "Do you want me to ring for a taxi?"

"You throwing me out already?"

"I thought you wanted to go?" I really was rusty.

"Truth? I want to stay. All night." He said it gently.

I looked down at our knees side by side. His jeans, dark blue from the rain. My black jeggings, clingy with water. A shockingly graphic image of peeling them off flashed into my mind, not giving a shit about what was right or wrong, what was a decent amount of time to wait at age forty-three. Instead I concentrated on the sensation of feeling alive again, of moving forward with new experiences rather than beating time, waiting for the world to come crashing down again.

"Shall we get out of our wet clothes then?" I felt my eyes fly open as though someone else had spoken.

Alex's lips twitched. "Are you sure? I mean, it sounds like a fantastic idea to me but—"

"I'm really cold." And probably needed to add, pretty bloody drunk. I got up before I lost my nerve. "I'm going to have a hot shower."

Alex looked hopeful, but that was a step too far.

"You can go after me."

I chased upstairs. Instead of finding some common sense to stop me in my tracks, I found one of Daisy's razors and did a swift tidy-up of my armpits and bikini line. If only I'd known the evening would end like this. As I cleaned my teeth, I felt giddy with daring.

I shouted downstairs. "All yours."

By the time Alex appeared in my bedroom, wrapped in a towel, I was tucked under the duvet, my skin warm and damp from the shower.

"Can I come in?" he said, poking his head around the door.

"You can."

He peeled back the duvet. "You've still got your towel on." He pulled it from under me and touched the silver locket with its eagle engraving around my neck. It was my grandmother's and I never took it off. "Whose picture is hiding in here? The secret love of your life? Am I under threat?"

I smiled and kissed him again. "Just my parents."

"Good."

And then we didn't talk anymore. Just concentrated on touching. Alex's body was so different from Oskar's wiry build. Where Oskar had been slight, Alex was broad and chunky, his body hair soft and blonde. There was a gentleness in his touch that stopped me fighting him, stopped me holding myself back, that made me feel as though this wasn't a slapperish, desperate act from a woman who hadn't had sex in years but a giving and receiving of something that felt like love. Which, frankly, my mind knew was bollocks, but my body was all hearts and rose petals and *Love Is* . . . cartoons.

He pulled me towards him with more urgency and there was a definite moment when I chose not to think but to feel instead.

Afterwards, I lay cuddled up, wondering if that meant I'd finally drawn a line under Oskar. But the truth was, I didn't want to waste a minute thinking about Oskar. I wanted to absorb every second of Alex. Later, I'd think about how I'd done the thing I'd have gone bonkers about if Daisy had slept with a boy after one date, but not now.

He stroked my face. "Want me to go?"

"No. But you're going to have to leave early. Before Daisy comes home. She can't walk in on . . . this."

I set the alarm for eight. She'd never yet come home before eleven.

"That's fine. I need to go into work tomorrow anyway."

"On a Saturday?"

"Yeah. The wonderful world of journalism. Got some reports to read. Find it much easier to concentrate at the office."

I pulled away. "Gisela said you worked in TV?"

"I do. Investigative journalism. Miscarriages of justice, drugs barons, gang warfare, that sort of thing."

The shouting, the people crowding around my door, the cameras in my face, pushed into Daisy's pram, grabbing at me as I walked out to the car, calling my name, Oskar's name, the headlines—always Polish immigrant/Eastern European/immigrant family even though I was born here and had never been to Poland—our family's history, her family's history, comments from "friends" and "neighbours," photographs of me buying a bottle of wine in Tesco (as if that was at all relevant), and, of course, the worst thing of all: her side of the story, vicious and raw as though our friendship had been nothing. When to me, it had been everything, a mainstay of my whole life, since we met in primary school. I still missed her. Still felt that Becky-shaped gap in my life, where I took for granted that ability to bounce from one topic to the next without the need to fill in what went before. Still occasionally caught myself smiling at a memory much further back than 2000.

And now I'd had sex with someone who could, with a few keystrokes, a quick google, and the tiniest amount of luck, find out stuff about me that he'd never want to know.

That *I'd* never want him to know.

CHAPTER 18

Sally

Friday 15 December

My mother sounded mournful on the phone. "Audrey's had a fall and gone into hospital. Think she'll be in there over Christmas, so Bert's not coming on Christmas Day now, and your Uncle George has decided he's not up to the journey from Preston this year. So it's just me and your dad."

Any other year, I'd have braved Chris's rage and said, "Come to us." But I couldn't invite Mum and Dad when I wasn't sure Chris would even be here. I'd rather spend the whole day crying under the duvet on my own than tolerate Mum peering into the gravy, ready with the whisk at the first sign of a lump, sniffing, "You're sure he doesn't have a fancy woman somewhere?"

I didn't know what to think. Apart from the odd text about transferring money into the joint account, we'd barely spoken for a fortnight. When I couldn't stand it any longer and rang him, he was always just going into a meeting, waiting on an important phone call, anything other than available to talk to me. Sometimes I'd come home from work and I could see he'd picked up his post. Another jacket had gone from the coat cupboard, another pair of shoes missing from the wardrobe. Today, I'd looked into his office and seen that he'd taken his Modigliani print. That wasn't like picking up your dressing gown, or fetching your wellies—the stuff that made life more comfortable. That was setting up home somewhere else.

Maybe I was that woman, blundering along believing that her husband was just "thinking things through" when, in fact, he was adding up numbers, making lists and working out how to divide up assets. And once I had that thought, it ate away at me. I imagined calling up his work and one of the secretaries putting her hand over the receiver and hissing, "It's Chris's wife," with everyone knowing that he was shacked up with Amy on the sales desk or Britta from accounts, or any one of his pretty colleagues with their black trousers, white shirts, posh accents and enough youthful years on their side that the baby issue wouldn't even have made its first squawk in their consciousness yet.

I needed to know. *Had* to know.

I rang his mobile, which went straight to voicemail. "Chris, I need to talk to you. Please call me as soon as you can."

He called me back almost immediately. "Are you okay?"

Hearing his voice made my eyes fill. "Um. Not great. Just wondering if you are actually going to be here for Christmas Day or whether I should arrange something else."

"I can't talk now."

Even though there was apology in his voice, those words stepped on the landmine. "So when can you bloody talk, Chris? When? Or am I going to sit in this house for the next six months until I realise you've actually moved out completely without bothering to tell me? You will meet me tomorrow and tell me exactly what is going on."

"Tomorrow?" He was stalling. I could hear it.

"Yes. Here at home or in town? Your choice."

"Not sure if I can do tomorrow." His words were drawn out, distracted, as though he was reading something.

"Tomorrow is Saturday, you know, the weekend, so even you should be able to find half an hour to speak to your wife. If you can't, I'll have divorce papers on your desk by the end of next week. So I'll make it easy for you. Eleven o'clock at Costa tomorrow or the solicitor's on Friday." As the words came out of my mouth, I wondered whether I'd have the guts to see it through.

"Sal, calm down. I'm having to work weekends at the moment and there are people relying on me."

"I do not give a shit about your work. I give a shit that our marriage is falling apart and you're not even making a half-hearted attempt to find a Pritt Stick. I'll see you at Costa tomorrow. Soya latte for me if you get there first." I finished the call without waiting for a reply, feeling better than I had done for days.

Self-doubt and fear of what I might now have to know had replaced the liberation of taking control by the next morning. I arrived fifteen minutes early, the old habit of not keeping Chris waiting and sending him to a sulk not yet withering on the vine.

He came in five minutes after me.

I studied him for signs of another woman's touch, a reformatting of my husband before I even knew he'd left me. He looked the same.

I beckoned him over to the little booth I'd found for us, trying to release the big swell of emotion that had ballooned in my chest without resorting to tears. His face was soft and apologetic. For some reason, a memory of the undertakers when my nan died popped into my head, that weird "feeling your pain" face when they were probably wondering if they could recycle the brass handles on the coffin without you knowing.

He made no attempt to hug me, just reached for the cappuccino I'd ordered for him, licking the froth off a spoon. "How have you been?"

It should have been such a simple question to answer. One that didn't cause a swell of rage and grief to collide somewhere around where love used to sit, lazily, smugly, without a thought for tomorrow. "It's been pretty shit to be honest. Mum keeps asking when you're getting back from your business trip. Gisela keeps trying to get a date for you to go golfing with Jack. And I feel as though you've made a decision about us but have forgotten to tell me."

He put his hand out to touch mine, then snatched it back in before it reached me. "I think we want different things, Sally."

I stared at him, the shouts of "flat white," "skinny cappu" echoing around me.

"So where does that leave us?" My voice sounded as though it was coming from somewhere else; a stupid question that no one in their right minds would want to know the answer to.

"I'm not sure."

A swirl of the cappuccino foam.

I couldn't sit in the unknown, balancing on a rotten bridge, uncertain whether we were going to make it to the other side or plunge howling into the abyss. "Do you want a divorce?"

He closed his eyes. "I want to be happy, Sally."

I could have thumped the table in frustration. "We were happy. We could be happy."

"But I don't want children. So I need to let you go so you can find someone who does."

I stared at him. "That's it? Thirteen years, most of my adult life, and you're letting everything we have, everything we've worked for, go, just like that?"

I dabbed my eyes with the useless little napkin.

"Don't cry."

I could hear it. Not "Don't cry because I can't bear to see you upset" but "Don't cry *here*. Don't make a scene. Don't let life be untidy."

I swallowed hard. "Is there someone else?"

Chris's eyes flicked to his phone as though a rogue text might come pinging in and betray him.

"It's complicated."

I tried to laugh, but tears were clogging my throat. "I'll take that as a yes, shall I?"

"Nothing has happened."

His face was a complete blank but the unspoken "yet" rang out like bells on Easter Sunday.

"What then? You want it to? You don't know if she likes you? What? Do share what this nothing that hasn't fucking happened is."

Chris did a little moue of disapproval at my language, which made me want to run through every single word he hated to hear me use, especially if there was anything northern about it: "Sally, I know it's where you're from, but it just makes you sound a bit ill-educated." Right now I wanted to reach back to the Yorkshire lass I'd been, before I airbrushed myself, working on my vowels and trying to fit in with that southern snobbishness, far away from my mum and dad's bungalow on a seventies housing estate, where currently every other house would be a light-up, blow-up medley of Father Christmases and flashing reindeers. I realised I'd missed the ritual of my mum shouting up the ladder to my dad not to fall off, when every year he took his life in his hands to hang Father Christmas legs out of the chimney. And my dad shouting down for Mum to stop mithering him. As soon as I turned eighteen I couldn't wait to escape to university but now, that familiarity, that predictability seemed like a haven compared with this see-saw of uncertainty.

Chris still didn't speak.

I struggled to keep my voice even, to remain calm. "Who is this person? Is it someone at work?"

"I haven't known her long. She's not from work. I met her when, you know…"

I didn't know. I didn't know anything. I certainly didn't know how the hell he'd had time to meet anyone.

I flicked my hands open for clarification. "Is it serious? Do you love her?"

Asking that question caused something to twist in my stomach.

Chris screwed up his face. "No! It's not like that."

I waited for him to shout, "And, of course, I love you."

He didn't. He looked irritable and said, "She's just a distraction."

"A distraction? *Coronation Street* is a distraction. A John Grisham book is a distraction. Another woman is a threat to your marriage, Chris." I lost the battle to sound reasonable. The words came out, strangled and tight, as though they were forcing themselves through a clump of anguish. "Are you having sex with her?"

"She's just someone to talk to, who's not trying to make me into something I'm not."

"I'm not trying to make you into someone you're not." I could have listed five hundred and fifty ways Chris had tried to file and shape me into someone better-spoken, a more sophisticated cook, someone who "didn't tell our business to all and sundry." And I'd gone along with his version of me, the one that I thought the world would find more attractive, less abrasive, more palatable. Apparently, it still wasn't enough. "Are you coming back for Christmas?"

"I think we need a bit of distance to see things clearly. Shall we talk again in the new year?"

"We haven't talked now. I'm none the bloody wiser, except there's some woman, who's conveniently popped up out of the woodwork the second you've left me, and I've no idea whether you're trying to find a way back to me or hoping I'll chuck you out for good."

I stomped out of the door without looking back, tears pouring down my face. I wasn't paying attention to where I was going and ended up in the Christmas market, picking my way through the throngs of people snapping up festive figures made out of old flour sacks, Christmas chutneys that would rot in the fridge till next November and wicker baskets of beeswax cosmetics.

The crowds, with the wives tapping their husbands' arms to point out a quirky clock, a rainbow wall hanging, a carved bowl, made my loneliness so acute, so tangible, I felt that everyone walking past must be tilting their head in sympathy.

I was just turning down a sample of beer from a boutique brewery when Chris appeared.

"There you are. I thought I'd lost you." He put his hand on my arm. "Don't go off like that, Sal. Please. I don't want you to be so upset."

I started hissing so only he could hear. "I'm not sure how you expect me to react when you tell me that you're 'seeing' someone else."

"You've blown it all out of proportion. She's just someone I talk to."

Before I could clarify how far out of proportion I'd got him sharing his problems with another woman rather than his wife, the owner of the stall thrust bottles of beer into our hands. "Take a selfie and put it on Facebook, tag us in and we'll pick a winner for a Christmas crate of beer."

I hesitated.

Chris looked as though he was about to give his back, but the bloke said, "Please, I'd appreciate your support. We're a new business. If I don't make this work, God knows what I'll do."

I grabbed my phone, put my arm round Chris and raised the bottle to the camera.

"Cheers!" I said, as I clicked, smiling as though my biggest worry was forgetting to buy the goose fat.

I'd blame the cold wind for making my eyes red.

Photo: Chris and Sally, clinking bottles of beer.
   Caption: Festive cheer at Windlow Farmer's Market.
   #ChristmasFayre #MyFavouriteTimeOfYear
#TisTheSeasonToBeJolly

CHAPTER 19

Gisela

Christmas Day

Since I'd seen the ultrasound, the overriding emotion when I woke up every morning was disbelief. Every day Ollie lived at home, right up until he went to live with Natalie, he'd wandered downstairs bleary-eyed: "Make me a smoothie, Mum? Don't put any of that odd shit in it." I'd hopped to it, because that need when he was at primary school to tick off his five a day still resided in me, that urge to protect, to keep him healthy, to be a good mum. So even though he was twenty-one, I was still there with my blueberries and flax seeds, my chia seeds, a shake of pomegranate, sneaking in a bit of avocado and kale when he wasn't looking. When I got away with my rogue ingredients, watching as he slugged them down unnoticed, I felt a burst of pleasure that money couldn't buy.

And now, in a way my little brain could not comprehend, he would be responsible for making sure that a baby didn't get too hot, too cold, for stopping the pram rolling off down a hill, for putting on tiny socks. Just a year ago he'd phoned me from a station near Brighton, slurring, "Missed my stop. Can you phone a cab for me? Haven't got any money. Will you pay?" And I'd had him on one line and an increasingly irritated cab controller on the other, while I tried to get some sense out of him. "Which station? What can you see? Where did you start from?"

Perhaps it was a good thing Natalie was so much older. Fleetingly, I had a moment of sympathy for her, those tough months of early motherhood ahead with Ollie just about remembering to change his own underpants, let alone thinking ahead to make sure they didn't run out of nappies. I didn't dare contemplate the relationship-enhancing strategy of struggling to work a washing machine but no doubt still being keen to have sex. After having a team of minions running about to do her bidding at work, I imagined the shock it would be for Natalie, suddenly at the irrational beck and call of a baby, not even able to squeeze in a shower without urgent cries making her think a tragedy was imminent. I wondered about offering to go and stay. Just thinking about Ollie and Natalie tottering off to bed together made me feel weird in a way the various girls that had come home from uni draped over him on the sofa hadn't.

But today was Christmas Bloody Day and I was going to play my role of a chubby-cheek-squeezing upcoming grandmother, whatever it took. I'd already had to swallow the fact that Ollie and Natalie were driving down on Christmas morning—"Our first Christmas together—and the last one on our own. We just want to wake up in our own bed. And don't get any lunch for us on Boxing Day because we're heading off after breakfast to see Nat's cousin."

I'd scribbled a little congratulations card to Natalie: "So delighted to hear your news and cannot wait for the forthcoming addition to the Anderson family" and tucked it under her Christmas napkin. I'd debated over whether to do a stocking for Ollie as I always did—somehow impending fatherhood didn't seem a natural bedfellow of snowman-covered boxers, singing socks and chocolate novelty dumb-bells. In the end, I figured traditions were the mainstay of making memories so hung it up over the fireplace as usual.

I dashed about basting the turkey, frying the bacon for the

sprouts, making sure the roasties were properly crispy before
steaming upstairs to change into my Christmas Day dress—
red, obviously. Jack was nowhere to be seen. I hoped he was
already dressed because I wanted him to fetch in some more
logs, so we wouldn't have to faff about when we were all dozy
in front of James Bond later on.

"Jack?"

No answer.

I could hear some mumbling from his office.

I opened the door.

He waved at me, shooing me away. "I'm just doing my
mindfulness. I'll be fifteen minutes."

I felt the rush of air as the words I didn't say left my mouth.
Mindfulness. On Christmas Day. Please God next time let me
be a bloke who sees a slot to take twenty minutes for essential
headspace while the woman of the house gives herself a hernia
lifting the Le Creuset out of the Aga.

"I'll give you bloody mindfulness. You do pick your
moments. Who do you think I am? Bloody Hecatoncheires?"

"Who?"

I knew he was going to say that. I'd googled a many-handed
mythical creature the night before so I could bring it out all
nonchalantly in front of Natalie, as though I was well-read in
Greek mythology. She wasn't going to trot off with the impression the only thing I knew about was how to pick out a rug to
match the sofa.

"Yes, you know, the creature with fifty heads and a hundred
hands."

With a sigh, he pressed the pause button on his iPad. God
forbid the mundane details of getting everything ready for
Christmas with our son's pregnant—older—girlfriend should
get in the way of his inner Zen.

"Could you get some more wood in, please?"

"There's already half a basket."

I must have looked suitably ferocious as he flipped the iPad cover shut, his headspace looking distinctly cluttered with the untimely trappings of family life, and headed downstairs.

He disappeared into the garden and I rushed back into the kitchen, wondering where the last half an hour had disappeared to when I had been running bang on time. "Hannah, just do the dishwasher for me."

She sagged in the middle. "I'm having breakfast. Get Ollie to do it when he comes."

I briefly entertained the idea of flipping the bowl of cereal into her face. "No. Dad is doing the logs, I'm doing every other bloody thing and you can help out. Why are you having breakfast now?"

"Cos I'm hungry?" Hannah's face was a direct contrast to the one she'd used when she was trying to persuade me that the latest iPhone was a must-have if she was going to comply with the cookery course suggestion of starting a food blog. "My phone takes crap pictures. I can't put those on Instagram. Who's going to like them?"

Of course, now she'd got what she wanted, the sunshine and "Can I do anything to help?" had disappeared behind a storm cloud.

My attempts to cling onto Christmas Day joy at all costs reminded me of the squirrel trying to shinny up the bird feeder pole after Jack had squirted it with WD40. When the doorbell announced Ollie's arrival, I practised my smile, walking down the hallway. He gave me a huge hug, lifting my spirits.

I waved to Natalie, who was already lugging cases out of the boot.

"Ollie! Give Natalie a hand. She shouldn't be lifting heavy things at the moment."

Natalie ignored me and brushed off Ollie. "I haven't suddenly become a little frail waif who can't carry a bag."

I tried to backtrack. "Perhaps they've changed the advice since I had my kids. We were told not to lift anything heavy."

"Nobody's said anything about that to me," she said.

"Anyway, Happy Christmas, Gisela. Sorry it's such a fleeting visit."

I waved her in. "That's okay. It's so hard to keep everyone happy."

I smiled despite being utterly pissed off that Ollie had let slip that they were staying two nights with her cousin—"Not even immediate family." Jack had laughed and said, "Her cousin's probably like a sister to her if her parents are dead. Shall we get a stopwatch out and see who clocks up the most hours over the year?" which moved him a step closer to meeting his maker.

I took her coat. "You've got such a neat bump, but you're really starting to show now, aren't you? You look so well, though. It's such a special time when you're expecting a baby."

"So everyone keeps telling me. I just feel fat and knackered all the time."

I wanted to say, "Just wait till the baby actually arrives," but instead I said, "Well, if you want a little nap this afternoon, don't stand on ceremony."

"I'm not missing out on Christmas!"

Natalie was one of those women who had that ability to dictate the mood of the room. I bet she was horrible to work for. I'd be afraid of getting things wrong but terrified to ask for guidance because she'd tut and say, "Use your initiative." Thank God I was forty-four and not twenty-four.

Given my mood since I heard the happy news, she was in for some stiff competition if she thought she was coming in here and getting us all hopping to her tune. I marched over to the table and opened a bottle of Veuve Clicquot, poured everyone a glass, then said, "And what will you have, Natalie? I've got tonic water, ginger beer—that's very good if you feel a bit queasy—or sparkling water?"

"I'll have a glass of champagne, please."

I willed my face muscles not to jolt in surprise. I'd had the occasional glass during my pregnancies, but not in front of my in-laws or anyone I wanted to convince that I would be the best mother in the world. And certainly not with my first baby. I might have been a bit more lax with Hannah.

"Could you get another bottle out of the fridge, Jack?" I was doing that thing of making a pointed remark in such a light voice I'd be able to claim paranoia if anyone picked me up on it. I was beginning to think that mothers-in-law from hell were a much-misunderstood breed. I bet half of them were people I'd love to have coffee with and compare notes about our sons' hideous lack of judgement.

Jack wasn't catching my eye or showing any solidarity that the mother of my grandchild should stay off the bloody booze. In fact, he made sure her glass was topped right up to the brim.

"You go through and relax in the sitting room and I'll just finish off here, then we can eat. But let's just have a quick family photo of all of us before we forget."

Everyone lined up and Hannah did the honours with her selfie stick. I deliberately stood partly in front of Natalie so you couldn't see her bump. I'd deal with my friends in my own time.

Then they all trundled through to the sitting room, while I put the plates in to warm, sieving through my feelings. I'd never taken against any of Ollie's girlfriends before, but then I'd never expected any of the skinny little wisps to bear my grandchildren. I had to make this work. I had to.

I took a big swig of champagne, topped up my glass and called everyone through.

"Sit down, sit down. Hannah, you put the carrots and Brussels on the table, Jack, you carve."

"What can I do?" Natalie asked.

"Could you give the gravy a stir, please?"

Natalie came over, saying to Ollie, "Go on, help your mum with the plates. You needn't think our son if we have one is going to sit around while all the women run around, whipping out the carving knife now and then after they've done all the hard work."

I glanced at Ollie to see if he was rebelling. But he jumped to his feet and started scurrying round with plates and jugs of water. I should applaud Natalie. I'd failed to get him to put his glass in the dishwasher when he lived at home. When the kids were little, I'd been adamant I'd bring up my son the same as my daughter, that there was no such thing as "woman's work." Over the years, the effort required to get Ollie to hoover properly, hang up a towel so it would dry or clean a loo to my satisfaction meant it was easier to ask Hannah.

Now, contrarily, I wanted to tell Natalie to stop having a go at him.

Once everyone was served, there was a little pause in the conversation after the general murmurs of "This looks very nice" and the stupid British thing my mum used to do and I'd been determined not to: "I hope it's all right." Since I'd been slaving over it for approximately five hours, if they thought they could do any better, they should keep it to themselves.

We pulled our crackers and Hannah insisted on us all putting our hats on. I did wonder who started that particular tradition of everyone wearing cheap paper crap on their heads after spending all morning making their hair look nicer than usual because "it's Christmas."

Dutifully, I took pictures of us all—"Say cheers!"—and, of course, of Jack carving the turkey to document the one moment over the whole holiday he voluntarily got off his backside without me nagging.

"So, Natalie, when is the baby actually due?" I asked.

"First week of April."

"At least the worst of the winter will be over. Just before your finals though, Ol."

Natalie rushed in with, "It's no problem. I'll do everything to start with so Oliver will be able to study. He can spend the summer catching up with the baby."

"You'd be very welcome to come and stay here for a bit. Or I'll come down to you and help out," I said.

Natalie smiled. "We'll be fine, thank you. We've decided not to have anyone to stay until Oliver's finished his finals."

I'd never been in a position of negotiating to visit my own son before. Even Jack's rhino hide must have registered a small dart as he started offering more vegetables to everyone, like a waiter hustling for tips. "More carrots? Have another potato, they're so crispy. Gravy?"

His distraction gave me a chance to recover myself. "So, how long are you going to have off for maternity leave? It's all changed now, hasn't it? Do you get a year?"

Natalie glanced at Ollie, then said, "We're not sure what we're doing yet. The maternity package at my work isn't very generous because it's an American company." She stabbed a sprout. "Obviously I'll have some time off, but the statutory pay after six weeks is only about one hundred and fifty quid, which isn't going to keep us for very long."

"Perhaps we can help you out a bit to start with? I'd like to buy some of the things you'll need at the beginning—a pram, the car seat and all that sort of stuff. It would be our pleasure, wouldn't it, Jack?"

Jack didn't answer, just speared another potato and raised an eyebrow.

Ollie didn't meet my eye, instead mumbling a thank you through a mouthful of turkey.

It was as though everyone had suddenly taken the "no speaking with your mouth full, chew fifty-five times before swallowing" to heart. Our Christmas table sang not with the excited conversation of a family with a new baby on the way but with the noise of everyone masticating a parsnip to oblivion.

I glared at Jack in the language peculiar to a long marriage, the sort of stare that hisses rather than gently conveys a message.

Jack stopped his mechanical digger shovelling of swede and said, "With any luck, Ollie will get snapped up for an engineering job and you'll be able to take a back seat on the work front for a bit. You can ask to go part-time now, can't you? Or maybe you could do a job share?"

Natalie looked horrified. "Oh no, I want to work full-time. Everyone who does part-time in engineering gets all the rubbish departments to cover. I've fought very hard to get to where I am and it would be silly to give it up now."

My stomach clenched as I imagined this poor baby shipped off to nursery at seven in the morning, reclaimed like a lost umbrella at seven at night.

"You'll miss out on such a lot, though. The time goes so quickly. You'll be able to go back to work when he or she goes to school. I wouldn't have missed those early years for anything. Ollie was such a sweet baby, I thought I was a brilliant parent because he slept through the night at about eight weeks. Hannah got me back, though. She didn't sleep until she was about three."

The shutters came down on Natalie's face. I knew I should stop talking.

Jack tried to help out. "I'm sure they'll work it out, Gisela. We didn't have much to start with, but we managed."

"I know, I just don't think they realise how hard it will be, rushing to get a baby to a nursery or a childminder every morning. Ollie doesn't even know where he'll be working. He's not necessarily going to get a job on the doorstep, is he?"

Ollie slammed down his knife and fork. "Mum! Stop having a go at us. I'm going to stay at home with the baby while Nat goes to work. We'll manage."

Hannah clapped her hands. "You're going to be a house husband? That's hilarious! I can just see you poncing about in a pinny with the baby in a sling!"

She laughed and laughed, bits of bean and carrot on display in her mouth.

I stared at Ollie. "You mean you're not even applying for jobs after you finish your degree?"

"No, Mum. I'm going to look after my son or daughter. Later on, I'll work."

I slumped back in my chair. "Oh, Ollie."

Natalie stood up. "Sorry, but I've had enough of this. Why are you actually so horrified about Oliver staying at home? It's his baby too. Why should it be just my responsibility? It's not the 1950s."

"Because he's twenty-one! Because he probably didn't want a bloody baby in the first place! Why should his life be ruined because you didn't sort out your contraception? Why? And now you've got everything you want—a baby, a full-time nursemaid to look after it for free and your glittering career."

Jack put his hand on my arm. "Gisela! Calm down." The greatest phrase ever invented for inflaming a situation further.

"I'm not going to calm down. Natalie's had her opportunities and, by the sounds of it, she's grasped them with both hands, and good for her, but it's not right that Ollie doesn't even get a shot at a career. It's bad enough that he's weighed down with this responsibility so young without being stuck at home with a baby all day."

Natalie put her hand on her hips. "The thing I find incredible in all of this is how you assume that Oliver and I can't find a solution for ourselves. As though we're a couple of kids who need our parents to decide things for us. I'm thirty-four, not seventeen. I run a team of twenty-five people without asking anyone what to do."

I took a deep breath. "Ollie, is this what you really want? Because if it is, I'll shut up right now. If it's not, I don't think you should throw your life away without considering all the other options."

Ollie's face was pink with emotion. Unlike Hannah, he hated confrontation, would do anything to avoid it. "Did I want a baby right now? Not really, but actually I'm quite excited by the idea now I've got used to it. Do I love Nat and want to stay with her and be a good dad? Yes."

I shook my head, wanting to shout that looking after a baby wasn't as easy as it appeared in the movies, that it can be boring and isolating and it would be harder for him because there wouldn't be a ready-made group of other men staying at home, especially not as young as him.

Natalie walked out to the sitting room.

Hannah pulled a face. "That went well, Mum."

Jack turned on her. "If you haven't got anything helpful to say, just shut up."

"Woo. Happy Christmas to you too."

I sank down into my chair, pressing my fingers into my eyes to stop the tears escaping. "This is not what I wanted for you, Ollie. You're too young. She's lived her life, had all the fun, then wanted a baby before it's too late and trapped you before you've even had a proper job."

I tried to explain that responsibility came so quickly once you had children. That the days of doing whatever took your fancy were over. For the next two decades. My heart ached at the idea of him tied to one measly fortnight's holiday a year before he'd had the luxury of trotting round Europe with a rucksack, sleeping on beaches, drinking cheap beer and never thinking beyond tomorrow.

Ollie got up. "But I love her, Mum." As though love was ever enough.

Natalie stormed back into the kitchen. "I'm driving home. Are you coming with me, Ollie?"

The indecision on his face hurt me more than if he'd sworn and spat the remnants of the chestnut stuffing onto the floor.

Jack stood clutching his glass of wine, looking to me to find the right words to rewind us all to a happier place. I didn't have any words.

Natalie whirled out, a six-foot massif of fury.

I turned to Ollie, trying not to sob. "You go with her, love. I'm sorry. I should have handled that better."

He hugged me tightly, looking more miserable than I'd ever seen him.

I watched him walk out.

"Love you."

He didn't turn round.

Photos: Everyone raising a glass of champagne with obligatory silly hats.

Shiny presents with ostentatious bows under the Christmas tree.

Caption: So lovely to have everyone home today.

#Christmas #LoveMyFamily

CHAPTER 20

Kate

Christmas Day

I watched the activity at Gisela's house. Jack fetching the wheelbarrow out of the garage. Hannah dancing in her bedroom. Ollie and his girlfriend arriving for lunch with an armful of presents. Gisela rushing out to the car to hug everyone. No wonder Daisy loved their house. Yet again, here we were, just the two of us, with our quiet "Happy Christmas," the crushing responsibility of finding the perfect present for each other, the mocking sparseness of the turkey crown next to a couple of crackers, served at three in the afternoon so we didn't have a long evening ahead with nothing to fill it. This year was even worse because Daisy had the excuse of her A level mocks to avoid joining in with any of the usual preparations—buying one new spectacular decoration for the Christmas tree, finding the white chocolates we loved to hang on it, singing, "All I want for Christmas is my two front teeth" when we had our first mince pie. "I need to *revise*, Mum," accompanied by the little "Oh my God, you are so stupid" headshake I'd seen Hannah direct at Gisela on numerous occasions.

I put my Christmas carol CD on, singing "Once in Royal David's City" as though today was a day full of promise. But the truth was, since that night with Alex, when I'd reached into that cobwebby space inside me where hope and love existed, I felt total despair. The sort of despair I thought I'd consigned to the past. I could no longer tell myself that as long as Daisy was happy, my world was complete. All the feelings I'd compressed so tightly had finally wriggled free. With Daisy on the cusp of adulthood, I was squinting into the abyss and hoping my future held more than an encyclopedic knowledge of TV scheduling.

Daisy eventually emerged at eleven-thirty. I made our ritual Christmas Day hot chocolate with marshmallows, wanting to love the comfort of our traditions, to convince myself that we didn't need anything—or anyone—else. We exchanged Christmas presents—the usual array of nail varnishes, make-up and toiletries for Daisy, with her exclaiming over every pot of goo. "That smells gorgeous!" "Yay! I love this Body Shop pink grapefruit!" I put on the lovely rose-patterned scarf she'd bought me—"Do you like it? Really? Not too girly?"—and then we were done.

Just like an ordinary Sunday, I started peeling vegetables. Once everything was in the oven, we sat over the *Radio Times*, circling our choice of films. Daisy thought it was hilarious that I still bought it: "You can just get the times of the films online." I liked the commitment of marking out *The Sound of Music* and *How the Grinch Stole Christmas*. This year I wasn't sure I could cope with our usual diet of *Dirty Dancing*, *Notting Hill*, *Love Actually*. I wanted a real-life fairy tale.

I surreptitiously looked at my phone to see if Alex had sent me a message. Nothing. He'd tried to contact me so many times since I'd made excuses not to see him again. He'd rung—with all the not taking no for an answer that came with his job. I'd picked up once.

"You're avoiding me. I want to know why that is."

I'd tried to fob him off with being too busy at work, with it not being the right time for me to start a relationship, with lame and lukewarm bollocks that he spotted a mile off.

"I will work it out, you know. There's something you're not telling me."

I'd finished the phone call quickly, telling him that I wasn't ready to get involved with anyone.

Weirdly, I then had a searing need, bordering on an obsession, to speak to him. Every day since, I'd picked up my phone at least once a day, usually more, to call. I even toyed with telling him the truth. He worked in investigative journalism. Maybe he was the one person who'd understand, who could find the unbelievable believable. He'd have come across lots of grey areas in human behaviour. But I'd lied for so long.

The laptop called to me in case he'd dropped me a line on Facebook. While Daisy went to set up the films to record, I muttered something about double-checking the turkey cooking times and quickly logged in. Straight up there in the feed were the smiling faces of Gisela's family, holding their glasses aloft, followed by some pictures of beautifully wrapped presents with glittery ribbon and bows. Even if I had the money and time, I couldn't be bothered with that. I felt a stab of envy at the thought of reading out a cracker joke and having a whole audience of people throwing out mad answers rather than just Daisy and I sitting opposite each other, saying, "I don't know, you'll have to tell me."

And there was Sally up in York, looking so slim. God knows how she'd managed to lose weight when she was always travelling and eating out. She obviously wasn't stinting herself today, though, judging by the fact she was waving a sixpence from her mum's homemade pud. I wondered if Chris had managed to make it back. No doubt he'd have sent some show-stopping present if he hadn't. And anyway, Sally was still with her mum and dad. Lucky her.

The second year for me without my mum. I closed my eyes and pictured her baking away, cutting out Christmas shapes in the pierniczki dough on the little Formica worktop in her kitchen. I could almost smell the cinnamon and nutmeg. My heart ached for her. She'd never stopped believing in me. "I'm very proud of you," she said as though I'd followed a traditional path through life with no more of a blip than a few failed fairy cakes in my home economics lessons. I wish I'd taken the time to appreciate what strength her words gave me, how they filled the empty spaces inside me where loneliness now seeped like a cold liquid, burrowing into every crack that my heart hadn't manage to seal over. In the eighteen months since she'd died, the grief inside me had not only expanded but gathered pace. Since we'd moved away from Manchester eleven years ago, I'd cut down on my visits to Mum, sneaking back to her after dark, terrified that her neighbours would see us and word would reach Becky. I couldn't risk being followed. And now, I'd never see Mum again.

I opened my eyes as wide as they would go until the urge to cry passed. I clicked on my messages despite there being no icon showing that anyone had tried to contact me. No Alex. I went onto his page, hoping he'd have posted a photo with a #broken-hearted #unrequitedlove hashtag. Instead there was a picture of him on his motorbike clearly missing the #mymidlifecrisis.

Right on cue, Gisela posted a collage of various photos of her with members of her family, all smiling and hugging, with the caption: "Love is most of all the feeling that these are the people you are meant to be with. #FoundMyTribe."

I shut the laptop, wishing I could creep back under my duvet and sleep until New Year was over. My tribe was as lost to me now as the Sapanahua in the Amazon.

I got up to switch on the Christmas tree lights. The road outside was quiet, apart from the rain pattering down, everyone secreted away in their houses, pouring wine, dragging up memories of Christmases past, making new ones to recall and argue about in the future. "That was the year Mum forgot to switch on the oven." "Dad fell asleep in his bread sauce." "Uncle Arthur got locked in the loo." All we'd ever be able to offer up was a comparison of M&S crackers versus Tesco's. "A much better quality of key ring." "Significantly louder bang." "Nasty little nail clippers."

I couldn't wait for Christmas to be over.

CHAPTER 21

Sally

Christmas Day

I'd driven up to York to Mum and Dad's on 22 December, unannounced. I'd intended to spend Christmas binge-watching box sets with the curtains shut, but the closer I got to Christmas, the more the quiet of the house made me feel I was just one step away from smashing up the place like a drug-crazed vandal. As I turned the car into my parents' street, the place I'd ridden my bike, walked hand-in-hand with my boyfriend from school, practised three-point turns in my dad's Fiesta with him saying, "Take it slow, love, take it slow," I felt that visceral sense of belonging.

I could turn up and I'd be loved. Imperfectly, sometimes critically, often in a way that I found irritating. "I don't think you're eating enough," "Do you need a coat?" "Is it safe for you to take the tube at night?" But love was waiting for me. And lots of it, even if I interrupted their viewing of *Long Lost Family*. Of course, I'd have to suffer Mum's: "See. Even women in their eighties never forgot about the babies they gave away. Nothing more special than children. Nothing." I'd probably have to absorb the realisation that something everyone else took for granted was going to pass me by. That unique yet common act so many people managed without trying, without even wanting, often without much debate, as though bringing another little person into the world was of no consequence. Intellectually, I could understand the feral, primeval love a mother felt for a child. Emotionally, I'd have to imagine it. Or, preferably, never imagine it.

I'd walked up to the door, with a sense of staggering towards a finish line where I could collapse in a heap and have someone else take over. I rang the bell.

My dad had answered. The huge smile that greeted me took the lid off my guilt for not visiting sooner.

"Our Sally! Come in, love, come in! Did your mother know you were coming?" He'd scooped me into his arms. And there it was. My soft landing. I'd tried not to cry, but the bit of me that still thought my parents could fix things was obviously not as evolved as I'd hoped. "What's wrong, love? Just a minute, I'll get your mum. Marge! Marge! Our Sally's here. Come on, you come through here. I'll make us a nice cup of tea."

I'd sunk onto the sofa, the bulky TV that Generation Flatscreen had passed by, showing the snooker. I'd rubbed my palm over the crimson velour that Chris disdained, comparing my parents' house unfavourably to his family home, where, in my opinion, all the minimalist furniture was designed to move you on, rather than encourage you to linger. The saggy old cushions of my parents' sofa carried the comfort of nights watching the *Generation Game* and *Blind Date*, drinking the Batida de Coco my mum had brought back from Majorca and eating Frazzles, without a smoked almond in sight.

Mum had come bustling in with her apron and a nailbrush in hand. "Sally! Why didn't you let me know you were coming? I could have made a lemon meringue pie!" She'd stopped. "Are you all right, love?"

"No. I'm not."

The words—an admission of failure after so many years of shutting out my parents with my success—were a relief after all these weeks of chatting away giving them the impression my biggest worry was whether the first edition I'd ordered for Chris about Winston Churchill's early life would turn up on time.

My mother's face took a second to adjust after her mind accepted what her ears had heard. Everything was always fine. Chris was fine, work was fine, the house was great. It was years since she'd needed the concerned face, last seen circa 1997 when a string of A* GCSEs was blighted by a single B in history, an event that had me hiding in my bedroom for a full forty-eight hours, convinced of my worthlessness and stupidity. That clenching of the hands and furrowing of the brow had made a rare appearance since, but as I'd got older I'd become better at putting on a front when things got tough. Better at lying.

Now, my heart felt as though someone had funnelled acid into it, stripping away all the coating, all the barriers that I'd used to defend myself over the years against the disappointments, the injustices, the betrayals.

"Is it work, love?" Mum had asked, as though she'd been waiting for me to climb too high and come crashing down ever since I got a Saturday job in the knicker department in BHS— "Will you be able to work the till all right?"

I'd shaken my head. "It's Chris. He's left me."

"Left you? Whatever for? You've just bought that lovely house. I haven't even seen it yet."

At this rate, my mother would be able to get intimately acquainted with it when she helped me move out. She sat on the one straight-backed chair in the room, as though this was far too serious to be lounging in an armchair.

Dad had come in with the tea. "I've put in a spoonful of sugar for the upset. Have a garibaldi."

"Chris has left our Sally."

Thankfully, Dad didn't join in with real-estate lamentations. "Well, that's a stupid thing to do. He'll not find anyone better."

Mum's cup rattled in its saucer. "He's not got someone else, surely?" as though most divorces came about because one person was more interested in chess than the other.

"I don't think so. I'm not really sure." Which was close to the truth, though I had spent a huge amount of time scrutinising all the work photos on his Facebook page to see if any women popped up next to him too often. So far, Rupert from accounts was the only one who featured in close proximity on a regular basis, so I was none the wiser as to who the *distraction* might be.

Dad picked at the raisins in his biscuit. "I thought you were happy. What's brought all that about then?"

I'd wanted to say it. I'd wanted to tell them. How every time someone announced they were pregnant at the office, I had to hold my breath to stop myself crying. How when I signed the "Congratulations on the birth of your baby" card, something horrible and resentful hardened within me, leaving me unable to write more than a cursory note. How every time I encountered a woman with a young child, I judged whether I could have been a better mother. God, how I judged. I'd never have given in to that tantrum over Pom-Bears. I wouldn't have let him drink juice from a baby's bottle—think of his teeth! I'd never have let my kid have a green, snotty nose. Yet their partners loved them enough to trust they'd be good mothers. Unlike my husband.

I wasn't ready to scoop out that vulnerable part of me for anyone to see. I couldn't stand the thought that, going forward, my mum—and probably Dad too—would tag on an "uplifting" fact to the news that Joyce down the road's daughter/the girl I was friends with at primary school/the shop assistant who we all thought was fifty-five had had a baby—"But she's never travelled like you," "But her house is nowhere near as big as yours—the kitchen's tiny," "But they can't even afford a weekend in Whitley Bay this year."

Dad had shifted in his seat, as though my hesitation at answering might be related to something horribly embarrassing, to do with my "downstairs" or Chris's "undercarriage."

"I don't honestly know, Dad," I'd said, reflecting on the vagaries of the English language that meant people often said "honestly" when they meant the exact opposite. Dad, bless him, had looked relieved that he wasn't going to be taken on an impromptu tour of stuff he never wanted to imagine his daughter doing.

"Well, if you don't know, I imagine it's one of them midlife crises. Your mother was lucky that I discovered golf. Some of the silly buggers down at the club start buying fancy cars and chasing around after the ladies."

My mother chipped in. "Dad's right, you'll see. He'll be back once he sees which side his bread is buttered. It'll be fine. Something and nothing. Crikey, if you could have seen some of the silly tiffs your dad and I had when we were younger…"

And with a bit of yarn and a laugh about the time Dad had backed into the garden wall because he'd hurt his neck and couldn't turn round and Mum was guiding him but confused her left with her right, my parents convinced themselves that Chris would soon see the light and we'd all be cruising off into the sunset in a shower of stars.

Mum had slapped her thighs with the finality of having made sense of it all. "You'll be staying for dinner then, shepherd's pie?"

I'd swallowed. "I was hoping I could stay for Christmas."

A glance carrying the panic of "This is more serious than we thought" had swirled between them, before my dad cleared his throat and said, "Right. Right. Have you got a case with you then, pet?"

The relief of striding out to the car with a case-carrying purpose was in direct contrast to Mum's fluttering over the Christmas pud that she wasn't sure would stretch to three— "We made a tiny one this year because we didn't want lots of leftovers, and you know your dad with his waistline." Yep. Poor old Dad and his waistline had long been the subject of Mum's attention, but it was still there. And still expanding.

I'd put up my hand in a gesture of surrender. "I don't need any Christmas pud. I'm not even that keen on it."

That didn't suit Mum either. "You must have a spoonful. You might get the sixpence."

"Whatever works, Mum."

She'd patted my arm. "It's so lovely to have you here, love. I know we live a long way away and you're so busy, what with work and the new house, and Chris," she added with a meaningful "It's not over till it's over" dip of the head. "But Dad and I are proper made up to have you here." She started, as though she'd sat on a drawing pin. "I'll just pop up and air your bed."

I'd never aired a bed in my life. If you changed the sheets with every new guest, I wasn't quite sure what you were airing. Unless, of course, like my mother, you "didn't hold with all this endless changing of beds," then I supposed you were allowing all the ancient farts to dissipate into the atmosphere.

Over the days leading up to Christmas, though, despite the "You're not having another bath, you'll wash yourself away" from my dad and the "Put some slippers on, you'll get chilblains" from Mum, I felt more relaxed than I had since we moved. I kept dropping off to sleep in front of the TV, "just like your father." By the time Christmas Day came round, Mum had almost convinced me that Chris would be waiting at home when I got back. She turned out to be surprisingly cunning. "Don't you be telling everyone that Chris has gone and left you high and dry. When he comes back, you don't want every Tom, Dick and Harry whispering about how he went off. You keep it quiet. Tell them he's off on one of his work trips. They don't need to know all your business."

"I think the neighbours will start to notice it's just me and my takeaways for one, Mum."

"I never have understood why you don't get yourself a slow cooker. It's so easy—a bit of brisket from the butcher, some chopped-up celery and carrots..."

My arms itched and ached with not putting my head in my hands.

Mum was on a roll. "Husbands go off all the time. You give

Chris a few weeks to see what life's like on the other side. He'll soon be back. I mean, that Samantha down the road, her husband went off with some dolly bird he met at the races, but he still came home when he ran out of money, and no one was any the wiser."

Despite resoundingly disproving her theory, Mum was a rolling stone gathering absolutely no moss.

"Anyway, who does he think he is, leaving you in the first place? I mean, he might come from a bit more of a la-di-da family, but they're a right rum lot if you ask me. His mother never even managed so much as a sniff on your wedding day."

I smiled at the memory. I'd said my vows to the plaintive refrain—interspersed with sniffing—of "Doesn't she look lovely? Such a clever girl too." My dad had walked me down the aisle with the air of someone who felt like the most important person in the room for the first time in his life. Just before we'd left for the church, he'd said, "Them other parents might have a bigger house and that, but they haven't got you. Look at you, love." And he'd kissed me, very gently on my forehead, in a gesture that contained pride, love and protection. All the things I'd hoped to be able to transmit to a child of my own one day.

On Christmas Day, I restricted myself to a simple text: *"Happy Christmas, Chris. Thinking of you xxx."* I didn't add, *"And I hope you're not with the bloody distraction and are at this very minute asking yourself why on earth you're not with your wife."*

He rang me immediately, my heart leaping with hope and dread. "It's odd not being together, isn't it?" he said.

I tried to sound casual. "It is. Where are you?"

"I'm having a long walk in Richmond Park. The world and his wife are here actually."

There was a moment of silence. The ghost of the question, "Is she with you?" hung in the air.

I filled the quiet, babbling on about my mum and dad and what we'd been watching on TV. Eventually, my words ran down until there was only one direction to go.

"Have you managed to think things through at all?" I asked.

"I think I'm getting there. Anyway, better go, before I get knocked over in a deer stampede. Take care, Sally."

His tone was tender. How two lonely people who loved each other couldn't find a way forward was beyond me. I ran into the bathroom to splash my face with cold water before texting, *"Miss you"* to Chris and receiving a single kiss in reply. That would have to do.

As I helped Mum with lunch, she whispered to me, "You won't mind me asking, will you?"

I shrugged. "Depends what it is, Mum."

"Chris going off isn't anything to do with what's going on upstairs, is it?"

My mind strayed to the attic conversion Chris and I had discussed if I got a decent bonus. I decided that it wasn't secondary staircases bothering Mum. "Do you mean—" I couldn't bring myself to say the word *sex*—"in the bedroom?"

Mum nodded furiously. "Because when we were young, your father liked—"

I butted in before I heard words I'd never be able to delete from my brain. "No, no, Mum, that's not an issue."

She'd clearly decided that her maternal duty was not yet at an end. "All I'm saying is that men have needs, dear. And if they're getting beef steak at home, they won't be going out for no beefburger with skinny fries or whatever it is you young ones eat these days."

It was ironic that one of the items I'd recently declared to be so old-fashioned as to be irrelevant turned out to be such a lifesaver.

"Mum! Where's the gravy boat?"

Photo: Sally holding the silver sixpence.
    Caption: Lovely day with my family and I found the sixpence too!
    #Myluckyyear #Happydays

CHAPTER 22

Kate

New Year's Eve

I was standing peering out at the street about ten o'clock, wondering whether to try to find a film to watch or to give up and go to bed when I saw Gisela pop up at her living room window. I did a double take. When Hannah had called for Daisy on their way to the rugby club earlier, she'd told me her parents were going to a party. I waved to her and we smiled, slightly embarrassed, as though we were the only two people in the world with nowhere else to go. The next thing I knew she was whipping across the road in her slippers and ringing my bell.

I opened the door. "Is everything all right? Hannah said you were out tonight."

"Everything's fine. Just wasn't feeling the love for partying tonight."

"That's not like you, is it?"

And with that, she burst into tears. "Sorry, sorry. I was only coming to see if you wanted to pop over for a drink. I've had such a shit Christmas."

"Come in for a moment," I said, leading her into the living room and scrabbling around for a half-decent bottle of wine.

"I can't stay. I've left Jack on his own. He's already grumpy with me for not going out. I don't even bloody like New Year's

Eve, all that clustering round the TV waiting for Big Ben to chime before having to hug people you probably won't see again for the next year."

As she glugged down most of a glass of wine in one go, she told me what had happened. "The reality is I couldn't face going to some crappy party and having to field all those questions about how the kids are, what they're up to. Right now, I feel like I might never see Ollie again, let alone my grandchild."

Gisela's honesty was refreshing, coming as it did as an insight into the house that Daisy found so "You just don't get it, Mum, it's so chill." I couldn't marry up the disaster of her Christmas Day with what I'd seen on Facebook. It certainly shot our low-key day up the enjoyable stakes. I did have a little intake of breath at Ollie shacking up with a pregnant thirty-four-year-old. Like Gisela, I'd sort of assumed it was a phase, a young man flattered by an older woman's attention. He looked like a kid to me, more suited to skateboarding in the local park, not gearing up for the responsibility of parenthood. But maybe they'd make it. Who knew which relationships would survive, what challenges we'd face? Oskar and I had been smug in our closeness, talking about what we'd do when we retired when we were in our early twenties. We'd never anticipated that something so big, so shocking, could rock our world, leaving us scrabbling around for flotsam to save ourselves, every man for himself, with nothing left to keep our joint venture afloat.

I patted her hand. "In the end, you're a really close family. You'll find a middle ground once the baby's born. Natalie won't want her child to grow up not knowing its grandparents."

"I hope you're right. Don't tell anyone, will you? I'm not ready for everyone else's opinion yet."

"Your secret's safe with me. I haven't got anyone to tell."

Gisela dabbed her face. "Please come back with me for a drink so I don't have to look at Jack's miserable mush on my own. There's loads of bubbly..."

I laughed. "You don't need to feel sorry for me. I'm quite used to spending New Year's Eve by myself."

"Please?"

I hesitated. It was quite nice to be wanted. "Will Jack mind?"

"God, no! He'll be thrilled to have some new blood. I don't think twenty-four/seven togetherness suits our family."

Sure enough, when I walked in, Jack leapt to his feet. "Kate! Lovely to see you. Happy New Year. Champagne?"

I could see why Daisy loved their world. I could get used to it myself.

Jack handed a glass to Gisela. "Alex has texted. He was supposed to be at some fancy TV celeb party this evening but fell off a ladder and has just come out of A&E. I told him to get a cab straight here, that he could stay the night if he wanted."

"Great. Beds are made up. You'll have to help him up the stairs, though." She turned to me. "You remember Alex, don't you? The tarantula at my birthday party?"

I tried to ignore the sudden rush of heat to my face. "I think so, I'm not sure, I talked to so many people that night." I didn't quite manage to meet Gisela's eye.

She clapped her hands. "Who needs to go out? We've got our own little party right here." She bustled off into the kitchen and came back with little bowls of olives and nuts.

I sat perched on the edge of her cream sofa, wishing I'd put on some make-up and something a bit more glamorous than jeans. I didn't even have time to dig about in my handbag for a stray lipstick because a cab pulled up, the door slammed, Jack rushed into the street and I saw Alex limping up the drive on crutches.

My stomach dropped as an image of his naked chest rushed into my mind.

Jack's voice boomed out in the hallway. "You poor bugger. Expecting to spend the evening cavorting with actresses and singers and getting stuck with us."

"I'm bloody lucky you're so unpopular that you were sitting

at home on New Year's Eve." I loved how his tone belied his words, that affection of long friendships allowing for outrageous insults.

Jack laughed. "You cheeky sod. I was invited to three parties, I'll have you know."

"And now you're so middle-aged you'd rather stay in and watch *When Harry Met Sally*?"

Before Jack could reply, Alex hopped into the sitting room.

His face froze as he saw me sitting in an armchair. He blinked a few times as though, if he was lucky, I might be an inconvenient mirage. "Kate. Nice to see you again. How are you?"

"Good, thank you."

Gisela raced over to him, saving me from having to come up with anything more substantial. "What were you doing up a ladder, you daft sod? Don't tell me you were cleaning windows?"

"Oh ye of little faith. I was actually hanging some paintings and obviously don't have the co-ordination required for balancing and drilling at the same time."

Jack's shoulders started to shake. "You were lucky not to drill through your eyeball when you fell."

Gisela frowned. "Since when did you do anything as homely as hang pictures? The last time I came to your flat, you were using newspaper as a tablecloth."

Alex looked sheepish. "Gisela, you should be applauding me, not berating me. I've decided to become a grown-up."

"Don't suppose you're in the country long enough to go shopping for some decent curtains? I'll always come and help if you need a woman's touch." Gisela paused. "Or are you hanging pictures *because* there's a woman on the scene?"

I held my breath. It was nothing to do with me anyway. Though that didn't stop me clenching all the muscles in my face so I wouldn't give myself away.

Alex said, "Maybe. Maybe not."

Gisela batted him with her hand. "Ooooh, is there someone? Oh my God, Alex is in love. We haven't been to a wedding in years. I could do the flowers."

Alex shook his head. "I say 'maybe' and you start banging on about flowers. And you wonder why I don't tell you anything?"

Gisela wagged her finger at him. "You're going to die a miserable old bachelor taken hostage by one of those gangs you insist on hounding."

"International criminals, you mean."

Gisela waved him away as though drug barons were just cuddly old fellas dabbling in the odd bag of white powder.

She turned to me. "I love a good wedding. I could get a hat."

Jack tutted. "You love an excuse to spend money."

"Have you noticed how tight Jack's become, Alex? There was a time when he was all 'you spend what you want, my darling.' If we're not careful, he'll be trying to trick me into drinking Prosecco instead of champagne."

I knew Gisela was being outrageous for the sake of it, but the atmosphere had shifted as though an argument was happening under the cover of a bit of marital banter. I wanted to escape, run away from all the odd tensions in the room. Run away from Alex. Or towards him.

He looked at me properly for the first time and raised a sympathetic eyebrow. "I wondered if I'd see you dashing in and out of A&E today."

My ability to read whether that was a "I was disappointed not to see you" or a "This is awkward, I'd better plug on with some neutral conversation" appeared to have flapped off into the sunset.

My words nailed themselves into my throat. "I wasn't working today." I just managed to stop myself launching into a nervous and detailed rundown of the paramedic holiday rota.

Out of the corner of my eye, I saw Gisela flounce off to the kitchen. I fumbled about, desperate for a topic that could include Jack and divert me from studying every little detail of Alex. Those hands and the things they could do. That alpha-male toughness combined with an unexpected gentleness. I breathed out. I couldn't weaken now. Not after all the effort of creating another anonymous life here. The "human interest" element—death, divorce, shattered friendships—was gold dust to a journalist. Every time a similar story hit the headlines, my picture cropped up, the details raked over. I couldn't risk letting the silt get stirred up again. The price for that was staying away from Alex. It was ironic that every nerve ending in my skin was straining towards him.

"When are you back at work, Jack?" I asked.

"Next week sometime, don't want to think about it. I don't know why so many people wait all year for their holidays to come and, when they do, all they talk about is how many days left they've got, instead of enjoying their time off."

I felt myself blush, as though I'd been told off for being parochial. "Sorry. Second nature to me, because work sched-ules dominate my life." I wanted to add, "And I don't have the luxury of a husband to pick up the slack," but I didn't want to look desperate.

Jack harrumphed something and went off to fetch some wine. I was pretty sure he'd gone to find Gisela and hiss, "Come and help me out, it's awkward in there with that weird friend of yours."

I looked at the floor for a moment, scared to see the bemuse-ment in his face, not sure I could lie if he asked me a direct question.

He broke the silence. "I didn't know you were here tonight."

"I wasn't supposed to be." My words came out grumpily as though I wouldn't have come if I'd known he was arriving.

"Have I spoilt the evening?"

I couldn't help myself. "No."

Alex clapped his hands together. "Kate, you fascinate me. And frustrate me." He smiled. "If I beg, will you come out for another drink?"

Gisela and Jack bowled into the room before I could answer, twirling in with more Moët "to toast the New Year."

When it came, unlike the others singing at the top of their voices, I self-consciously mumbled along to "Auld Lang Syne." We hugged, with Alex whispering, "Happy New Year, lovely lady" in my ear. And despite everything my head knew, my heart was cheering, clutching onto the silver silk of hope threading its way forwards, in a place where love had died, but, with exactly the right temperature and perfect amount of watering, it might grow again.

CHAPTER 23

Sally

Tuesday 2 January

I'd texted Chris to let him know I was coming home on the Tuesday after New Year. I parked the Mini on the drive, brushing away the stab of disappointment that his car wasn't there. I reminded myself of all the times he'd parked around the corner and leapt out to surprise me when he'd come home early from a trip.

As I pushed open the door, it jammed on the build-up of letters. I wrestled them free and scurried in with my case. Now was not the time to bump into Kate or Gisela. No one would ask for details of my Christmas if I didn't see them until the fifteenth of January.

I waited with my back to the front door, listening for movement, still half expecting Chris's face to peer round the sitting room door despite the evidence that he hadn't been near the place. The house was silent. The bolstering up that my parents had managed in their primitive way, convincing me that every marriage had these "silly little storms in a teacup," was already seeping away.

With a sinking of spirit, I dragged my case through to the kitchen and flicked through the post, alert for anything with Chris's spiky left-sloping writing. Nothing. There was one handwritten letter with an Argentinian stamp.

K. Kowalski, 17 Parkview. Kate's house. Kowalski? That sounded Polish. To be fair, Kate looked as though she could be Polish, with those high cheekbones, so did Daisy. Then I remembered how prickly she'd been when I suggested her dress could be Eastern European at Gisela's fancy dress party. If I had exotic roots like that, I'd tell everyone. I frowned. Maybe it was a letter for her ex-husband. Perhaps he was foreign. Kate was so guarded, I could count the things I knew about her on one hand, despite living next door to her for six months. She didn't seem to have any friends coming and going, and I'd never seen a boyfriend. Maybe I'd end up being quoted in the paper one day: "Neighbour Sally Gastrell, 36, said Kate Jones and her daughter Daisy kept themselves to themselves, quiet and polite." Followed by a shocked statement about how I had no idea she was an East European drug dealer/supplied teenagers to a brothel in Warsaw.

On the other hand, the truth was probably far more banal, though she did go a bit fidgety whenever anyone mentioned her looking Slavic. My mind ran through the possibilities. Wrongly addressed letter? Illegal immigrants? Brexited out and decided to call themselves something else to avoid being harangued about their right to be here? It was so much easier to speculate about Kate's life than to face the reality of my own—that Chris wasn't here and I had no idea when—or whether—he'd be back.

I stuck the letter on the windowsill by the front door and emptied my case, unable to shrug off Chris's habit of unpacking everything and putting the washing machine on the second we walked through the door. In a burst of rebellion, I made tea in a mug and, without bothering to get a plate, ate a slice of the Christmas cake my mother had foisted upon me ("Otherwise your father will eat it all, and I can't have that").

The doorbell went. My stupid heart leapt with hope, even though Chris would use his keys.

I opened the door. Gisela. So much for hibernating until the middle of January.

"Welcome home! How was Christmas?"

That simple question made my heart constrict. I wanted to wail, "Chris has left me. Might be shacked up with someone else." Instead I said, "We had a lovely time, thank you, doing all the traditional things with my parents. How about you?"

Gisela laughed. "So many people in and out, Ollie and his girlfriend, Hannah and her friends, Jack's no-hoper mate from university days... It was like running a restaurant and being a chambermaid all rolled into one."

Mothers did this a lot. I noticed it at work. The joy of family life, of having people who needed you, of nurturing with food and time and love, disguised as a moan about how hard it all was.

I pushed myself to join in with the "Gosh, it must be exhausting for you" face, rather than shouting about how she could have been lying in a single bed at her parents' home with a hot-water bottle and the same bloody rose-flecked wallpaper they'd put up when she was thirteen.

"Anyway," Gisela said. "Jack is a bit down in the dumps—I don't know if it's because he's back to work tomorrow—but I wondered if Chris would invite him out for a drink?"

My brain wouldn't work. I couldn't tell her. I just couldn't. The downside of Gisela's friendliness was that I suspected she was the street's town crier. Anything I told her would soon be bouncing from house to house, until the whole cul-de-sac was abuzz with "You know that Sally, the one with that wine job and the husband with the purple sports car, well, he's only gone and left her." No doubt soon to be followed by "Poor thing. Never had any kids. Though probably for the best. Much easier to split up if there aren't any little ones to consider."

If I had a baby or a toddler or even a teenager, I'd have a purpose. I'd have to keep going. I'd be like my mum, putting on a brave face, jollying everyone along. Rather than giving in to the temptation to eat doughnuts and microwave popcorn until I got stuck in one of those narrow armchairs that Chris had chosen, designed to embarrass people with ample backsides.

Gisela was standing in front of me, eyebrows raised, waiting for an answer to a not very difficult question.

"He's not around at the moment. He's abroad for work. I'm not sure when he'll be back. I'll tell him, though. See if they can work something out."

Gisela frowned. "I thought he'd been away for several weeks before Christmas? It must be so hard on you both if he's already had to go off again."

"It is."

Gisela waited for me to elaborate.

I countered with my own question—a technique Chris had honed and perfected. "Why's Jack down in the dumps?"

"I don't know. Probably reached that age when he's bored with running the business and wondering how many caravan parks he'll have to buy and sell before he can retire. He envies Chris, zooming all over the world with work. Bet Chris would like to be at home more with you, though? Grass is always greener, isn't it?"

I did one of those mumbles that could have meant anything and diverted her by reaching inside for the letter addressed to the mysterious K. Kowalski. "Kate doesn't have another surname of Kowalski, does she?"

Gisela shook her head. "Not as far as I know. That sounds sort of Czech or Bulgarian, Eastern bloc, doesn't it? Think she was born in Manchester, though I suppose she could have been married to a foreigner. She's never mentioned it, though. Maybe the letter's not for her."

"But it's from Argentina, where Daisy's dad lives."

Gisela shrugged because, unlike me, she wasn't all suspicious, reading things into it. It was just a Post Office mess-up, not a mystery to be solved.

I waved her off, agreeing to catch up for coffee in a week or so, just as Kate got out of her car and hurried to her front door.

I shouted for her to wait and ran over with the letter. "This was delivered to my house by mistake. Is it for you?"

She stood in the doorway, her eyes darting about. "That stupid postman. It says number seventeen on it quite clearly." She put her hand out for it. "God knows why that's come here."

I almost got into a tussle over it, unwilling to relinquish it until I had an explanation. Kate never felt the need to justify anything. In fact, she was one of those women who seemed friendly, always quick with a wave, to shout hello from over the fence, but she never offered any insights into her life, nor asked for any into yours.

"Do you know this person? Can you forward it or shall I open it and see if there's a return address?" I asked.

Her face tightened for a second, then she smiled. "I know where to send it."

Just at that moment, Daisy appeared behind her, the complete opposite with her greetings and chatter. "Sally! How are you?"

We picked over the bones of Christmas, mine a lot fleshier than the reality, before Daisy noticed the letter in Kate's hand.

"When did that arrive?" she asked in a voice that held a hint of accusation.

"It was delivered to Sally's house. I said I'd send it on to the right person." Everything about Kate was rigid, warnings ringing out in her tone as clearly as an air-raid siren.

Daisy scowled and muttered a goodbye to me before disappearing back inside. Poor Daisy. It was hard enough being a teenager without a mother as closed and difficult to talk to as Kate. If I'd had a teenager, I'd never have worked such odd hours, leaving her to fend for herself. If parents never made the time to be at home, to talk and create opportunities to understand what was going on in their lives, then it wasn't surprising their kids got their kicks from weed and vodka Red Bull. Several times a week, I saw Daisy walk up the street eating cheap takeaway food. I resisted the urge to run out and offer her something decent—beef casserole, asparagus risotto, even a bit of cheese on wholegrain toast would get a few vitamins into her, instead of all those transfats and God knows what else. Hannah was just as bad, probably worse, considering she was training to be some top chef. She'd actually been sitting on their front wall eating candyfloss the other day. I couldn't believe it even existed anymore.

Kate was edging backwards. "I'd better go and put dinner on, you know what these teens are like, constantly eating. Must be wonderful to leave something in the fridge and find it sitting there when you get back."

I tried not to take her words as a slight on my childlessness, though I wanted to bellow that my fridge would be overflowing with strawberries, blueberries and avocado and I would never make my daughter feel bad about how much she ate.

I nodded at the letter. "I'll leave that with you to send on?"

Kate's face had closed down. "Yes, I'll sort it out."

She didn't quite shut the door in my face.

Photo: Picture of a bed with a perfectly ironed white duvet cover and a stack of intellectual books on the bedside table.

Caption: After a brilliant Christmas, it's lovely to be home again.

#NoPlaceLikeHome #HomeIsWhereTheHeartIs

CHAPTER 24

Gisela

Thursday 18 January

By the middle of January, we still hadn't had any communication from Ollie. I couldn't mention it to Jack without him waggling his head and saying, "What do you expect? You made it quite clear you don't like his life choices. I expect he'll come round in time."

I wondered when we'd stopped being a team. We'd always sat down and discussed disastrous grades in maths, Hannah's tricky friendship groups, Ollie's lack of confidence at speaking in class. All the little details of our children's lives that mattered to the two of us and no one else.

In fact, every time I mentioned Ollie, Jack looked distracted, as though he was having to make an effort to remember he had a son. Whereas every night I went to bed wondering whether he was curled up with Natalie, stroking her stomach, envisaging a life that we wouldn't be part of. Could that really happen? Could I have poured twenty-one years of love into my son, my mind constantly gathering data about his well-being—vegetables, winter coats, dental appointments—for that to be severed forever? I couldn't contemplate it. I'd expected Ollie to do more or less what we did, just better and later, with more opportunities. I'd had a hazy image of him taking us out to dinner in ten years' time to tell us that he was marrying a kind, intelligent woman who made him laugh, slim, with long brown hair and a shy smile. Maybe a job in PR or an art gallery. But not someone like Natalie. Never Natalie.

It was a relief when Jack went back to work a week after New Year and Hannah huffed off to college looking as though she was in for a day down the mines so I could let my face fall into deep gloom without being told to "Cheer up!" It also allowed me to order lots of lovely bargains in the January sales, unseen by Jack.

I'd forgotten about today's delivery when the doorbell rang. A young man was unloading four large cardboard boxes. I was getting quite sneaky at shuffling stuff into the garage until the coast was clear. If Sally was away, she didn't mind me using her recycling bins for the packaging: "Makes the place look lived in."

Chris was hardly ever there. I occasionally saw him pop into the house, but it never seemed to be when Sally was around. Funny way to lead a married life, though Sally told me they FaceTimed every evening. Probably spoke to each other more than Jack and me, given that every time I asked him something he looked as though he'd been on the verge of solving a tricky crossword clue before I disturbed him. There'd been a few times when I'd nearly blurted out, "Is there something you're not telling me?" But I kept shying away. Me. The person who was never afraid to confront things. After the debacle with Ollie, I didn't trust my own judgement. I had no idea what I would do with a yes answer to "Are you having an affair?"

I hauled my boxes inside. The Union Jack beanbags Hannah and I had decided she couldn't live without for her bedroom. The only time she really communicated with me was when we were buying stuff online. I always fell for it. She'd sidle up. "Will you just look at this coat/cushion/pair of trousers with me? What do you think? I don't mean you to buy it for me."

I was so desperate for the one child who was still speaking

to connect with me, that I'd wink and say, "I don't suppose Dad will notice if I stick it on the credit card."

Her face would light up, the clouds and the unfairness and the general shittiness of her life, wasting her time learning "how to stuff a bloody crab claw," would dissipate. It lasted for about half an hour, until I asked her to help unload the dishwasher, pick up her shoes or eat something that wasn't pasta with pesto. Then the shutters would bang down again and I'd feel duped and taken for granted, the person no one liked unless I was trading things for affection.

I was flattening the packaging when I heard a car pull up. I peered out through the diamond in the porch door. Jack. Shit. I ran to shove the boxes into the utility room. God knows why he was home at midday, but if he was having a bad day I didn't want mine to get worse with a lecture about getting a job at John Lewis: "You'd be a millionaire just from the profit share generated by this household."

I watched him get out of his car and walk up the drive. He had the same lacerated look he'd had when he took the phone call telling him his dad had died. This wasn't about a phone left in a cab or forgetting to collect his card from the cashpoint.

What now? What else could be heaped on my plate? Maybe Jack really was going to tell me he was seeing someone else and that had somehow become public knowledge. A little knot of dread unfurled in my stomach. I couldn't imagine Jack making eyes at another woman in a candlelit restaurant, discussing the merits of sea bass over the mussels. I probably had that mistake in common with a large percentage of women opening their decree absolute at this very moment.

But who? Maybe that marketing manager of his, though I would have thought she was a bit humourless for Jack. I never liked her, way too much "Jack's the most professional person I've ever worked with, so meticulous. Such a clever man." It took me all my restraint not to blurt out that last summer I'd found a ham sandwich with maggots in it practically on the run across his desk. Meticulous with figures maybe, a bit half-hearted on the clearing-up front. Though if all you were seeing were hotel rooms and restaurants, then the domestic detail wouldn't impact on Jack's easy charm.

I steeled myself to open the door, hoping that my life wasn't going to change any more than it already had. The sight of him shuffling up the drive, looking as though he barely had the strength to carry his briefcase, frightened me. And as always when I was frightened, I defaulted to shouting, which at forty-four I should have learnt was the option least likely to get me the answers I wanted.

"Why are you home? What's happened?"

Jack stared at me, his eyes heavy as though he'd run out of energy to hold up the lids. He held his hand up and walked past me into the kitchen. "I've had enough people having a go at me today."

I followed him in and put the kettle on, then turned round to look at him slumped over the table, his forehead resting on his palm. I tried to sound gentle and calm when the words "Pull yourself together and tell me what's wrong" were hovering on my lips. I took a deep breath. "Just tell me what's happened, love." My voice went small. "Are you going to leave me for someone else?"

"For Christ's sake! When would I have time for another bloody woman?"

Not the most gracious reply, but I still felt tears of relief spring to my eyes. I cleared my throat. "Have you been sacked?" I said the word "sacked" as though the idea was completely bonkers and anything else he told me would be much lighter on the catastrophe scale. But he didn't screw his face up with shock that I could even—momentarily—have entertained the idea.

Jack breathed in noisily, a big intake of air as though he was trying to reinflate his thinking. "I've been suspended."

Again, a rush of anger chasing out fear. "What for?"

I'd always hoped to be the port in a storm, a hand gently patting his arm and saying, "We can get through this together." Instead, I wanted to shake the answers out of him. None of that "in your own time" bollocks. If our lives were going to implode, I wasn't a fan of the long, slow burn.

I imagined humiliating half-naked scenarios in the board-room loos, crashing the computer server through excess porn download, lecherous behaviour on the wrong end of too many glasses of corporate champagne.

"Well?"

The effort it took for him to look at me made my stomach flip with fright.

"I've been stealing money."

My heart shot up and back down again. Jack was the one who would always tell a restaurant if they'd left a bottle of wine off the bill. The one who got outraged about big bosses taking huge payouts for jobs they'd failed at.

I almost laughed. It was so unlikely. I didn't know which question to ask first. Why? How? What for? How long?

I made some tea and pushed the mug towards Jack, wondering whether I'd have felt more or less shocked if he'd told me he'd had a threesome on the photocopier with way too many genitals squashed against the glass and presented as evidence.

He sipped his tea, looking wretched.

I found the right question to ask. "Are the police involved?"

"Not yet."

"Will they be?"

"Depends on Mike."

"Only on Mike? Would he really shop you to the police after all these years?" Mike and Jack had worked together for fifteen years, building the company from a few run-down parks on the south coast to more than twenty mid-range facilities across the UK.

Jack didn't answer immediately. It was like trying to get to the bottom of one of Hannah's airbrushed accounts of exactly who did and didn't take drugs at the party that got busted, who supplied them and why she was there in the first place.

"Mike's the one who realised that the accounts didn't tally. As MD he's going to have to speak to the shareholders, otherwise it puts him in a compromising position. More of a compromising position than he's already in. He did say he'd try and keep the police out of it, but who knows?"

"Will they find anything?"

Jack nodded. "I've taken about fifty thousand pounds."

"Fifty thousand pounds? Whatever for?"

He put his head in his hands and sobbed.

I ran to him. "Don't cry. There'll be a way through this. I promise. We'll pay it back."

He shook his head. "We can't pay it back. There's no money, Gisela. The credit cards are maxed out, the mortgage is the most I could borrow, I've sold the few shares I had. I can't keep up the repayments on anything."

"Why didn't you tell me?"

"You'd given up your chance of going back into education because you got pregnant. I felt as though I owed you the big house, the holidays, the restaurants. I was already struggling while we were at our old house and borrowing a few thousand to keep us going. I thought I'd be able to pay it back when I got last year's bonus, but then it was one of the wettest summers on record and the arse dropped out of the caravan holiday market."

I thought back to last year, how irritated I'd got with Jack and his endless weather bulletins. I'd assumed he was just being middle-aged, obsessing over whether he'd need to water his flipping lupins. I didn't realise a downpour was the deciding factor between him jamming his fingers in the till or not.

"Why did you agree to move if you knew we couldn't afford it?"

"By the time it clicked that I was in serious trouble, we'd already put down the deposit for this house. I got carried away, thinking you'd be so proud of where we'd got to in life that maybe you wouldn't mind you'd never gone to university, that you'd see that your support, you taking care of the family while I worked, had been worthwhile." I leant towards him to catch his words. "I sort of stuck my head in the sand, telling myself that Hannah would be finishing private school so I wouldn't have the fees and somehow we'd make other savings elsewhere."

As much as I wanted to plant myself on the moral high ground and polish my pointing finger, I had to admit I'd never taken any responsibility for where the cash came from, childishly assuming that there was a vague money tree somewhere that Jack kept watering and pruning. I wished I could rewind back to the moments when I'd gone on about him being tight, when I accused him of trying to control me, when I'd stood with my hands on my hips saying, "I work just as hard as you, except the difference is I don't get paid and no one values anything I do. If I wasn't doing what I do, you couldn't do your big 'I'm so important' job and you'd all be wiping your backsides on newspaper and ferreting about in bargain buckets of KFC." And then I'd ordered a new handbag to spite him. Or some moisturiser guaranteed to "turn back the clock" at £100 a pop, though judging by the tramlines sitting between my eyebrows, I'd wasted my money.

"I'm sorry," I said.

Jack pressed his fingers into his eyes. "I'm the one who's sorry. I should have told you we couldn't afford things."

"You did. I didn't listen."

"I wanted to give you everything. I wanted Ollie and Hannah to look up to me, to think I'd done well, that I was a good role model for working hard. Now I'll probably go to prison. And they'll be ashamed of me forever."

"It won't come to that, surely?" I was having to make a mental switch from the sort of people I thought went to prison, the type you saw on TV, big bruisers with a gold tooth and "cut here" tattooed across their necks. Not people like Jack who used interdental brushes, oiled the lawnmower blades and put suet balls out for the birds. I shuddered at the thought of all those keys and clanging doors. I'd be terrified to stand next to half the women visiting their husbands. And despite Jack insisting on having a gym in the garage, the last time I'd looked, his dumb-bells were weighing down the tarpaulin over the barbecue. "How will that even happen? Will they arrest you? Will they come here?" I had a vision of a car turning up with blue lights flashing, everyone in the street peering out of their windows.

"I don't know. I don't think white-collar crime is a top priority for the police, so I don't think they'll do a dawn raid."

Frankly, if it hadn't been on *Vera*, we didn't have a clue.

Jack sighed. "I suppose the police will probably call me in for an interview or something. If it goes that far."

"Was Mike furious? Do you think he'd take it to the police to punish you?"

Jack started crying again. "Not furious. Devastated. He kept saying, 'I don't understand why you didn't talk to me. We might have been able to arrange a loan.' I let him down, Zell. I let all of you down."

I was shaking my head. "Until we find out what's going to happen, no one is to know anything about this. We'll say you're on gardening leave and looking for a change in career direction before you're too old to do something else." In a much smaller voice, I said, "I do love you, you know."

"I love you too."

Photo: Union Jack beanbags.

Caption: Look at these beauties that have just arrived! Just need a cup of tea and the latest copy of Homes & Gardens and all is well with the world.

#Snuggleup #LoveACuppa #LoveMyHome

CHAPTER 25

Kate

Saturday 2 February

Since Daisy's letter from Oskar had arrived a month ago, she had perfected the art of speaking without communicating, replying to my questions without answering them. Today's conversation was another variation on how I'd tried to engage with her over the last four weeks. "So what does this weekend hold for you, darling?"

"Just schoolwork really."

"Are you going out with Hannah at all?"

"We haven't made any plans yet."

Although her tone was light and pleasant, I could feel an invisible arm pushing me away, batting me back into my corner.

On days when I was at work, I'd hare around in the morning, making her tea and toast to get rid of my guilt at rushing off before she left for college. She'd thank me, but I'd find it on the side untouched. Rejection by a thousand toast crumbs.

Daisy, like me, had become an expert at telling people what she wanted them to know and not a word more. My heart ached for her pre-school self, those bright eyes flicking around her world, seeing friends to be made among the random strangers at the supermarket, in the library, at the park, walking up to everyone and saying in her lispy little voice, "You're my friend." Over the next few years, the world knocked that naivety out of her. "Sam said his mother told him to stay away from me." "Lily said she's not allowed to come to my house for playdates." "I shouldn't tell anyone you used to have a best friend called Becky, should I?"

I'd hug her, so sad that my little girl—who couldn't yet get the "i" and "e" the right way round in the word "friend"—already knew that some friendships weren't allowed and that some even grew so toxic it was better for people not to know about them.

Now she'd chosen Hannah as a friend, a person who as far as I could see liked talking about herself so much that Daisy wouldn't have to work very hard to sidestep any awkward questions.

When Daisy retreated, I waited it out, knowing that her stubbornness was more than a match for my detective skills. But this morning, following another "No, haven't had any feedback from course work lately," I snapped.

"I know more about bloody Hannah over the road than what's going on in your life. Have I done something wrong? Are you in trouble? Are you behind with your studies?"

The colour rushed into her cheeks. I braced myself, forcing my irritation down into something kinder and caring. Her eyes filled.

I stretched out my arms to her. She came to me but stood like a totem pole while I tried to cuddle her. "Can I help with anything that's going on? Did your dad say something to upset you?"

And by the look on her face, I'd scored the perfect bullseye, but she just said, "I miss him, Mum. It's two years since I've seen him."

"Perhaps he'll come and visit soon. I know he misses you too."

"Don't think that's very likely, is it?"

I glanced at the clock, not wanting to make her late for

college. "Maybe we could go halves on a ticket to Buenos Aires?" I asked, needing to make it right despite knowing that every penny I earned for the next six months was already accounted for.

Her reply, when it came, was definite. "I'm not going to Argentina."

She shrugged out of my hold.

"I can't even really remember him now. I hardly know anything about him except what he tells me on Facebook. It's not like we actually have a relationship."

And from her manner, I was a long way from making up for the shortfall. I never wanted her to feel like this. When she was growing up, I tried to explain how he used to point out the flowers in the garden, help her touch different textures when she was little, sit with her at the sandpit, creating palaces and castles. She deserved a sense of family history, however fleeting. But my feelings for Oskar were so tied up with everything else, that even saying, "Your dad used to..." filled my chest with a sensation so toxic it lingered all day, dragging me down, away from the calm I'd fought so hard to achieve.

"You can ask me anything about him, really you can. I don't mind."

She narrowed her eyes. "Yeah, right, Mum." She pushed past me. "Doesn't matter."

But it did. It really did. I didn't know how Oskar could close his eyes at night and not feel his heart break over the distance between them; I missed Daisy when she stayed over at Gisela's house for two nights in a row. I glanced out of the window, wondering whether to write to Oskar myself, to beg him to visit. I couldn't have him here, though, jabbering away in Polish to Daisy, with all the neighbours wondering who he was.

As the front door banged, she shouted, "And when I leave home I'm going to change my name back to Karolina Kowalski!"

Bloody Oskar. It was all right for him in Argentina, not

having to shoulder any of the burden of making sure Daisy didn't become the talking point—"Isn't she the daughter of that woman who was in the news?"

He'd gone mad when I told him I was changing our names. "But Kowalski is our family heritage, her heritage." Followed by a history lesson in how when our families came here from Poland they expected future generations to learn English, to speak without an accent, to grasp every opportunity—but "not to deny who we are and where we came from."

Oskar wouldn't accept it. "For me, she is Karolina Kowalski. You can be Kate Jones if you want, but you are not giving my daughter a new name. She has nothing to be ashamed of." I tried to believe I didn't either, but plenty of people didn't share my view.

It didn't matter how much I argued and pleaded, he wouldn't budge. I couldn't understand his reasoning. The five years of abuse we'd had in Manchester—letters, phone calls, scuffles in the street—had broken him. The systematic snapping of every raspberry cane he'd planted in our back garden was the last straw. Still I refused to go to the police. That tiny thing, coupled with the gradual realisation that the clients for the carpentry business he'd built up didn't want to be associated with him anymore, had driven him out. And once he'd left, I had no reason not to move myself, which is what I'd suggested all along. Daisy and I had a glorious break from Becky for a couple of months when we moved to Leeds and then nearly a year before she found me in Peterborough. Then the letters began again, dropping onto the mat with sickening regularity, the phone calls that went dead as soon as I answered. When Mum died, leaving me enough money to start again, I decided I'd have one final attempt at disappearing and took the first decent paramedic job that came up.

If Oskar didn't like me changing Daisy's name, too bad. He didn't have to live with the fear that Becky might carry out her threats, that they weren't just the ramblings of a tortured mind. He didn't have the reflex of scanning the post, with a little jolt of relief when that large, rounded lettering wasn't there. No, he'd taken himself off to Argentina nearly twelve years ago, where he could huff and puff from afar about ideals and standing up for ourselves, and holding our heads high, without having to face the stomach-churning reality of what that meant. So Izabela Kowalski and Karolina Kowalski became Kate and Daisy Jones.

Which had worked very well until Oskar had decided to stick his oar in at the very moment the postman had decided getting home for his lunch was more important than shoving letters through the right door.

Since the letter had arrived, I'd restricted my interaction with Sally to a wave as I dashed into the car in the mornings, hurrying up the driveway looking at my watch as though I had something urgent to do in the evenings. My fledgling social group seemed to have died a death before it began—even Gisela had gone a bit quiet over the last fortnight.

So when Sally rang the bell about fifteen minutes after Daisy had left, I wasn't expecting a neighbour.

"Long time no see, Kate. How are you?"

"Fine. How are you? How's Chris? Haven't seen him for ages." I was doing the thing Daisy hated. Standing blocking the doorway with both hands against the doorjamb.

Sally shrugged. "Neither have I! He's working so hard, he's always away, the States mainly." She looked down, then said, "Could I come in for a minute?"

I frowned but stood back and let her in. "Is everything all right?"

I felt obliged to put the kettle on, but I wanted to get my big broom and sweep her out of my house before she started poking into my business.

She put her hand on my arm. "I've really wondered about whether to tell you this, but I thought you should know."

"What? Is it Daisy?" A familiar surge of adrenaline took me from low-level watchful to red alert in seconds.

Sally nodded.

My mind jumped to its default position. Becky. Becky had been here. In an instant, I could see everything I'd worked towards falling apart again. "Has she been threatened? Has someone been here?" The thought came out before I could catch it.

Sally looked puzzled. "Threatened? By whom?"

"Oh nothing, just a bit of trouble she had a while ago." I waved it away as though it was a silly idea.

Sally carried on. "It's just that a couple of weeks ago, I was driving back from work and I saw Daisy walking home, so I stopped to see if she wanted a lift and she was crying, really sobbing."

I hadn't seen Daisy cry in years.

"Did she tell you what was wrong?" I could hear my voice rising.

"She made me promise not to tell you, so please don't let on I've been round."

My daughter trusted this woman more than her own mother. "She's not pregnant, is she?" I knew I should have been stricter, not let her copy Hannah with her barely-there clothes.

"No, nothing like that. She'd heard from her dad. I gather you're not in touch with him anymore. I think he wrote a letter to her a few weeks ago?" She paused, peering at me as though she was waiting for a reaction. I'd had years of keeping my face neutral. "As far as I understood it, he'd got married again and let her know he'd had a son."

I attempted to fall back on my tried and tested technique of looking blank and disinterested however close people got to uncovering a fragment of my story. But the shock made me blurt out: "What? Are you talking about Oskar? My ex-husband? He hasn't got married again and had a baby, has he?" My voice was squeezing through my throat, out of the tiny gap not strangled by hurt.

And there it was, that recognition, that sick rush of

understanding that all of Daisy's little barbs about "making the right choice, not the easiest choice," "not waiting for the storm to pass but learning to dance in the rain," stuff that I'd thought was the result of parroting all the self-help quotes she'd seen on the internet, were founded in this horrible truth. Oskar. The man I'd dreamed of having four children with. The man who'd always wanted a son. Who now, apparently, had what he'd wished for. With another woman.

If only it had been Gisela who'd bumped into Daisy. I couldn't put my finger on it, but Sally gave me the impression that her concern went hand-in-hand with disapproval.

"Daisy seemed pretty sure about it. Kept saying that he'd love Mateusz more than her." She studied me as she made an effort with the Polish pronunciation. I didn't comment, though the knowledge he'd used the name we'd talked about if we had a boy made my chest go tight with resentment. She carried on, "I hope you don't mind me telling you. I felt so sorry for her. She seemed so lonely. I know it's not easy, with you being a single parent and having to work long hours. I think she just needed someone who had time to listen to her."

It took all my willpower not to grab her ears and rattle her head. My voice was calm—that shaky, menacing calm that precedes a total loss of control. "I do listen to her. I do ask her if she's okay. And, do you know what, nine times out of ten she shrugs and walks out. What am I supposed to do? Tie her to the chair until she tells me what's going on?"

Sally was waving her hand in apology. "I didn't mean it like that. I was trying to help."

I was beyond listening. "Well, it sounds like you think you could do better. I don't choose to work for some kind of self-fulfilment—I *have* to work so I can pay the mortgage without a husband to rely on. And sometimes that leaves me with less time than I'd like with Daisy. Parenting isn't as easy as it looks, you know. It's all right for you, with your child-free holidays and Michelin-starred restaurants. When you've walked a mile in my shoes, raised a child on your own, carried the whole responsibility of keeping another human being alive and happy, feel free to comment on how I bring up my daughter."

Very quietly, she said, "You have no idea about my life and how lucky you are," then turned on her heels and walked out of my house.

CHAPTER 26

Sally

Monday 11 February

For the last week, I'd been double-checking that I wasn't about to bump into Kate when I got out of the car. I missed her more than I thought I would and wondered whether to go and clear the air. If I looked deep into my heart, maybe there was a bit of me that thought I could do a better job than she was. But her words were so cruel, so oblivious to how much I would love to have a daughter like Daisy.

I was so busy replaying the argument in my mind, I didn't notice that the lights were on at home when I got back from work.

Chris was waiting in the kitchen. I'd got so used to walking into an empty house, I had to stifle a scream. "Jesus Christ. You scared me to death." Which weren't exactly the words of love and longing I'd rehearsed.

I stood with my handbag looped over my arm, wanting to go and freshen up after a long day of meetings and sales figures, but, equally, every bit of me wanted to fold myself into him, to feel that shape of the man I married fit into all my angles.

"Are you here to see me or to pick something up?"

He put his head on one side, looking unsure of himself. "I've come to see you."

I searched his tone, looking for clues about whether he was here to impart bad news, but he sounded wistful. I knew I couldn't hurry him, so I blustered on.

"How did you know I wasn't away?"

"I phoned Marion, who was more than happy to map out your every move over the next two months for me."

Bet she was. Least discreet secretary to ever walk this earth. I couldn't stop smiling even though I should have been raging that he'd just turned up out of the blue after two and a half months of erratic text messages and the occasional phone call, which more often than not left me confused for days. I felt a surge of delight.

I concentrated on keeping things light, not scaring him off. "Your hair's grown. What's with the struggling artist look?" I loved the idea that he might become less rigid. A man who could saunter around a medieval Mediterranean town and take a punt on a restaurant we liked the look of, rather than pore over the various recommendations on TripAdvisor and book seven weeks ahead. A man who might, one day, tolerate the chaos of children.

"I've been so busy, I haven't had time to get it cut," he said, sounding offended, as though only idle layabouts had the headspace to concern themselves with hair length.

"It really suits you."

Silence.

I defaulted to my mother's solution to everything. "Tea?"

"Shall I make it?" he asked.

The way he tugged the fridge gently to release the suction before pulling it open, the deadheading of the orchids on the windowsill while he waited for the kettle to boil, the precise levelling of the loose tea was so familiar, like settling down to watch a film you'd seen twenty times before. Maybe he was going to come back.

It just came out. "I've missed you," I said.

He turned round. "Really?"

"Yes, really."

It was like being in one of those locked rooms where only the solving of a complex puzzle would reunite you with the outside world.

For a second, he looked vulnerable, then something clouded his face and he went back to the tea.

I slipped my phone out of my handbag and took a photo of his back, his head bent to one side as he stirred the tea. The sight of him doing something so ordinary made me want to cry. Cry for who we used to be. The man whose ambition encompassed both of us—"You'd be great. You could do that, no problem." The woman who saw a cultured, clever man and realised she could learn from him. There had once been a softness between us, a kindness, the sense that we had each other's backs. Over the space of a decade, we'd chiselled it into something steelier, less yielding, where we parked ourselves in opposing corners, each concerned with defending our territory, our right to be independent, to forge ahead at work without being held back by demands at home.

"Can I have a hug?" My voice came out uncertain, unsure of where I stood on the tactile front, after all these years.

He looked surprised, as though I'd given up something he hadn't expected. He hesitated, then put his arms out to me. He held me loosely.

I tipped my head back to look at him. "You didn't explain what you were doing here."

His eyes locked onto mine, softening as though he was reminding himself that we'd laughed and loved as well as fought.

He didn't answer. Just bent his head and kissed me, his eyes slowly closing, his lips gentle, almost as though he was retrieving a memory. Not a memory of a passionate night when we'd explored each other's bodies into the early hours but of when the thing—maybe the only thing—we were sure about was that we wouldn't hurt each other. At some point in the past, there had been that moment and now we were no longer in it, but still not so far from shore that we couldn't remember it.

I didn't know how long we kissed for. Not hasty nor demanding but connected, as though we were about love, not who was winning in the career stakes, who did or didn't want a baby, just that sweet melting into each other. He was no longer holding me lightly like a fragile edifice of glass but tightly, as though he was transferring the love from his heart to mine.

Eventually he raised his head, breathing out with a big sigh. "I just wanted to see you, to try and sort my head out."

"And what about the other 'distraction'?" I failed to keep the sarcasm out of my tone.

He shook his head imperceptibly.

"Did it ever come to anything?"

Again a slight headshake.

I was in danger of ruining the moment, but I had to know. "Did you want it to? Come to something, I mean?"

His answer, when it came, was raw, as though something festering inside him had split open. "No, no, Sally. I didn't want it to come to anything because I wanted my marriage—*our* marriage—to work, for us to be happy. Again."

I looked at the floor as his arms dropped to his side, just his fingertips touching mine. I felt as though I was on a see-saw, suspended in a precarious equilibrium where my next words would send me flying high or plunging back down to earth with such a bump, I'd rebound twice. "Have you missed me?"

He nodded. "I've missed us."

"The us before we were having discussions about a family?" I paused. "Or the us that hasn't resolved the issue but is prepared to work towards it?"

I made myself look him in the eye.

"The former, mostly."

He wasn't hostile. He was sad.

I wished I could fix him.

"Are you staying the night? Or going back to the flat?"

"What do you want me to do?" He stroked my elbow so tenderly, I wanted to fall into him and promise I'd never mention children again, that I'd just be grateful to have him back, that he'd be enough for me. But I knew from my row with Kate a week or so ago, the sheer agony of regret and longing her words seared into my heart, that within a month, maybe even a week, I'd be back on my endless loop, trying to persuade him.

I still said, "Stay."

Photo: Chris making tea.
   Caption: Lucky me! Chris back from a work trip unexpectedly.
   #LittleThingsMeanSoMuch #BestSurpriseEver #MissMyHusband

CHAPTER 27

Gisela

Sunday 11 March

In the lead-up to Mothers' Day, I'd always said jokingly that low expectations were the key to greater happiness, but this year I really meant it. I didn't know whether to hope for the sound of something flapping through the letter box or not, since within weeks of Jack being suspended, all forms of communication felt toxic. I dreaded the phone ringing and hearing the HR manager ask for Jack. Every time the post arrived, every envelope made my heart leap as I imagined letters from the police, from the court, from lawyers nestling there ready to invade our lives with a summons, plunging us into a bewildering world we'd hoped never to inhabit.

Increasingly, how we'd arrived at such a position consumed me. I thought back over the last few months, the last few years, to see where it all went wrong, but more often than not, I'd drift back to our twenty-year-old selves lying on the grass, cloud-watching in the park on one of Jack's frequent trips home from university to visit me. Whenever we talked about the future, our answers were always the same.

Me: "Two kids. A great big banger of a house. A sports car. Dogs."

Jack: "I just need you. And a university degree so you can have what you want."

I'd swipe at him and say, "Where's your imagination?"

But in the end, he'd been the one to persuade me to retake my A levels while he was in his final year. "You can definitely do it. You're bright enough. If you become a lawyer and I set up my own business, we'll make a brilliant team."

We'd stayed up all night drinking before watching the sun come up on a hill overlooking the South Downs when I'd got the grades I needed to study Law at Southampton. We'd agreed he'd go travelling for six months, then try to find a job near me on the South Coast.

The week before I was due to leave for uni, I discovered I was pregnant.

So instead of my going to university and Jack backpacking off to Thailand, we were married within six weeks. Jack took the first job that came his way. My dad—"thought the whole point of you doing your A levels again was to get a degree so you'd actually do something other than stay at home with kids"—stumped up for a deposit on a flat.

We'd been so determined to show them we could make a success of our lives. Until a couple of months ago, I thought we'd pulled it off. It was a tiny consolation that my parents were no longer alive to witness Jack's disgrace.

He alternated between humble—"I'm so ashamed, I don't know what got into me"—and furious—"I kept telling you we couldn't afford it, but you had to have the best."

Sometimes I'd hold his hand and say, "Whatever happens, we'll manage." I could be that wife supporting her stupid but essentially decent husband. I could look the world in the eye and dare them to comment.

Then sometimes, when he tried to blame me, I'd blow up. "Why the fuck didn't you just tell me the truth? How was I supposed to know you were borrowing money left, right and centre when you never said a word?"

I'd imagine leaving him to rot in jail while I disappeared off to a little cottage by the sea with Titch, inventing a mysterious past for myself, far more glamorous than the sordid truth of my husband going to prison for bankrolling our lifestyle by thieving from his business partner.

The day before, I'd said, "I think we should tell the children," as Hannah slammed out to go and see Daisy, shouting at me for changing the password on my John Lewis account and calling a halt to the endless packages of make-up that plopped through the door.

Jack had jumped to his feet. "No. No. Not yet. Ollie's got enough to worry about with his finals and a baby on the way. And Hannah, well, she's in a funny place already. I don't think she's found her calling in cookery."

I'd tried not to bristle, tried not to take it as a slight that I'd found a solution that hadn't been a glittering success. While everyone else had sat around, gob open, putting forward precisely no solutions.

"If anything becomes more official than just a suspension, then we should tell them."

The humiliation of letting the kids down had dragged across Jack's face, making him look so despairing that I'd changed the subject without, however, managing to steer us onto a cheerier topic. "Have you heard from Ollie?" I asked, swallowing back the sadness that he'd chosen Jack to send his terse little texts to, ignoring my little notes to his home, my messages telling him to keep communicating, to stay in touch, that I knew he was angry but I'd always be there for him.

Jack shook his head. "No, just what I told you the other week. That he was okay."

"What do you mean 'okay'?"

Jack sighed and found the text for me on his phone. My heart wrenched at the familiar sight of Ollie's number.

Jack: *"How's it going?"*

Ollie: *"We're okay."*

Jack: *"Do you need anything?"*

Ollie: *"Just a bit of respect."*

"That's Natalie talking," I said, shoving his mobile back at him and stomping out, with Jack doing a "Don't ask if you don't want to know the answer" face.

So, when Mothering Sunday dawned, while Jack was in the shower, I clung to the slim hope that he'd squirrelled away a card from Ollie ready to wave out of the ether like a great big olive branch. Hannah had stayed at Daisy's the night before and had probably forgotten altogether. I lay in bed, scrolling through the Facebook feed on my phone. And immediately hated my life just slightly more.

First up was the picture from bloody Sarah, the woman who hadn't spoken to me since I'd done the post–A level rant about university not being for everyone.

Of course, she had a handmade card. From her eighteen-year-old! Not some unrecognisable flower of pink tissue paper squashed onto white card, but a flipping hand-drawn work of art. And inside a poem about how her daughter would be "so happy if I could just be a tenth of the woman you are." I thought I might put the pillow over my face and keep it there. Hannah always looked absolutely horrified if anyone ever said, "You're so like your mum."

I should have had the sense to put my phone down right away and stop looking at the pictures of heart-shaped toast presented on a tray with little posies of roses. The collages of photos in silver frames. The jokey posts about the army of children it took to cook a Sunday lunch and how much washing-up there would be afterwards. And, of course, the husbands who'd thought ahead and booked a lovely restaurant "as a big thank you to my wonderful wife. Our children are lucky to have such a fantastic mother."

Even in the good years, I'd be lucky to get a card that Jack hadn't bought for them. And even luckier if he wasn't shouting at them to write the damn thing at eleven o'clock, while I resentfully clattered cutlery into the drawer in the kitchen, saying, "It doesn't matter. Commercialised nonsense," through gritted teeth.

Jack came back through, his towel round his hips. With the antenna of a man who's been married a long time, he sensed my anticipation without being able to identify the source. He was looking around the room for clues.

I decided to put him—and me—out of our misery. "No letters arrived for me yesterday while I was out, did they?"

Jack was very quick to get to the post these days, a sort of ritual superstition to make sure that he was first on the site of bad news. He frowned. "Didn't I leave it on the kitchen table for you? Or maybe by the bread bin?"

"I didn't see anything." I hopped out of bed and went downstairs as quickly as I could, trying not to alert Jack to my desperation.

Amazingly, he had tucked a couple of letters between the bread bin and the knife block. I scrabbled them up, my spirits soaring, then plunging. Nothing that looked like a card. A circular from Majestic. One official-looking envelope. My heart skipped a little as I wondered whether the powers that be would try to implicate me in Jack's theft. I'd always thought the wives must know what was going on. I ripped it open. It was a letter from Hannah's catering college.

> *We regret to inform you that owing to an absence for the entire spring term without providing any supporting documentation for mitigating circumstances, we will be rescinding Hannah Anderson's place at the Darling Cookery College with immediate effect.*

Happy bloody Mother's Day.

I stampeded upstairs and thrust it under Jack's nose as he had one leg in his boxers and one out, leading to a comedy hop around the room as he tried to balance and read.

"For God's sake! Thousands of pounds a term and she hasn't even bothered to go."

It did slightly make a mockery of all the photos I'd posted

of her in our kitchen every time she so much as picked up a wooden spoon.

I snatched the letter out of Jack's hand, threw some clothes on and, without even bothering to clean my teeth, I stormed over the road and hammered on Kate's door. She looked surprised to see me as I never arrived unannounced.

"Are you okay?"

"Oh, you know, the usual family dramas to get Mother's Day off to a good start."

Kate rolled her eyes. "Unlike me who's mother of the year. I actually had someone knock on my door to tell me what a shit job I was doing with Daisy."

"No! Who?"

"Someone who didn't have children."

"Well, I'd be a bloody brilliant mother if I didn't have children. God, the nerve. Did you get to the bottom of why she thought you were doing a shit job?"

"It's all very boring. My ex moving on and Daisy feeling left out. I'll tell you one day when you've got nothing else to do."

I was convinced that Kate's story was exceptionally interesting, but it didn't look like I was going to hear it today. I'd have given anything to think about someone else's misery rather than my own.

"Anyway, I'm after Hannah. Is she here?"

Kate put her hand on my arm. "Yes, she's in Daisy's bedroom."

I tried to make my voice calm, but instead I started shouting up the stairs, angry and aggressive. "Hannah! Hannah!"

She appeared on the landing with that dull-eyed insolence I'd been seeing more and more. "What?"

I waved the letter at her, swallowing down the huge roar of fury in deference to not being in my own home, where I would have been making the rafters rattle. "I just wanted to talk to you about a letter from the cookery college. Could you get your things and come home?" I felt hot air whistle out of my nostrils. "Please?"

Hannah's shoulders slumped, then rallied, her head snapping up and her chin lifting in defiance. She glanced at Kate, and I hoped that the old not washing your dirty laundry in public would save us all, but no. She looked at me with what felt like hate. "I guess they're saying my attendance hasn't been too good? So fucking what? I couldn't give a shit about puff pastry, shortcrust pastry or hollandaise bloody sauce. I never wanted to learn to cook, but would you listen to what I wanted? No. You were so busy being ashamed that your daughter fucked up her A levels, you just wanted something to tell your friends that would make me seem less of a big fat failure."

The stab of injustice drilled into my heart. All I recalled from last summer was Hannah sitting there with her chin resting on her palm, saying, "How should I know what I want to do? I'm only eighteen. You didn't go to university and now you're making such a drama out of the fact that I'm not."

I hovered between polishing both barrels and pointing them in her direction and the embarrassment that we were in Kate's house having a right old ding-dong when I'd never heard Daisy say a single swear word.

"I'm sorry you feel like that." I wasn't actually sorry, I thought she was an entitled, arrogant little toad in that moment, but I didn't want Kate to think I was a worse mother than I was. "Anyway, get your stuff and we'll go home and talk to Dad."

Daisy was standing behind Hannah with her eyes on stalks. She'd only ever seen me as the fun mum, who'd knock on Hannah's bedroom door with a little dish of chocolates—"keep your spirits up." And deep down I'd loved presenting myself as that mum, sorry for Daisy that she spent so much time fending for herself. I'd encouraged her to spend loads of time at ours—"You're welcome any time!"—Daisy's enjoyment of the banter and boisterousness of our family giving my pathetic soul a boost.

I turned to Kate. "Sorry for bursting in like this. We'll leave you in peace."

Kate smiled. "Don't worry at all. Pop over for a glass of wine one evening if you need a breather."

Wow. I must have looked in a state if Kate was inviting me over to hers. Sally had commented on it the other day. "Have you ever been over to Kate's?"

The way she'd said it made me want to protect Kate. "No, but of course she works full-time. And when she's not at work, I think she likes to spend time with Daisy."

Sally hadn't let it go. "That poor girl spends way too much time on her own as it is. Anyway, I just think it's rude to keep accepting invitations and never reciprocating."

Frankly, the thing I couldn't stand was people keeping a hospitality tally of every cup of coffee, every Bourbon biscuit, every tomato-stuffed olive, racked up on the abacus of "who owes what and I'm not inviting them back until…"

I'd pulled a face. "I don't really keep count. I invite people when I want to see them. Anyway, Kate's quite private. I don't think we should take it personally. She's not a big party person, I don't think."

But Sally had been in one of those funny moods, huffing away about how she wasn't a party person either but still managed to get everyone over for drinks now and again. Privately I thought that was probably to keep her company because Chris was away so much, but I wasn't going to win. Which made me look forward to taking Kate up on her offer so I could post a big picture on Facebook to prove Sally wrong.

In the meantime, I needed to find out what the hell was going on with Hannah. I all but frogmarched her over the road, attempting to look all loose-limbed and "just a little something that needs sorting out" while resisting the temptation to clamp my fingers around her upper arm and yank her through the front door. Clearly my Mother's Day card was still in WHSmith.

I expected Jack to be sitting in wait in the kitchen, ready to do joint battle with me, but he was upstairs. All the fury I'd tried to hold in at Kate's erupted with full volcanic force.

"Jack! Jack! Are you going to come down and help me sort the little matter of your daughter playing truant for ooh, a mere three months, or are you going to sit upstairs feeling sorry for yourself?"

Hannah scowled. "What's the matter with Dad?"

Shit. Yes. We hadn't got that little joy out on the family dining table yet. "He's just got a few things going on at work."

Jack appeared at the top of the stairs. "I'm coming."

We all sat round the kitchen table, the tension between us like barricades. I put on my mature negotiator voice. "So, can you tell us what's happened at the cookery school?"

Hannah raised the eyebrows she'd pencilled in like comedy caterpillars. "Not much to say really. Haven't been." The insolence in her words made me want to go upstairs, pack all her belongings into a bag and hurl it and her out of the front door, shouting, "If you're so bloody brilliant and we're so fucking stupid, why don't you go and live somewhere else and see how you get on?"

Thankfully Jack stepped in. "Hannah, you can cut the smart-arse comments. We're not angry," he said.

I nearly choked trying to hang onto the words—"Not angry at all, just so furious I think my blood might boil out of my ears."

Jack carried on. "But we are really worried and I'd like to know where you've been every day for the last few months if you weren't at college."

Hannah did that hooded eyelid thing. "Nowhere. Around."

I loved Jack for the fact that he could suppress the fear that he might go to prison enough to find a voice filled with kindness for his daughter. "It's okay if you've done something you're ashamed of."

"I'm not ashamed. Everyone's been so bothered about Ollie and what he's up to, there was never a good moment to tell you what I was doing, so I just got on with it. I didn't want the aggro of telling you and Mum," she said, with special emphasis on the tediousness of telling "*Mum.*"

Jack sat back, patient in his chair.

"I've been going to the college Daisy goes to. I'm training to be a plumber."

My God. I had one son who was almost qualified to be an engineer but had chosen to become a house husband. A daughter who could barely change the head on a toothbrush training to be a plumber. And a husband whom I'd thought was a captain of industry but apparently was just a thief.

And me—a bit lippy, a bit of a spendthrift, a bit short-tempered and probably not that bright—but I'd considered myself fairly solid as a wife and mother.

Instead I'd turned out to be the person no one trusted enough to explain what was really going on in their lives.

Happy Mother's Day to me.

Caption: Happy Mother's Day everyone! Can't post a photo as my phone has decided to stop working, but raising a glass to all the hard-working mums out there! Have a great day!

  #Blessed

CHAPTER 28

Kate

Tuesday 3 April—the day after Easter

Easter was the devil's spawn for people like me who had no partner and only two friends I actually saw—Sally and I had apologised to each other in a very British "Sorry about the other day" way rather than getting to the heart of the matter and were back to waving across the road and liking each other's Facebook posts. Even having Daisy was no distraction as she'd decided to cash in on bank holiday overtime on a supermarket till rather than curl up and watch films with me. When she wasn't working, she was off with Hannah. I'd spot them walking down the street together, Daisy lit up with a vibrancy, a liveliness, that I never got to witness when it was just the two of us.

Without her peering over my shoulder to see what I was doing on the computer, there was no barrier to my Facebook addiction, my laptop singing to me with stories of what Alex might be up to if I just clicked onto his page—again. If I saw he was loved up with someone else, someone who wasn't lugging such a barrowload of baggage that the future would be a series of rabbit holes to fall down and snap an ankle, I'd be at peace. An uncomfortable peace, but it would stop me longing for a man who could have done any job but had to be a flaming investigative journalist. On New Year's Eve, with my champagne head on, I'd nearly convinced myself it would be worth the risk. Against my better judgement, the occasional message on Facebook had started to become a bit of regular banter. But the row with Sally had made me wary. She obviously had her suspicions about who I really was. I was living in cloud cuckoo land if I thought I could have a proper relationship. I would never be able to be honest. I'd have to remember everything I said, running behind myself with a blackboard rubber to keep my past smudged and blurry, terrified of the day when he might link Kate Jones to Izabela Kowalski. So a couple of weeks ago, I'd pressed "send" on a message telling him it had been lovely to bump into him again, but I wasn't in the right frame of mind to start a relationship with anyone and I wouldn't be messaging anymore. It was the right thing to do.

It was just that my heart wasn't accepting that decision—not at all.

I still squinted at him, clicking on the photos, my nose inches from the screen, scanning them for a square of handbag poking into shot. Tortured myself over a picture of him grinning against a backdrop of Pembrokeshire coastline. I wondered who he was with. The idea of hiking with him, sitting on a wall, surveying the scenery then ending up in a pub for a well-deserved dinner was so appealing, I became aware of an ache I hadn't felt since Oskar left me. Oskar who, as Daisy had confirmed with dismissive grunts, had firmly, categorically, moved on. While I was still here, dumped like a half-eaten takeaway on a bench.

I scrolled through Sally's timeline. Lucky her, living it up in Chile in between her rendezvous in Europe with Chris. Those two lived the life. They were hardly ever at home. Must be easy to keep a relationship fresh if your weekends were composed of trying out four-poster beds in capital cities rather than irritably shouting down the stairs to "come and give us a hand with this duvet cover." No wonder they hadn't rushed to have children. Even though I didn't give a hoot about sitting in restaurants fawning over the celeriac purée or trying a bit of my partner's "mouth-watering" tempura prawn #swapsies, I couldn't help wishing that, just for once, I could have a weekend away with someone who knew so much about me that I never had to filter an unguarded thought.

Across the street, I saw Gisela and Jack strolling along together, holding hands. Just yesterday I'd seen her stop, turn to him and say something so earnest, before leaning over to hug him. Their body language held mutual respect—the acceptance of compromise, the underlay of caring, the practicality of co-existence. He really was a tolerant man. Oskar would never have put up with all those people in and out of the house. Gisela was always posting pictures about her friends over from Canada, her chief bridesmaid hopping over for a few days from Ireland, Hannah having ten people round for a sleepover. I hadn't noticed anything about Ollie lately. I must remember to ask Gisela how he was getting on. Their baby must be due soon. She'd be a brilliant grandma—if she could get past the fact Natalie was so much older than Ollie. I didn't dare say it to her, but if the worst that happened to her was her son getting together with a woman she didn't particularly like, she was bloody lucky.

It was a sad reflection of my life that I was relieved to step out into torrential rain and go to work when everyone else was wishing the bank holiday could go on forever.

At half-past four, we were en route to see to an eighty-year-old woman who'd fallen off a ladder while changing a light bulb when the call came to divert us. "CAT 1, A22 towards Caterham." The type we dreaded. Life and limb. A pile-up on a busy stretch of dual carriageway. Four cars, three walking, two seriously wounded. We were a couple of minutes from the motorway turn-off and hammered down the hard shoulder. The slip road was backed up right to the M25 and despite our sirens going and the lights flashing it was incredible how slow people were to react and pull over.

Pete was cursing, inching through the traffic, hampered by torrential rain that made it hard to see even with the windscreen wipers on full pelt. We were just behind another ambulance and it looked like the police had only arrived minutes before us as they were still checking the cars and securing the scene. The police directed the first ambulance over to a sports car that had its front end caved in under the rear corner of a truck and the back shunted by a Range Rover. I could see a man sitting dazed at the steering wheel with blood on his face. A police officer pointed us to the grass verge, where a group of four or five bystanders clustered around a woman lying on a pile of coats, some standing over her with umbrellas. A little crowd was starting to gather on the other side of the road. It never ceased to amaze me how many people stood and stared but didn't actually help. I reserved a special place in hell for the two or three people I could see taking photos and videos.

As soon as Pete managed to squeeze onto the verge next to the sports car, I grabbed my bag, the fear of what lay ahead kept at bay with the knowledge that I had the experience to deal with it. As I jumped down in my high-vis wet-weather gear, I was repeating to myself "Airways, Breathing, Circulation, Disability, Exposure." Even after all these years, it calmed me to say it to myself, reminding me what to look for first.

The police officer moved everyone back a bit apart from one man, who introduced himself as Geoff. He peered through misty glasses, desperate to tell me what he knew, tripping over his words. "I was in the car behind. It was the truck. It didn't indicate. I couldn't stop in the rain. I didn't hit them hard, though. The roof ripped off and she was half hanging out, so we lifted her out. I don't know if we did the right thing. She's twenty-nine weeks pregnant. Her leg's bleeding—it looks broken—we wrapped it in a bandage from a first-aid kit that was in one of the cars. She's losing so much blood."

I'd seen these sorts of expressions so often: the childlike relief that we'd arrived to take over.

I didn't blame them, but I wished they hadn't moved her. "Thank you. The police might ask you to give a statement later."

I knelt down.

"Hello, I'm Kate and I'm a paramedic. We're going to get you into the ambulance as soon as possible so we can have a proper look at you. I know it's wet and cold out here." Blood was oozing down one side of her face and her curly hair fanned out in wet clumps. In other circumstances, she'd have been one of those women who turned heads—uniform features, all beautifully arranged.

There was a rumbling among the group gathered about her catching her death. One woman was shouting at me to get to hospital. "Why didn't a helicopter come? Can't you see she needs proper treatment?"

I looked up, ridiculously tempted to list all the many courses I had to do to qualify as a paramedic. "I need to make sure we don't cause more harm than good before I move her. The helicopter can't fly in this weather."

Pete ran over to join me. I covered her with a silver blanket. While he checked her airways and breathing, I pulled out the blood pressure monitor.

"Can you tell me your name?"

The woman grunted. "Sophie. Is the baby going to be all right? I've got stomach ache. Where's my boyfriend? Is he okay?"

Geoff indicated the man in the sports car. I looked over to him. The police had managed to wrench the door open and the crew were lifting him out. He was groaning. "My chest's killing me. It really hurts."

"Sophie, he's being looked after. My colleagues are with him now. Just keep calm for me."

We could hear him moaning in pain through the rain, his panicky voice just reaching us. "Is she all right? What about the baby? Is she bleeding? Are you taking her to hospital?" followed by the soothing tone of the paramedic reassuring him.

There was something familiar about his voice that I couldn't quite place. My brain was almost finding an answer but not quite getting over the finishing line. The rain was funnelling into my hood and running down my back.

Although he was in obvious agony, he was trying to crane his neck to see her, despite the paramedic's instruction to stay still while he checked him over. Every now and then, despite the blood pouring down his cheek, the flashing lights still illuminated the expression I'd seen so many times before, particularly on men. The sheer terror that there was something they couldn't fix, for someone they loved. It was the great leveller of humanity—no matter whether you lived in a house with a bathroom for every bedroom or one loo for all, had Ocado deliver the groceries or clipped every coupon out of the paper to survive—none of us was immune to losing someone so dear that you couldn't imagine how tomorrow could even think of showing its face without them.

Sophie was whimpering. I could see she was trying to be brave but couldn't quite manage her pain. Pete and I decided to do all the other checks we needed once we'd got her onto the stretcher and into the ambulance out of the rain.

We hauled her up into the van and I attached her to the heart monitor.

"I'm just going to give you something to ease the pain."

"Will it hurt the baby?"

I drew up a shot of morphine. "No, not as a one-off. You'll be fine."

I grabbed the kit to cannulate her so I could start pumping in some fluid to stabilise her blood pressure.

I heard Pete's voice raise as he ran to grab the rest of the kit from outside. And then: "You're the scum of the earth, you lot are. How would you like it if someone was photographing you in a smashed-up car? Ambulance-chasing arseholes. Get out the way and get lost."

Pete slammed the doors shut. It didn't matter how bad the

accident, even when people were lying dead on the motorway, some idiot would always be thrilled to capture other people's misery on their phone and plaster it all over the internet. He started the engine and the ambulance lurched as he manoeuvred between the various bits of wreckage onto the dual carriageway.

Sophie was writhing in discomfort, slurring out her words. "I won't lose the baby, will I?"

Her blood pressure was falling, which meant she was losing a lot of blood from her leg wound. I could feel the stirrings of alarm.

"Just stay calm and keep talking to me. Tell me where you were going when you crashed."

"Shopping centre to look for a cot for the baby. Just picking up some groceries from Waitrose in Caterham on the way."

I could feel the effort she was making to talk, as though she was fetching the words from somewhere far away.

"Bluewater? My daughter loves it there."

She squirmed.

"Lie still for me if you can. I know it hurts." I tried to distract her. "So, was it a day off work?"

"No, I'm a vet and I just did the morning shift today."

I was only half listening, more interested in how she spoke, the exertion to get her words out, rather than what she was saying. I worked methodically, pushing down the adrenaline triggered by the knowledge that not one but two lives were depending on me.

"Vet, that must be an interesting job." I peeled back the makeshift bandages that were by now soaked through and put some fresh dressing around the deep gashes on her right shin, wincing at how grey and clammy she looked under the bright ambulance lights. I could see right down to the bone. The little bee tattoo on her wrist caught my eye and I realised she was the woman I'd met at Gisela's barbecue who'd been house-sitting. I didn't say anything. This wasn't the moment for meet-and-greet.

Pete contacted the trauma centre to get an obs and gynae team on standby.

"Have you felt the baby move since the accident?" I asked.

"I think so. I'm not sure." She tried to sit up.

"Just lie back for me, so I can feel for the baby. My hands are a bit cold." I rubbed them together. In the second before I made contact with her skin, I sent up a wish to the gods I didn't believe in that her stomach wouldn't be rigid. I'd never seen it firsthand but I knew that a car crash could cause the placenta to rip away from the uterus wall, in which case we were in trouble. Panic was threatening to derail my focus, my mind clawing at me, images I resolutely refused to remember pushing hard to regain colour and sound. As my hands made contact with a soft stomach, the rush of relief brought me straight back into the moment. One tick on my list. I pressed my palm down, desperate for some sign of movement, and was eventually rewarded with a wriggle.

I smiled, hoping that I'd hidden my own fear. "He or she is taking everything in its stride. The best thing you can do is stay calm."

I was just gathering myself, taking a second to run through the checks in my head, when Sophie's low and constant moaning dialled up to a new intensity. She started screaming. "I'm wet between my legs. Am I bleeding?"

I dug out my softest voice. "Sophie, just breathe deeply, while I see what's happening. How many weeks are you?" I asked.

Even though Geoff had already told me, it didn't seem right to delegate the proper fact-finding to a guy who probably sold pet insurance for a living.

"Twenty-nine weeks. It's too early. It can't come yet." I couldn't agree more. I couldn't be responsible for a baby.

But it seemed I was going to be. Sophie's waters had broken and unlike Daisy who'd taken eighteen hours to arrive in the world, this baby showed every sign of being in a hurry.

Sophie was thrashing about. "I can feel it coming. I want my partner. Where is he? I can't do this without him!"

I hooked her up to the gas and air. "Listen to me. He's in good hands and getting the best possible care. Right now we need to concentrate on keeping you and the baby safe. Keep breathing."

I shouted through to the front in the calmest tone I could manage, "Pete, I think the baby's on its way."

Sophie was panting, her face contorted.

I might as well have been a forklift truck driver unexpectedly in charge of the delivery room. Every single bit of medical knowledge I'd ever had flapped away. I reached for a delivery pack, reluctant to open it, to pick out the apron, gown and pads, to make the whole bloody thing real. I pulled myself together, focusing on my training, knowing I had to establish the baby's position. This was not the time for a tricky breech birth. I tried to distract her, asking her about her partner, how long they'd been together, what names they had for the baby. Eventually the effort of speaking became too much for her and I fell silent, remembering how I'd wanted Oskar to keep quiet and let me focus on my body and its job of delivering our daughter safely into the world. I was frightened to trust my judgement but after what seemed like forever, hampered by Sophie writhing in pain, I was as sure as I could be that the baby was head down. I shouted the news through to Pete, who yelled back to be ready for things to move quickly because "early ones often don't take as long."

With a false brightness to my voice, I told Sophie that she'd saved herself hours of labour but she only managed a groan in return.

Pete was weaving in and out of the traffic, which kept grinding to a standstill in the evening rush hour. It was always the same when it rained.

Sophie was squeezing my hand. I started to count the time between the contractions.

"Pete, quick as you can."

He was responding through gritted teeth, "I'm getting there, it's a bit busy, doing my best."

"We should be at the hospital long before the baby comes, but let's get you into the gown." With the contractions speeding up, coming less than five minutes apart, I wasn't sure that was the case. I put on the apron and cut away the rest of her trousers. "Is it your first baby?"

"First, yes...Are we nearly there?"

Her voice was draining away, as though she was floating off from me. I looked at the new bandages I'd pressed on her leg, which were already turning red. Her pulse was climbing.

I wasn't sure what fully dilated looked like but I knew Sophie couldn't be far off. I passed her the gas and air. She bit on the end as another contraction wracked her body, sucking in the Entonox with a swooshing noise.

"How long, Pete?" I could hear my voice rising.

In the ten years I'd been working as a paramedic, I'd never had to deliver a baby. Thank God Sophie was so scrunched up with pain, she couldn't see my face. I felt paralysed, afraid to look down in case the baby's head was crowning, in case I had to see a baby that was the wrong colour or not breathing. Eleven weeks early. Those tiny little lungs that I'd be responsible for keeping beating in and out. I reminded myself that babies survived much, much younger than that. Quickly followed by the thought that was usually because they were in a unit with specialist equipment and years of collective knowledge gathered round them.

"I reckon forty minutes."

I was going to have to do this. I tried to be in the moment, tapping into my training. "Sophie, take deep breaths and only push if you need to. You're doing really well."

Sophie was crying. "Don't let my baby die. Please don't let it die." Of course, people had begged me to keep their spouse or parent alive before. I'd had an eighty-eight-year-old man sit holding his wife's hand as she died from a stroke, saying, "I've never spent a night away from her and never want to. You can't let her die," as though we were little gods with the right to choose who stayed and who left. I'd thought about him for weeks afterwards, imagined him shuffling upstairs to a lonely cold bed. I wondered if he lasted the year. But even his anguish had nothing on this. Sophie's urging was primeval, so raw that I wanted to do the thing we were taught not to: I wanted to promise her that it would be okay.

Despite being an atheist for nearly two decades, I was praying that baby was going to stay put. Praying that some super-capable midwife would dash to the ambulance and take over. But before we turned off the motorway, the head started to crown. I was practically shouting at Sophie to stop pushing. "Little breaths. Blow out through your mouth! Nice and slow." Just as we sped down the main road towards the hospital, Sophie gave a primitive wail and in a gush of blood and fluid, a tiny body slithered into my hands with a speed that almost took me by surprise. I wrapped up the baby, willing it to move and cry.

"Is the baby all right? Is it?"

My heart was racing out of my chest. I rubbed her little daughter with the towel, trying to get a reaction, some sign that she was alive.

After a whole lifetime condensed into a few seconds, the sound we'd all been waiting for—a frail little wail, like a kitten trapped in a garage. I went wobbly with relief that I wouldn't have to do CPR on that tiny chest. My voice threatened to give way to sobs as I said, "It's a girl." I placed a blanket around Sophie then opened her shirt to put the baby on her stomach, skin to skin to keep her warm. I marvelled at how Sophie's face had shifted from one of fight, drawing on every resource available to her and beyond, to the electric mix of tenderness and ferocity of maternal love. Before I had time to dwell, the ambulance came to a halt. Instantly, a throng of people burst in, giving orders, directing and scooping up like white knights from a fairy tale, whisking Sophie and her daughter away.

I stumbled out of the ambulance after Sophie disappeared into the depths of the hospital on a trolley. As soon as the adrenaline subsided, my legs seemed to come unhinged at the joints, as though they had lost the ability of forward motion and were flicking randomly in unpredictable directions.

I headed to the loo, shouting for Pete to wait for me. I trailed my hand along the hospital walls to keep me upright. I threw up, great heaving retches from the depths of my stomach. I considered calling my manager to say that I needed to go home, but I hadn't been here long enough for them to know that my reaction really was a one-off. I didn't want to get sidelined into the curling tong burns and twisted ankles. Heart attacks, strokes, bleeding, injuries where you could see right to the bone—I could deal with them all.

I washed my face in the sink, gritted my teeth—actually stood in front of the mirror and set my jaw—then staggered back to the ambulance, light-headed and dejected.

Once we'd completed the handover, Pete drove me back to the station mess, high on the drama. "Bloody hell. You did well. That baby was tiny, wasn't it?"

I felt as though I didn't have enough blood circulating around my body to feed my brain. I crumpled in the front seat, images flashing in and out, bringing questions about whether I should have got Sophie into the ambulance earlier, whether we could have got to the trauma centre more quickly, whether I'd done enough for the baby to survive.

When I got back to the station mess, I wanted to ask whether anyone had heard how they were, whether we knew how Sophie's partner was doing. I kept forming the words but not quite getting enough forward thrust to push them out of my mouth. I didn't know how I'd ever get back in an ambulance if the baby died. But as I walked in, my colleagues started clapping—"You were brilliant, Kate."

Then there was that excited swapping of stories, the first time I'd really been in the thick of things, where everyone wants to relive their moment of a similar experience, that knife-edge between disaster and triumph, the perfect balance of adrenaline, luck and knowledge that—against all odds—brought a happy ending to this world.

I didn't know what the final outcome would be. And I was scared to hope.

I couldn't join in. I wanted to. I yearned to be part of something, of the belonging other people took for granted. I had too many sounds and images crowding into my mind—the desperate love and terror on Sophie's partner's face as he sat trapped in the car, the howl coming from deep within her, that baby, a tiny pink miracle of life, my hands in the latex gloves, poised over that doll-like chest.

I shook my head to push back other images, older ones fluttering out, sepia memories I'd tried to leave behind, always sitting on the sidelines like a flock of seagulls biding their time for a chip. I never wanted to hear that agonising howl of grief again.

Martin, who'd been looking after Sophie's partner, walked in. He came straight over. "Heard you got the baby out alive. Good work. Do you know how the mother's doing?"

"No, not yet. She'd lost a lot of blood from the leg wound. The little girl was tiny. I hope she makes it." I swallowed. No one was used to seeing any emotion from me. "How about the bloke? Looked like he had chest injuries?"

Martin looked down. "He did. Head injury too."

My shoulders slumped. Sometimes I hated this job. The bloody arbitrary nature of it all. No one set out on a little trip to the shops, excited about a new baby, and expected to be lying in intensive care a few hours later. I tried not to let my mind roll back to the day when one minute I'd been singing "Baa, Baa, Black Sheep" and the next I'd been sitting in a police cell.

"How bad was it?"

"He didn't look too bad to start with—just thought he'd cracked a rib—he didn't even want us to ring anyone, kept saying he was fine and no one needed to know, no point in frightening anyone, the usual stuff. But later on, he was getting all confused, having trouble remembering his surname and date of birth and kept telling us to contact someone called Sally and getting all aggressive, you know how they do sometimes when they've had a bash to the bonce." Martin frowned. "He said it was his wife. I think he must have meant sister, given that his partner was giving birth in the ambulance next door."

I went cold. I suddenly knew why his voice seemed familiar. Sally. Purple sports car. The one that had sat on the driveway beside my living room window for months. A Lotus something or other. And *Sophie* the vet. Us all standing in Gisela's garden at one of her parties. My mind was fighting to insist that all of these elements were just coincidence instead of an ugly truth I did not want to accept.

Martin carried on, oblivious. "We sedated him. I guess they'll keep him out for a few days, see if they can get the swelling down." He shrugged. "Poor bloke. Doesn't even know he's got a baby daughter."

I had to ask. "Did you discover what his surname was?"

Martin frowned. "Found it on his driving licence. Gassomething. Gastrol? It was an odd name."

I thought back to every conversation I'd had with Sally. The Facebook posts of where she was meeting Chris for a weekend. The endless photos of wine glasses here, there and everywhere. Had I made a mistake? Had I somehow got the wrong end of the stick and assumed that the father of Sophie's baby was the bloke in the car? Martin clearly thought he was. I replayed the conversation in the ambulance. Had she called him by name? Or did she say "partner"? She had told me they hadn't been together very long.

Martin was peering at me, waiting for an explanation of why I was asking. I burst out with, "Just going to grab a tea before the next call." His expression took on that weary look that people often got around me, when they thought they were getting to know me and the drawbridge clanged up without warning.

I needed to sit on my own and work through what I knew before the next call came in. I'd only got as far as "Had Chris left Sally and she just wasn't telling us?" when I was called out to a forty-two-year-old man who was having heart palpitations. He turned out to have drunk too much Coke and coffee before a stint on a very violent PlayStation game.

When my shift finished, I drove home feeling as though my head was going to implode with the dual loop of wondering how Sophie was, whether her baby had survived, interspersed with puzzling about the Sally, Sophie and Chris triangle and the shit stew they found themselves in. Usually I calmed my mind with the mantra of "Not everyone dies and not everyone survives," but that didn't seem to be anywhere near enough today.

CHAPTER 29

Sally

Tuesday 3 April

Photo: Waitresses with bottles of wine, waiters with cana-
pés of mini beef Wellingtons and goat's cheese quiche
with beetroot topping.
Caption: Not a bad way to spend a day at work!
#Work #LoveMyJob

It was eight o'clock when I got in after a long day at work,
finally escaping the "voyage of wine discovery" event put on
for restaurant sommeliers, during which time they sampled
everything and I drank water, finding it harder and harder to
deal with the misogyny surrounding the fact that a woman, not
a man, might have the perfect palate for being a senior buyer.
I'd run upstairs and flung off my suit, which had become a bit
tighter without Chris's junk food vigilance. I'd have to get going
on a diet: we'd started texting and speaking so much more
since he'd stayed overnight a month and a half ago, with our
last conversation about how much history we shared and how
he was finding it difficult to imagine leaving all that behind. I
didn't ask him outright; I didn't want to scare him off, but I took
it to mean he might be warming to the idea of having children.

He'd asked to have dinner with me next week at the Ginger

Hen, which I'd taken as a good sign. It was our special place, the scene of many birthday and anniversary celebrations. If he was going to end our marriage, what would be the point of a three-course meal, waiters hovering about, "Any more water? Any more wine?" dragging out the agony? No. Chris didn't like drama. I was pretty sure he'd have suggested a cup of coffee if that was the case so maybe he'd realised that what we had was worth saving, after all.

I was just settling down in front of the TV in my pyjamas when the doorbell went. I did miss not being able to send Chris rottweiling out to deal with callers. He didn't feel the need to be polite to Jehovah's Witnesses or door-to-door salesmen in the same way I did.

I hated anyone coming to the door in the evening. Goodness knows how vulnerable the elderly felt. I considered ignoring it, but then I knew I'd be lying awake, paranoid about burglars thinking no one was home, bracing myself for the shattering of a window at the back.

I shouted through the front door. "Who is it?"

"It's Gisela."

Of all the people I could bear to see, she was probably top of the list, suitably superficial but jolly and generous. I had to be in the mood for Kate, with her odd mixture of assertiveness that could easily tip over into being abrupt and the sort of shyness that meant she looked as though she was never quite sure if it really was okay to stay for a coffee. Not to mention her capacity to be ferocious. I wouldn't make the mistake of passing comment on her parenting again. At least Gisela was straightforward, and I never felt that panic of lining up five topics of conversation the second I saw her in case silence started to engulf us.

"Hello, come on in," I said, opening the door and mentally running through which wine was cold and whether my fridge might contain some cheese that wasn't mouldy.

I stood back to let her through, feeling a mixture of curiosity and, despite considering myself pretty lonely, a thread of irritation. I'd got used to my uninterrupted evenings, my little routine of catching up on work emails, watching a box set, having a bath and an early night.

"Sorry for barging in, Sally, but I saw you drive up and wanted to check you were okay?"

"I'm fine, thank you." I tried to soften the snappiness in my voice. "I've just come in, long day today, hence the dressing gown." I was never quite sure whether Gisela thought I was a rubbish wife for working away so much or secretly envious I had a career.

She scratched her nose, frowning as though I'd said something really odd. My mind was racing, trying to understand what had sparked her concern, why she'd come scuttling round now. I'd been on my own for four months, since the beginning of December, though I didn't know how she could have found that out. Perhaps she'd just guessed because she hadn't seen Chris in so long.

I didn't want her here. I was too bloody tired to sift through my words before I spoke and I'd planned to spend the evening browsing the internet for a new outfit for my big date with Chris next week. Something sexy, perhaps a little more overt than he—and I—were used to. "Was there something you needed me for?"

She blinked hard. "I might have got completely the wrong end of the stick." She puffed out her cheeks as if she was affirming in her own mind what she thought she knew. "Have you heard from Chris this afternoon?"

"I've been in meetings all day. He's away at the moment anyway. We'll probably FaceTime later on before bedtime." My words were pouring out of me, tumbling over themselves in order to sound convincing. Hopefully next Wednesday he'd be back and we'd never be the subject of Parkview gossip again.

As Gisela's face fell, my focus swung away from my own lies, and the uncertainty in her voice began to make headway.

"Sally, I might be completely wrong about this, but I was on Twitter trying to find out if there's a Wagamama coming to where that old pizza place in the high street used to be." She looked a bit embarrassed, as though it was an admission she really didn't have enough to do. Her voice came out in a rush. "When I put in the hashtag Windlow, it brought up some photos of an accident between here and Caterham. I'm sorry, but I think Chris was involved. There was a pile-up on the A22 and one of the cars looked like his purple Lotus. You could see the beginning of the number plate. His is CLG 2 something, isn't it?"

I stared at her. "Are you sure? Is he hurt?"

Panic flitted over Gisela's face. "I don't know. There weren't any details, just a video and some photos of the ambulances arriving and the fact there was a pregnant woman in one of the cars."

"Show me."

Gisela fumbled with her phone and, after scrolling about for what seemed like forever, pulled up a picture. She made it bigger. It definitely looked like his car—what was left of it—squished between a truck and a Land Rover.

"Oh God. Surely if it was his, someone would have got in touch by now? If it was posted at 4:30?" I picked up my mobile, remembering too late that my boss had kept me tied up for an hour listening to his ideas for a new range of wines when I was rushing around trying to check all the last-minute arrangements. "Shit, the bloody battery's flat. I've been meaning to get a new phone for ages. It never holds its charge."

I ran to the landline, an old-fashioned telephone with a dial—Chris's attempt at retro irony—and rang his number, which went straight to voicemail. The thought that he might be dead, that I'd never speak to him again, never say all the thousands of things we had yet to resolve, flashed through my head. I'd always prided myself on being calm in a crisis, but my mind was blank.

I ran into the kitchen to stick my phone on charge, pushing past Gisela, who looked as helpless as I felt. I shouted to her, "Can you look again and see if there's any more information? Where will they have taken him?"

"I don't know. East Surrey? Croydon? Epsom? Or one of the London ones? Should we try and ring round the hospitals? I thought the police always contacted the next of kin."

Through the front window, I saw Kate draw up and get out of her car. "There's Kate. She might know what to do."

I snatched up my keys and we tore out of the house through the rain, me still in my dressing gown. I shouted to her and her face dropped, as though I was the last person she wanted to see.

Gisela filled her in on what we knew and showed her the Twitter feed. "Did you hear anything at work?" Gisela asked.

Kate hesitated. She was finding it hard to meet my eye. She could hardly stay still long enough to talk to us. "No. No. I've been over at Betchworth this afternoon. All serious road traffic accidents go to the major trauma centre, which is at St. Benedict's, just past Croydon. If you give them a ring, they'll be able to tell you which ward he's on." She blushed and corrected herself. "If it's even him, of course." Her voice petered out. "It might not be."

She didn't sound at all convinced.

I turned to Gisela. "I'm going to drive up there."

Kate said, "The weather's terrible. Why don't you ring to make sure he's there first? If they're treating him, you won't be able to see him anyway. You might be better waiting until tomorrow morning."

Wait till tomorrow morning? What normal wife would sit at home when her husband might be in a critical condition?

I looked at her expectantly. I wanted Kate to tell me she'd make some phone calls, that she'd find out what she could. Despite our row about Daisy, I'd always felt that, at heart, she was a kind person. Now she looked like she just wanted to get inside to her beans on toast rather than help me out in my hour of need.

Before we could get any further, a police car came round the corner and I felt my knees give. We all stood there in complete silence for a second. As it crawled past Gisela's house, obviously searching for the numbers in the rain, I ran over, my legs unsteady and uncooperative. Gisela followed me, but I registered Kate disappearing through her front door.

A policewoman in her thirties got out. "I'm looking for Sally Gastrell?"

"That's me." I shut my mouth before the scream at the back of my throat escaped into the air.

"Can we go inside?"

Gisela turned to me. "Shall I come in with you?"

I nodded. My hands were shaking so much that the police officer took the keys from me to unlock the door. We walked into the sitting room and sat down.

The officer spread her hands on her knees. "Could you tell me whether you are related to Chris Gastrell?" She sounded as though there was some doubt in her mind.

"He's my husband, we've been married for ten years. What's happened?" My voice came out louder than I'd intended. My mother would definitely have given me a glare for not being deferential enough. A huge sob was welling up in my chest.

The policewoman frowned as though she'd been expecting a different answer.

"Is he okay? Is he hurt?" Oddly it felt more important than ever not to let on that we'd been separated for a while.

The policewoman pulled herself together and explained about the accident, that she'd been one of the attending officers and that Chris had asked her to contact me before they had to sedate him. "He's been taken to St. Benedict's."

"Is he in intensive care?" I stumbled over those horrible words, conjuring up a picture of wires and tubes. "Is he going to die?"

The policewoman looked apologetic. "He got good treatment at the scene. I don't know any of the medical details, though. They'll fill you in when you get to hospital. Do you know where your husband was going?"

"He wasn't even supposed to be in the UK today. I thought he was in Paris. Maybe he was on his way back from the airport?"

She shrugged. "I don't know. He was on the A22 near Caterham."

Which was sort of Gatwick way, but not quite. Maybe the M23 had been closed. I didn't see how where he was going mattered.

"I'd like to go to the hospital now."

The policewoman nodded. "Are you all right for transport?"

Gisela put her hand on my arm. "Shall I drive you there?"

I was about to argue, then realised I was a bit unstable on my feet.

"Would you? Thank you. I'll just go and get dressed."

Gisela said, "I'll nip next door and let Jack know what's happening."

The policewoman hesitated in the doorway as though she had more to say.

I didn't have time for her dithering. I pushed past her and opened the front door. "Goodbye then, thank you for coming."

Eventually, she stepped outside with Gisela following. I left the door ajar and bolted upstairs, scrabbling in my drawers for clothes, not caring that everything I'd learnt to fold so carefully since I'd been married to Chris was spewing all over the floor.

By the time I ran downstairs again, Gisela was back.

She was screwing up her eyes as though she was struggling to make sense of something, then marched towards the car and said, "Are you ready?"

We leapt into her Beetle and she roared up the road. I studied her out of the corner of my eye. There was something about her expression that frightened me. It was the same expression I'd seen on my dad's face when he'd told me that my granddad had cancer. The sort of expression that meant they had to tell you the truth, but if they could have lied their arses off and got away with it, they'd have done that instead.

Eventually she broke the silence. "Can I tell you something before we get there, in case there are any misunderstandings at the hospital?"

My heart did a little flip. "What?"

Her words came flinging out like she just had to get them out into the air and away from her. "While I was waiting for Jack to come out of the loo, I had a quick look at Twitter. Some bloody ambulance chaser has taken a photo of Chris's car and tweeted, 'Praying that this guy's pregnant wife is okay.'"

I felt a jolt of anger. I swallowed the sour saliva that surged into my mouth. "What idiot would even stand and take photos of an accident? Must have been a work colleague or someone he was giving a lift to."

Gisela fixed her eyes forward. Her face was telling the story, though. That the fact she hadn't seen Chris in months had not escaped her notice.

I laughed, a scratchy sound. "I can tell you for definite that a pregnant woman is nothing to do with him. He would never have a baby. He can't stand children."

Although Gisela didn't say anything, her lack of response told me she wasn't convinced.

More to myself than Gisela, I said, "We're supposed to be going to Ginger Hen on Wednesday. That's not going to happen now."

I leaned back on the headrest.

Gisela drove, uncharacteristically quiet. My mind veered, wildly, between wondering how injured Chris was, whether he'd ever make a full recovery, to sifting through the policewoman's conversation, that slight hesitation, as though she was trying to find out something from me, as if my place in Chris's life wasn't quite as clear-cut as you would think. Every now and then, a thought would escape me, a random rant. "You'd think that there'd be some law against putting photos of accidents on the internet. Why didn't the police move them away?"

"I suppose when the accident first happens they're too busy

making sure other cars don't pile into the back of it. I think people are so used to taking photos now that they forget they are videoing real people's lives."

I sensed a reluctance, some kind of holding back, in Gisela as we got closer to the A&E reception. Maybe she was one of those people who couldn't stand to be around illness. "Do you want to wait for me outside?"

"Not if you're happy for me to come in." She stopped and put her hand on my arm. "Come on. It might not be as bad as you think."

I pushed open the door, the faces of the people lined up on the chairs a blur, not caring whether someone had gashed themselves on a greenhouse or thought they were having a heart attack. My bad news was confirmed. I had a husband in intensive care.

I walked up to the desk. Gisela stood back to let me deal, but as the words came out of my mouth, "My husband was in a car accident earlier and I think he's in intensive care" and the receptionist's face switched from "There's at least a three-hour wait" to a gentle "Could you just tell me his name and date of birth?" I started to cry. Sobs that blocked my breathing, as though a conker had lodged in my windpipe.

Gisela took over, her hand on my shoulder, and steered me in the direction of the neurological intensive care unit. I hoped she'd absorbed the turn right before X-rays, through the double doors and whatever else stood between me and reaching for my husband's hand. Whatever—*whatever*—had got lost in translation between his desire for freedom to climb as high as he could in his career unencumbered by family demands and my yearning to have and to hold the next generation, he'd failed, succeeded, and bluffed alongside me as we made our way through the world. He'd been the one to witness those precious mid-twenty to mid-thirty years when I'd made the important transition from the person who knew it all to the person who realised the right answer took time to arrive at.

And I loved him.

Eventually, I found myself in front of a reception desk with my eyes boring holes into the back of the nurse's head who was in the corner tapping away at her computer. She looked up and smiled.

In a voice that didn't sound like mine, I said, "I'm here to see Chris Gastrell."

"And you are?"

"I'm his wife, Sally. Can I see him? Is he okay?"

"His wife? Just bear with me a moment." Again, that puzzled face. Did most wives get the message their husbands were in intensive care and go, "Shame. I'll pop up in a few days when I've finished my *Killing Eve* box set." It was like they didn't expect me to come. "I just need to check something." She nodded towards a little room further up the corridor. "Take a seat in there for a minute."

I sank onto a plastic chair to a backdrop of her feet scrabbling along the corridor at speed.

Gisela looked as though there was so much she wanted to ask. Her eyes were round with concern. "Are you all right?"

I wonder if people of other nationalities would reply, "How the fuck do you think I feel?" Luckily for Gisela my Britishness was very pronounced. Tears were beading along my lower lash line. "Do you think he's dead? Do you think she's gone to get someone to tell me?"

Gisela made shushing sounds. We sat dumbfounded, the noise of trollies rattling along the corridor, groans of pain, bleeping machines. A macabre soundtrack to a life I didn't want to know. For someone who could rival my mother in chattering on in any circumstance, even Gisela was at a loss.

After about five minutes, I couldn't sit there not knowing whether he was dead or alive for one second longer. I leapt to my feet. "I've got to find out what's going on."

I started off down the corridor, with Gisela trotting behind me, wondering how I'd find out which ward he was in.

The nurse appeared with that whole "give me a bedpan to

empty any day" face going on. "Someone's with him at the moment. Won't be long."

"But is he okay?"

"The consultant will talk to you tomorrow. He's sedated just now, which means he's unconscious. We're monitoring him really carefully. Pop back and have a seat in the side room for a minute. I'll call you as soon as I can."

I sensed she was trying to shuffle me off, tidy me away. I'd never felt untidier, less held in.

Gisela pulled gently on my arm. I wanted to swing round and shake her off. "Come on, let's sit down."

"What do you think the problem is? Why can't I just go in there?" In a minute I was going to run down the corridor barging into wards until I found my husband.

I let Gisela guide me back to that sparse little room with its pale blue curtains and insipid picture of a hayfield.

Just as we got there, a porter pushed a woman with her leg up in a wheelchair past us. "Don't cry, love. He'll be fine. You'll see. Right as rain in a few days. He'll be rocking that little baby in no time. Let's get you back to orthopaedics before that matron gives me a rollicking. I told her we'd only be ten minutes, max, just long enough for you to tell him he's a dad. I bet he heard you. Come on, no more crying. You need to look after yourself for that little girl of yours."

On and on he twittered, while she sat slouched in a miserable silence, still managing to look pretty—her hair a halo of blonde corkscrew curls—despite the huge tears rolling down her face. Pretty and familiar. She'd obviously been in the wars herself, though; her face was covered in cuts and bruises.

The penny dropped. I whispered to Gisela. "Isn't that the vet woman from your party? Sophie someone?"

She swung round. "Who? The girl in the wheelchair?"

I should have known better than to think that Gisela was capable of the tonal moderation required to talk about someone four feet away.

The woman jerked her head round, then looked away quickly. It was definitely her. It didn't feel appropriate to shout "Coo-ee" and say, "So what happened to you?"

At that moment, the nurse came back and beckoned us in.

"He's just through in this ward. Now, he's been sedated, so he won't be able to speak to you, but he might be able to hear you." She explained that he had swelling on the brain caused by the impact of the car crash, as far as they could tell from the CT scan so far. They were keeping him sedated to relieve the intra-cranial pressure. "Basically to allow the swelling to go down."

I gasped when I walked in and saw the tube down his throat and various other monitors attached to him.

Gisela pulled the curtain around us and said, "I'm going to wait outside. Give you a bit of privacy."

I held his hand. I expected it to be cold, but it was warm. I watched his chest rise and fall. I looked at his hands, his fingers with the sparse dark hairs at the base of them, trying to imprint the shape of them on my brain in case this was it. In case I really was going to spend the rest of my life without him. I'd wanted a baby so much, I'd pushed him away. Now I might not have him either. I thought about the last five months. How when he did call, I'd let the phone ring and snatched it up just before it clicked onto voicemail. How I'd make myself wait a couple of hours before texting back. How I'd deliberately post pictures of me out drinking, in restaurants with my colleagues, in vine-yards all over the world raising a glass. Invisible hashtag: I ain't missing you at all.

What a fool I'd been.

CHAPTER 30

Kate

Thursday 5 April

I couldn't settle. I had to know. Did that baby survive? I'd become so good at shutting myself off from patients that it was years since I'd been unable to shake off what I'd seen. But images of that tiny body burned into my brain when I tried to sleep. That pitiful cry from those underdeveloped lungs. And, most of all, the look in Sophie's eyes. The shift from pain to protection the second she held her baby. Every time I remembered that, I thought of Becky. Even now, when her face came into my mind, I had to chase it away. I couldn't allow myself to think about seeing her agony in physical form, a knotting, clawing grief consuming her whole body.

As always, whenever my thoughts wandered down the dark alleys I was usually able to barricade, I wanted to hug Daisy more tightly and issue far more detailed instructions than the "Be careful" I restricted myself to every time she left the house. I was having to fight the feeling that every day she might be taken from me. Would she know how much I loved her? At the moment, we resembled enemies living in an uneasy truce. For the last two mornings I'd got up especially early to make scrambled eggs, as though somehow she'd feel the love stirred in. It was fair to say it hadn't yet produced the effect I'd been hoping for.

This morning was no different. "Why are you suddenly getting up early to cook breakfast for me?" There was no longer any such thing as a simple conversation in our house. Every sentence, every question Daisy uttered felt as though it had accusation threading through it.

"I think you're working really hard for your A levels and I like to know you've started your day with some goodness inside you before I go to work."

I tried not to feel criticised. Daisy wasn't the sort of girl you could pounce on, address a problem and deal with it there and then. She was so much more like Oskar—you had to peel back the surface to reach the emotions beneath, like a forensic pathologist excavating soil, searching for clues. I'd brought up what Sally had told me about Oskar on several different occasions, trying to tick the perfect parenting box of "creating opportunities to talk." But Daisy made me feel as though I was single-handedly responsible for his new baby and lack of contact with her. In fact, I'd begged him to be properly involved in her life. In the end, after a few more jibes about how it was "so difficult for Dad to get back to the UK," I grew impatient and said, "I do understand how horrible it is to find out you've got a new half-brother and a whole other family that you're not part of at the moment. But the reality is he left us behind and chose to go and live in Argentina." I tried not to sound self-pitying, but I felt a great rush of anger. "I'm sorry about what happened. No one wishes more than me that we were still at home with your dad, leading normal, boring lives. I know it's easy to blame me, but in the end, I am the one who's been here for you, day in, day out. I wouldn't want it any other way, but your dad hasn't taken responsibility, I have."

After a lifetime of stepping lightly around each other, afraid to be a mother and daughter who shouted out truths, Daisy put her hands on her hips and said, "You've no idea how hard it is to have a name that's not even yours. To have no family identity at all. Not even to be able to talk about where you grew up, which schools you went to, who you sat next to in Reception. To have you monitoring what I'm posting on social media, who I'm telling what, never feeling I can invite people round, let alone—God forbid—have a party. It's not my fault that your life turned to shit and took mine with it. And how's it going to work when I have my own kids? Are they going to lie about where they came from? How will I ever have a relationship if I can't tell my boyfriend who I am? It's so stupid. I can't even have a bloody smartphone in case someone realises where I am." She slammed down her Nokia and stormed out.

For the hundredth time, I cursed Oskar for finding his first family too complicated and taking the easy way out by having a second go with someone else.

I allowed myself to imagine coming clean with everyone. Watching their faces fall, backing away in case my tragedy became contagious. Half of them expressing sympathy, the others quietly repelled, suspicious. Could I really go back to catching the curious glances in the street, the insults shouted at me underneath my window, the sense that certain call-outs at work were being diverted to other crews? Nothing I could prove, nothing I could take up with the management, just a feeling that I was being slightly sidelined without anyone ever bothering to hear—or be entirely convinced by—my side of the story.

I could never come up with an answer. Never escape the feeling there wasn't a solution. Before I could go and find Daisy, she slammed out of the house. I watched her ring the bell at Gisela's. How I wished the only thing I had to worry about was my daughter failing to learn how to double-bake a soufflé.

Thankfully, work was so full on, with a call-out to a diabetic coma, an asthma attack, plus the usual time-wasting on a bad back, ear infection and a child who'd swallowed some bathwater, that I didn't have time to weigh myself down with unhelpful thoughts. The last call on my shift was to a suspected stroke and as we pulled in to the trauma centre, I saw Elaine, one of the A&E nurses who'd been there when Sophie had been admitted. "Do you know how the woman who had the baby on Tuesday got on?"

"Baby's in NICU but not heard how she's doing. Think the mother ended up on the orthopaedic ward."

As soon as my shift finished, despite telling myself that Sophie, her baby, plus the whole Chris drama was none of my business, I headed back to the hospital. I walked through the corridors feeling strangely vulnerable without my paramedic's scrubs. I went up to find Sophie.

I explained who I was to the nurse at the desk in her ward.

"I'd better check she's happy to see you. She's only been seeing family for the moment." She huffed down the corridor.

Her tone made me feel as though I was a builder who was going back to justify doing a bodge job rather than the person who'd probably saved a life. *And please, please, her baby's life too.*

She emerged from her room. "You can go in for a few minutes."

I slipped in through the open door. "Hello Sophie. I'm Kate. I'm the paramedic who brought you in."

She nodded. "I remember. A little bit anyway. You were really kind. And you saved my baby. And me as well, I think. They're taking me down to her in a minute."

I walked over to the window so she couldn't see the tears in my eyes. "How much did she weigh? Have you named her yet?"

"Three pounds eleven ounces. Chris wanted to call her Lola, so I've gone with that." She swallowed and I thought again how often I saw joy and grief walk hand-in-hand in my job. She cleared her throat and carried on. "She looked so tiny to me, but they said she's doing fine, though they're still having to monitor her breathing and her heart. She had a tube up her nose."

I paused to gather myself before replying, "That looks very frightening, but it's to make sure she's getting all the right nutrients. She's in the best place. You'd be amazed how quickly babies turn a corner. And what about you? How's the leg?"

"OK, I think. I saw the consultant this morning and he

didn't seem too concerned. I had a blood transfusion yesterday and the nurse seemed happy with all the stuff they checked this morning. I don't care about myself. I just want to hold my little girl, make sure she's okay."

In those few words, she summed up the truth of motherhood.

"Do you know how Chris is?"

I shook my head, feeling a total traitor to Sally. "No. Have you seen him?"

"They wheeled me up really late on the first night. They wanted me to rest, but I refused to go to sleep until I saw him. I was only allowed to stay for a few minutes. Do people really get better from brain injuries? They just kept saying they'd have to see if the swelling on the brain went down and then they'd take him off the drugs and wake him up."

"I don't know anything about his condition, but people can recover very well. He'll be getting the best care." Despite the opposing rush of loyalty to Sally, I still hoped Sophie and Chris would get their happy-ever-after. No daughter should be without her dad.

She looked so desolate. "I can't bear it if he never sees Lola. If she never knows her dad."

I took her hand, feeling a little flare of rage that Oskar had chosen not to share his daughter's life when some people never even got the opportunity. "I know it's hard, but try and take it one day at a time. You're going to be a great mum. You'll soon be on the mend. Chris too, hopefully."

She put her head on one side. "Have we met before? I mean, apart from you scraping me off a grass verge? You look really familiar."

I nodded. "I live in Parkview, where you were house-sitting last year? We've met a couple of times at Gisela's parties."

She scanned my face. Realisation dawned that I knew her secrets. The sort of secret we'd all like the time and peace to stage-manage, to repackage with different angles to show ourselves in a much better light.

She looked down. "We didn't mean for this to happen. He was going to tell his wife next week." She met my eyes, though her voice faded away. "Does Sally know about me yet?"

"I've no idea what she knows," I said. I could have voiced my opinion on Sophie having an affair with a married man, let alone being so careless about contraception. I wanted to defend Sally, to mark Sophie's card with my disapproval of her behaviour and Chris's. But I knew what it was like to be judged. I knew how much people in possession of approximately ten per cent of the facts liked to spout about things that were nothing to do with them. And I also knew how identifying the precise ingredients that made the difference between a love affair turning sour and growing into something that could withstand the bashing and buffeting of life was like trying to understand how a drop of vinegar or a pinch of salt changed the whole dynamics of a recipe.

"My job is to save lives, not to judge them. You need to rest. Take care."

"Thank you. I'll do everything I can to keep Lola safe."

I walked away. Because of me, a mother had her daughter. And I desperately hoped the daughter would have the luxury of getting to know her father. More than ever, I believed that one mistake shouldn't mean you were punished forever.

Maybe one day I'd even forgive myself.

CHAPTER 31

Gisela

Thursday 5 April

Photo: Gisela holding baby Ollie while a young Jack smiles broadly.
Caption: Happy birthday, Ollie! Goodness knows where those twenty-two years have gone. Have a wonderful day.
#SoProudOfYou #WorldAtYourFeet

It was late evening when I got back from checking in on Sally, who was strung out and tearful after a frustrating day at the hospital, where she'd missed the consultant and had no clearer idea what was happening with Chris. The strength of her grief made me blunder out with platitudes such as "Modern medicine can work miracles these days." I just managed to clamp my teeth shut before I said, "He'll be fine," on the grounds that it seemed rather arrogant to claim to know more than the neurologist might have been able to tell her.

As I walked in the door, Jack rushed downstairs. My heart clenched with apprehension. I missed the days when I assumed someone stampeding through the house was to report good news: Jack getting an offer accepted on a new site, Hannah passing her driving test, Ollie getting into university, even a celebrity like on Instagram. The thrill that a "like" from

Brooklyn Beckham could bring was now replaced with the fear of the unknown. Fear of what bloody thing would be coming to do me in next. Fear of Jack being arrested. Fear of losing the house. Fear that Hannah would become one of those lost people, never quite finding her way in life, drifting about until bitterness and resentment replaced all her potential to be proud of her place in the world. Worse than all of these was the terror of never seeing Ollie again, never hugging him and feeling all my love for him safe and solid between us. I hadn't even allowed myself to think about what would happen when his son was born. Was it really possible that I could be a grandmother who never knew her grandchild? Who would eventually have the word "estranged" in her vocabulary?

Jack clattered in, waving his phone. "Natalie's had the baby."

"Oh my God! What does it say?"

Jack's face clouded, then he handed it to me.

"Alfie Oliver Webster, born 6 a.m., 5 April 2018. 7.5lbs."

Fifteen hours ago. My son had a baby and I'd found out fifteen hours later.

I looked up at Jack. "Born on Ollie's own birthday."

Jack nodded. "Doesn't seem possible that he's a dad, does it? Seems like yesterday he popped out himself with all that hair. Didn't go for our surname then."

As Jack wiped his eye, I had such a mix of emotions flooding my mind. The surname was the least of it, though it gave my furious dislike of Natalie a gratuitous lick of polish. None of my feelings matched the nebulous idea I'd had about the joyous moment of becoming a grandparent. I'd thought I'd be in my fifties at least, not witnessing my man-child becoming a father. The boy who less than eight months ago was arguing with Hannah over who ate the last Magnum. Did he grip Natalie's hand while she pushed out her baby? Reassure her it would all be okay when she was screaming? Hold his son and whisper that he'd never let him down? I simply couldn't imagine Ollie in that role. Whenever Titch was sick or had diarrhoea, Ollie was the first to start retching. If I hadn't felt so miserable, I'd have laughed, imagining his reaction to the placenta plopping out.

Beyond the shock and disbelief was grief, surging to the top like a swimmer at the end of his breath. Pure unadulterated sadness for all I'd lost, for the fact that Natalie had taken Ollie from me so quickly, so deftly, that I'd scarcely recognised the threat. I'd been stupid enough to think I could compete, that my mother's love given freely over two decades could have the upper hand over a relationship barely a year old. And now my son, *my twenty-two-year-old son*, had his own child and I wasn't part of it. No warning that the baby was on the way. No crack-of-dawn phone call to announce his arrival. Not even our bloody surname.

I wondered if he'd even received the letter I'd put in with his birthday card. I supposed there was an outside chance he'd been at the hospital for more than a day if the labour was long and hadn't yet seen it. I'd apologised, unreservedly, on paper at least. I'd told him I'd been wrong and bigoted. That the thing that mattered to me most in the world was that he was happy, that I'd made my choices, as imperfect and flawed as they were, and, of course, he needed to make his. I told him I'd overlooked the fact he was a grown-up because to me he'd always be my little boy, and maybe he'd understand that now he was going to be a parent himself. And everything I'd said came from a place of love, though it would be hard for him to see that right now. Could we just talk?

I put my arms round Jack. "Not even a photo. Not even a bloody photo of my own grandson."

He rubbed his eyes. "Give it time. Let him realise that parenthood isn't the perfect science he thinks it is."

I made us some tea. We sat immersed in thought, caught in a weird trap of being devastated about something joyful. "I hope Ollie's all right," I said, to myself more than to Jack. "Having a baby's such a shock to the system." I wondered when Natalie was coming out of hospital.

Just as I was contemplating spending the rest of the evening curled up on the sofa feeling so damn sorry for myself that I didn't even have the energy to forage in the cupboard for some emergency chocolate, the phone went. Jack's solicitor, Graham. I recognised him immediately from his ridiculously cheery tone, the thought of charging an exorbitant fee for identifying mitigating circumstances for Jack—Spendthrift wife? Runaway house ambitions? Ideas above his station?—lighting up his life.

My throat went dry. "Jack. Phone for you." No solicitor rang at 9 p.m. in the evening without something important to report.

I could tell by the way Jack moved towards me that he knew who was on the other end of the line.

"Two weeks' time? Will you be there?" He sounded like a young boy off on an overnight school trip for the first time. He nodded a few times, with the half-closed eyes of someone who was struggling to believe this was his real life.

He handed the phone back to me. "Mike has gone to the police. They want to interview me at five-thirty a week on Thursday." He dropped into the armchair. "Jesus. I didn't think Mike would actually go to the police. So much for fifteen years in business together."

I wanted to be sympathetic. I wanted to pat his hand and agree that it was unfair. But it wasn't unfair. Jack had stolen the money. From someone who was a friend. Not directly out of his wallet, but out of the business they ran together. As thieving as running into a bank and emptying a safe. Just not as brave or as worthy of sneaking admiration.

I'd hoped to be that wife who stood by his side, all belt and braces but with better skirts, the sort of wife you saw standing next to disgraced politicians, not simpering, not deluded, but dignified, intent on holding the family together with her head held high, exuding "people make mistakes but we're solid as a rock." Instead I wanted to shout about the stupidity of the man, rage about not seeing my son or my grandson, scream about Hannah and the squandering of her expensive education, which if I'd sent her to the local school would have saved us way more than fifty thousand, with change to spare for some bloody marvellous holidays. I was searching for some words of comfort, for something that could make it better, when Hannah appeared waving her iPad.

"I'm an auntie! Did you see the photos Ollie posted on Instagram?"

I rushed over to look. I pushed away the insulting irony of seeing my grandson for the first time on Instagram. A gorgeous little bundle in a soft blue sleepsuit, sleeping with his arms stretched out above his head, defences down. Ollie cradling him, pride written all over him. I studied the picture of Natalie, smiling but exhausted.

My whole body ached with the desire to reach into the picture and touch that soft skin, feel the downy hair on his head, breathe in that newborn smell, the scent of family, of the next generation, of inexplicable, inescapable love. A peculiar sense of loss lodged in my heart, as though I was grieving for someone I hadn't yet lost.

If I had to beg to see him, then that is what I would do.

In the meantime, I had a husband to keep out of prison.

CHAPTER 32

Sally

Friday 6 April

I intended to hold off phoning Mum and Dad until I could say the words, "Chris has had an accident" without bursting into tears. I'd spent the last couple of days in and out of the hospital, the time ticking past in long boring stretches while I watched Chris sleep, wondering what would be left of him when he came round. I'd managed one snatched conversation with the consultant on Wednesday, who had obviously taken the "not offering false hope" to the extreme, delivering matter-of-fact details about the CT scan showing swelling on the brain without helping me understand how serious it was.

"Is it possible he could be completely okay?" I'd asked.

He'd shrugged. "Possible, yes."

When I'd tried to quiz the nurses, they'd encouraged me to be patient and to rest assured that they were doing everything they could.

By Thursday evening, I still couldn't get any answers definite enough to satisfy me. I wasn't sure I was ever going to get through a phone call to my parents without blubbing, so I'd bitten the bullet, sobbing out my misery to my mum, who for once did more listening than volunteering opinions. They'd offered to come down, but I'd refused, saying I'd keep them informed and perhaps they could visit in a week or two when I had a better idea of what was happening. My mother's conspiracy theories would be an added stress I wasn't yet ready to manage. By midday on Friday, just as I was leaving to go to the hospital, she turned up with Dad, a big jar of Nescafe—"I knew you'd have one of those machines, and I don't think the coffee's anywhere near as good"—and twenty-four Tunnock's teacakes—"You need sugar for the shock. Your dad wondered whether the Lotus's brakes failed? Those sports cars are all very well until the weather's not good."

I tried to explain that the truck in front hadn't indicated. Mum nodded knowledgably and went into a long story about how a bus had clipped the corner of the café down the street from her. There was no relevance, except both vehicles in question had four wheels. I began to wish I'd never told them.

She and Dad pottered about the house, remarking on the built-in shelving in the shower—"How lovely not to be tripping over the shampoo"—the electric garage door—"Thank God we haven't got one of those. I'd be afraid it would chop the car in half"—the microwave hidden in a cupboard—"You'd never know it was there, would you?"

Mum was very keen to come to the hospital, saying in a rare moment of self-awareness, "I can jabber on and give you a rest from thinking of things to say." I told her that they'd only let in one person at a time on the off-chance that despite being unconscious he could hear us speaking and find out what my mother really thought of him.

I drove to the hospital, wondering how this had become my life. A week ago, I'd been imagining our reunion at the Ginger Hen. How it would all feel new and exciting. How I was sure Chris would have booked a room upstairs, our favourite with the tiled fireplace and four-poster bed. And now I didn't know whether he'd ever recover enough to lead a normal life.

I was buzzed through the double doors, already feeling that sense of familiarity after just three days. As always, there was a hive of activity, with the nurses wheeling monitors, writing on charts, calming down anxious relatives. On the ward, I pushed open the curtain to Chris's cubicle. There was a woman already in there, holding Chris's hand, her head leaning on his arm, murmuring to him. I wondered if she was a volunteer visitor, someone the hospital organised to keep people in an unconscious state company. Before I could finish the thought, her head shot up.

Her face was bruised and now I looked, she was in a wheelchair. The woman we'd seen when I'd first arrived at the hospital with Gisela. "Is it Sophie? The vet?"

She nodded, her eyes wide. She let go of Chris's hand.

"Sorry, I don't understand... what are you doing here?" I reminded myself to keep my voice down.

Her voice was little more than a whisper, but there was a definite determination in her tone. "I was involved in the same accident as Chris."

"Were you in the same car? Gisela said she'd seen on Twitter there'd been someone else in the car, but the police didn't mention it so I thought she'd got it wrong."

She looked surprised, as though I hadn't asked the question she was expecting.

There was a beat of silence when we stared at each other, that tiny moment before realisation dawned. Her face changed from watchful to defensive.

My hand flew to my face. "Oh my God. It's you. You're having an affair with him. That's why you were in his car."

Her eyes filled. "I'm sorry. We didn't mean it to happen."

"How long? How bloody long? Was he going to leave me? Was anyone actually ever going to tell me?"

"He didn't want to hurt you. We wanted to be sure. It was so complicated because..." She swallowed, her whole face crumpling. Her voice trailed off, leaving a space for my anger to fill the gap.

"He didn't want to hurt me? Well, it didn't bloody look like it! What an idiot I was. Hanging on in there, giving him space to make up his mind. Believing his lies that he wasn't seeing anyone else. Did he tell you we had sex a few weeks ago? Did he? Did he say we were going out for dinner next week?" Silence. "No. I bet he bloody didn't."

Before I could say any more, a nurse came bursting through the curtains.

"What's going on? This is the intensive care unit. You can't shout in here. I'm sorry, I'm going to have to ask you to step outside until you calm down."

I shrugged her off. "I'm just going, don't worry. I'll leave my husband's floozy to it."

I marched out, sobbing in the distressed way that had the people coming into the ICU standing to the side respectfully as though I'd just had the bad news none of us wanted to hear. It wasn't until I got to the lift that I remembered a snatch of conversation as the porter wheeled her past us on the first night. Something about "just long enough to tell him he's a dad." And Gisela had showed me that weird tweet about the person who was praying for the pregnant wife. I wracked my brains about whether Sophie looked as though she was expecting a baby. I didn't recall seeing a bump. Had she already had the baby? I had to know.

I turned on my heel and buzzed to get back through the ICU doors.

This time a nurse met me at the door. "Sorry, you can't go in there now. He needs to rest."

With great effort, I managed to get the words out. "Has she had a baby? Has she had my husband's baby?"

The nurse kept her face completely neutral. She reminded me of those magnetic drawing games I had as a child where you could wipe the screen clean with a slide of a button. "I'm sorry. I can't discuss other patients with you." But the shift in her tone from her earlier irritation to kindness scared me. Could it be true? Could it be that Chris had had the baby I'd longed for with someone else? I couldn't compute that. Why her and not me, if so?

"Please tell me. Please put me out of my misery. This is cruel. Really cruel."

She took my arm. "The best thing you can do is go home and rest. Come back after the weekend." There was a finality in her words.

There was no fight left in me and I allowed myself to be propelled towards the exit. I blundered out, tears blinding me. I drove straight to Gisela's to ask her what she remembered of the porter's conversation, hammering on her door with an urgency that frightened us both.

She hauled me inside, waving at Jack to disappear, and sat me down at her kitchen table while I burbled out a confused story that, to her credit, she appeared to have no difficulty following, hardly blinking at the news that Chris had been having an affair with Sophie. On another occasion I might have found the energy to be insulted that what was astonishing to me came as no surprise to her.

She couldn't help me with what I really needed to know— the details of the porter's conversation with Sophie.

"I didn't really hear any of it. I didn't pay any attention until you pointed her out to me. Is it even possible, though? I think they only met for the first time in July."

We went backwards and forwards, with none of the answers fitting what either of us knew of the world. Maybe that first night at the hospital she was on her way back from telling him she was pregnant, that he was going to become a dad? But how would the idiot who took a photo of her know that she was pregnant? And if she'd had the baby, they must have got together about a week after they first met, when Chris and I hadn't even started discussing having a family.

In the end, I couldn't think anymore. Couldn't separate what I knew from what I imagined. Eventually, Hannah came in from college, Jack started making noises about what they were doing for dinner and despite Gisela's protestations that I wasn't holding anything up, I went back home to face my mum and dad, wondering how some people had such simple, straightforward lives.

CHAPTER 33

Sally

Monday 9 April

I spent the weekend holed up in bed, sleeping for hours at a stretch. Every time I woke, Mum was either whispering with Dad outside my bedroom door about calling the doctor or peering in to see if I wanted a poached egg to keep my energy up. I felt as though I had flu. Everything ached. I kept telling myself I needed to get up, make my way to the hospital, find some answers, but the sheer effort of swinging my legs over the side of the bed made me weak and shivery. I didn't have the strength to do battle. And if Chris hadn't been brought out of sedation, there were no answers to get. But by Monday, the desire to know the truth forced me out of my pit.

Dad offered to come with me. I couldn't face anyone witnessing my humiliation if it turned out to be true.

"Thanks, Dad. I think this is something I have to do on my own."

He'd obviously given Mum a good talking-to about not badmouthing Chris. With great restraint, she managed to say, "You haven't heard his side of the story yet, love, so don't be jumping to conclusions."

I parked the car at the hospital and checked my lipstick. Maybe I'd stand more chance of finding out something if their fingers weren't hovering over the call-security button.

Before I went in, I gave myself a stern talking-to. There'd be no shouting today. I'd be the calm rational woman whom everyone would want to help.

As luck would have it, I hadn't come across the nurse who buzzed me in before and she was busy on the phone.

I walked straight into Chris's ward, steeling myself to see Sophie holding his hand, where I should have been. But his bed was empty and, as far as I could see, none of his stuff was there.

I ran out into the corridor to the nurse's station. Eventually, the nurse finished her phone call. "I've come to visit Chris Gastrell, but he's not in his bed." I could hear the tremor rippling through my words. "Have they taken him for a scan?"

The nurse looked puzzled. "Chris Gastrell? I don't think he's on this unit anymore."

"He was on Friday. He was sedated, the one who came in after a car accident."

She frowned. "You are?"

"His wife. Sally Gastrell?"

Her eyebrows shot up. "Sorry. I've just come back from holiday today. Let me go and check."

She flurried off down the ward, gesturing to another nurse, who backed into what looked like a cupboard. And there they stayed for several minutes, while I didn't know whether or not my husband was on a trolley heading to the mortuary.

The nurse I'd seen before came scuttling down the corridor. "He's been moved to the high dependency unit. They've brought him out of sedation. They'll be able to tell you more down there."

Breath flowed back into my body with the relief that he was still alive.

She gave me directions and failed to disguise her happiness that my dirty laundry was going to be washed elsewhere.

I found my way to his bed on a small four-cubicle ward. He was sitting up in bed, unshaven and grey.

"Oh my God. You're awake. Are you all right? When did you

come round?" There were so many questions I wanted to ask, but tears were clogging my throat, though I'd have been hard pressed to identify whether sadness or anger had the upper hand.

Chris looked at me as though I was the last person he expected to see. "Friday afternoon." His tone was flat and weary. So different from the man whose voice usually carried such authority.

A nurse bustled past and put her hand on Chris's shoulder. "Are you up to visitors now? You might need to rest."

I burst in with, "He can sleep. I'll just sit with him."

The nurse had an odd expression on her face. "It can be very tiring when people first come out of sedation. Sometimes they prefer to be on their own."

Now I was here with the answers tantalisingly within reach, I wasn't going to let this nurse be a gatekeeper. "I won't stay long."

Eventually Chris said, "I'll be all right."

The nurse adjusted his pillows and pulled the curtains round us. "Just a few minutes then."

I sat myself in the armchair, torn between hugging and hitting him. "How are you? You frightened me there. God, when I got up to the intensive care unit and saw your empty bed, I nearly keeled over." I knew I was babbling.

Chris put his hand up. "Sal, I need to tell you something. There was another woman in the car accident with me. I think you met her the other day."

I nodded. "I recognised her. I guess she was the 'distraction.'"

He looked up as though he was making a huge effort to pull up his eyelids. "I was going to tell you next week. She was pregnant and the accident made her go into labour, eleven weeks early."

"Was the baby yours?" I felt my brain pushing outwards, repelling the information he was telling me, recognising that eleven weeks early might be the tiny piece of jigsaw that obliterated all hope.

He nodded.

The despair that I'd driven back into its box through sheer dint of will was spreading through me again, thick muddy sludge washing away the future I'd been clinging onto.

I was hissing, desperate not to get ejected before I dug out the truth. "No. You didn't want children! That was the whole point."

He sighed and I heard the effort he was making to speak, his voice rasping out, "We didn't plan it. I'm sorry."

I should come back later, but I couldn't. I couldn't leave without knowing. And I shouldn't be haranguing the man who, a few days ago, I thought might die.

I breathed out, folding my lips together, feeling the scaffolding of my face threatening to dissolve. It seemed another lifetime ago that I'd seen the mother of his child being wheeled past me, taking everything from me, commandeering the life I craved and I'd just watched her go, oblivious. "Was the baby all right?"

And there it was, all I needed to know, the instant softening of his face, the catch in the voice of the man whose first filter when booking a holiday online was always "adults only."

"She's hanging on in there. She needs help to breathe at the moment and they're worried about infection, but she's a fighter." Ten years of marriage had taught me to recognise the tightness in Chris's voice when he was trying not to cry.

A daughter. The little girl I'd imagined. Her tiny wellies next to mine in our hallway. Her best drawing on our fridge. Ladybird slippers by her bed.

I never knew heartbreak was a physical feeling before. I grappled to protect myself. I'd been braced for him leaving me. But not for this. Never once for this.

I stayed silent for a moment, studying the pride and fear in his face and sifting through my own competing strands of thought, the mix of hurt, humanity and, of course, love for him, that bloody love thing that wouldn't just keel over and die on command, despite the rage consuming my body. I blurted out the first thing that came into my head.

"It won't make me feel better if she doesn't make it."

I saw, should have known, that Chris wouldn't have even acknowledged the possibility to himself, let alone allowed anyone else to say it, that he would have focused firmly on the positives. "Don't even talk like that."

"Sorry, I didn't mean…I meant I hope she's fine. She will be fine, I'm sure she will."

"We don't know yet."

I stopped talking, recognising I was just giving out platitudes. I actually had no idea about premature babies, no barometer for understanding what might happen.

Chris ran his hand over his face. "I would have done anything for this not to have happened."

I was trying to trap the sobs in my chest, but they were stronger than me.

I swiped at my tears. "It's such a shock. Was it me you didn't want? Or a baby with me?"

He closed his eyes for a moment and I nearly got up to leave, feeling guilty about putting him under interrogation when he'd taken such a hammering. But he looked at me with a real purpose as though he'd decided to make sure there was no room for misunderstanding.

"I loved you, Sally." Of those fourteen letters, the "d" stood out like an out-of-tune trumpet in the middle of a violin solo. It landed deep in my stomach. His voice was slow and deliberate as though he was having to use every bit of energy to put his words in the right order. "I really did love you. But I never wanted a child with you. Never felt as though the family dynamic could work for us. I can't explain why. Maybe we met too young and I was used to having you all to myself. Whenever I tried to imagine the future, I could only see us. Never us with children."

"And you could with her?" I swallowed, hearing the crackling in my ears.

"I didn't plan it. I promise I didn't go looking for it."

"How long? How long after we moved into the house? After Gisela's barbecue in July? Before?"

"It doesn't matter now."

"Perhaps not to you, but I'd like to know when it all started to go wrong. When you gave up on us. Or when you decided not to involve me in the fact that you'd met someone else?"

Chris was screwing up his eyes as though thinking was a physical effort. "I kept bumping into her at the gym after we'd met at Jack's first party, the barbecue."

And there was me, all encouraging, thinking the exercise would make Chris easier to live with, less pernickety if he was filling himself with endorphins.

"We were still having sex in February. You came back that night. I thought you might come back permanently."

"I was so confused. I didn't want to leave you just because Sophie had got pregnant. I still had feelings for you."

He had the grace to look ashamed that his feelings weren't enough to stop him having the affair in the first place.

"And now?" Those two words stuck in my throat, rushing out on a moan of despondency.

"A baby changes everything, Sally. I'm sorry."

The question I knew I shouldn't ask burrowed its way out, searing my throat with the bile and bitterness attached to the death of a dream. "So if I'd got pregnant by accident, you'd have stayed with me?"

"It wasn't really like that."

And suddenly I was too, too weary to know how it was. Too full up with the details I already knew. Too heartbroken to bear anything else, because nothing would ever hurt me more than "I never wanted a child with you" when I could see already how much he loved his daughter.

I stood up as the nurse came to check on him. "Sorry to interrupt, but he really should rest now."

"Don't worry. I'm going." I turned back to Chris. "I don't know what to say to you. I hope it's all worth it. I really do."

I stumbled along the corridor, trying to absorb the fact that Chris had become a dad. To someone else's baby. When I'd begged him, pleaded with him, to turn us from a couple into a family. I felt as though I'd been drinking on an empty stomach, reaching that tipping point where I wasn't drunk but thoughts were taking a bit longer to process.

I turned left, past a whole swathe of outpatient departments—oncology, X-rays, ultrasound—places where a waggle of the finger of fate could drop your life off a cliff. I headed past another building on the way to the car park. The maternity unit, where several heavily pregnant women were puffing away outside. It took me all of my restraint not to run up to them and snatch the fags out of their fingers, shouting, "Look at me! Look at me! I'd give anything to have a baby! And you, you're just taking it for granted. Don't you care that you're harming your baby?" In fact, for one moment, I could feel the muscles in my legs contracting, ready to push me forward. I swallowed, contenting myself with giving them a dirty look.

Was Sophie in there? Breathing in Chris's daughter and revelling in her good fortune? Her face pressed against soft hair? Staring in wonder at tiny toes? His words, "I just don't see myself as a father. I'm too selfish. I love my life the way it is," were looping round and round my brain.

I took a shortcut through the east wing of the hospital, past the little M&S store and café housing a few lacerated relatives, their faces a hospital grey like some kind of poor man's Farrow & Ball, carrying the strain of long weeks on the roller coaster of dashed hopes and disappointment. By the time I reached the car, my legs were leaden with the thick wet sand of misery. And there it was. The knowledge I could no longer deny. The maths was simple: if the baby was eleven weeks early, by September, a couple of months after we'd moved into Parkview, another woman was pregnant with the baby I longed for, that Chris refused point-blank to let me have.

I collapsed into the car, sitting with my knees tucked under my chin, every last bit of me curling around the agony inside, the empty realisation Chris had probably never lived in the company flat, never even boarded a train to King's Cross, let alone a plane to the U.S. every other week. Probably just popped in to see me on the evenings Sophie was away on a course. Phoned me from the car on his way home from work. Texted me when she'd gone to the gym.

I drove home, wondering why he hadn't told me the truth and ended our marriage rather than throwing me little scraps of hope, just enough to keep me hanging on, while he worked out, what? Whether she was going to keep the baby? Whether they had a future or were simply friends with benefits and inadequate contraception?

I couldn't face Mum and Dad yet. I stopped at the top of the road, a good distance from my house and texted Gisela: "*Could I come round for a minute?*"

No reply. I couldn't bring myself to get out of the car. Once I'd told Mum, it would be real. Far too real. I rested my head on the steering wheel and stayed there for well over an hour. Every time I geared myself up to go home, the thought of saying the words "Chris has had a baby daughter" set me off crying again.

There was a knock on the window. I looked up, expecting it to be some territorial neighbour moaning at me for parking in front of their house. It was Kate, on her way home from the corner shop.

I opened the door slightly.

"Sally? Are you all right?"

"No, not really."

"You're going to get cold sitting out here. Would you like to come in for a coffee?"

I allowed her to lead me up the road. I stood out of sight while she unlocked her front door. She checked my parents weren't looking out of the window at my house and beckoned me in.

Over several hot drinks and a whole packet of ginger nuts,

I told her my story, tears I hadn't the energy to be ashamed of rolling down my face until the neck of my jumper was soaking.

She kept shaking her head. "You poor thing. What a horrible shock. And there was me envying you your freedom and all your travelling, your exciting job. I just assumed—wrongly, obviously—that you never wanted children."

"Why would you think anything else? I'd tell anyone who listened I loved being child-free, but in all honesty I couldn't bear people asking. I hated people for not realising how jealous I was. I couldn't listen to women who had kids, with all their stories of how their children didn't eat their broccoli or crept into their bed at four in the morning. I just felt jealous all the time, but not normal 'that would be lovely, I'd like what you've got' jealous like you do when someone has a new car or a nice kitchen. Sick jealous, like I never wanted to speak to them or see them again. As though them having what I wanted made it even less likely that I'd have a child eventually." Admitting the truth felt like finally managing to pick out a splinter that had been sitting under my skin for years, uncomfortable when pressed, always threatening to flare up and fester into something bigger.

"It must have been hard keeping all that to yourself, though. I didn't realise he'd actually left. I was just in awe of your jet-setting lifestyle."

"I did tell my parents, but they think we're being silly and if we grew a few tomato plants together and started playing bridge we'd be fine." I tried to laugh, but it turned into a choke of despair.

At six o'clock, when I was so tired I thought I might fall asleep mid-sentence, Daisy came bursting in. She waved hello, then said, "Guess what? Hannah's an auntie! Ollie's girlfriend has had her baby. Can I buy him a present? It's a little boy."

Kate smiled at her. "That's great news. Yes, start thinking what we could send him. Now, I'm just sorting something out with Sally so give me a few minutes and then I'll get dinner ready."

"Isn't it ready yet?"

Kate's face was a mask of apology as Daisy stomped up the stairs.

I shrugged. "People have babies all the time, Kate. I just have to get used to it. I'd better go. Thank you. Thank you for listening to me." I got to my feet. "When Gisela and I came running over to you the other night, you already knew Chris had a girlfriend, didn't you?"

Kate nodded. "I'm sorry I couldn't prepare you. We can't talk about patients at all. I'd lose my job."

"I probably wouldn't have believed you anyway. I'm still struggling to get my head around it now. I'm sorry about lying to you and Gisela about where he was." I still felt stunned as though extraordinary things didn't happen to ordinary people like us. That drama like this only came to people who sought it out, who flirted, drank and had secret mobiles at the ready, primed for opportunities and affairs.

Kate patted my arm. "Sometimes it's very hard to be totally honest." A shadow flickered over her face and I waited. There was definitely more to her than met the eye. Then she leapt up. "Come over any time you want to let off steam."

I crossed over the road to my house, glancing into Gisela's sitting room as I walked past. A lovely husband, two children and now a grandson.

I wished I had her life.

CHAPTER 34

Gisela

Thursday 19 April

While Jack showered and shaved to go to the police station, I went downstairs. Me sitting there with a face with "We're doomed" written all over it wasn't going to add value. I knew he'd go through the ritual of picking out the dice cufflinks he wore when he needed something to go well. I wasn't sure if I could raise the smile to acknowledge it while tremors of panic were coursing through my stomach. How would I go to bed every night without Jack? How would I even begin to get to sleep imagining his face pressed up against the wall in a little cell, all that clanging and shouting in the background? I'd been dashing through life, sorting out the kids, assuming Jack would be there to take up where we left off twenty-two years ago when the heavy lifting of child-rearing was done.

Now he might not be.

All those years waiting for me to ask him what *he* wanted for dinner instead of having to go along with the chilli con carne without the kidney beans (Hannah) and the risotto without the garlic (Ollie). And gone along with it he had, with everything, starting conversations about work and money, which never really got going because Hannah would have some drama about not being able to find her purple bra or Ollie would call from university and I'd keep him on the phone as long as possible, wanting to know all about his studies, his friends, his love life—always the shortest discussion.

"Have you met anyone nice?"

"I've met loads of nice people."

"You know what I mean."

"Early days, Mum, early days for a babe magnet to be settling down."

I'd laughed, scarcely noticing that Jack had stopped waiting for me to finish on the phone and taken himself off to his office, staying up there till late into the evening before I shouted up, "Are you actually joining us this evening or shall we start dinner without you?"

If only I'd listened. If only I'd *heard*.

I tried to blot out my fear by looking at Natalie's Facebook feed for information via Hannah's profile. For once, I was thankful that Hannah could never sit near any piece of technology without logging into something. More often than not, she was utterly careless about logging out. Now I was using it to my advantage to stalk my own grandson.

My need to understand what was happening with Ollie and his son far outweighed the guilt I felt about snooping. I scrolled down Natalie's feed. Alfie in the bath, Alfie asleep on Ollie's chest, Alfie in the cot, his tiny little Babygros flapping like bunting on the line. I studied the one of Ollie holding Alfie right next to his face. The baby was unmistakably his. The line of his mouth, the arch of his eyebrows. I sat back to stop my tears dripping into the keyboard as I read the comments underneath.

"So gorgeous, hun! Lovely to see your little family."

"Can't wait to come over and meet the bubba!"

"Will pop in on Weds afternoon. Are you coming to the NCT meeting this week?"

I was really beginning to understand the grandparents who went to court to fight for access rights to their grandchildren. All of these people, half of them acquaintances, casually dropping in to meet my grandson, while I didn't even know whether they'd received the little dungarees I'd sent—I scrutinised the washing line photo but couldn't see them. I forced away the idea of all these strangers I'd never heard of touching his tiny toes, watching those chubby little legs kick up and down. I'd kept Ollie's old train set for this day, his tiny toy cars, the Micro Machines he used to line up on the floor, his cheek pressed on the carpet, lost for hours in his own little world. I'd refused to let Jack throw them out when we were clearing the attic to move here.

Scroll, scroll, scroll. I peered into the background of the rooms. Obviously Natalie had been leaving the tidying up to Ollie, judging by the sweatshirts cluttering the sofa and the amount of mugs I could see on the table. She looked shattered. I remembered that sheer exhaustion of nursing a baby through the night, scared to go to sleep in case I had to rouse myself five minutes after I'd dropped off. That bone-weary malaise of wondering whether I'd ever feel normal again, ever be able to have a glass of wine without collapsing into a slumber after two sips. I hoped Ollie was helping. I wasn't sure he understood what hormones could do to a woman, though he'd lived with me for long enough.

Whatever Jack said, I'd have to drive to Bristol and camp outside their door until they let me in.

I downloaded all the photos, desperate to post the one of Alfie next to a baby photo of Ollie. He was definitely an Anderson, regardless of which surname he'd been given. But I couldn't risk Natalie finding out I'd somehow been looking at her page because it was my only way of seeing what was going on as Ollie had obviously unfriended me or blocked me somehow. I carried on flicking through my feed, looking at the pictures people had posted of their holidays. I wished people with ugly feet wouldn't share photos of them poking off the edge of a sunlounger. Everyone I knew seemed to be somewhere with an infinity pool, palm trees or a bloody cocktail—and found it necessary to show us their stubby toes.

Jack came in. "Can you just sort out my collar at the back?"

I slammed down the laptop lid, feeling guilty for not sitting upstairs in the bedroom with him.

He looked so drawn and nervous, I leapt to my feet.

"You look like an upstanding pillar of society. You'll be fine, love. Just tell the truth. Whatever it is, we'll get through it."

Jack pulled me to him. "Thank God for you, Zell. I wish I'd been a better husband. I've let you down."

He had no idea how much I wished I'd been an economy wife.

"Are you sure you don't want me to come to the police station with you?"

"No. I want you completely out of this. I don't want there to be any suspicion that you knew anything about it. Graham's picking me up."

"I don't think driving my husband to the police station makes me look guilty," I said, pressing my cheek against his, still trying to get my head round the fact Jack had sat down one day to work out a way to siphon a chunk of money into a personal account every time a caravan was sold.

Jack held me at arm's length and looked right into my eyes. "I don't know if I'll go to prison." His voice started to catch, but he took a deep breath. "Just promise me you'll wait for me. That's all I ask. I know I'll get through it if you don't leave me."

"I won't leave you. I won't." I hugged him to me, wondering how that floppy-haired student who hitched home to see me, saving his train fares to take me out for dinner, had become this forty-four-year-old facing a prison sentence.

I'd manage. I'd have to, even if I couldn't quite crush the thought that a jailbird grandfather wouldn't increase my chances of Natalie coming round to the idea of us being ideal grandparents. Before those unhelpful thoughts reached the air, Jack's solicitor was at the door.

"Right, good luck. Ring me as soon as you get out."

I glanced at Graham. "They won't keep him in overnight, will they?"

"Very unlikely. He's just helping them with their inquiries at the moment."

My lip threatened to wobble. "See you later. Love you."

The words fell away.

I watched the car move away, marvelling at the stealth with which real life creeps up, nibbling away year by year at everything that is carefree and leaving weights in its place. Feathers at first, a sprinkling of responsibility, so light that it seems a privilege. A flat of our own, an exciting business opportunity, an independence way ahead of our peers. And with it, ambitions for more, bigger, better—the acceptance of longer hours, harder work, less time to ourselves—until we were pinned down by shoulds, by ought-tos, by must-haves, selling off bits of our souls without even noticing.

Where was she now, that girl with beaded ankle bracelets, who'd lie with Jack, whispering her dreams and starspotting all night at the beach and go straight to work, yawning as she typed invoices at her desk but unable to resist smiling at a remembered caress, a promise, a plan for the future?

Here she was. Sitting at the bespoke oak table, jealous of every person who posted about their fantastic lives on Facebook, estranged from the son who'd got a Rolex for his eighteenth, barely communicating with the daughter who'd gone to a school where they played lacrosse, waiting for her Financial Director husband to find out whether he was going to jail.

Funny how life turns out.

Photo: Daffodils, wood anemones, hellebores.
   Caption: First spring in our new house and everything's coming up roses! (Boom, boom!)
   #LoveMyGarden

CHAPTER 35

Kate

Monday 14 May

God knows why I'd found Sally so up her own backside. Since the whole Chris thing had come out, I felt guilty for how I'd judged her. I should know better than anyone that what people showed to the world might be a big smokescreen hiding all sorts of fears and insecurities. For the first time in forever, I had a regular visitor to my house. I'd even met her mum and dad a couple of times. Her mum was a hoot, relentlessly finding the upside to Sally's situation: "He always did cut the grass far too short. It encourages weeds, you know. Our grass doesn't have any moss or dandelions. You wait and see what your lawn looks like next summer when Dad's worked his magic."

I'd forgotten how lovely it was to have a friend with whom I could relax, sit in silence or watch TV without feeling the need to perform. She always came armed with excellent wine and I'd drunk more in the last month and a half than in the whole of the preceding year. In typical British fashion, it was the oil that greased the path to Sally's secrets. The more she drank, the more she repeated how she never felt good enough as a child, that she'd spent her whole life waiting to fail and now she had.

"Mum and Dad thought I was a genius because I did well at school, but that's just because I worked so bloody hard." She'd kept shaking her head. "Everyone will be talking about me. The whole road probably saw him coming in and out, fetching his stuff when he knew I was away for work. He was actually living with his pregnant girlfriend when I had convinced myself he was about to come home and we'd all live happily ever after." After the second bottle, she'd simply say, "I must be stupid, really, really stupid."

Today I'd been especially glad of Sally's company because I was on tenterhooks waiting to see how Daisy's psychology AS level retake had gone. She should have been home about five, but she'd texted to say she was going to "chill" at Hannah's for the evening. I didn't argue. I still felt the need to make amends for spoiling her focus last year by arranging to move the day after she finished her exams.

My text asking how she'd got on had gone unanswered. I tried not to rush into the hallway the minute I heard the door open at nine o'clock, but I couldn't help it.

"How did it go?"

"Don't know really."

I thought I might implode with frustration. I'd spent about half a month's wages on every highlighter, flash card, special sparkly pen, particular gel pen, every flipping writing implement a person could possibly need for any situation. I'd tested her until I could have explained every detail of the amygdala myself. I'd given her omega supplements, cooked loads of fish and tried to work shifts that allowed me to get home to ensure she went to bed at a decent time. My reward for all that was a "Don't know really."

I struggled to control my impatience. "Could you answer all the questions?"

"Sort of. It's not really like that," she said, shaking her head as though I was a bit too limited in brainpower to grasp what an A level might entail.

She pushed past me into the living room. "Oh, hello, Sally."

Sally waved, a little uncoordinated as she'd drunk most of

the first bottle of wine and had insisted on uncorking a second. "Hello. Sorry. Sorry. I'll be going soon. How did you get on?"

Blow me, if she didn't start discussing the paper question by question with Sally, asking her if she thought that "episodic memory" was correct. If I ever dared to suggest an answer on the rare occasion I was allowed to know what was in the holy sanctity of any A level paper, Daisy would pretend to listen before saying, "That's not what I put."

Sally was struggling to connect the wine glass to her lips but was still making a great effort to chat to Daisy.

"What are you revising tonight?"

"Personality disorders."

Sally barked out a short sharp laugh. "You could do a study of me—is there a term for someone who is completely deluded and turns out to be lying to themselves and everyone else about the life they are living?"

I winced, wanting to protect Daisy from the reality of what had happened to Sally. She had a bad enough view of relationships as it was.

Daisy tucked her hair behind her ears. "Not exactly. There is a thing called Dissociative Identity Disorder when people have more than one identity, sort of multiple personalities, almost like different people are in charge of you at different times." She glared at me.

Sally screwed up her eyes. Her face was a picture of concentration. "I've read about that. I don't think that was me, though. I think I was just stupid."

Daisy was looking puzzled and irritated.

Sally slurred on. "Doesn't that thing you said happen when people have suffered from some sort of terrible experience that they can't cope with?"

Daisy nodded, raising her eyebrows at me. "It's more common than you think."

Goad, goad, goad.

I wanted to shout at her that I didn't have a personality disorder, that what I'd done wasn't because I was ill, it was because I didn't have a choice. And it wasn't so much having multiple personalities as having to ditch the old one and adopt an entirely different one to protect us all. How could it be that I was permanently in the wrong, when I was trying so hard to make it right?

I wondered if Daisy remembered cowering behind me on the stairs when she was about six, while I tried to jam the front door shut in the middle of the night. I'd attempted to calm Becky down, nearly let her in, the old habits of comfort and care refusing to die. She went for me, shouting, screaming and scratching, with Daisy whimpering in fear behind me.

And all of that history Becky and I had shared as kids, the giggling sleepovers, the copying each other's maths homework, running in and out of each other's houses, knowing where to find the orange squash, the biscuits, even the spare loo roll, being able to bounce from one topic to another without having to fill in what went before counted for nothing.

Then the letters started, the silent phone calls, Daisy casually announcing that she'd seen Becky walk past her school. Oskar was long gone and I was too scared to let Daisy play in the back garden on her own, frightened to let her go to other people's houses in case she somehow disappeared. We'd moved to Leeds in the end, but she'd found us eventually.

Sally was looking from Daisy to me, as though her fuddled brain was attempting to make sense of all the little innuendos and barbs Daisy was firing my way.

Daisy picked up her bag, her face set as though she'd proved a point to an audience that didn't even know there was a point to prove. "Anyway, I must go and revise. More psychology tomorrow."

Sally stood up. "I must go home. Sorry to intrude on your family time."

I had to suppress a snort at that; Daisy sulking in one room replying to me in monosyllabic mutters wasn't the happy-clappy family time Sally imagined.

"I know it doesn't feel like it now, but good things will come from this. You just can't see the shape of them yet," I said.

Her shoulders sagged. "I hope you're right."

"I know I'm right."

The worst thing had happened to me and I'd survived.

She didn't need to know how hard it would be.

CHAPTER 36

Sally

Thursday 17 May

For a few weeks after the accident, I still nurtured a hope I couldn't have admitted to anyone that Chris might come back to me. In ridiculous moments of extreme optimism—usually after a glass or four of wine—I thought I might end up with my baby after all, now he'd set a precedent. I could get past the affair. I'd probably be able to accept his daughter being part of our lives, especially if I had my own child. I thought back to the last time, three months ago, when he'd stayed the night, when we'd made love so tenderly I'd felt as though it would be criminal to toss everything we had aside, convinced he felt it too. But the truth was, Sophie was already pregnant. Five and a half months pregnant. Had he been thinking of coming back? Had she been considering a termination at that late stage? Or had he just been bloody bet hedging?

If I'd heard a woman trying to justify what Chris had done, even looking like she might think about giving him a second chance, I'd have shaken her. "Stop fooling yourself. Look at it for what it is. You're ridiculous!"

As much as my brain was urging me to cauterise everything capable of carrying any feeling towards Chris, my heart was still sitting on the sidelines, like the girl in her best dress at the school prom, hoping this would be the day he realised she was the one.

In reality, the end of our marriage had all the oomph of a helium-filled balloon shoved in a cupboard after a milestone birthday and discovered a fortnight later. About a month after I'd seen him at the hospital, he'd texted, asking me to pack up his clothes, his books and Bose speakers and he'd send a van from work to fetch them in a few weeks' time. Obviously far too busy to come and sort his stuff out himself. Probably purée-ing broccoli or ordering every Bugaboo accessory known to man. Another outlet for his love affair with a label. I'd eventually crawled and hauled myself to the moral high ground and phoned him. I thought I should at least know whether my not-yet-ex-husband had recovered properly from a serious accident. He told me he was on the mend, his voice softening as he said, "We all are." I covered my hurt at the "we" by asking him what he wanted to do about dividing up the rest of our belongings.

"I don't need anything else from the house. I'm streamlining my life." "Streamlining" from the man who was always brows-ing for the next big thing. I should have been grateful, but to my ears, it smacked of someone who was so intoxicated by love and life that material possessions had become trivial fripperies that only his shallow first wife had bothered herself about.

That was two weeks ago and I kept walking past his ward-robe, terrified to open it in case the impulse to get the garden shears to the suits and shirts he hadn't taken when he first left got the better of me. It didn't matter how often I repeated, "Dig-nity, Sally, dignity," to myself, the urge to screw every shirt into a tiny ball and deliver them shredded in a bin bag seemed to grow stronger as the pick-up day approached.

When I confided in Kate, she clapped her hands together. "The sooner you get rid of his stuff, the better you'll feel. Come on, I'll help you." I tuned in the radio to some country and west-ern station—all those songs about cheating hearts and boots under a stranger's bed tapping into my wronged-wife state. I sang along to cheesy songs such as "Lucille"—yep, there never really was a fine time to leave anyone—trying to turn my sadness into rage at the injustice of all these years fighting Chris's resistance to having kids and then him ending up with the one thing I'd so desperately wanted.

Thank God for Kate, who turned out to be so much more irreverent than I'd given her credit for. She laughed when she packed up his books about "smart" workplace strategies and "effective" motivational management. "What sort of a person buys these?"

I'd always listened to Chris reading nuggets out of these books, feeling guilty for ever wishing I could lie in until eleven-thirty without him somehow considering me lazy and unambitious. I'd seen them as evidence that he was smart and destined for great things in his career. Kate's take, although she was too polite to say it, was that he was a bit of a knob. Right now, that made me feel a bit better.

She helped me pack his suits. "Don't give him that case. He can have this one over here with the missing wheel. And the Chelsea holdall," she said, dusting down a bag I knew Chris would see as a relic from his youth, not something he would ever sport in his role as senior executive.

Kate was so good at sensing any weakening in my motivation, any suggestion of doubt. "Come on, you chuck his shoes into this bin bag and I'll make tea."

When she came back, I'd decided. I'd float my fragile idea past her. It was the only thing I could think of that might stop me becoming a bitter old hag. I couldn't voice it to anyone else for fear that other people's opinions might crush the tiny transparent chrysalis underfoot before it had a chance to throw out a wing.

It seemed so rash, so bold, so not me, that I blurted it out. "I'm thinking of putting the house up for sale and moving to Italy. Up in the hills outside a little town called Castelfiorentino in Tuscany. I've found a property to renovate."

"Wow."

Shades of the old Kate. That ability to keep silent and let everyone else fill the void. I wished I hadn't mentioned it. I wanted her to beg me not to leave, tell me that she'd miss me, that the estate wouldn't be the same without me.

I pressed on. "I have thought it through. Sort of." My voice was small.

"So how would that work then? Could you still do your job?"

I nodded. "I've been offered the role of overseeing Italian wine buying and it would actually be easier if I lived out there. For a while, anyway. Later on, I might start doing Airbnb and see how I get on."

I explained how I couldn't stay here and risk bumping into Chris and his daughter, how I couldn't face my parents driving the four hours to see me on a regular basis, concern and worry disguised under Swiss rolls—"can't beat a bit of cake with a cup of tea"—and bags of compost—"your pots need freshening up." That it was something I'd dreamed of, but Chris had always waved away: "Italy's nice for a holiday but not to live." I'd always thought that living somewhere where you could sit outside more than five nights a year wouldn't be too shabby.

Kate smiled. "Moving can be very cathartic. It's always good to reinvent yourself so that you don't get pigeonholed into how you were when you were twelve, twenty or even thirty-five." She looked down. "I'll be sorry to see you go, though. But I do get it. You can choose who you tell your story to, rather than being the 'woman who...'"

The way she said that, with such conviction, caused me to stop pairing up Chris's shoes and to look at her properly. "You say that as though you have some experience?"

She nodded.

I picked up a pair of designer flip-flops that Chris had only worn once because they'd rubbed up such a blister between his toes. I waited, wondering whether she was going to creak open the cupboard on the secrets of Kate.

She sighed. "Moving is a good thing, but it's lonely. Do you know anyone in the village you want to move to? Do you speak Italian?"

I pushed away the stab of disappointment that she still wouldn't confide in me. "I'd be lying if I said I wasn't terrified, but Chris would only ever buy brand-new houses and I've always fancied having a go at renovating a wreck. And now's my chance. I speak enough Italian to get by. I hope you'll come and visit? With Daisy? Once I get the plumbing sorted anyway."

"Really? We'd love to." She cleared her throat. "This is the first time I've had any real friends for a long time. Well, local ones, anyway." And as though the words had skipped away from her, untethered like a kite snatched out of her hand by a gust of wind, she blushed so deeply I considered leaving the room to let her gather herself. And then this unfathomable woman started to cry, proper sorrowful tears that I didn't understand but joined in with anyway.

When we both ground to a halt with the crying, interspersed with a bit of embarrassed giggling before it all took off again, I said, "You've been really good to me. Thank you. I wish I'd helped you a bit more but..." I didn't quite know how to say, you're a difficult person to help because you're always so self-contained and actually I'm not even sure you are who you say you are. Her reaction when I'd taken round the envelope with that odd foreign name on it still disturbed me. I rushed on: "Gisela will still be here. She's much more sociable than I am, so you'll have party central over the road."

Kate shook her head. "I haven't seen her for ages. Not even a Facebook post. I feel as though she's avoiding me."

"Do you? I thought it was just me because she didn't want to get involved in the whole Chris situation. Perhaps she's one of those friends who thinks divorce is contagious?"

Kate shrugged. "I don't think she's like that. I've always found her pretty non-judgemental. Perhaps she's just busy."

"Not like her to be off Facebook though, is it?" I said.

Even when she wasn't posting photos, she was sharing stupid "find your hippie name/pole dancer name/what you'll die of" quizzes. Barely a day went by without her proclaiming her hippie name was Sweetpea Hailstorm, or that her pole dancer name was Pixie Pervy or letting us know that she'd die having sex.

Weirdly, although I was secretly disdainful about her having so much time on her hands she had time to test herself on the latest maths GCSE questions, tell us her Elf name was Gisand—"you can do it too—the first three letters of your name and surname!"—as well as posting lists about the names of women most likely to eat all the chocolates before Christmas, I discovered I missed her presence. There was something joyful about her chirpiness, with her LOLs and PMSLs and mad GIFs of women drinking a whole bottle of wine out of one huge glass.

"Maybe she's got a lot going on. I think Hannah can be a handful," Kate said as she stuffed a load of belts into a bag.

I tried not to look as though I'd love that kind of problem, but just thinking that I'd never have a teenager to tut over set me off crying again.

Kate sighed. "This will pass. You're strong."

"Am I? I burst into tears at the doctor's the other day when they were double-checking my next of kin. I feel as though everything I thought about the world has been turned on its head, all the things I took for granted—like having a husband, like eventually having children, like staying with Chris forever—have been ripped away and now everything feels so uncertain."

"You'll learn to live with that."

Her belief in me almost made me believe in myself.

Perhaps a move to a house in Italy with some dodgy plumbing and wild hens living in the courtyard would be within my capabilities.

Maybe, one day, this would be the best thing that ever happened to me.

Just not today.

CHAPTER 37

Gisela

Monday 21 May

It turned out the police were going to do a full-scale investigation to decide whether or not they were going to pass the case to the Crown Prosecution Service. Creaming off a few grand from the sale of caravans and lodges didn't appear to be a matter of urgency, though, and a month after Jack had come back from his big scary interview we were no closer to knowing how long it might take.

"Weeks? Months? Years? Why didn't you ask?" The idea of having the whole thing hanging over us not just for the summer but Christmas, maybe even beyond, made me sick to my stomach. I wondered if we'd get used to living like that, find a way of pushing it to the back of our minds.

"Did they say you'd have to go to court?" I asked, queasy at the idea of sitting in the public gallery, while Jack was questioned in the witness box. Was that even how it worked, or had I been watching too many re-runs of *Judge John Deed*? What if we were photographed going into the court? Our pictures published in the bloody *Evening Star*, the whole road beaking away?

"They didn't really tell me anything. Just said they would investigate further and let me know whether it was going to the

CPS. Graham said it would go to the Magistrates' Court first, if they do decide to press charges."

"What if we paid the money back?" I asked. "Would they drop the case then?"

"I don't know, but how could we pay the money back? There is no money."

I didn't dare say, "I could get a job." After all these years, I'd feel ridiculous offering to fill the family coffers. It would take me forever to earn fifty grand. "We could sell the house."

Jack sighed, a sigh so despairing I went over to hug him.

He threaded his fingers through my hair. "I'm sorry."

"No, I'm sorry. Sorry you couldn't talk to me. Sorry you felt under so much pressure to provide. Sorry I made you feel I couldn't be happy without all this." I gestured around at the stupid cushions I'd bought at seventy-five quid a pop, the hi-tech speaker system for a couple of thousand—so temperamental that we often used the £30 speaker I'd bought as a stocking filler—and, the biggest white elephant of all, the massage chair in the sitting room, five grand. For a brief moment I'd hoped it might earn its keep when Hannah had a bad back from twisting under sinks and U-bends, but she refused point-blank to use it and insisted on going to the osteopath at sixty quid for half an hour. In fact, I couldn't remember the last time anyone had bothered to plug it in, let alone find fifteen minutes for a massage.

"The thing is, Zell, we wouldn't be able to sell the house in time to stop it coming to court anyway. It could take us six months or a year to move."

"What about the cars then?"

"You love that car." I did love my Beetle, especially now the warmer weather was here and I could have the roof down.

I could feel my temper rising. "For God's sake! If selling the car means you don't end up in bloody prison, then that's what has to happen. We'll get rid of yours as well and buy something smaller."

And what a cliché Jack turned out to be. Suggesting that

he left the house in anything less than a Jaguar was a eunuch moment. "I'm not selling my car."

"You could get a second-hand BMW or even something practical like a Fiesta."

It was as though I'd suggested he run around on a unicycle.

"I am not selling the Jaguar." He folded his arms.

In that moment, all those candlesticks that seemed so essential to my life a few months ago looked like they could come in useful as murder weapons. Even though I knew he would eventually see sense, that rigid mindset enraged me.

"Fine. You sit there and wait for the handcuffs. In the meantime, I'll get on and flog my car, and as you're going to be at home for the foreseeable future, perhaps you won't mind running me around in your Jaguar. Then I can drive that when you're in jail."

And, to prove my point, I shot outside, fury at Jack's intransigence making me dramatic. Within minutes I'd uploaded photos while Jack stood by, face set.

Photos: Vintage Beetle. One with roof up, one with roof down.
    Caption: Anyone fancy this vintage beauty? £15000 ono. Decided to get fit and be a bit kinder to the environment. Walking everywhere from now on! #WalkTheWalk

My timeline filled up with comments instantly:

"No! Not the Beetle!" followed by lots of sad-faced emojis from my old cleaner.

"I'm sure you could offset the car pollution by using your compost bin!" from the mother of one of Hannah's schoolfriends. She'd come to dinner and nearly fallen on the floor when she'd seen me chuck all the leftover vegetables into the kitchen bin—"Don't you use your kitchen compost bin?"

I'd laughed it off. "Not likely. I don't want maggots crawling around on my work surfaces, thank you."

Despite turning up to many of our parties without ever feeling the need to reciprocate, and on this occasion feasting on smoked salmon, Gressingham duck and chocolate lavender pots, she still felt entitled to lecture me on my selfishness. It was very tempting to write: "And I'm sure we could reduce CO_2 emissions if you kept your big mouth shut." I replied with an emoji laughing so hard it was crying.

How I hoped she opened the lid of her kitchen compost one day and a big fat rat was sitting buck-toothed in the remains of her purple sprouting broccoli and quinoa crumbs.

Kate liked the post. "Any time you want to swap it for the Mini (ten careless owners and a spilt yoghurt smell but quite economical), just let me know!"

Kate always made me feel a bit better.

Jack going to prison would act as an automatic friendship cull. I could hear it now—"He was no better than a thief. She must have known about it." I hoped Kate wouldn't be in that category. I wasn't sure about Sally. Before I could get any further down that spiral of misery, my phone went. Ollie. No direct communication in nearly six months. I had no idea whether this would be good or bad.

I fumbled to slide the button before he rang off.

Ollie plunged straight in. No "How are you? Sorry I haven't been in touch." Just "Mum, it's Nat. She won't stop crying." His voice cracked. "I'm supposed to be doing my finals, but I can't work and I don't know what to do to help her."

And there it was. All that maternal love that had been swilling around for months with nowhere to go leapt to attention, relieved to have an outlet. "Is Alfie okay?"

"I don't know. I think so. He cries a lot. Sometimes he doesn't sleep all night."

"That's normal, love. Babies can be contrary things. Have you seen the health visitor?"

"She's visited a few times, but Nat won't tell her how bad it is. She drags herself out of bed when she knows the health visitor's coming, but otherwise half the time she doesn't even get up. She's worried the baby will be taken away."

I took no satisfaction in hearing that having a baby wasn't quite the picnic they'd both predicted at Christmas. "Shall I come?"

Relief rushed into Ollie's voice. "Can you come soon?"

"I'll leave this afternoon."

I finished the call, impatient to get going.

"Are you joining me?" I asked Jack.

He heaved out a big sigh. "I'd love to come with you, but I daren't leave in case I get called back into the police station."

"Do you mind me going?"

Jack managed a smile. "So if I said, 'No, stay with me,' you'd text Ollie and say you couldn't make it? Go on, off you go. Let me know how he is." He hugged me and buried his face in my shoulder. "Don't tell him that I'm in trouble with the police, will you? I'll have to come clean at some point, but I don't want him to be ashamed of me. Not yet, anyway. Let him think his son can be proud of his granddad, for the moment, at least."

"They will be proud of you. The kids love you."

"What about you?"

"Me too, of course."

But as I said it, I wondered how many wives loved their husbands more than their children. When pushed to the extremes, with resources for just one of them, how they would pick. I hoped I wouldn't be put to the test.

I drove as fast as I dared up the M4, my boot full of baby mobiles, baby gyms, books that squeaked and rustled and a bottle of champagne. One of the last bottles left since austerity had set in. It seemed as good a time to drink it as any.

I drew up outside their flat in the Redlands area of Bristol.

I didn't get as far as ringing the bell. Ollie appeared at the door with a baby in a sling.

Primeval was the only way to describe it. That sense of wanting to scoop him up and fix him and keep him safe. Of a desire to absorb all of his burdens and hand back that carefree feeling, reverse time to the twenty-year-old Ollie of two years ago, the constant opening and closing of the fridge—"Where's the meat?"—the lounging in bed till midday before parking himself in front of the TV, one hand on the PlayStation controller, the other on his phone.

"Mum!"

There it was. The one syllable that defined and exasperated me. The word that made me who I was, even when I didn't want to be, even when the demands of the role were too many, too painful, too bloody hard. The title that meant I could never be free again. Nor would I want to be.

I put out my arms. "My son. And look at him, your son." I kissed the top of the softest head, a bit of me immediately rushing to identify his double crown, the shape of his chin, that perfect little nose, as coming from the Anderson side of the family. "He's beautiful, Ol."

Ollie stood there, tears pouring down his face. "It's been awful, Mum."

"I can help. We'll sort it out. Come on. You can do this."

Just like that, I had a purpose.

Ollie waved me into a large sitting room with a Moses basket on the sofa and a distinct smell of rotting nappies. The mess reminded me of the first time I'd seen his room on campus and realised that eighteen years of zipping about with bleach and kitchen spray had not rubbed off on him at all.

"Where's Natalie?"

Ollie pointed to a door that was shut. "She's in bed. She's had a terrible time feeding." He looked down as if he was wondering what was appropriate to share with his mother.

"Is she breastfeeding?"

He nodded. "But it's not going very well."

"Poor thing. I don't know why people say it's the most natural thing in the world. You couldn't get the hang of it at all."

Ollie looked vaguely appalled at the image that had created in his head.

"Shall we get things shipshape in here and leave her to sleep until Alfie needs feeding again? Can I have a cuddle first? With Alfie, I mean. You can have a hug as well, if you like."

Ollie really seemed like he wanted one. Everything about him looked battered, as though being a full-time adult had taken a toll. He was so gentle with Alfie, though, love in every gesture. And confident. I didn't know what I'd expected. That he'd be afraid to pick up his own baby?

"Can I hold him?"

Ollie lifted him carefully out of the sling.

I moved a pile of Babygros and muslins to one side and sat on the sofa. "Come to me, my little lovely." In that moment, my heart swelled to add someone else to the list of people that I'd die for. "He's just gorgeous, Ollie. Did you love him as soon as you saw him?"

"I did, but I felt a bit frightened as well. Nat had had a load of pethidine and fell asleep after she'd given birth. I just sat there holding him for about two hours." He smiled, the tiredness around his eyes easing for a minute. "It's a bit scary being responsible for something so little, isn't it?"

"Yes. It is. But I'm sure you're a brilliant dad."

Ollie's whole face darkened and tightened as he struggled to keep his emotions in check. I had to stop seeing that eight-year-old goalkeeper struggling not to cry when the fifth ball had gone rushing past him. "I hope so."

"Now, one thing that might help Natalie feel better is if we have a bit of a clean-up here. Can you put the sling on me? You can go and have a shower and I'll make a start on the tidying."

Ollie put the sling over my head.

"Are you sure that's tight enough? I don't want him falling out."

"It's fine, Mum, honestly," he said, reminding me of how irritated he used to get when I insisted on using apostrophes and commas in text messages.

With Ollie in the bathroom and Alfie lolling, snuffling gently if I moved too quickly, I found a pleasure that had previously evaded me in scrubbing work surfaces and folding clothes. A complete contrast to the days when I was stuck at home with my own babies, hanging out yet another bloody basket of washing, while Jack was off scouting for caravan sites, moaning about the shitty hotels he had to stay in, when the idea of being in any room, even a tent, without someone wetting themselves or getting a head stuck up their nose seemed like the height of luxury.

Ollie appeared, looking so much better now he'd had a shave.

I opened the fridge. It was all I could do to stop myself rolling my eyes. No wonder the poor girl was knackered if she was existing on a diet of Coke Zero, sausage rolls and yoghurt. "If Natalie's feeling under the weather, we need to make sure she's getting plenty of good food. Alfie will be taking a lot from her. Why don't you pop out to the supermarket and I'll stay here with Alfie and carry on having a bit of a spruce up?"

I scribbled down a list, reaching for my purse.

Ollie put his hand up. "I can pay, Mum."

"I'm happy to treat you."

"No. I'm not sponging off you. But if I buy some carrots and coriander, can you make me some soup?"

"I should think so," I said, rejoicing in the idea of getting some vegetables into Ollie, who judging by the contents of the bin had been surviving on kebabs and Starbucks sandwiches. "Off you go then."

He hovered, his lips twitching as though he didn't know how to find the words he needed. "We haven't left Alfie with anyone yet."

"Don't worry. If there's a problem, I'll wake Natalie. I promise I will take really good care of him. Honestly. Looking after a baby is like riding a bike." I paused. "Look at you. I didn't do so badly. You go and have five minutes to yourself. Here, take some carrier bags."

He pulled a face. "Nat doesn't know I called you."

I sat on the sofa, feeling a wisp of tension tighten my stomach. I stroked Alfie's little foot, watching his toes flex up and down. "Will that be a problem?"

"I don't know."

My poor boy. Twenty-two and juggling a partner who didn't like his mother and a baby of his own before he even knew how to roast a chicken and where the wool cycle was on a washing machine.

"Listen, as soon as she wakes up, I'll explain I'm just here to help. Don't worry. I promise, absolutely promise, that I won't fall out with her. Take your time."

Ollie had been gone about five minutes when Alfie started to cry. I jiggled, rocked and soothed, showed him the trees, distracted him with the crinkly ears of the elephant. I kept glancing at the bedroom door, willing it to stay shut, singing "The Wheels on the Bus" to him, quietly, marvelling at how the words were burnt into my brain two decades later.

A memory of me arguing with Jack crept in, him standing in the hallway in his suit, back from a few days away with work, both children fighting over a rabbit with one ear that nobody had ever looked at before and me shouting, "I'd bloody love to go to work, use my brain, instead of singing 'Wheels on the Bus' fifty times a day!"

If only I'd embraced it rather than railed against it. Realised what a privilege it was to be at home with my kids and how quickly it would go and how much I'd wish I could turn the clock back and do it better, with more grace and patience. Instead of feeling I'd lost out, robbed of a university education, the opportunity to try out in the world of work, seeing if I could cut it, if I was smart enough to make my mark.

If I wasn't careful I'd become that person posting "In the end we only regret the chances we didn't take" on Facebook against a sunset. Most fitting for me would be "Would have, could have, should have, but did not." I'd probably get everyone commenting, "Are you okay, hun?"

Before I got further down the hundreds of ways I'd messed up, the bedroom door opened and Natalie burst out in a greying nightdress that I was pretty sure wouldn't have been her first choice of garment to confront me in. Her hair hung in strings as though she hadn't washed it in weeks. She bore no resemblance to the tall, poised woman who was no doubt used to issuing commands and having them obeyed. I'd always stumbled over the latter part, usually feeling as though I was barking a wish list into the wind.

"What are you doing here? Where's Ollie?" She rubbed at her eyes as though it was a surprise to her that it was two in the afternoon rather than the morning. With a gesture I recognised as protective instinct, she stepped towards me. "Let me have Alfie."

I explained where Ollie was as I tried to lift Alfie out of the sling to give him to her, unfamiliarity making me clumsy. He started to scream.

"For God's sake. I told Ollie I didn't want anyone here." She snatched Alfie from me. His fists went up and his mouth opened for the perfect bellow.

I weighed up my words, trying to work out which way to lean for safety. "I'm sorry. I don't want to intrude, but everyone needs a bit of help when they first have a baby."

Alfie was reaching ear-splitting levels, his little face turning purple with rage.

"Look, I'll go if you want, but let me just help you calm Alfie down. Have you got any feed made up, a bottle I could give him?"

"I'm feeding him myself," Natalie said, her voice starting off defiant and then ending in a sob.

"Oh, bless you. What can I do to help? Please let me do something."

Natalie slumped onto the sofa, with Alfie snuffling around the front of her nightdress. I recognised the weary resignation of someone who hadn't yet come to terms with the utter dependence on her of another human being.

"Do you want me to go into the kitchen while you feed him? I'll make you a drink."

She nodded.

I darted out, relieved to have a task.

The screaming didn't abate. In fact, it became more and more hysterical. I was desperate to peer out, each fresh yell leading me to hover behind the door, pulling faces in sympathy. In the end, I just couldn't bear it.

"Shall I hold him for a minute?" The words were out of my mouth before I'd worked out what I'd intended to say.

But Natalie pushed him at me without a word, collapsing back onto the sofa in tears, struggling to clip up her nursing bra, then giving up and sinking down, great rings of milk staining her nightdress like targets.

I stuck my little finger into Alfie's mouth, which gave us a tiny lull in the screaming.

In between sobs, she said, "Everything's so sore and I just can't seem to feed him properly. He never seems to get the right position, the health visitor said he's not putting on weight. I can't do anything right."

"You're doing a brilliant job. Look at him. He's gorgeous. I remember feeling like this with Hannah. She was a fussy baby and never seemed to settle. I got quite hysterical about it, thought I was such a rubbish mother that I couldn't even feed my own baby properly."

"Did you?" Her face brightened slightly. "Everyone says it's the most natural thing in the world, it's such a bonding experience, but honestly, I dread every feed."

And the irony of it all was that a good ten-minute discussion about cracked nipples and cabbage leaves neutralised the animosity between us far quicker than a cards-on-the-table discussion about our respective grievances. By the time Natalie had shown me her poor sorry nipples—"Oooh, that looks na-asty"—and I'd texted Ollie to pick up some Kamillosan and nipple shields as a "matter of urgency," I'd gained in confidence enough to suggest that she expressed some milk after this feed and I'd try him on a bottle while she got some rest.

I passed Alfie back to her and it seemed that the idea she might get three consecutive hours of sleep relaxed her enough to wince her way through the feed.

"Here, give him to me and you go and have a bath or have a sleep."

She hovered uncertainly.

"Go. I'll be fine and so will he."

I popped him over my shoulder, gently patting his back.

"I'd love a bath. I can't even have a shower unless Ollie's here, but he's revising for his finals so he spends lots of his time at the library."

She didn't even make it as far as the bathroom. Within minutes, Natalie was snoring gently on the bed, her limbs sagging into the duvet as though she'd melted into sleep.

I bathed Alfie and swore he'd smiled, though it was probably wind. I was nervous, testing the water with my wrist three or four times. Eventually, clean and sparkling in one of the Babygros I'd brought with me, he fell asleep in my arms. I sat watching his little mouth twitch, the tip of his tongue flick out, his eyes moving beneath the lids. I didn't yearn to get up and make a cup of tea, to pull a book within reach, to flip on the TV as I had in the long hours of looking after my own babies. For reasons that escaped me now, I couldn't wait to pop them in their cot so I could rush around with the Hoover, put some washing on, make dinner, have five minutes without another human being wanting something from me.

Ollie came back with groceries. I raised a finger to my lips and pointed to their bedroom. He smiled and rolled his eyes with relief.

"Was she okay with you? How did you get her to leave Alfie with you?" he whispered.

"We bonded over the joys of breastfeeding. I persuaded her she could trust me."

His face softened. "Thank you."

I stretched out the arm not supporting Alfie and grabbed his hand. "I'm sorry for making everything so difficult. Really sorry. My reservations came from a place of love. It's so hard for me to realise you're a grown-up, that you know your own mind. I still want to protect you, stop anything bad happening to you."

Ollie shrugged. He glanced down at Alfie and his eyes filled. "I sort of get that a bit better now."

I squeezed his hand. "Would you like me to stay for a couple of days? I can do some of the night shift if Nat expresses? Then you can both have a good night's sleep. If you trust me, I'll sleep in here with Alfie in the Moses basket. Then tomorrow I can have a proper tidy-up and get the washing done."

Ollie swiped a hand over his face. "I'm not great at all that stuff."

I resisted saying, "Tough shit, you'd better get good at it" and went for the baby step of "It all takes a bit of practice."

Ollie plonked himself into an armchair. "I think this is the first time I've sat down without Nat or Alfie crying since he was born."

"So shall I let Dad know I'm not coming back tonight?"

Ollie nodded.

"First, though, just take a few photos of me with Alfie so I can text them to him. Phone's in my bag over there."

"Is Dad okay?"

"What makes you ask that?"

"Dunno. He doesn't really communicate with me. If I text him, he says everything's fine but doesn't tell me anything else."

Honestly, I loved the pot-kettle-blackness of it all. This was the boy who texted "*Still alive*" every time I asked how he was in his first year at university.

I decided not to hit him with the full family catastrophe. There was plenty of time to be wretched. "He's fine. Concerned about you, obviously. And he'd love to meet Alfie."

"He will, Mum. It's just been a bit of a tricky time. Nat thought it would be easier than it is. *I* thought it would be easier than it is."

In that moment he looked so lost, the ten-year-old waiting at the school bus stop when I'd been delayed, thinking I'd forgotten to pick him up. "Parenthood is hard. Much harder than it looks. I was a wonderful mother before I had kids." I rocked Alfie as he whimpered. "You'll do brilliantly. Alfie's lucky to have you." For bridge building and hope for the future, I added, "Lucky to have both of you."

That was quite enough emotion for Ollie for one day and he got up to take photos. I sent them to Jack who rang me immediately.

"Whatever happens, love, promise me that you'll keep talking about me to Alfie so he knows I exist. Tell him I wasn't all bad."

Ollie frowned as the tears I'd been trying to cork in for months started to fall. "I've got to go, darling, but you can bet your life Alfie is going to love his Granddad Jack." I forced a smile after I ended the call. "God, Dad and I are getting so emotional in our old age. Now let's have another look at those photos. Do you mind if I put them on Facebook so my friends can see Alfie?"

There it was, that great blaze of pride on Ollie's face. He knew that his son was the most gorgeous one in the whole world. And I knew my grandson was.

Photos: Ollie with Alfie, Gisela with Alfie
   Caption: I couldn't love my son or my grandson more.
   #Cutie

Within moments, the comments ran down the page like an expanding ladder of surprise and shock.

"Didn't know you had a grandchild on the way! Congratulations."

"Congratulations! You are the youngest and most glamorous granny I know." I decided to take that one at face value. They'd better not be making a jibe at how young Ollie was to have a baby.

"Where did this beauty pop up from? Is he Ollie's son?"

"Grandson? Whose son?" This from Sarah, the woman who had the ding-dong over universities with me.

Reply: "Ollie's."

Bloody Sarah: "Wow. I didn't realise he'd got married so young."

Reply: "Not married, just lucky to have found a lovely woman and to have had the brilliant fortune to have a gorgeous healthy baby." I wrote, then deleted, #SoStickYourBigFatOpini onsIntoYourBigFatPipe.

I did find a bit of satisfaction when my comment immediately attracted five likes.

I sat waiting for Sarah to offer a comeback. Then Alfie stirred and something shifted in me. The first time I'd ever met my grandson and I was wasting time arguing with a tit on Facebook whom I never ever saw in real life. I pressed the unfriend button and said to myself, *Now I am a grandma I will be more dignified.*

Then gave the screen the finger as a last, immature me, hurrah.

CHAPTER 38

Kate

Wednesday 23 May

I hadn't seen Gisela to speak to face-to-face for a couple of weeks. I wasn't used to being the one reaching out to people anymore, especially popular, lively people like Gisela. I tried not to take it personally. When I'd looked at her Facebook page on Monday, apart from her post selling the Beetle, which in itself was odd, there'd been nothing for weeks. None of the usual lunchtime rocket/avocado/quinoa creations that made me feel guilty about going to the drive-through McDonald's if we managed a ten-minute lunch break. No arty pics of glasses of wine next to a cheese plate. No reminders of wedding anniversaries, no newly painted toenails in brilliant blue, no cute little weekend cottages on the "most perfect lake."

Maybe she was away, but if she was, she usually came over with a bag of stuff from her fridge even if Jack was at home— "He wouldn't know how to cook a courgette if it bit him on the bottom. You might as well have all of this before it rots." Daisy and I swooned over the barrel-aged feta, the white nectarines, the pots of ready-peeled mango while trying to guess how much she spent on food a week. But although the Beetle wasn't on the drive, she hadn't let me know she was going away. Perhaps she'd sold the car already and really was walking everywhere.

It was ironic that I'd spent all this time slightly unnerved about her habit of popping over to invite me round to something that was happening in the next twenty minutes—"We've bought too many steaks. Do you fancy one?" "My bloody brother has cancelled on us yet again. We're wading around in garlic prawns over there...do you want to join us?"

Now I caught myself glancing out of the window, longing for the familiar sight of her, trundling over in a pair of Jack's Crocs or Hannah's fluffy slippers, rarely resembling her endlessly updated profile picture. Maybe she was offended by my own lack of hospitality. Somehow I never seemed to find the right moment for that whole "Come over for my very average cooking and some wine from a vineyard I've never heard of, let alone visited—unlike Sally—and by the way, are you sure Jack won't feel awkward because I don't have a husband to entertain him?" Perhaps she was put out because I'd been spending so much time with Sally without inviting her too.

I shook my head at my own ridiculousness. All these years without any friends had buggered up my ability to juggle all the dynamics. With a sigh, I flipped open the laptop and logged onto her page.

There was my answer. She was in Bristol with her *grandson*. Explained her absence at least. The stab of hurt surprised me. The last I'd heard, she was in a standoff with Ollie and Natalie and didn't know whether she'd ever meet him. It was so long since I'd got to know anyone well enough to expect to know their news as it happened. Then I told myself off for being over forty and still competitive about who knew what when. It was a good sign that I'd got close enough to anyone to notice. And brilliant that Gisela had managed to build bridges. She'd be an amazing grandmother.

It certainly explained the lack of activity at the house. I was so used to seeing people in and out, boxes delivered, oven cleaning specialists, takeaway orders. And sometimes, Alex. Of course, Alex. The little flip of my stupid heart when his motorbike roared up the road. I hated myself for remembering that he'd once told me he usually came to the Andersons on a Wednesday for fish and chips—"You know Gisela, she likes to make sure I've eaten properly once a week. I'm her surrogate son now Ollie's left home." I found it a bit easier to get out of bed midweek, knowing I might be rewarded with a glimpse of him that evening. Sometimes even a quick chat if I plucked up the courage to go and fetch something out of the car before he disappeared into their house.

I wondered how long it would be before I stopped noticing it was Wednesday, stopped glancing round when I heard a motorbike engine. It was like being a lovesick teenager but with the upfront knowledge that there was never a fairy-tale ending. Gisela had made it clear she thought we were perfect for each other. "Just give it a chance. How do you know whether you're ready for a relationship unless you try?" And then after several glasses of wine, "For God's sake, Kate, while you're sitting about overthinking all this, you could have been having sex!"

This week, to my embarrassment, I was standing gazing out of the living room window when Alex drew up on his bike. I was too late to duck out of sight and, for reasons known to nobody, picked up the vase on the windowsill and turned it over as though I was choosing an item for *Antiques Roadshow*.

Alex took off his helmet, started up Gisela's drive, then turned round and walked directly to my front door. The study of the perfect chemical combination of desire and fright could have kept scientists in work for a decade. I just had time to run my fingers through my hair before he rang the doorbell.

That smile.

"Is Daisy home?"

"No, she's at work. Why?"

"I wanted to talk to you for a minute. Can I come in?"

I nodded. Two non-family people in my house in less than a week. Get me. "Tea? Or a glass of wine?"

"Just water will be fine, thank you."

Water. The drink of someone who doesn't intend to stay long.

I dug in the cupboard for a glass that hadn't gone cloudy in the dishwasher and filled it up. "Have a seat."

"I've been stuck inside all day. Can I be really cheeky and ask to sit in the garden?"

I nearly tripped over my own feet in the race to get some air and space between us.

Outside, he sat down, his eyes flickering over me in a way that made me want to pull a face to break the awkwardness of thinking about someone for weeks, then being overwhelmed with a compulsion to flee when they presented themselves in the flesh.

Alex leaned back, his tall frame making my lime green "bistro" chairs look tiny. "So, how have you been?"

"You know, the same, working, looking after Daisy, trying to stay out of trouble. You?"

He bent forward, elbows on his knees. "I've been making a documentary." Those grey eyes holding mine, thoughtful. And something else. Inquiring. Curious. There it was, that warning flare of alarm, buzzing at the back of my brain like a sleepy fly on its last legs.

I put my face into neutral. "Sounds like you've been busy. Are Gisela and Jack around? I haven't seen them for a few days," I said, even though I knew exactly where Gisela was.

His face shuttered for a second as I changed the subject. "Jack's here. Gisela has gone to see Ollie."

"That's great. I kept telling her to go and visit him. She's been so sad about falling out with him."

Alex nodded and sipped his water. "This documentary was about cot death, Sudden Infant Death Syndrome, to mark the fifteen years since Angela Cannings was acquitted."

I swallowed, feeling everything in me flop and freeze.

"I was interviewing mothers who lost their babies to it. I interviewed Becky Haughton."

I started to shut down. That familiar pulling-away feeling, the need to sever ties with anyone I cared about. I didn't respond. I wanted to leap up and run out of the gate but instead I sat there, helplessly, watching the avenues of escape close off around me.

Alex carried on. "She kept talking about Izabela and her daughter, Karolina, the Polish family she'd known all her life. She showed me some photos. At first, I just thought it was someone who looked a bit like you and didn't think anything of it. Then she talked about growing up in Manchester and how close you were and I noticed that locket in one of the photos. It's quite distinctive. The eagle. The hexagonal shape."

I put my hand to my throat. The evidence was hanging there for him to see. I closed my eyes, wishing I could hug my mum again, have her tell me that one day this nightmare would end. "Please tell me you didn't say anything about me. Or Daisy. Or where we live now."

"I didn't. I wasn't a hundred per cent sure it was you because it seemed so unlikely. Then I did some digging around when those names didn't show up anywhere and everything started to make a bit more sense." A tiny apologetic smile hovered on his lips.

I couldn't smile back. Despair washed through me, a familiar flood. I'd never be free. I couldn't go through all this again. Couldn't face everyone gossiping and pointing the finger ever again. "I suppose you don't believe me either?"

Alex took my hand. I left it there without responding to his squeeze. "Can I hear your side of the story?"

"No. No, actually you fucking can't," I said, snatching away my hand. "I was cleared of murder, and of manslaughter, you know. And here I am, sixteen years later, justifying myself to you, hiding from the world. Changing our names. Terrified she'll get me back, that the girl I'd known all my life, my best friend for twenty years, will somehow find a way to get to my daughter. To ruin my life the way she thinks I ruined hers."

I jumped up, knocking over my chair. "I can't do this anymore. Please, go away and pretend you never realised who I was. Please. I've moved three times to escape this and I can't uproot Daisy again. We just want to live in peace."

I was sobbing now, all those star-crossed lover thoughts, stupid fantasies of the truth coming out, with him championing me, believing in my innocence, dead in the water. Instead he wanted the inside track for his shitty documentary, the salacious details for an audience baying for blood, who'd comment on internet sites: "Scum of the earth," "Hanging is too good for people like this," "Thank God for Brexit, get control of our borders and keep murderers like this in their own country."

God knows what fucked-up finger of fate had brought me to live opposite his best friends. The same one that had led me to volunteer to look after Becky's baby when she went back to work. "Would you really, Iz? That would be such a weight off my mind. I'm such a fusspot, I can't bear the thought of leaving her. I know you'll love her as much as I do." We'd taken photos of our baby girls together, born just a month apart, and talked about how they'd be more like sisters and grow up really knowing each other. For me, it was an added income. We weren't rich, but Oskar and I were in total agreement. He would work and I would look after Karolina and Cara. Becky would pay me to childmind. It was a brilliant plan.

Alex picked up my chair. He put his hand out to me. "Kate! Listen to me!"

"No. I know what you'll do. I've tried over the years to tell my side of the story, but in the end, it all comes back to 'No smoke without fire.' You'll listen to what I say, nod like you believe me and then report shit about me—how I was a good-time girl, how I liked to party, how our house was always full of people. It was. I was happy, I loved having people round, we both did. And yes, sometimes I'd drink too much wine—but, Jesus, nothing like anyone round here. But in the press, I was the drunken Polish immigrant—even though I was born here.

They made it sound like I was on bloody moonshine at breakfast, then dozing on the sofa while Becky's baby gasped her last on my watch."

Something was ripping inside me, the years of grief wrenching apart everything I'd carefully stapled back together to make sure it wasn't all for nothing, to keep Daisy safe and happy.

Alex kept trying to move towards me, but I was batting him off, fury and fear making me spin around like a feral cat undecided between fight or flight.

"Sit down. Just for ten minutes, then I promise I'll go."

In the end, I took the path of least resistance and sat, determined that the old journalist charm wouldn't suck me in. I'd seen it all before—"We won't print anything you're not happy with" equalled "Polish childminder says she didn't kill her best friend's baby."

"Please, just listen to me. Firstly, I'm sorry. I know you won't believe me, but I didn't want to upset you and I am definitely, definitely not here for a story."

If he heard my snort, he ignored it and plugged on.

"I've thought about you so much since that night we went out together, and then when I saw you at New Year, I just couldn't understand why you wouldn't have anything to do with me. What you were saying didn't match what I was feeling from you, if that makes sense? And I kept raking it all over, trying to work out where I'd messed up."

Somewhere something softened inside me. In different circumstances, I might have admitted to stalking his Facebook profile. I shrugged. But it seemed that a middle-aged woman looking less than receptive to his charms wasn't going to put him off easily. He didn't show any signs of retreat.

"Becky showed me a photo of you with the babies—you haven't changed much. Lots of photos actually, from when you were teenagers." Again that wisp of a smile as though he was about to remind me of the canary-yellow pantaloons or the glittery elbow-length gloves then thought better of it. "When I thought about it, I realised you'd gone funny when I said I was a journalist." He rested his chin on his hand. "Am I right?"

I nodded and saw his body relax as though he'd finally turned over a matching pair of lightbulbs in a child's memory game.

He frowned. "Becky sounded as though she misses you."

"Misses me? That is such bollocks. She and her husband did everything they could to press charges. They accused me of *murder*. My family had to put up bail for me. I had to stand in the witness box and give evidence. I loved little Cara. I'd just put her down to sleep, did all the right things, feet to the foot of the cot, not too hot, Daisy was sleeping in the cot next to her. Becky accused me of murdering her, saying I'd lost my temper with her when she was crying. She was a fussy baby, hated to be put down, but of course I didn't kill her. I'd spent all morning walking around with her in a sling. The case only came to court because I'd broken a rib when I was doing CPR." I closed my eyes against the memory. "I was so desperate to save her."

Alex shifted on his chair as though he was trying to match up what I was saying and what he'd heard from Becky. I wasn't going to be painted as the bad guy again. Fuck *that*.

"Did she tell you about the 'birthday card' she sent Daisy every year? Reminding her that her mother was a murderer and couldn't be trusted? And that every year instead of celebrating her little girl's birthday in July, she sat in the park where we used to take our babies and wondered how I could live with myself? Not to mention the silent phone calls, the long rambling letters about how she'd counted on me all her life and now I'd robbed her of any joy. Ever again."

Alex shook his head. "You poor thing. Why didn't you go to the police? Report the harassment?"

"She'd lost her baby, Alex."

He splayed his hands as though my answer didn't make sense to him.

"I felt guilty. Her baby died in my care. It never bloody

leaves me. I still wonder whether it was anything I did, something I can't think of, whether if I'd checked on them both ten minutes earlier, Cara would still be here. I sort of felt—still feel probably—that I deserved to be punished." I rubbed my eyes. "Irrational heart triumphs over rational head. I couldn't call the police on her. 'Sorry your daughter died while I was looking after her, but what you really need is to spend time at the police station and get a criminal record for harassment.' I'm not going to lie, I nearly did it loads of times, but I knew she needed help, that it was just the grief making her mad. Who knows what I'd be like if I lost Daisy?"

I'd spent months, years, trying to show her I understood her reaction, that it would take time, that I would always be a painful reminder of the little girl she'd lost, but I hadn't caused this. I'd written back, begged her to have some counselling, asked her to let me help. The replies were so vicious, so cruel, but then so heartbreaking in parts, almost reaching out to me—"I'm broken, Izzy, just broken"—that I couldn't add to her problems.

When Daisy started in Reception and Becky turned up shouting abuse at the school gates, I knew we needed to move. The cards, the letters, followed us to Leeds—"I wish I could escape what you did to us so easily"—bringing me back to the past, on a monthly, sometimes weekly, basis.

Alex put his head on one side. "But you wouldn't have behaved like that if it had been the other way round."

"None of us know what we're capable of when the worst thing happens to us. I hope I wouldn't have needed to blame her if the boot had been on the other foot, but who knows? It's human nature to want to find a reason for everything. I don't think we're very good at accepting 'it's random bad luck.' I see it at work all the time."

"Have you had any support?" Alex asked.

"What do you mean? Counselling?"

He nodded.

"I just wanted to forget about it. I was trying to keep things normal for Daisy. I did consider it when Becky turned up in Peterborough on Daisy's thirteenth birthday—I'd had to go to work for a few hours. Becky had gone when I got back, but Daisy had let her in because she'd brought a birthday present for her and was all 'I'm an old friend of your mum's, I knew you when you lived in Manchester and I was just passing...' She didn't remember her, of course, because she'd only been little last time she'd seen her. According to Daisy, she'd just wanted to wish her happy birthday and stayed and chatted for about an hour. I went completely potty for a few months, obsessing about locking the door, keeping the curtains shut, following Daisy to school in case she was kidnapped. I was afraid that if I started counselling, I'd have to get worse before I'd get better. I couldn't risk having a breakdown because there was no one to look after Daisy. So I plodded on."

I still flinched at the memory of screaming at Daisy for letting in a stranger when I wasn't there. Of snatching up the photo frame Becky had brought and ripping out the picture of Daisy and Cara as babies while Daisy stood there, tears pouring down her face, saying, "Sorry, Mum. Sorry. I didn't want to be rude because she'd brought me a present for my birthday. I thought you'd be cross if I didn't invite your friend in."

"Have you told anyone at all? Does Gisela know about it?" His shoulders slumped. "Sorry. Stupid question. No one knows, do they? That's why you've changed your name."

"I changed it when we moved here. Daisy is eighteen in a couple of months and I couldn't stand the idea that even as an adult, we'd be looking over our shoulders, waiting for Becky to come round the corner, harassing us, dragging up the past, telling everyone what I'd done. What she *thought* I'd done. Who wants everyone thinking she's the daughter of a baby killer? I'd tried moving, keeping a low profile, staying off social media, jettisoned all my old friendships, my old connections, but she'd always found me."

I looked at the grass, wondering when we'd last had rain. "I loved Becky. I loved Cara. It hurt me so much that Becky never accepted I hadn't harmed her baby girl. She wouldn't believe that Cara could die like that, out of the blue with no warning. Even when the expert gave evidence and said Cara's death was unexplained, a tragic event where no one was responsible."

I shook my head to stop myself seeing that floppy pale body, to block out the noise of my footsteps on the stairs, the ragged gasps of my breathing as I flew down to the phone, the mixture of terror and disbelief in my voice as I rushed out "Ambulance, my baby's stopped breathing." Of course, it wasn't my baby, but she was like a daughter to me. My desperate efforts to resuscitate her had become the focus of the court case, the rib I'd cracked as I'd tried to get her breathing again, pressing on her chest, my legs shaking, every millimetre of me willing her brown eyes to fly open, her body to take in a great suck of air.

Alex was blinking as though he was straining to process what I was telling him. He sighed. "What a burden to carry. Does Daisy know what happened?"

"I've told her the bare bones. She's already had to put up with so much of my paranoia about social media and being deliberately vague about where we live. She goes along with it, but she thinks I'm being dramatic. I've never voiced my fear that Becky will try to hurt her. In my heart of hearts, I don't think she would, but I'm not sure enough to risk it."

"When I spoke to her, she didn't mention that she'd been stalking you, funnily enough. She was very eager for me to find you 'so I got a rounded picture of what SIDS means for everyone, the carers too.'"

"I bet she did. Presumably she was quite keen for you to let her know where I was if you found me."

He frowned, as though he was replaying the conversation in his mind. "She almost gave me the impression she'd be happy to be interviewed alongside you."

"Promise me you'll never admit you know me. Please, please don't tell her where I am." I pressed my fingers into my eyes to stop the tears.

"I'm not even going to run the interview with her. I'll tell my editor that the story wasn't strong enough."

A weight lifted, just slightly. "Won't you get into trouble?"

Alex grinned. "Probably. I can cope."

"Thank you. Thank you so much."

The atmosphere shifted. The intensity, the rawness inside me faded as though someone had turned the volume down. My arms went loose.

"You've been through enough, Kate. Or Izabela?"

"Izabela doesn't exist anymore. Well, only in my memories."

Alex leant forward, running his fingers through his dark hair. "Is there any tiny chance you'd consider making new memories with me?"

I held my breath, waiting for the question that would prove he wasn't a hundred per cent convinced I was telling the truth.

But he just said, "Well? Would you?"

"Do you believe what I've told you?" I asked.

He shuffled his chair towards me and kissed the top of my head. "I believe you."

The sweetest three words I'd heard in so long.

CHAPTER 39

Kate

Wednesday 30 May

A whole week had passed since I'd told the truth to Alex. Instead of feeling vulnerable, I felt safe. After all these years of building up my barriers, I now had moments at work, even when I was mopping up blood or dodging splatters of sick, when I'd get a rush of emotion that made something soften in my hard old heart. Seeing him propped against the wall opposite the ambulance station, that recognisable shape—the angle of his knee, the lean of his head as he checked his mobile—that I'd quickly learnt to pick out from a distance, made the trials of the day diminish in an instant. Hope. Excitement. Joy. All the instinctive reactions that disappear after tragedy felt as though they were sitting in the petri dish of my heart, ready to regenerate again. Today he'd brought a motorbike helmet and a jacket for me.

"I can't leave the car here, I need it for the morning."

"I'll bring you." He saw my face. "Don't worry, I'll pick you up early. I'm working from home tomorrow."

I argued that it was too much trouble, but he put out his hand to me.

"Come on. We're going to make the most of a sunny evening. Fish and chips with a view."

"Daisy finishes her shift at Tesco at ten. I ought to be home by then."

"You will be, Cinders, you will." He smiled and the little pull of concern that he might not understand she had to come first faded.

I relaxed and clambered up behind him, feeling ridiculously teenage, wanting my colleagues to see that the reliable Kate, the one who always volunteered to work bank holidays, who never complained but never chatted much either, actually had a bit more to her than they thought. I leaned into his back, inhaling that masculine smell of leather, with the last vestiges of his morning aftershave. I expected him to head through the North Downs to a country pub, but instead I found myself roaring down the M23 towards Brighton, clinging onto him with a mixture of exhilaration and fear.

An hour later, we were sitting on the beach eating fish and chips in the early evening sun, watching the seagulls swooping over a calm sea. After we'd thrown the last scraps to the birds, Alex pulled me to my feet.

We walked along the shoreline, my hand in his. After Oskar, I hadn't dared imagine I'd experience that again, that my palm would sit comfortably in the cradle of someone else's, intense communication without a single word, that a simple act would hold so much optimism in its grasp.

I worked hard to enjoy the moment, not to let clouds of worry roll in. I was so used to blocking off my feelings, to rationalising rather than releasing them to wander at will, I wondered whether I'd ever have the courage to believe that daring to love didn't always end in disaster. I'd made a good start, though. Over the last week, I'd been more honest with Alex about my life than anyone else in almost two decades.

We sat on a low wall, commenting on the warmth of the evening, the buzz of Brighton, the quirky little art galleries under the arches.

"It would be great to spend a weekend here," Alex said. "Do you think you could manage a night away?"

"Maybe."

"Is that a 'maybe, I'd like to but I won't leave Daisy on her own overnight,' or is that a 'maybe, I'll see whether I like you enough'?" He was so good at teasing the truth out of me, though it never felt critical or unkind.

"The first one."

He turned my face to him and kissed me. The hubbub of parents pushing their babies in prams, the kids racing past on their scooters, the call of the gulls receded. My ability to think seemed to collapse, folding into itself and surrendering to unfamiliar sensations, which frightened and thrilled me with their intensity.

When he finally pulled away, there was a desire for more, the sense that we could stay until the early hours of the morning, listening to the waves lapping the shore, and never feel the need to go home.

As always, real life intruded. My eyes flicked to my watch.

"Do you need to get back?"

"I don't like Daisy coming into an empty house more often than she needs to."

"She's nearly eighteen, isn't she?"

I pulled my hand away. "In two weeks' time. I still prefer to be at home when she gets back, even now."

Alex laughed at me. "Don't get all defensive. I wasn't saying you shouldn't be there for her. I was just thinking out loud and didn't quite finish off the thought that she'll probably go off to university in the autumn and then you'll be the one in an empty house."

I relaxed. "She's definitely hoping to go. It will be so odd without her."

"What are you doing for her eighteenth?"

"I haven't got my head round that yet. I'm too busy trying to accept that, at eighteen, I've got to let her have a smartphone to replace her old Nokia, one of those pay-as-you-go push-button things."

For about the last four years, I'd been fighting a battle that raged continuously about moving to a smartphone from the dinosaur Nokia that only allowed for texts and phone calls rather than internet access. I couldn't cope with the idea that she might get Snapchat and, at a push of a button, anyone could see where she was on Snap Maps.

"Mum, I get left out of everything because I'm not on Whats-App or Snapchat. No one invites me to parties because I'm not in the groups."

I'd argued back. "What sort of friends don't invite you to parties because you don't have the right phone? Why don't they *ring* to invite you?"

Daisy would stomp off, shaking her head at my ignorance. In a moment of guilt when yet again Daisy missed out on some last-minute gathering because it had been announced on WhatsApp, I'd told her I'd buy a smartphone for her eighteenth. I'd hoped she'd forget about it, get over it, but she'd counted down the months, then the weeks and now she was ticking off the next seventeen days.

Alex squeezed my hand. "It's a miracle you've managed to make her stay with the Nokia for so long."

I frowned. "I'm doing a brilliant job of sucking all the joy out of getting it, though, by telling her over and over again that under no circumstances is she ever to turn on her location."

Every time I looked at the much-lusted-after white package hidden in my wardrobe, my heart lurched. I didn't understand how all the apps worked, but I knew for sure that they'd make it so much easier for Becky to find us.

"Presumably the lack of online presence is part of your hiding strategy?"

I nodded. "It's not just that. Daisy's birthday is a tricky time. Cara was exactly a month younger, so in my mind, they're very interlinked."

I explained how when I lived in Manchester, when I still hoped Becky would see sense and let us live our lives in peace, she'd drive up and down the street outside our house on every

red-letter day—Cara's birthday, the anniversary of her death,
Christmas Day—her silver Volkswagen creeping past, not even
doing anything, just lurking until I closed the curtains, put the
TV on, baked cakes, anything not to dwell on her pain, my guilt.
And eventually my fury that I'd tried to help her by looking after
Cara so she could go back to work but instead I'd had to carry
the blame for something that I couldn't prevent. Forever.

Alex listened as so many of the things I'd tried not to think
about bubbled out. Then, quietly, gently, he said, "I don't think
you can hide forever, Kate. You've paid a huge price for what
was effectively bad luck. I've read the reports and the judge said
in his summing up that the inescapable reality was that some
deaths remained unexplained."

I remembered those words. I remembered glancing at Becky
as he said them, my knees trembling with relief. She was shaking her head, rejecting the possibility that no one was to blame.
That there wouldn't be an answer. My heart accepted her hurt,
tucking it into that place within us where someone else's pain
crosses the threshold into our own world and lives there so
boldly that it defines us nearly as acutely as it defines them.

"But it's so awful, so frightening, to see letters from her
drop through my letter box, all that vitriol, all that grief and
blame, wondering whether I'll suddenly see her drifting past
my front window. It makes me so anxious. It's like having an
intruder in the house. Anyway, you don't want to listen to all
this shit. We should go. Daisy will be home soon."

He put out his hand to touch my forearm. "This is important
and I absolutely do want to listen to it."

"It's a bit tough on you taking me to the beach for an
impromptu burst of sunshine and having to listen to the voice
of doom and gloom."

Alex scuffed at a pebble with his toe. "My next documentary
is about abuse in care homes. I'm in the wrong job if I'm looking
for cheery." He took both of my hands in his. "Eighteen years is
a long time to suffer for something that wasn't your fault."

"I feel as though it was. She thinks it was. And plenty of others do too."

"Look at you. You've almost been on the run like a criminal. What if you just stopped? If you decided that people can think what they like about you?"

"I don't want Daisy to have to deal with it."

Alex frowned. "But she is already dealing with it. She's hiding away under a different name."

I pulled my hands away. "I've done what I thought was best." That sick feeling of getting it wrong, of not being able to make him understand, was mounting. "It's not that easy. Do you think I haven't thought about every bloody possibility, every different way of making sure that Daisy didn't have to pay the price?"

This was why I could never get close to people.

Alex spoke softly, as though he was talking to an animal hovering between retreat or attack. "I know that, I'm not criticising you. Who knows what anyone would have done in your situation? You were between a rock and a hard place." He made little circles on the wall, swirling the sand with his fingertips. "I wish I could fix things for you."

My irritation dropped a notch. "I wish you could too. But you can't." Though it was such a novelty to feel someone even cared what life looked like for me.

He leaned forward. "I've got an idea for making you the best role model for your daughter in the whole world. And very cool to boot."

Irritation shot up again. "I'm never going to be cool and that's probably number seven hundred and ninety on my list of priorities." And I was also thinking, *For a bloke I've been kissing for a week, that's a bit bloody presumptuous*, followed by the thought that it wasn't surprising that snappy old me hadn't had a whiff of interest from a man in over a decade.

He rested his chin on his hand, his brown eyes never leaving mine. "Kate, let's get a few things straight, because I'm sensing they're a bit of a deal-breaker. Number one, I'm on your side.

Number two, I've absolutely no idea how you've managed so well and what I would have done in your situation. Number three, it is possible that other people have some good ideas and that allowing someone else to help you doesn't make you weak, pathetic or ridiculous. It makes you someone who is strong but who needs a bit of support now and again. Like all of us."

He said it with such charm, such kindness of tone, such a complete lack of accusation, that I managed to say, "Sorry. Shall I start that again? What would make me very cool in the eyes of my eighteen-year-old daughter?"

He held up his hands in surrender. "Don't shoot the messenger. Let her have a party at home. I'll come and be your bouncer and I'm sure Gisela and Jack would help out."

"I can't. I just can't."

"Why not? If Becky wants to find you, it won't be because some spotty eighteen-year-old knows where you live. I did a documentary on millennials and they're far more worried that the degree everyone told them they should do was a complete waste of time and money and they'll never be able to get on the property ladder than helping someone settle old scores."

I shifted on the wall, already fidgety at the thought of lots of people trooping through my house. "I wouldn't know where to start with organising a party for her."

He did that very blokey thing of clasping his hands and cracking his knuckles. "But I do, and so do your neighbours."

I picked up my bag. "You are food for thought, Mr. Fitzgerald, but I need to go."

"Kate, she's eighteen. It's a really good time to nail the lesson that one tragedy doesn't define who you are."

We hurried back along the beach as the sun dropped lower in the sky. I climbed onto the motorbike, pulled on my helmet and allowed myself to imagine that could even be possible. Not for me, maybe. But Daisy?

Perhaps.

CHAPTER 40

Gisela

Wednesday 30 May

I didn't want to leave Ollie. Looking after Alfie, cooking for them both, cleaning the flat and making sure Natalie got some rest gave a routine to my days, a purpose I hadn't felt in a long time. Ollie had gone to work in the library every day and I'd held Alfie while Natalie showered and got dressed in peace—"Wow! I'd forgotten what it felt like to wash without someone screaming." But a nine-day guest—even someone who took over some of the night-time feeds—was plenty in a one-bedroomed flat. I was battling to hold in the temptation to ask Ollie whether he needed to get an early night to be fresh for his revision in the morning when poor Nat, even with my help, was only getting three or four hours sleep in a row. I had to let him grow up. That meant going home.

I hugged them all goodbye, touched that Nat held my hands and said, "Thank you. Thank you for being so kind."

I waved it all away, big smiles and "just let me know when you need a burst of Mary Poppins again." Then got into the car and sobbed all the way from Bristol to Reading, finally arriving home looking as though my world had ended.

When I stepped through the front door and saw the state of Jack, that didn't seem too much of a ridiculous notion.

The kitchen had that distinct odour of bins that needed emptying. There were several empty wine bottles by the sink and Jack himself was unshaven with something of the Great Uncle Arthur in a not very diligent nursing home about him. I gave him a brief hug, wondering how the hell that preppy young student who never turned up without a liberal dosing of Lynx became this broken man smelling like the morning after a party. Of course, I wanted to say, "Are you okay? You look terrible," but my long-term chivvying-everyone-along role was harder to shed than I'd bargained on. I only managed, "How long have you been wearing those clothes for? Have you had a shower since I left?"

He sank onto a kitchen chair, put his head in his hands and wept. "What if I go to prison, Zell? How will I survive? How will you?"

A shiver of dread passed through me. Jack was the sorter-outer, the ballast of the family ship. I was more the decider of bedroom colour schemes, provider of aftersun and instigator of Friday evening dance-offs.

I took a deep breath.

"Jack, we don't know what will happen yet, but we will sort it out. And if you do go to prison, we'll just have to deal with that as well. But you're not using that as an excuse to stop showering. Go and put some clean clothes on. We're not going to live as though the sky is going to fall in until it does. If it does."

He nodded and shuffled upstairs. I raced about the kitchen, picking up plates and mugs, bleaching the surfaces, frowning at the fact that Hannah had used a huge Pyrex dish for her cereal rather than rinse a cereal bowl or put on the dishwasher. I gathered up a pile of letters and found one from the bank saying we'd missed a mortgage payment and to get in touch urgently "otherwise your house could be repossessed." I felt a rush of self-pity. I told myself not to be pathetic, to grow a backbone, but I couldn't hold back my fear any longer. If Jack went to jail, I couldn't live here. I didn't know what the numbers were, but I knew enough to be sure I'd have to move.

I lifted up my laptop lid and scrolled through the replies to my Facebook post advertising the Beetle. I messaged the ones that were interested. Jack would have to sell the bloody Jaguar whether he liked it or not. And, of course, instead of choosing a calm moment to chat that through with him, I started shouting about it the second he appeared at the bottom of the stairs, still unshaven, still in a pair of tracksuit bottoms but with what appeared to be a clean T-shirt.

"Stop going on about the bloody car!"

"What do you suggest then? Sorry to point this out, but you're the one who decided to walk off with fifty bloody grand and I can't see you making many plans to pay it back."

"You don't get it, do you? I'm not asking you to sell all that crap you've bought over the years, the flaming antique ottoman, the Designers Guild this, that and the other, the marble birdbath all the way from sodding Carrara."

A huge rage rose inside me, so white-hot and engulfing that I picked up my handbag and walked straight out of the front door. My kids didn't need two parents in the dock—one for theft and one for murder.

I saw the light on at Kate's house and stormed over there, my body rigid with self-righteousness, already justifying to myself how I had the headspace to deal with the bureaucracy of importing a birdbath from Italy but overlooked the fact that Jack was spending more and more time locked in his office upstairs and always seemed to be just closing down the computer whenever I went in. I hoped Kate would have wine. Otherwise I'd run down to the Londis.

I rang the doorbell.

She opened the door. "Hello, stranger! How are you? I haven't seen you for ages. I see Ollie couldn't resist the charms of introducing his son to a very glamorous granny in the end. I saw the photo on Facebook. Isn't he gorgeous?"

I nodded. "He is. Really lovely. Ollie's finding it a bit of a shock to the system."

Kate stood across the door without inviting me in. She carried on, "Babies are hard work in the beginning, aren't they? He'll get used to it, though. And it's brilliant he's so young. He'll have loads of energy when the baby's a teenager. Unlike me."

I sighed. "That's one way of looking at it."

We stood awkwardly. I couldn't go home, not right now while I could still feel fury buzzing through my veins. "I wondered if I could come in for a minute?"

A little beat of silence. Kate looked away, then said, "Yes, of course, um, Alex, you know, Jack's friend, your friend, Alex, has just popped in for a minute." She blushed.

"Oh, okay, if you don't mind me joining you?"

Alex appeared in the hallway. "Hello, Zell! How's it all going?" He moved to give me a hug but not before I caught the glance between them. A mixture of amusement, embarrassment and tenderness. Alex resting his hand briefly on Kate's back. That invisible but indisputable aura of togetherness. I felt a wave of understanding, followed by the odd sensation of being an outsider despite knowing Alex for over twenty years. Lucky them, having all that glorious getting to know each other to come. He stepped towards me and kissed me on the cheek.

I raised my eyebrows. "I didn't see your bike outside. Don't tell me you've finally realised how dangerous motorbikes are?"

"I parked it in the alley."

"Trying to travel incognito?"

"Something like that." He couldn't stop himself grinning, which made me envious and pleased in equal measures.

Kate gathered herself. "Come in, would you like a drink? Tea? Wine?"

"Wine, please. It's been that sort of a day. That sort of a bloody month actually," I said, sitting in the chair she'd pulled out for me in the kitchen. To my shame, the tears I'd been containing burst their banks in a spectacular fashion.

As Kate busied herself opening the bottle, Alex murmured, "Is everything okay, Zell?"

Why did blokes say that to a woman who was crying?

"No, it's bloody not! It's all absolute shit!"

Alex looked non-plussed, as though he wanted to back away, saying, "Dodgy drug dealers, yes, hysterical swearing women, no."

Kate put a couple of glasses of wine down. "Why don't you go and talk to Alex in the sitting room?"

Alex reached up and put his hand over hers, as if to say she didn't need to leave. A distant part of me marvelled at how quickly brand-new love affairs took priority over long-term friendships. Though if there was one woman who could keep a secret, it would be Kate.

I said, "Stay. It's only a matter of time before everyone knows anyway. I bumped into Jack's secretary in the supermarket and she talked to me like someone had died. You might as well decide now whether you still want to be friends with us."

Kate sat completely still while Alex asked all the right questions, with the ease of old friendships, starting with whether we were splitting up or if one of us was ill.

I sighed. "Nothing like that. Though I feel like divorcing him for being so bloody stupid." I paused. "Jack's probably going to end up in prison. He borrowed—who am I kidding?— stole—fifty thousand pounds from Painted Wagon Holidays."

Alex clapped his hand over his mouth. "Shit. He said he was in a bit of bother about money, 'run up a few debts,' when I spoke to him the other week, but he was all 'nothing I can't sort out.'"

I saw immediately why Alex was so good at his job. He fetched a notebook from his rucksack in the hallway, then got right to the heart of the matter without ever sounding judgemental, just neutral, on the quest for information. How long had it been going on for? Where were they on the police investigation? Was there any chance of the charges being dropped if partial repayment was made? Meanwhile, Kate bustled about fetching more wine. I daren't look at her face in case she was mouthing *Fifty thousand pounds!* over and over to herself.

No doubt she was wondering the same as me: how someone stole that amount without anyone noticing?

Half an hour earlier I'd have happily got into the car and left Jack to sort out his own shit, but now I had a bizarre urge to defend him. "I feel so guilty. I wanted more, more, more. Private schooling, a better house, the biggest house."

Kate hadn't said anything up until then. "You didn't steal the money, though, Gisela. Don't put that on yourself."

Alex was making notes. "Start thinking of who you can call as character witnesses. See if you can transfer the house into your name. Sorry to dig into your finances, but have you got any money to pay it back?"

I told him about the cars.

"He always did like a good label. He's going to have to get over that if he wants to stay out of prison. I'll talk to him."

I stood up. "I'd better go. Thank you." I turned to Kate. "Could you keep this to yourself for the moment? Everyone will know soon enough—it will probably be in the papers—but we need to tell the children first."

She hugged me, a great big warm hug that I didn't know Kate was capable of. "I thought you'd fallen out with me, I hadn't seen you for so long. Hang on in there, you'll get through it."

"I wish I had your confidence, Kate. I feel as though everything about our lives is a complete sham."

She shook her head. "No one has a clue what people's lives are really like. I was looking at Sally's Facebook feed and thinking she had the most glamorous life in the world. I feel guilty for not realising what was really going on. How could we know that she'd lost weight because her heart was broken?"

I nodded. "Not many people are going to stick up a photo of themselves in a bikini and say, 'Look at me, I've put on two stone' or write 'I'm really disappointed in the way my son or daughter turned out and I don't like them very much.' When did you last see someone admit 'My family holiday was shit because we can't stand being together 24/7'? Never!"

Kate leaned forward, her eyes serious. "But that's just it. We're all getting sucked into the whole 'everyone has a perfect family/wonderful holiday/beautiful home.' It's no wonder we feel like crashing great failures all the time. Me included."

"Why do you feel like a failure? I know you never post anything, but I'm always looking at your life and thinking it's so straightforward. Okay, you don't have a husband..." It didn't escape my notice that Alex squeezed her hand and Kate blushed for the second time during my visit. "But you've got a good job, you're putting something back into the community, Daisy is gorgeous and a real credit to you. I get the sense that sometimes finances are a bit tight, but you still seem to enjoy yourself and you're not bloody stealing money or wondering whether you'll end up with any friends if your husband goes to prison."

Kate let go of Alex's hand. He reached out and pulled it back towards him. He nodded, almost imperceptibly, his eyes holding hers. Her whole face was shuttered, resistant, and then suddenly she put her shoulders back and held her head up. My brain was too tired to decipher it all.

She looked me straight in the eye and said, "Gisela, I will always be your friend whatever happens."

The strength of conviction in her voice made tears spring to my eyes.

"Thank you. I hope you don't change your mind when you hear all the gory details."

She put her glass down. "I won't." She took such a deep breath I heard the air suck in. "I was put on trial for murder nearly eighteen years ago. I don't think a bit of theft will frighten me."

If I could have videoed myself in that moment and posted it on Facebook, I'd have had a face like a goggle-eyed goose set to a soundtrack of ancient machinery with badly oiled cogs whirring and cranking into place. #Stunned

CHAPTER 41

Kate

Saturday 16 June

Daisy's eighteenth birthday party was the first time we'd had more than three or four people in the house since she'd started school. I was fluttering about, fiddling with the beer and wine bottles in a big trough of ice, moving the bowls of crisps an inch one way and back again, checking on the sausages for the fiftieth time. I straightened the birthday card from Oskar. He'd offered to pay for her to visit next summer. It had made her day and I'd managed not to piss on her party by huffing about him being a part-time dad.

Upstairs, I could hear Daisy laughing with Hannah and a couple of girls from college, the scent of competing perfumes drifting down into the living room with two hours still to go until kick-off. Alex had promised to come straight from work. My relief when he drew up on the drive made me ashamed of how quickly I'd come to rely on him.

I let him in and he gathered me into a hug, kissing me. For a second, I melted into him, that warm, heavy sense of belonging spreading through me. At the sound of a door banging upstairs, I pulled away, feeling like a teenager whose parents might suddenly walk in.

He raised his arms in surrender. "Sorry. Just too tempting."

He walked into the living room, gesturing to the balloons, streamers and fairy lights. "Wow, this looks lovely. Aren't you clever?"

"Gisela and Sally helped me. It was quite the afternoon—Gisela filled in Sally on what's happening with Jack. She was much more shocked than I expected, but she was pretty definite that she'd stand by them both. It was a bit like a scene out of *The Three Musketeers* in the end—'All for one, and one for all.' "

He put his hand on my waist. "Did you manage to tell her your story?"

"I did."

"And?"

"She was lovely about it, actually." My throat constricted as I thought about the horror, then sympathy on her face. "She said she'd always wondered if there was more to me than met the eye, and that she'd sensed I was holding something back. She also said some really nice stuff, like she couldn't believe how I'd coped with it all on my own and managed to bring up a daughter as well-adjusted as Daisy."

"See? People aren't as harsh as you think."

I untangled the silver cord on one of the balloons, twiddling the ends round and round in my fingers. "It's learning to trust that. I still feel as though there'll be a big crowd baying for blood outside my house if anyone finds out."

"I don't think that will happen, but if it does, we'll go to the police this time. You've effectively been in a sort of jail for eighteen years without doing anything wrong. Of course it's tragic for Becky, but you just happened to be in the wrong place at the wrong time. This is it now, Kate. You can't spend the rest of your life peering round the curtains." He stopped speaking, though I could tell by his face that he had something else he wanted to say. "I didn't know whether to bring this up or not now, but I got a letter for you at work. It might make you feel better about tonight."

"For me?"

"Well, it was to me, really, about you."

My heart started to thud. I wanted to run through the house, shouting that the party was cancelled, that they'd all have to go home. "What letter? Show me!"

Alex grabbed hold of my arm. "Sorry, I haven't expressed myself very well. It's not a terrible thing, might even be a good thing. Come into the kitchen so I can show you."

I followed him through, scraping out a chair and sitting down. I wasn't a big drinker but the Prosecco on the side suddenly looked very appealing.

"You know I interviewed Becky and rang her to say there wasn't enough story so we weren't pursuing it?"

A hot rush of fear rose up my chest. I nodded.

"She wrote to me."

He unfolded the letter and held it out to me. I wanted to snatch it from him and run off and read it, locked away somewhere where he wouldn't be able to see my reaction. I looked at the address on the top of the page, written in those rounded letters of hers, the writing of so many childhood birthday cards with cuddly bears and best-friend banners. 117 Garton Street. I wondered if she'd sat at the little pine table in her kitchen, the backdrop to so much of our early motherhood, rocking our daughters there, moaning about our sore nipples, our lack of sleep, our wobbly stomachs, and trying to drink cups of tea while they were still hot. Or would she have curled up on the brown leather sofa in her living room, where sometimes she'd doze for an hour while I minded our babies, oblivious to what was heading our way?

I hardly dared let my eyes drop down to the words.

> *Dear Alex,*
> *I don't know why you decided that the unexplained death of my baby wasn't a "strong enough story." It completely wrecked my life, nearly finished off my marriage and broke up a friendship—the best friend*

I ever had. What you told me on the phone—that your editor was looking for something "more women could relate to"—just doesn't sound right to me. What woman couldn't relate to letting her friend that she's known for over twenty years look after a baby and how awful the child dying while she was in charge would be?

Anyway, I don't suppose you'll change your mind, though I would have liked to tell people about what happened because I think it would have helped them— and me. The reason I am writing is because at the beginning you seemed really excited by the story when we met. I remember you saying something like, "This is very powerful. You lost two people. Your baby and your best friend." Then, as soon as I showed you the photos, you went all weird and "we've got a crowded schedule, so I'm not promising anything, we're just exploring possibilities at the moment." I keep going round and round with this in my mind. Maybe I've got completely the wrong end of the stick, but I felt like you were put off by Izabela, but I can't work out why. Because she was Polish and with all the Brexit stuff, you didn't want to look like you were having a pop at Eastern Europeans? Because it would take too long to track her down? Because there are too many poor sods like me who you could easily interview instead without going on a wild goose chase looking for someone who's probably changed her name? I got the impression you wanted to keep her out of it.

Maybe I shouldn't rake it all up again. One of the things that I didn't say when we met was that for years, I couldn't forgive her. We pushed to have her prosecuted for murder. I couldn't accept that Cara had died, fine one day and gone the next, out of the blue like that. Someone had to be responsible.

I wanted Izabela to pay for my pain, when she—as I saw it—waltzed off scot-free with Karolina, still alive with everything that should have been mine ahead of her—days out shopping, mother of the bride, maybe even grandchildren. Over the last few years, I've finally had some counselling—better late than never. It's coming up to what would have been Cara's eighteenth birthday and it just felt like it was time to try and make some sense of all of this. It was offered to me when she died, but all I cared about then was making Izabela pay.

Counselling has helped me see that some things are just bad luck, stuff we can't control and that we have to accept, however hard it is. It also made me realise that Cara's death and how I behaved afterwards to Izabela has probably ruined her life too.

So I just wanted to say, that if you ever decide to make a programme about forgiveness, then you should keep me in mind, though I wouldn't blame her if she doesn't feel like forgiving me for what I did to her.

Yours sincerely,
Becky Haughton

He pulled his chair right up next to mine and put his arm around my shoulders. "She doesn't sound like someone who is going to cause trouble anymore."

I pressed my fingers into my eyes. "I don't know what to think. I'm frightened in case it's a trick to get you to find me."

"When I interviewed her, she sounded like she missed you. She seemed genuine to me. I know she's been an absolute cow, but I couldn't help liking her when I met her," he said, as a sudden blast of "She Will Be Loved" blared down the stairs.

I swallowed. "Only one way to find out." I grabbed my phone, ran upstairs and shuffled the girls into a group. "Say cheese!"

They clambered onto the bed, making a pyramid of shapes, in the shortest skirts and tightest tops.

"Put your tongues in!" God knows why teenage girls thought they looked so gorgeous with their tongues hanging out. More like a bunch of beagles heading for water.

When they'd inspected the photos—"I look so ugly in that one!" "Look at my chins!"—and finally agreed on one where they were all satisfied with their appearance, I said, "Right. Half an hour, then you need to be downstairs to greet everyone. Not too much vodka before the party even starts."

I walked downstairs, loving Daisy's excitement, and the idea she was doing exactly what any other eighteen-year-old would be doing on her birthday. Adrenaline was buzzing around my body as I contemplated something that would have been unthinkable a year ago. I looked at Alex, my finger poised over the blue button on my phone.

He nodded, "Go for it."

Photo: Daisy and her friends.
  Caption: Happy eighteenth birthday to my gorgeous Daisy. I couldn't love her more. As we say in Polish, "Twoje zdrowie."
  #Cheers

CHAPTER 42

Gisela

Wednesday 21 November

In the end, Jack had not only realised that he wouldn't need a Jaguar in jail and selling it might keep his freedom, but we'd also put the house on the market at the end of June. Whether or not he went to prison, we needed to find a way to pay back the fifty thousand pounds—he'd been adamant that had to happen even if he wasn't ordered to by law—"just so I can look myself in the eye." There was also the small matter of staying solvent for however long it took for him to find another job. I never let myself say "*if* he found another job" out loud.

In the months before Jack's trial I'd intended to move away completely if he ended up in jail, perhaps nearer to Ollie. Jack disagreed when I suggested it. "Zell, far be it for me to tell you what to do, but if you move near Ollie, you're going to be supporting him rather than the other way round. They're still pretty chaotic. I think you're better off staying locally where you know people, if you can bear all the gossip. Kate and Alex will help you out. If you move to a completely different area, you won't be able to call on anyone if there's a pipe burst or you hear a noise in the night." He'd wept then. "I'm sorry. You shouldn't be in this position."

I'd gripped his hand. "You worry about you. I'm going to

be fine, whatever happens." Although the little voice inside my head kept threatening to shout the word "bollocks" out loud, Jack was usually so stoic about the prospect of going to prison, he dragged me along with him. At least until three in the morning when I'd lie staring at the ceiling, tears running into my ears, wondering how I'd cope with getting a removal quote, work out whether I was being ripped off, or even understand the survey report on a new house.

Sally and I found a solution in the bottom of a wine glass— "Why don't you just sell your house and move into mine?"—a rare occasion when our brilliant idea didn't seem ridiculous in the morning. In fact, it worked in everyone's favour: Chris bought Sally out so she could press on with the purchase of her house in Italy, he saved on the estate agent's fees and was happy to wait a couple of months while ours completed and we freed up money to survive and thrive if Jack went to prison.

Now I stood sandwiched between Kate and Alex in Guildford Crown Court waiting to hear what Jack's sentence would be. I still hadn't accepted that my husband, this ordinary man who oiled the gate hinge, flapped the leaf-blower about every autumn and renewed our breakdown cover, might be heading off in the back of a police van with no chance to say goodbye. He looked like he was ready for a meeting with the bank manager in his navy suit and pink shirt. I kept trying to catch his eye, to let him know that the great reserve of youthful love powered by energy, dreams and not knowing what we didn't know was still there. Dented, bruised from life's twists and turns for sure, but still solid at the core. He didn't look at me. He stared straight ahead, glazed, as though he had stumbled into a life that wasn't his, where someone would say, "Off you go now, back to your own world."

Suddenly we were all standing and the judge's words were rippling across the court, my mind a step behind the sound. "For someone who by most people's standards led a privileged life, your greed has led to your downfall. You abused your position and deceived a long-standing friend to the detriment of the business." He went on to say that he had considered the impact on Mike and the breach of trust. I knew those words would wound Jack. He'd prided himself on being loyal. I had always, always seen him that way. Otherwise we'd never have stayed together through university. Then he talked about reducing his sentence on the grounds of his guilty plea. I was still hoping he might get a suspended sentence or community service.

Nine months rang out. Nine months! Kate grabbed my hand and Alex slipped his arm under mine. I didn't cry. I was still waiting for the next bit, the bit that meant he wouldn't actually have to serve all that time. But then the judge was writing something down and the court official was shuffling his papers, putting the lid on his pen, and the people Alex had told me were journalists were filing out.

Jack turned to look at me as he was led away. I lifted my hand, not even having the presence of mind to blow a kiss. I watched the back of him disappear, his shoulders rounded, slight against the burly policeman by his side. I never knew that it was possible to be so filled with sadness without wailing and buckling into a heap.

Kate pushed me forward. "Let's go. Alex will fetch the car and pick us up from the front."

I nodded, relieved that someone knew what to do and I could just blunder along without having to think.

"Gisela, this is really important. If any journalists ask you a question, do not speak to them."

And sure enough, as we walked through reception, a man in his thirties called my name, "Just wondered if I could have a quick word about your husband's conviction?"

Kate practically pushed him out of the way. "No comment!" She hustled me down the front steps past two or three people, one girl about Ollie's age, with their tape recorders and notebooks.

I still felt rude ignoring people who were shouting, "Excuse me! Gisela!" but Kate was waving away a photographer and pushed me towards her car where Alex had the door open. I fumbled into the back seat. Alex drove off and I sat shaking my head, thinking, *I didn't see that coming*, quickly followed by, *Why didn't I see that coming?*

The sight of the prosecution's barrister crossing the road, light of step in the winter sun, unravelled me. I started swearing, terrible disgusting language, railing about Jack's useless defence team, then my stupid bloody husband. "As if I cared about a great big American fridge? I might have liked it for five minutes, but I didn't realise he'd have to go to prison to buy it! For fuck's sake!" before bursting into sobs that originated in my stomach and felt as though they were lacerating vital organs as they exited.

It didn't take long for word to get out. That smug cow at number seven dragged her three kids into the house whenever she saw me as though they'd found bodies under our back patio. The bloke at the corner shop folded over the local newspaper so that Jack's picture on the front page wasn't right in my face. People I hadn't heard a word from in years popped up on my Facebook page—"You okay, my lovely? Let me know if I can do anything," which felt like a thinly veiled "Please get in touch so I can hear about your disaster firsthand." Or "You can call me any time, even at three in the morning." When I sat in front of my computer thinking yet again, *I wouldn't call you at ten o'clock in the morning or five o'clock in the afternoon, let alone three in the morning*, I decided that Facebook was not where I was going to find support. I'd seen—and posted—enough photos of glasses of champagne, happy family holidays and way too many painted toes on sunloungers to know that *some* of it might be true but no one had the perfect life. I felt like posting a picture of Jack peering through prison bars and putting it next to the photos of my fluffy cushions, the bouquets of roses, the absolute bollocks that I'd shared with the world so they could look at me and think, "That Gisela, she's got a good life." Yep, a good life on money stolen from my husband's company.

I deleted my account.

CHAPTER 43

Six Months Later

Sally, Castelfiorentino, Italy

Saturday 18 May

That raw but resigned longing crept up so rarely now. It was the small gesture of Hannah arranging some olive tree twigs in an old oil tin for Gisela's bedroom that gave me pause. The casual thoughtfulness of it. Overall, I'd been thrilled to witness Hannah's excitement that her mum would finally see what she'd achieved—the two bathrooms renovated with a little help from Aldo, the local plumber who seemed to spend a lot of time throwing his hands in the air while Hannah sweated away with tile cutters and soldering irons. She had a great eye for what worked, encouraging me to choose an antique stone sink we'd found in a junkyard, persuading me into the terracotta tiles that had, in her words, "been a bugger to cut" but now looked both rustic and chic. I'd learnt not to dwell on the pang of envy that Hannah FaceTiming Gisela brought, especially when there was nothing huge to report, just a "seeing how you are," the giggle, the shared joke, the unselfconscious "Love you" signalling the end of the conversation. The belonging to someone without having to try, that glorious freedom to be any old self, knowing that who you really were would never stop the other person loving you, never make them leave you. Unlike husbands, who might find someone whose self they liked more. I would probably never have that, not with someone who shared my DNA, anyway, and I was beginning to accept that. There were other ways of belonging.

I would still love someone to pop a little jar of flowers into a bedroom for me, though, for no other reason than it would please me. I chased that thought away, wandering out to the garden with a glass of Vernaccia and sitting on my little terrace, with the bougainvillea winding round the pergola. I couldn't wait for Gisela, Kate and Daisy to arrive. And for Gisela to realise the plumbing course she thought was a disaster for Hannah had turned out to be the making of her. Last September when I'd suggested the idea, she'd said, "Really? You want Hannah to come out and help you? Well, she hasn't found any other work here." Gisela had raised her eyebrows. "She can be a bit tricky to get along with sometimes. I hope she'll be okay. If you're sure, the timing would be perfect, then she won't have to be around when we go to the Magistrates' Court in October. Or the Crown Court for that matter, if it goes that far."

Hannah had jumped at the idea, impatiently wiping away a tear when I suggested it. "I don't want to be here if Dad goes to prison."

Over the winter, she'd lost that indolent air, that condescension that was so off-putting. Now she was lean and fit from months grafting in the old farmhouses south of Florence, whizzing around on her motorino, learning Italian and in great demand with the expats whose wine and food vocabulary didn't run to telephone conversations about broken loos and leaking taps. That odd superiority, her overconfidence, had matured into something earthier, something still outspoken but laced with an acceptance that there might be other opinions that counted, a debate to be had. I liked the idea someone was house-sitting when I was away travelling to wine fairs, feeding the little stray cat we'd adopted and called Strega, the Italian for witch, because she was so jet black.

I hoped in some small way I'd contributed to helping her grow up. That I'd offered a haven, an escape, when the rest of her world had caught, suspended in a catastrophe that had wobbled the foundations of her comfortable existence. She showed no sign of wanting to return to the UK and, selfishly, I was glad.

I leant over the little wall into my allotment and examined my tomatoes that were already ripening in the early May sun. Dad had helped me plant them when he'd visited with Mum a couple of weeks ago. "Nice place this, love. Feel like a king sitting on your terrace." Even Mum had perked up under Aldo's charming attentions.

I'd made this happen. It wasn't the future I wanted. Not before anyway. Though I was getting better at seeing it as a different path, not a second-best path, not a plan B because A had failed, just the one I hadn't seen on the map as early as the others.

The slamming of a taxi door broke into my thoughts. I ran around the side of the terrace to see Gisela, Kate and Daisy hauling their suitcases out of the boot. I managed not to be offended as Gisela flew past me to hug Hannah. I could sense the rush of love and relief between them, Hannah launching into how much Italian she'd learnt, dragging Gisela into the house to show her what she'd done, Gisela laughing and telling her to slow down, that she wanted to hear all about it, but she needed the loo first.

I was already hugging Kate and Daisy and asking about Alex when Gisela turned to me and grabbed my hands. "Your house looks amazing, Sally. And, honestly, I can see already that Hannah's happier here with you than she's been in the last two years with us. You did me such a favour, getting her out of the way while, well, all the stuff with Jack."

I waved her away. "It's just timing and the opportunity to do something she enjoys. All the rather gorgeous Italian boys down at the bar in the village are good for her soul too, no doubt." I turned away, busying myself with helping with the suitcases so she couldn't see how much her words meant to me. Then I took a deep breath. "How is Jack? He's coming home soon, isn't he?"

"Two weeks."

I didn't have to ask how she was feeling. Her face lit up with longing. There'd be more to that story, the inevitable jiggling round, adjusting back, dealing with unexpected fallout while everyone found their places in the family again.

Gisela had never wavered. "I was nearly as much to blame. We were both really stupid."

Although I always wanted to say, "But the difference is you didn't steal any money!" I envied the fact she could find that level of forgiveness when, even now, the thought of Chris lying to me, having sex with me, then going home to Sophie and her burgeoning bump while declaring he still loved me, could fill me with a white-hot rage. Today, though, today wasn't that day.

I ushered everyone through, with Kate saying, "What a gorgeous kitchen. And look at your basil! That beats those weedy little supermarket packets any day. It's like a triffid!" There were more exclamations about my lovely blue and white ceramic table, the view over the olive groves, the sun hot enough to have everyone peeling off layers. It was so long since I'd had this sense of contentment, with no agenda licking at the edges, just an awareness of well-being, of sharing in the delight of my friends loving everything I adored about my new home.

As Hannah fetched chilled bottles of Prosecco and bowls of sundried tomatoes and goat's cheese, filling in Daisy on the local talent, and Gisela and Kate brought me up to date on life back in Parkview, I had a thought. A thought I hadn't had in years. I might not have everything I wanted, but I was happy being me.

Photo: Everyone holding a glass of Prosecco against a backdrop of olive groves.
    Caption: Am always delighted to see Kate Jones, Daisy Jones and Gisela Anderson anywhere in the world but especially in my new home where Hannah Anderson has worked so hard to give us hot showers!
    #Italy #GoodFriends #LuckyMe

CHAPTER 44

Gisela

Monday 3 June

Kate sat in the car while I stood at the prison gates. My stomach was flipping, just as it used to when I waited at the station on Friday nights, craning my neck to catch sight of him with his rucksack hanging off one shoulder. Back then, we took so much for granted. We didn't know the answers and we didn't even worry about finding them. We just assumed that life would go our way.

Now I had to keep lifting every rock to find my certainty. It hadn't been my intention but I'd created a life without him. I loved my job at Laura Ashley. He'd wrinkled his nose when I'd told him. "I'm sorry you didn't get to become a lawyer." He tried to smile. "Might have come in useful."

I'd felt angry, deflated, because I wanted to show him I wasn't just sitting around, that I was at least doing something to bring in a bit of money. When the visiting time was up, I'd left, seething with resentment as I walked out past the other men, some with huge biceps and thuggy haircuts, who cuddled their babies with an intensity that made me weep, the sort of men we'd probably forgotten existed in our gilded lives. Others with pale faces and straggly hair looked as though they wouldn't dare take a library book back late, let alone commit an imprisonable crime. Jack was one of them.

Standing here today, waiting for him to emerge, I counted the hours I'd seen him since he went to prison. About three hours, sometimes four a month, fewer when Ollie took one of my visits. That brightly lit hall was the enemy of honest conversation. Neither of us wanted to hurt the other with the reality of our lives. I didn't want to tell him that sometimes I drank wine with Kate and didn't think about him for a whole evening while we swapped stories from our week. I couldn't say I almost dreaded the phone calls from him because of the pressure to say important things, but somehow knowing he was standing in a corridor with other prisoners milling about made my mind go blank. It didn't seem very kind to tell him I'd got into a new routine of walking Titch in the woods every morning, when Jack was lucky to be allowed out into the prison yard. Nor did I spell out how often I stayed with Ollie and Nat. I didn't want to make him feel bad for missing out on Alfie, with his toothy smiles, the best antidote to an aching heart. I wanted to bottle that gorgeous giggle to curl around on days when I imagined Jack sitting on a mean little bunk in his cell. It was hard to remember how devastated I'd been when I'd opened the ultrasound on my birthday. Just watching Ollie calm, playful and loving even when Alfie was crying or throwing up over him filled me with a pride that a hundred top jobs or first-class degrees never would.

Equally, I didn't want to hear that Jack cried when he got letters from Hannah. That sometimes he felt frightened of other inmates. That if the PIN for his phone card wasn't working, it seemed like the end of the world. I didn't want to know how bad it was. And I was pretty sure he didn't tell me.

Then, suddenly, the gate opened and Jack was there, clutching a bag of belongings, looking thin but smiling, a bit shy.

I hesitated, unprepared for this moment I'd been thinking about for so long now it was here. Then we ran towards each other. I hugged him, breathing in the smell of cooking, of alien soap powder, of stale air but still underpinned by a trace of the scent I recognised as my husband. I had the sensation of standing on one of those wobbly wooden bridges. Swaying. A bit unstable. But still a bridge that, with a fair wind, would take us safely back to shore.

CHAPTER 45

Kate

Saturday 22 June

Photo: Kate and Alex on their wedding day.

Caption: I hardly ever post photos, but this man has made me so happy, I'm going to make an exception.

(P. S. My life is not usually so perfect—I'm normally running around late for work, shouting at Daisy about the state of her bedroom and never, ever have painted nails. But it was my wedding day.)

#Hope #Future #Love #Don'tUsuallyLookLikeThis

Look for more compelling and emotional fiction from Kerry Fisher!

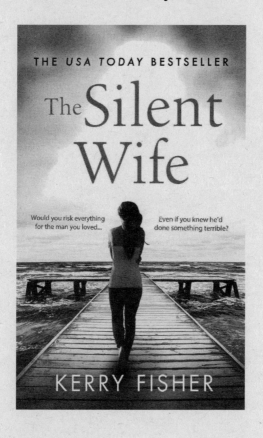

READING GROUP GUIDE

THE INSPIRATION FOR *THE WOMAN I WAS BEFORE*

Dear Reader,

One of the questions I'm asked a lot when I speak at festivals or reading groups is where did you get the idea for your books?

Almost always the answer is from talking to people—my friends, people I get chatting to in cafes, on trains, buses, sieving little fragments from conversations with my mum (who can't stand in a queue without delving into someone's life history: "I met a lovely man at the supermarket checkout—he bred ferrets for a living"). All of my ideas come from what I see around me—and more specifically, from the things that impact families, and especially women, who often seem to carry the lion's share of the burden of keeping family life on an even keel.

I grew up in a pre-internet era, so I still regard participating in social media as a choice rather than the simple fact of life it appears to be for most teenagers, my own included. Occasionally, I see a quote on Facebook that says something like, "Do you remember a time when we could go through a whole day without taking a photo?" It seems quaint and old-fashioned now that posing for pictures was once reserved for Christmas, holidays and red-letter days.

This phenomenon of documenting our lives in such detail, right down to what we eat for breakfast, coupled with the human tendency to try to present the best version of ourselves—our exotic holidays, thoughtful birthday gifts, perfect family occasions—gave me the idea for the social media aspect of this book. My family holidays tend to be more of the "Ugh! We're not going to any more museums, are we?"/"Will there be any Wi-Fi?"/"I thought you were bringing the driving licence" variety, plus some shouting from me to get out of the house and to the airport on time. I don't see too much of my reality represented on Facebook, so I wanted to explore that sense of comparing your own life with the impossible perfection presented on social media in more detail. It's so easy to feel as though your world is humdrum and mundane and everyone else is having a much better time. I was also interested in how what we see on Facebook is often only part of the story—not necessarily a lie, but a snapshot in time that represents a highlight rather than the day-to-day reality.

I felt particularly strongly about the difference between what we put on social media and what our real lives are like because six months before I started writing this book, my seventeen-year-old son had been diagnosed with cancer. During that time I didn't post anything personal or talk publicly about his diagnosis but I did carry on with work-related promotion. The book preceding this one, *The Secret Child*, came out in November 2017 when he was right in the middle of treatment. I posted a jolly video of me reading the first chapter and talking about my new novel. Anyone looking at my social media posts would probably think I didn't have a care in the world, when in fact, the following day, he was going into hospital for chemotherapy. Now, two years on, I do post happy family photos of us all because I am so grateful that he's in remission and still here. (Though, sadly, just for balance, I must add that I still haven't become the perfect parent and he is a normal twenty-year-old with many wonderful qualities and a few imperfections.)

This brings me to the other huge inspiration for this book: the strength that can be gained from friendship. All three women in *The Woman I Was Before* benefitted from discovering they could be honest with each other and allow themselves to be vulnerable. They found that at their lowest moments, someone else could be their strength until they could support themselves. Over the past few years, I've relied hugely on my womenfolk to lift me up and comfort me in the toughest of times and I wanted to celebrate the treasure that friendship can deliver in the darkest moments. I loved seeing Kate finally realise that after all she'd been through, she could relax in the company of Sally and Gisela and not hide away; that she could bring the secret she had considered shameful for so long out into the light, where in the warmth of friendship, it lost its power to dominate her life.

I also wanted to examine parental expectations in this book and how family relations come under strain when an adult child takes a different path from the one their parents advocate. Sally's mum wanted grandchildren and was unintentionally hurtful in her hints that Sally should get on with having a baby rather than focusing on her career. Gisela was keen for Hannah to go to university because she regretted not going herself and found it difficult to see that Hannah might be happier doing something else. And finally, from so many conversations with friends and also readers, I was interested in examining the fallout when a child chooses a partner that doesn't meet with family approval. In this case, Gisela was worried about the impact of the age gap between Ollie and Natalie but that could easily have translated into differences in class, religion, education, earning power... the hundreds of ways that parents project their hopes onto their children and struggle to adjust when they fall in love with someone who doesn't tick the right boxes.

Throughout my life, I've been fascinated by men and women in long-term relationships that fall apart because they cannot agree over something fundamental, such as Sally's desire to have children and Chris' equal determination not to. I've often observed that the partner who refuses to get married or have children then seems to turn up with someone else sporting a wedding ring or a baby within a very short space of time, as Sally witnesses with Chris and Sophie in *The Woman I Was Before*. Equally, by sending Sally to live in Italy, I hoped to show that it's possible to recover from the ending of one dream and to discover another to pursue and the strength to do it.

Most of all, I wanted to write about survival. Surviving when you find yourself in the eye of a sudden storm. Of hanging on and keeping the faith that one day, it will all be behind you and good times can come again. Kate finally found peace. Gisela's life veered off its comfortable tracks, especially when Jack went to prison, but she discovered ways to keep going, to appreciate the joy in small things—a steady job, time with her grandson, seeing her daughter stretch her wings and work in Italy. And Sally was stronger than she gave herself credit for, forging a different but satisfying life.

On that note, I'm acutely aware that some readers might have suffered the terrible loss of a baby to sudden infant death syndrome—my heart goes out to you. I hope I struck the right balance between being sympathetic to both Kate and Becky, who experienced the tragedy in different ways.

Finally, one of the biggest privileges of my job is receiving messages from people who've enjoyed my books—and, of course, social media is wonderful for facilitating that. Sometimes readers have shared their own personal stories when they identify with an element in my novels. I am absolutely humbled by the raw honesty of some of these messages and the trust you put in me. Thank you.

I hope you loved *The Woman I Was Before* and would be very grateful if you could write a review if you did. I'd love to hear what you think, and it makes a real difference to helping new readers to discover one of my books for the first time.

I love hearing from my readers—you can get in touch on my Facebook page, through Twitter, Goodreads or my website. Whenever I hear from readers, I am reminded of why I love my job—pure motivational gold!

Thank you so much for reading,
Kerry Fisher

QUESTIONS FOR READERS

1. Should Kate have gone to the police to stop her friend harassing her instead of moving around the country trying to avoid her? What did you think about her attempts to protect Daisy by banning her from social media and changing her name? Was she right to do that?

2. Was Sally weak for not giving Chris an ultimatum early on or strong for giving him space to think things over? Do you think she was in denial about what was really happening?

3. Was Gisela a controlling mother who wanted to dictate who her son fell in love with, or was she just a mother who wanted to protect him from making a big mistake? Did Gisela and Kate both try to control their children in different ways and did you have any sympathy with them?

4. Did you think Jack's approach—that Ollie would come around eventually—was the right one or did you think he needed to be more proactive?

5. Did Gisela's and Sally's posts on Facebook stem from a desire to convince themselves that they had a good life rather than a deliberate intention to mislead those around them? What do you think people's motivation is in general when they post on social media? Is social media a negative or positive influence on society?

6. Should Gisela have left Jack when he went to prison or was she right to stand by him?

7. Should Kate have made contact with her childhood friend,

Becky, to talk things through at the end of the book? Did you understand Becky's actions even if you didn't condone her behavior toward Kate?

8. Which woman would you like to be your friend and why?

9. Did you ever feel sorry for Sophie, despite the fact that she'd stolen Sally's husband?

10. Who did you want to have a happy ending the most?

YOUR
BOOK
CLUB
RESOURCE

VISIT
GCPClubCar.com

to sign up for the **GCP Club Car** newsletter, featuring exclusive promotions, info on other **Club Car** titles, and more.

ACKNOWLEDGMENTS

With every book, the list of people to thank seems to grow, which makes me a very lucky author. I'm going to start with where the magic happens and words get turned from the first inklings of an idea into something readers might want to read! My lovely publishers, Bookouture, have a fantastic team working so hard to get books out into the world in the best possible shape. There are so many things going on behind the scenes without the authors even realising. I do have to say a special thanks to my brilliant editor, Jenny Geras, with her meticulous attention to detail, and to Kim Nash and Noelle Holten for the many hours they dedicate to helping our books find an audience. A huge shout-out to the author community at Bookouture too—it's a privilege to be part of it. Thank you also to the wonderful Forever team at Grand Central Publishing for bringing *The Woman I Was Before* to US readers.

Thanks—as always—to my agent, Clare Wallace. I appreciate her wisdom on all things publishing, and her kindness in everything. I'm also very grateful to Mary Darby and Kristina Egan at Darley Anderson, who have worked wonders in getting my books out into the wider world.

As always, the bloggers and FB book groups have been a force to be reckoned with—they do an amazing job in spreading the word about new books and give up so much time to read and write reviews.

I've had some great help on medical facts and hospital procedure from Emma Edgar, Rick Strang and Anna Collins—any mistakes remaining are entirely down to me. Lindsay Bocking did a brilliant job of guiding me through the speedy birth of a premature baby. Thanks also to Helen Rice-Birchall for advice on employment law and Samantha Lewin who took time to put me straight on police procedure.

I also have to mention Jan Sowa, who helped me to get the Polish background right—thank you for that and so much more.

The writing of this book coincided with my son's A levels, my daughter's GCSEs and some very noisy building work, so much gratitude due to Caroline Bennett and Caroline Harris for offering me refuge in their spare rooms. And also to my husband, Steve, who steadied the ship during the children's exams to allow me pockets of creative thought. (And for generally being a great support during recent turbulent times.)

Finally—a huge thank you to all the readers who buy, review and recommend my books—and especially anyone who takes the time to contact me personally. Those messages never fail to lift my day.

ABOUT THE AUTHOR

Born in Peterborough, England, Kerry Fisher studied French and Italian at Bath University. She lived in Corsica, Spain, and Italy before returning to Britain to work as a journalist. She now lives in Surrey with her husband and two teenagers and writes fiction full-time. When she's not writing, she can be found in her garden or walking her lab/giant schnauzer on the Surrey Hills.

You can learn more at:
KerryFisherAuthor.com
Twitter @KerryFSwayne
Facebook.com/KerryFisherAuthor